Dr. Todson's Home for Incorrigible Women

ALSO BY RILEY LASHEA

Historical Romance
Club Storyville

Erotic Romance
Night Falls on the Piazza
Behind the Green Curtain

Romantic Comedy
The Meddling Friends Trilogy
(The Wish List, The Four Proposals, The Island Getaway)

Fantasy
The Black Forest Trilogy
(Kingdoms Fall, Magicks Rise, Stories End)
The Innocents

A Special Gift From Gram V

Dr. Todson's Home for Incorrigible Women

Riley LaShea

Dr. Todson's Home for Incorrigible Women © 2021 Riley LaShea

Midnight Jasmine Books

Paperback Edition April 2021
ISBN: 978-1-955155-01-4
Printed: Monee, IL 2021
Library of Congress Control Number: 2021935930

For the women who cling to the scales.

Inconvenient

Chapter 1

Caroline

1886

Caroline woke on the edge of memory. All vibrant hues and resentment. Contradictory, the beauty crafted by her mind's eye and the utter rage that accompanied it. Like a delicate lyric set against a strident melody.

Somewhere, in the far reaches of her consciousness, a thought shivered. Danced and provoked. She almost opened her eyes to see it. Almost raised a hand to reach out.

But the stillness, warm and soft, it coddled her. Sang to her amidst the color and fury. Rolling over and under, Caroline billowed and soared, lifting out of the world. Yet, she could still feel the world beneath her, its silken, downy comforts. Somehow, she was both above and below. In her body and not in it.

"Hello." She heard her own voice murmur in the darkness. She couldn't recall opening her mouth.

And no one answered her.

The only sound was the soft hum of a household in use. The only scent spiced honey - her own perfume. Nothing noxious to nose or ears. Only silence. And solitude. Serenity, shimmering slowly around her - seductive and sumptuous - she let it drag her back down into her dreams.

The sunswept hills of the English countryside burst with an outlandish display of color - reds, purples, oranges, blues, yellows - stretching in arcs and patterns as far as the eye could see only to be swallowed up in an endless cerulean sky.

It was a deceptively idyllic setting for betrayal.

Watching the puffy, white clouds drift by overhead from the window of the landau, Caroline knew the only souls who traveled this road were either betrayer or betrayed, or those being paid for their services - servants or commissions. Since she was neither servant nor commission, she could only assume she was one of the former, and since none of the day's events had been planned or promoted by her, she supposed that left her only one possible role in all of this.

Let's overnight in the country, Dear. I'm told the tulips are not to be missed this year.

Caroline wished she could feel some measure of surprise, a smidgeon, a soupçon, but she wasn't addle-brained. No doubt she would prove much less problematic for Thomas if she were. She also wouldn't be in this position, keeping calm and passive through the middle of the rolling landscape, knowing she was headed toward a firing squad. Figurative, of course. Thomas couldn't really off her. Not without a load of questions. His one lethal plot, he had already used up. He would be a madman himself to try it again.

I've told Mack to take us back by a different route.

Dear god, she hated him. She may not have been a skilled navigator, but Caroline *could* tell which side of the carriage the sun was on as they left the small inn and continued moving in the same direction - away from London, not toward it.

She could also read, and had watched Thomas as they passed the sign warning them they were entering private property. His moment of panic. The quick dart of his eyes her way. As if he feared she might suddenly know. As if it would make any difference if Caroline did know.

Well, she knew. Had known for months. She wasn't immune to Thomas's hints, dropped to and for others. To friends, family, neighbors, the vicar, anyone who would listen to him talk really.

She reads all the time. Or has her maid read to her. She doesn't want to do much else it seems. I think she likes her stories more than real life. Said in jest.

Yes, of course, please come for a visit. But could it wait until next month? Caroline doesn't always allow the staff to clean. She goes through these phases. Whispered.

If you wouldn't mind praying a bit extra for my wife, Vicar. I worry sometimes she isn't well. A plea for sympathy.

'Setting the stage,' they called it, from the theater lingo meaning to prepare the set for an actor about to put on a big, heart-wrenching performance. Thomas, no doubt, would emote his insides out onto the floor. He had been rehearsing non-stop for weeks.

"Are you warm? I'll open another window."

She could still run, she supposed, leap from the carriage and dash through the wayward impressionist painting that had co-opted the Surrey Hills. But what would that accomplish but to provide further evidence? Assure all those who witnessed it that, indeed, Thomas was a very put-upon man and was doing the only thing he could do given his difficult circumstances.

No, she would not be doing him such a favor. If she had any intention of physically resisting, she would have done so back in London when the carriage pulled up with a hired driver instead of Floyd. But she was tired, frankly, of the wait. The prolonged knowledge of Thomas's intentions for her was torment. And a bit of an annoyance, really. Like a fly buzzing nonstop around her head. If what was going to happen was going to happen, she wanted to get it over and done with, rather than wait for whatever brute squad her husband might call to drag her from her bed in the middle of the night.

"Is there a problem?"

Thomas was the one who was anxious, sweaty, tense, and fidgeting, demonstrated now by the swipe of his sleeve across his brow and the brisk manner with which he threw open the carriage door, causing it to groan at it hinges, the instant they rolled to a stop.

"Private property, Sir." The hulking man who halted their carriage stood in Thomas's open door, and Thomas jerked another glance Caroline's way.

My, what a razor's edge he had been on all day. A shame. Truly. He probably hadn't even noticed the flowers or the sky or that the cucumbers in the sandwiches Mary had made them the morning before were still perfectly crisp and deliciously flavorful. They went in perfect combination with the fresh-baked brown bread and hint of basil oil. If Caroline could say one thing about Thomas's distant cousin who had come to keep house for them, and for whom her husband had been pining every moment since, it was that she was outstanding in the kitchen.

"Only a precaution. Could I have your name, Sir?"

"Yes, of course. It's Ajax. Thomas Ajax."

"Ajax. Yeah, all right. Open the gate! Have a good day, Sir. Miss." The hulking man stepped away, and with an unsteady nod, Thomas pulled the carriage door closed, glancing to Caroline once more.

Caroline stared back, not sure which was more insulting, that he was doing this to her or that he thought her completely oblivious of it up until this point.

No answers or pleas forthcoming, Thomas's guilt at last got the better of him and he turned his eyes away.

The second time Caroline woke was to a song - a boisterous, spontaneous melody not far beyond the silent sphere in which she had been left.

It's a party
I'm the party
Dancing in the night so gay
Music, food, a lady new
Banquet, ball, a big soiree

Eruption of laughter trailing after the lyrics, it churned some cognition out of Caroline. Blew some of the cobwebs off her gauzed brain.

Lady new? That had to be her, didn't it? She was the most recent arrival there. Had to be. But the lyric couldn't possibly be a literal one. No one would be throwing her a welcome party here, a banquet, ball, or soiree.

It was ridicule, she realized. Ridicule to go along with her confinement. They would ensure, since she wasn't mad when she arrived, she would be by the time she left. Maybe that was the true meaning of a "madhouse," a place where one was driven to madness.

That seemed exactly the sort of outcome Thomas would hope to achieve by bringing her to this place.

This institution.

This mansion of illusion.

This palatial country estate that looked like a dream, but could only house nightmares.

It was a thought that required action. A fighting spirit. Whatever vim and vigor she had left inside of her. But, first, Caroline had to open her eyes. And, in trying to do so, she found her will already starting to fade. To break. To kiss her mockingly on the cheek and flit off into the atmosphere.

It was easier to just give in. To the emptiness. To the apathy. To the sleepiness. If only for a short while.

At some point it would wear off, whatever substance they had forced into her veins. The abyss would disappear, the lull would sharpen, and she would feel the full, brutal gravity of her abandonment. It would yank her back down to Earth with an excruciating thud.

Prospect utterly unappealing, Caroline chose to delay it. To allow her muscles to relax and to sink once more into oblivion.

A mile or so after the forbidding iron gate opened and closed behind them, a sprawling manor house came into view, nothing at all like Caroline was expecting. Where there should have been drab, dirty stonework and iron bars, the house was as bright as a sunray with its yellow skin and crisp white accents.

Clouds hanging big and unnaturally perky in the blue sky behind it, Caroline waited for the winds to change. Where was England's signature gray? Its spitting rain? The thunder and lightning that threatened to unleash God's eternal damnation over the land?

Ominous things should be backed by ominous skies.

This place, with its bright exterior and green-slated dormers and gables, was a picture postcard meant to lure visitors to the Surrey Hills. Caroline could imagine its caption:

Come! See our beauty!
Drop your women off along the way!

On the front lawn, those women worked, the ones who had come before her. Dressed in common, matching frocks, they had to be residents of the place, made to keep the grounds clean and ornamented so the men who rode up to dispose of their wives or mothers or daughters had something pleasant to look at. Whether that pleasant sight was the gardens themselves or so many women down on their knees was up for debate.

"Caroline." Disembarking from the carriage, Thomas held out a hand in the shadow of the door.

Yes, God forbid I break my ankle on the walk to my own judgment. Caroline brushed past him, stepping onto the hard-packed dirt drive of her own free will.

Sunlight hitting and warming her instantly, she understood the place's appeal, even as she pulled on her sun hat to shield her eyes. The house presented itself as a retreat. A perfect country getaway. It was designed to make such an impression. An estate so lovely and charming that men like Thomas could garner respect and adoration while doing their very worst.

You must be a saint. Caroline could imagine their society acquaintances patting him on his poor martyr head. *To spring for such a lovely place for your crazy wife when Bedlam is right here in the city.*

"Mr. Ajax." Descending the stone stairs outside the house's tall wooden doors, a sandy-haired man in thick spectacles and a plaid-accented suit shook Thomas's hand. "Welcome. I'm Dr. Rand."

"Dr. Rand? I thought I would be meeting with Dr. Todson today."

Yes, Thomas *would* think that. He would expect nothing less than to meet with the person whose name was on the plaque next to the front door.

Dr. Todson's Home for Women

- the nameplate shown through the ivy in polished and beveled bronze letters. How very quaint it sounded. Not 'Hospital.' Not 'Asylum.' Not 'Institution.' *Home.* Like a place women might actually choose to be. Caroline supposed 'Dr. Todson's House of Torture and Neglect' simply wasn't good advertising.

"Oh no, Sir. As you can imagine, Dr. Todson keeps a very busy schedule. I take care of the day-to-day matters in the doctor's stead, including the welcoming of potential residents. But don't worry, you'll still have your two signatures. Dr. Todson trusts my judgment."

Two signatures. That was all it took. To determine a woman too much of a burden and lock her safely away from polite society. The word of her husband, or any male relation, and two doctors' names on a slip of paper. The woman, for her part, didn't have to do anything. Anything, that was, but exist. Caroline could state that fact with some authority, because she had lived for more than thirty-five years doing scarcely more than existing.

"Mrs. Ajax." Dr. Rand moved past Thomas, and Caroline gave him her full attention. Her calmest, most rational attention. He was handsome, in an offhanded sort of way, as if he worried little about it one way or the other. His gaze surprisingly soft. "I'm Dr. Rand. It's a pleasure to meet you. How are you?"

Some sort of polite response typically in order, there was nothing typical about this. In fact, a typical response might be considered highly atypical in the moment. Crazy even. What sort of sane person smiled a reply as she was threatened with her own commitment? Realizing there was no good option - she was damned if she did, damned if she didn't - Caroline huffed a small breath, shaking her head, saying nothing.

"I imagine this must be very difficult for you," Dr. Rand gleaned from her silence, and it was a fine act, Caroline had to admit. He sounded truly sympathetic. "We'll try to make it as painless as we can. Please."

Lifting an arm, he indicated the way - up the stone stairs and through the wooden doors - and, gathering her skirts, Caroline ignored both the men who flanked her, looking up at the enchanting façade of the provincial palace, with its gentle colors and climbing ivy, cursing its deceit.

Three steps up, a small sound commanded her attention, and she glanced to the woman re-potting a plant next to the front door. Hair black, eyes black, the woman's face, slightly round and prominent of cheekbone, was striking. Soothing, in a strange sort of way. And most uncommon around London, its contours indicated she came from somewhere further to the east.

When it met Caroline's own, the stranger's dark gaze seemed to commiserate for a moment. To sympathize and to try to comfort. Before thick pink lips turned up in a subdued smirk, meant for Caroline's eyes alone, and Caroline felt the sting of her delight. This woman was glad to see her dropped off there, glad to see her marched through the front door of a madhouse to defend her own sanity.

Bruised more by the stranger's casual malice than by that of Thomas - perhaps, because she expected nothing better of him - Caroline tried to hold her head up. To retain her composure. She could be angry to a point, but she couldn't let her anger overwhelm her. She had one purpose now and one purpose only, to show them she had no business being there. No business being there at all.

"Mrs. Ajax," Dr. Rand began once they were formally seated in his parlor-like office. No desk, no examination table, just several armchairs and a fainting couch to swoon upon should the threat of her impending incarceration become too much to bear. "Or do you prefer Caroline? May I call you Caroline?"

"Call me whatever you like," Caroline said, and Dr. Rand's blue eyes flicked up as a resident of the house, made to serve as assistant, entered the room with tea. Lukewarm, Caroline did hope. They really shouldn't be arming the crazies with scalding hot beverages.

"Thank you, Margaret." Dr. Rand smiled as the woman left them, returning his attention to Caroline as the door closed behind her. "Mr. Ajax tells us you've been having some difficulties lately."

"What sort of difficulties?"

"I was hoping you would tell me that."

"I couldn't begin to read Thomas's mind."

A most proper response. To read Thomas's mind would be telepathy, and belief in telepathy was almost certainly grounds for immediate commitment. Of course, as a woman, just knowing the word "telepathy" was likely grounds. Even more so if they found out she had read it in the *Journal of the Society for Psychical Research*. So, channeling her life's training, Caroline schooled her expression to look as insipid and clueless as possible.

"Maybe not," Dr. Rand said. "But you can tell me how you've been feeling of late."

How she'd been feeling? Did people care about such things now?

Sit down, Caroline.

Wear this, Caroline.

Be nice, Caroline.

Don't look so dour, Caroline.

As far as she could tell, life was about one's observable actions, not one's feelings.

Assailed, though, by the question, Caroline couldn't help but formulate an answer. *How did she feel?* She felt like a ghost in her own life. Flitting through it. Observing. Having absolutely no impact at all. But that wasn't just "of late." She had almost always felt that way. "I feel fine."

"Ask her about the cleaning." Evidently dissatisfied with the speed or tack of Dr. Rand's questions, Thomas shifted uncomfortably in his chair.

"What about the cleaning?" Dr. Rand asked.

"What about it?" Caroline said.

"Mr. Ajax says you don't allow the staff in your home to clean."

Oh, Dear Thomas. Simplistic, absolute Thomas. That was one very clear-cut way of looking at something nuanced.

"That simply isn't true."

"Would you care to explain that to me?"

"The staff cleans when the house needs cleaning. They don't when it doesn't. I see no need for them to walk around polishing bookcases and

7

railings each day that have a layer of soot upon them again by the following morning. It's noisy, it stirs the air, and it's hopeless."

Throwing up a hand as if Caroline had just signed her own commitment papers, Thomas looked absurdly pleased with himself. Remarkable really, considering Thomas never looked pleased. Though, if he were to, it would certainly be with himself.

One might say it was he, Thomas, who demanded absolute spotlessness in his home, or perhaps just liked snapping at the servants for finding a speck on a mantle, who behaved in an absurd way. But pointing blame at her husband was certainly no means of talking herself into freedom, so Caroline withheld the recrimination, and Dr. Rand edged forward in his chair as if trying to find it.

"So, what does the staff do all day?" he asked.

"Their jobs. They do have other assignments."

"Those do not take all day," Thomas complained.

"You play cards and lose money at horse races! If you believe in leisure time, why shouldn't they?"

Thomas expelling a sudden, boisterous laugh, Caroline felt the cold melt of regret down her spine. She had made a mistake. Already. Thomas baited her, and she bit. Arguing on behalf of their servants, or even sounding as if she was, was certainly considered a condition of some sort in a woman of means, and Caroline floundered for a way to bring the focus back to herself.

"I get headaches." Looking to Dr. Rand, she found his eyes had never left her. Watching for her psychosis to reveal itself. "I get them often and they are unbearable. Too much unnecessary noise and dust makes them worse."

"Yes, your headaches. You take laudanum for those?" Dr. Rand asked.

"It was prescribed for me by my doctor."

"Mm hm."

Watching him make the note in his leather-bound book, Caroline felt her solid foundation begin to crack. He knew everything, she realized. Every fact Thomas could possibly use against her, Dr. Rand already had.

"Do you like reality, Caroline?" Dr. Rand stared into her eyes, and Caroline knew the right answer - *What else is there?* - but it would make no difference if she said it. Even if she executed it flawlessly. Not a flinch. Not an instant's hesitation. No mistake could put her in this place, and no stream of perfect replies could get her out. She didn't know why she thought they could. Why she thought it would be different for her. Why she believed, for a single instant, she could talk her way out of this, make anyone hear her reason. All that mattered was her husband said she was mad and was willing to pay this man to believe him.

Thomas giving a tiny scoff of satisfaction, because he had spoon-fed the doctor all the right questions and knew exactly how this was going to play out for him, the fury Caroline had tempered into vague interest all day consumed her. One glance at his smug, satisfied face, and all thoughts of self-preservation went straight out of her head.

"Ahh!"

Flying out of her chair, she saw the surprise on Thomas's face before she caught him by his shoulders and they tumbled together onto the floor. One knee thrust into his side, she dug her fingernails into his skin, feeling the warm, wet flow of satisfaction as she dragged bloody tracks down his cheeks.

"Mrs. Ajax." Dr. Rand rose to his feet, but made only a weak man's attempt to come between them. Or Caroline was just that strong at the moment. She could feel the slight tug at her shoulder, but it wasn't half the effort it would take to dislodge her. "You must stop this."

As if a verbal scolding could even begin to contain her wrath.

Thomas fighting back was far more effective, as he restrained one of her wrists, but, even then, Caroline got in another good swipe at him, taking blood and skin away with it.

"Go ahead." Through his pain, Thomas turned venomous, spitting the words in a whisper as Dr. Rand moved for the door. "You're only proving to them you're insane."

"They're going to put me in here anyway. You should at least feel pain."

"A little help in here!"

Seconds later, Caroline was wrapped up, arms closing around her waist and plucking her bodily off of Thomas.

"Took you a minute," Thomas said as Dr. Rand helped him to his feet, and Caroline watched the blood flow from the many wounds on his face with intense pleasure. She may not have saved herself, but at least she knew now how she would spend her next few days, praying some of those scratches would scar. Thomas should have a reminder of this. She certainly would.

"I hope you'll be well, Caroline." Thomas played the part of the grieving husband with flair and dramatics, and it set Caroline's hair on fire.

"I hope you'll ride off a cliff on your... way... bach... ta..."

Words starting to slur, she glanced down at the syringe that jutted out of her inner elbow. So much cold coursing through her, she hadn't even felt it go in. The ice in her veins.

Then, the warmth.

Then, nothing.

The next sounds that woke her were nearer. Neither voice nor song, they came in the form of thumps, soft but intrusive, not far beyond her feet, and it took Caroline's debilitated brain several seconds to recognize it as the sounds of someone coming through the door.

Shock bending her upright at the waist, her eyes flashed wide, but unfocused, and she reached out as she swayed, finding a puffy handhold to steady her as she struggled for awareness.

A small room with a door, at last she blinked into view. A cell of some sort? It had to be. The fainting couch she sat on was very much like the one in Dr. Rand's office, narrow and ornamental, but surprisingly plush, while soft light emanating from somewhere overhead revealed a lack of any additional furnishings.

All she had time to recognize before the door pressed open, Caroline tried to scurry backwards on the couch. Tried. But her compromised strength wouldn't carry her far, and it wouldn't matter if it did. There was no place to go. Whichever direction she moved, she had only as far as the four walls, and that would do nothing but prolong whatever was coming to her.

She had heard stories about places like this. One couldn't help but hear them. Madhouses were ripe sources of sensationalist gossip. Even with the new, gentler personas they were trying to promote. But though she had listened, along with everybody else, it occurred to Caroline now, with a stuttering heart and quivering bowel, she had never had any desire to learn how those stories ended.

"Caroline."

Nightmare scenarios vying for dominance in her mind, she didn't expect to hear her name so softly spoken, nor the voice of a woman speaking it.

She certainly didn't expect to see a woman she recognized, even if only in passing. But she did recognize the woman when she came into view. It was the same woman from the front stoop, the black-eyed, lovely-faced woman who smirked at her bad fortune as she had entered this place.

"It's all right." The woman wasn't smirking now. Crouching next to the fainting couch, she gazed up into Caroline's face, eyes once again sympathetic. "Are you all right?"

Certainly not all right, not even sure she was all right with the woman asking her that, Caroline stared back, wondering whether she might be hallucinating as the light cast its faint yellow glow down over them, sending golden streaks through the stranger's black hair, giving her an ethereal look like a displaced angel.

"I'm Lei," the woman said. "I need you to come with me."

"I can't. I'm..." Weak. Caroline was weak. Terribly and cripplingly so. And muddled. But she couldn't tell this stranger that. Who knew what havoc the woman might wreak with the information? "I'm sick."

"It's the serum. Now that you're awake, it will wear off more quickly. Can you walk?"

"I don't know. I think so."

"See if you can get up."

Searching for the floor with slightly numbed feet, Caroline made an attempt. Or, rather, she thought about making it. She didn't actually move at all. Not on her first or her second try. On the third, with considerable support, she was able to rise, but was so unsteady she fell instantly into Lei and felt like a puppet being pulled on strings.

"A little unsteady." Lei's voice was a breathy whisper against her cheek. "But I think you can make it."

"Where? Where are we going?"

"I'm taking you out of here."

Bizarre as the notion sounded, Lei looked perfectly serious, and remarkably calm, as Caroline looked to her in the low light of the room. "You can get out?"

"I can."

"How?"

"Come with me and I'll show you."

"What if they see us?"

"It will be all right. Trust me."

It was a very strange thing for Lei to say. What reason did Caroline have to trust her? To trust anyone in that place? What choice did she have not to? Too unsteady to walk on her own, she didn't even have the choice to move without assistance, and staying in that room waiting for whatever might come along next had to be a worse option, so she leaned on Lei all the way out the door of the fainting cell and down the darkened hall.

"This isn't the right door." Not entirely conscious of her surroundings or what was happening inside her own body, Caroline did know that. The wood door she had walked through to enter the house was taller with far more elaborate carvings than the wood door Lei led her up to now.

"We can't go that way," Lei said as she pulled the door open, and Caroline stared into the depths beyond it. The weakly lit stairs. The smell of earth rising up to tickle her nose.

"I don't..." Equal parts woozy and trepidatious, she put her hand on the doorframe to stop Lei from maneuvering her through it. "I don't want to go down there."

Lei glanced to her in the shadows, dark eyes searching Caroline's face, a soft smile coming to her lips that was less amusement than comfort. "It will be all right, Caroline. I won't let anything happen to you. I promise."

Again, Caroline had no cause to believe that. She was in a madhouse. Lei was in the same madhouse. And a complete stranger to her. Caroline knew no more than her name and her face and the words that came out of her mouth. Yet, she did believe her. She did trust Lei when she said it. At least enough to let Lei ease her through the door and down toward the underworld.

"Where are we going?" Chill seeping through her dress from the stone walls, fear bloomed, wild and rapid, inside Caroline's chest with every downward step. This was how she expected the place to look from the outside. Dank, inhospitable gray. Like a prison. Or a dungeon.

"Not much further," Lei said when they reached the bottom, and they walked on, passing through several narrow corridors, all with the same half-lit gloom, through a doorway to an empty room.

Empty, that was, but for a second door. Though, it was clear at first glance that door wasn't a way out. Crafted out of iron, giant gold wheel sitting at its center, an extensive network of levers and dials surrounding it, it was quite obviously the door of a vault.

"What are you doing?" Caroline asked as Lei settled her against a nearby wall to turn to the vault's switches.

"Just one second." Lei's eyes already scanned the levers and dials, tight smile jumping to her lips as she started to flip and to slide them. Mere seconds later, with a gratified spin of the wheel, she pulled the vault door open and light spilled from its interior, quite unexpected, but entirely welcome in the otherwise dreary space.

"Caroline." Lei held out her hand, and, pushing off the wall, Caroline shuffled unsteadily to her side, relying on Lei's strength and embrace when her knees gave out as she reached her.

Gold? Jewels? Her only guesses as to what might be inside, Caroline managed to be absolutely stunned by the vault's contents.

Dressed up like a room, or rather a portion of a room, with an armchair and an oval side table on a red Persian rug, elaborate floor lamp producing the light that filtered from its recesses, the vault held what had to be the most elegant specter Caroline could ever expect to see.

That specter was perched in the armchair, dressed in a dark green coattail jacket over a dusty rose bodice and a lighter green skirt, the absolute picture of grace and civility. The picture of grace and civility with a sly grin and a silver pocket watch clutched in her hand.

"Incredible, Lei. That's your fastest time yet." Sliding the watch into her jacket, the specter turned brown eyes on Caroline, and Caroline felt faint and afflicted under their focused attention. "Hello, Caroline," she said. "I'm Dr. Todson."

Chapter 2

Eirinn

1862

If daggers from the eyes were actual, physical daggers, Paul Browning would be dead in the middle of Tavistock Square. The sniveling little ratbag.

Perched on a bench at the edge of an abnormally balmy London day, Eirinn felt the chill of the shade at her back and the fire of fury upon her face. She knew envy only punished the sufferer, but she couldn't help but pick at her own wounds. Watching Paul Browning take his praise, the pats on his back, the boys clambering to be in his orbit for managing barely passing marks felt like a direct mockery of her and all that she wanted in the world. Not only was Paul Browning a bully who made a point of reminding Eirinn of her place every opportunity given him, he was also an idiot. An idiot who would succeed. Because polite society dictated that he should. He was simply too well-born, too connected, and too male not to.

"Want me to break any of his limbs for ya? Or all of 'em maybe?"

Hearing the footsteps approach from behind before they landed at her shoulder, Eirinn wasn't worried. While she had little doubt any one of these unlicked cubs would stab her in the back if they thought they could get away with it, she knew her back was well-guarded and the punishment for them would be quick and severe.

They knew it too.

Which was good.

Especially now.

This academic season had been a particularly vitriolic one. The new professor, Mr. Hays, recently transferred from King's College and a proponent of women in higher education, had decided to make an example out of Eirinn. To show the world women could, and should, learn just as well as men. To that end, he had the audacity to call on Eirinn frequently for answers, and, when he did, Eirinn had the audacity to answer correctly. It was a dangerous game with no clear-cut winners when Eirinn wasn't supposed to be officially playing.

"I can lure Braining around a building with the smell of slop. No one will know it was me who did it."

Smile quirking her lips - both at the insult and the offer - Eirinn glanced to where Rand stood amused with himself, but ever alert, behind her, like a soldier in service to a queen. A fact that was somewhat humorous in its own right. Were they at home, it would be Rand causing her grief and Eirinn doing the threatening.

"My God, Rand. I appreciate your willingness to take out Braining, but it's hardly worth the risk to your future. You're worth ten of him and a million more men."

"Yeah. Maybe." Coming around the bench's end, Rand sat down beside her, but at a respectable distance with his hands on his knees where any nosey passersby could see. Not for their own sakes - who cared what others thought? - but for the sake of Eirinn's parents. It was already a talking point that the Todsons allowed Rand to serve as her chaperone at all.

Can you believe it? A male servant, and a YOUNG man at that, they whispered to each other after church and over tea.

Everyone knew Rand's mother, Mrs. Ballentine - Bally to those who knew and adored her - would be the far more appropriate choice. But Eirinn's parents weren't particularly susceptible to arbitrary rules or idle gossip. Nor were they willing to take a risk. Many of the boys at University College didn't want Eirinn in their lecture halls, regardless of the fact she was only allowed to sit and listen and not to actually matriculate, but no one was going to make as much of a deal out of it with a six-foot-two pillar of protective muscle close by.

"You ready to head home?" Rand asked after a few quiet minutes.

"I suppose there's no reason to continue to sit here," Eirinn said.

That was the brutal truth of the matter. She could sit all day, glaring and brooding, but it wasn't going to change anything. The young men she had spent the past few weeks with would still continue on in their studies and be awarded their degrees to practice medicine, and Eirinn would be coddled for her shocking interest in human anatomy, given a

14

condescending smile, and be sent back to the home sphere to do womanly things with womanly virtue.

Dinner was at seven o'clock. Dinner always endeavored to be at seven o'clock in the Todson household, and Papa always endeavored to be in his chair on time. *What point is success,* he asked Eirinn once, bopping her on the nose, *if one isn't home to dine with his family?* And though she was only a young girl at the time, Eirinn had always remembered it.

Success was nothing, she supposed, to a man like her father if he couldn't keep to his own schedule. As a boy, he never got to eat dinner with his Ma, Pa, brothers and sisters. Half his family worked the coal mines and the other half the paper mills, each with their appointed jobs to do. Separated from sunup to sundown, they scarcely got a word in passing, let alone full meals together.

If success for Papa wasn't all that he had accomplished, burrowing his way from that shack outside of Langley Moor to their house in Mayfair through sheer, persistent digging, but eating with his wife and daughter each night, Eirinn and Mama could see to it. No matter how many times he told them to eat without him if he wasn't there on time. *We were playing Hearts and lost track of the hour.* Or *The roast took longer than expected,* Bally would lie for them. There was always some excuse to be found.

Tonight, though, tonight Papa wasn't just on time, he was home early, coming through the door with a whistle and time enough to change his jacket and comb his hair before he came into the dining room.

"You look nice," Eirinn said with just a tinge of suspicion. Papa, with his thick dark hair and easy good looks, cleaned up as handsome as just about any man in town, but he was far more likely to toss off his jacket and loosen his cravat around them.

"Thank you very much," Papa returned, running a hand down his checked jacket front, pleased that she had noticed. "I had to clean up somewhat. We *are* celebrating."

"Celebrating? What are we celebrating?" Eirinn asked.

"What are we...?" Glancing to Mama with a bemused expression, Papa seemed to hold the secrets of the universe in his very eyes. Papa often looked like that, on the verge of some great discovery. "You, of course."

"Me. Why me? What did I do?" Eirinn asked.

"Your last day of advanced medical theory." Much to her chagrin, he remembered. "We haven't the day wrong, have we? I was certain it was today."

"It was today." Realizing what was happening, and why Mama had been so chipper ever since she returned home from university, Eirinn busied herself with her napkin, taking it from its triangular fold to spread across her lap, wondering how she was supposed to eat with the pressing ache in the cavity of her chest.

"And? How did you fare?" Papa asked her.

"I fared fine," Eirinn said.

"Only fine?"

She had made it home in one piece with some new knowledge in her head. Given the circumstances, Eirinn wasn't sure how much better it could have gone. But Papa didn't just look as if he held secrets. He did have a few tucked up his sleeve. And he loved to do this, needle her about something he already knew and see if she would first confess. Tonight, at least, Eirinn had the luxury of knowing she had nothing worthy of confessing.

"I stopped by the university to speak with Everett on my way home."

"Ah." Small sound worrying her throat, Eirinn should have considered that possibility. Papa was friendly with Mr. Hays in a passing fashion, and an expert at getting information in roundabout ways.

"He told me, had you been allowed to test, you surely would have had the highest score in class."

"Did he?" Eirinn feigned surprise, despite the fact the information wasn't new to her. Mr. Hays announced it to the class that very afternoon. Eirinn was his shining example, his paradigm of female pupildom. A prototype. So, he slapped her publicly on the back and spread the target already there.

"Oh, Eirinn, that's wonderful." Mama smiled. Eirinn didn't look up to see it, but she could hear it in her voice. The affection. The pride. "And not at all a surprise to us. Why didn't you tell me earlier?"

"Because it doesn't matter, does it?" Frustration flaring, Eirinn's voice cracked on a sob, and she felt both of the emotions, the simmering anger and the utter hopelessness. She hated feeling this way, so sorry for herself. Self-pity wasn't going to get her anywhere. Only hard work and persistence would do that, and, even then, it could only get her as far as women were permitted to go.

"It may not matter now, or feel as if it does," Papa said, and if he were in less of a position to know, she might not have listened. If Papa had been born into this house, instead of clawing his way into it. But Papa knew exactly what it meant to be told over and over the odds were not in his favor, only to beat them in the end. "You will be a doctor one day, Eir, if that's what you want. Women in the United States are already being licensed as physicians. If all else fails, we will put you on a ship and educate you there."

Where I will have to stay if I want to practice, Eirinn thought. Because, degree or not, no hospital in England was going to employ a woman.

But she had no doubt her parents would do just what Papa said. They would spend every last penny they had in pursuit of the life that she wanted. But why should they have to? Why should her parents - her father who worked himself ragged in the mines at five years old, her mother who loved him before she dare should - have to spend all they had worked so hard to build together to get Eirinn exactly the same title as snotty Paul Browning who lived two streets over and was completely unaware of how stupid or lucky he was?

"All right." Eirinn forced a smile, not feeling it at all. "But, if this is a celebration, where are Bally and Rand? Shouldn't they be in here?"

"They'll be in after dinner with the cake," Mama said. Softly. Disappointed.

For good reason.

There wasn't a cake baked in their house by Bally alone. Mama was the hostess of many a party and celebration, and she liked to do the work that needed doing with her own two hands. She and Bally had probably spent the better part of their day trying to make this dinner special for Eirinn.

"Thank you, Mama," Eirinn said, and Mama forced a smile too, but there was a melancholy in her eyes Eirinn felt cruel for putting there.

And spoiled.

And selfish.

Papa grew up on the road and in the underground. He lit streetlamps at dusk and snuffed them in the mornings, working every waking hour between to rise above his meager beginnings.

Mama loved him before it was possible to love him. She waited years to marry, putting off other enthusiastic suitors, until Papa was able to make enough of himself to earn her parents' approval.

I knew who he was the first time I met him, she always said to Eirinn. *I felt like I knew him in another lifetime.* And Eirinn believed it.

Her parents had done all the hard work. They had built a life on her father's shoulders and her mother's devotion. The least she could do was be grateful.

Night fell on the house like a Poe story. Not entirely gloomy, but haunted with the memories of a young girl. Four years old, running half-naked through the halls, perilously curious. Nine years old, nose in a book, vexingly precocious. Fifteen years old, hands folded - quieter, sadder - fading confidence hiding behind perfect poise.

In the light of her lamp, Eirinn watched older versions of herself disappear into the shadows.

On the first-floor landing, she was startled by voices, intimately familiar, but unexpected at this time of night, and the murmured sounds drew her gaze to the soft glow of candlelight that still flickered beneath her parents' bedroom door. Guilty once more. Not only had she ruined their dinner, she was clearly keeping them awake. She knew of nothing else that could be so occupying her parents' minds, and, sure enough, the conversation proved out as she drifted toward their door, canting her head closer to listen.

"...to Everett. He has contacts in America. I'm certain some university there will admit her."

"We cannot send her to America, Simon. For God's sake. The country is at war with itself."

"Exactly. All those young men rushing off into battle. With the lack of available students, they should be happy to fill a vacancy."

"That is not funny," Mama said, but Eirinn could hear the trace of amusement in her voice.

It was fascinating, she had always thought, how differently people spoke to each other behind closed doors. The jokes they shared. The improprieties they indulged in. Millions of things that should never be said had to have been said between two people in intimate confidence.

"I know," Papa admitted, and it was followed by a long spell of silence.

Wondering if they were finished, knowing she should stop listening in regardless, that she should either knock or leave, Eirinn was just on the verge of sneaking off when Mama spoke again.

"I do wish you wouldn't get her hopes up like that."

Statement gluing her to the spot, she wished for a second that she *had* left. That was the problem with listening in on other people's conversations. One never knew what she might hear.

"I just want her to believe she can have anything she wants."

"Why, when it isn't true?"

Words striking her with the venom of a snake, Eirinn had to remind herself she was never meant to be in their path. She was the one with her ear to the serpent's mouth. Mama would never say these things in front of her.

"One day, it will be."

"Will it? I've been waiting more than forty years and it hasn't happened yet," Mama said, and there was a longing in it. A sorrow. Like some long forlorn acceptance. "You have done everything in the world to make this life for us." Her voice growing softer, Eirinn had to press recklessly close to the door to hear. "You have given Eir every opportunity. Do you know how helpless it feels that there is nothing I can do to open them up for her?"

Pained sob and shuffle of linens coming from behind the door, Eirinn knew Papa was embracing Mama as she cried. She shouldn't be listening to this. If her mother wanted her to know her concerns, her torment, she would tell her.

But it was also good she had heard it. Because she forgot sometimes. She forgot that all Papa had done, his personal glory, their family's great success story, he had done only because he had the right to do it. Mama was born into a far better life than him - all her needs provided for, no cause to work or scrap to survive - but was it a better life? Papa could drag himself through the grime of a coal mine into a lovely home and a gentleman's station, but what if their places had been reversed? Where would Mama be right now if she had been the one born into poverty? There was very little room for men to climb through the cracks of caste. For women, there was none.

I should leave. The thought went through Eirinn's mind again, but hearing Mama weeping through the door, she couldn't. She couldn't just let Mama cry on her behalf, and, almost reflexively, she raised her hand to knock.

"Yes? Who is it?"

"It's me, Papa."

"Eir, come in."

Putting on a brave face so they wouldn't know she had heard anything - everything - Eirinn pressed open the door to her parents' bedroom, revealing them just as she expected to find them, side by side in bed, separated just enough not to make her blush.

"Are you all right?" Mama looked much too worried, tears still shining in her eyes, like dew through a greenhouse window, and it struck Eirinn with inspiration.

Mama used to smile more too, it occurred to her. All their smiles were so much easier to come by when Eirinn was young.

"I'm fine. I was just wondering, could we go to Kew Gardens tomorrow?"

Joy instantly appearing on Mama's face, like a rainbow through the storm, it was everything Eirinn hoped it would be. Mama was so surprised, so instantly eager, it wiped out all traces of despair.

"I can't remember the last time we rode out there."

"I know. I think it's high time we did. My memories of our days there are so good. I think it would make me feel better."

"Yes. Of course, we can. I would love that," Mama breathed.

"Sorry, Papa. Since you do have work to do, maybe you can join us next time. After all, the museum is terribly behind shed-jule." Eirinn overemphasized the word as she had heard it from the mouths of Papa's stuffy fellow investors. He would always be a risk for them, the man who came from nothing managing their precious fortunes, and they reminded him of it, in small, petty ways, as often as they could.

"I am quite all right with that. You should have time alone with your mother. But I would love to see you on your way back through the city. You can route right through Chelsea. We'll have tea and I can show you the progress on the museum."

"That sounds nice too." Hand wrapping around Papa's arm, Mama gave it an affectionate squeeze. "Eir?"

"That sounds perfect," Eirinn agreed, and, watching her parents go from sorrow to delight in an instant, she realized she felt better already.

Chapter 3

Caroline

1886

Some instances of waking felt illusory. They might be waking from a dream into reality or waking from reality into a dream.

Caroline remembered waking the morning after she married Thomas, alone in a new house and a new bed, able to recall he had been there, but unable to grasp the peculiarity that her life should change so much from one day to the next.

She remembered waking the morning after they found Sarah and Nathaniel - and not waking - drifting in and out of sleep and consciousness, never quite sure which one was which.

Now, she'd had two of those wakings in a row - dream into reality, reality into dream - the first the night before when she startled awake on the fainting couch at Lei's appearance and now in the quiet, comfortable bedroom at Dr. Todson's Home for Women.

Stretching her legs beneath the weighted quilt didn't help matters. Its warmth, delicate and inviting. What sort of madhouse gave a woman her own, private bedroom with a well-stuffed mattress and beautiful appointments?

But this wasn't a madhouse.

And it *was* a madhouse.

Both had been proven the night before.

Awake and asleep.

Dream and reality.

Caroline recalled it like a mirage. The brightly lit hall, not as big or as opulent as a hall in a palace, but still quite grand and ornamental. Angels dancing in its friezes. Decorative tiles lining its floor. A bountiful spread on a large banquet table, women dancing and laughing around it, eating and drinking of its offerings. It might have been a debutante ball, if the women were, on the whole, younger. Or a harem, if the king wasn't particularly picky.

It's a party
I'm the party
Dancing in the night so gay
Music, food, a lady new
Banquet, ball, a big soiree

A woman in a nightdress with a full head of unruly gray hair twirled amidst the others, arms thrown open to the world.

"That's Imogen," Dr. Todson introduced from afar, taking a snifter from Dr. Rand, whom Caroline would soon discover wasn't a doctor at all, but the herbal specialist and Dr. Todson's oldest, dearest friend. At least, that was how Dr. Todson described him. "Here. Drink this. It will counteract the sleeping draught."

"Did you give me opium?" Caroline asked. It didn't feel like opium, not exactly, but given its undeniable effectiveness, she didn't know what else it could possibly have been.

"No. That was my own special formula," Rand said. "So is this. Healthy herbs. Non-addicting. Brewed from the plants in our very own gardens."

Not sure that made her feel any better, Caroline stared into the copper snifter, unable to determine the color of the drink from the metal, a rational, but troubling thought forming in her slowly-working brain. Testing on patients. That was certainly straight out of madhouse lore.

"Drink it, Caroline." Before she could refuse, Lei, who had been largely silent on their way back up the stairs, but ever in her reach, leaned over her shoulder, one hand pressing into the small of her back. "It's all right. You will feel better."

Dream, reality. Reality, dream. The line between the two was at its most blurry as Caroline looked to Lei, meeting her gaze at close range, and, not sure how she could get any more incapacitated, other than being unconscious again or dead, she drained the snifter of its contents, grimacing as the bitter taste enveloped her tongue.

"Yeah," Rand said as he took the empty snifter out of her hand. "It doesn't taste great. But you'll see."

And, over the next few minutes, Caroline did. The sluggishness in her muscles releasing, the clouds in her head clearing, she found normal, or a close approximation of it, as she looked around the room, finding everything exactly as it had been before. A woman in a fitted blue frock still played imperfect piano in one corner. Thirty or so women still ate, danced, and conversed as if they were at a society gala and not shuttered away in a madhouse in the countryside.

"All right. If everyone is in acceptable condition, I should get to bed. Enjoy the party. I'm on the top floor if you need anything, Caroline." Dr. Todson lightly touched her arm, and it was only as she was disappearing out the door that Caroline realized she had a head full of questions she hadn't gotten to ask.

She would get another chance, she assumed, that Dr. Todson, being the doctor of name on the building, would still be there come morning. But she couldn't be sure. Was Dr. Todson part of her reality or of her dream? The woman did have a rather dreamlike quality about her, despite the fact she turned out to be a flesh-and-blood human and not the ghostly specter Caroline first believed her to be.

"I'm up there too, if you have any problems." A few minutes later, Rand also retired, and, left alone in Lei's company, Caroline turned to her, gaze moving over Lei's uniquely attractive features, trying to detect any deceit or oddity that might be left for her that day.

"I know," Lei said, and just that, those two simple words, gave credence to everything Caroline was feeling. "It's a lot. I'm sure it feels unreal to you. You're confused and you're dazed. Rand is good with his potions, but they aren't magic. Might I suggest..." Hand moving slowly up her arm, Caroline felt a flimsy tether to reality. And an equal tie to her dreams. "For tonight, don't worry about real or unreal. Just enjoy the food and the music and know you are not where you thought you were going to end up."

"I sang to a staircase in Tunisia."

There were signs Caroline was exactly where she thought she was going to end up, and one accosted her the instant she opened the bedroom door.

"Caroline."

Dr. Todson's voice the next thing she heard, Caroline abandoned her notion of fleeing back into the room to hide and stepped into the hallway instead, finding Dr. Todson, flesh and blood, real and present, standing with Imogen next to a post in the banister at the top of the stairs.

"Good morning," Dr. Todson said.

"Good morning." Caroline felt utterly unprepared for human conversation. Especially this particular conversation.

"How did you sleep?" Dr. Todson asked.

"I slept well."

"Good. I'm glad. Are you hungry?"

Caroline wasn't sure whether she wanted to confirm or deny her hunger, to go forward into this brave new world or shelter away from it for as long as she could, but, at the mere mention of food, her stomach growled so insistently, so prominently, it practically echoed down the hall.

"Breakfast is downstairs." The hint of a smile flitted over Dr. Todson's face, and, in the light of the sun through the window, Caroline could see the lines that appeared around her eyes. In her cheeks. The strands of gray barely visible in her blonde hair. When she first saw Dr. Todson, the picture of seamless beauty down in the vault, she was certain the woman had to be younger than her. Now, in the light of day, she wondered if Dr. Todson wasn't a few years older. "Did Lei show you where the dining room was last night?"

"No, she didn't," Caroline said.

"It's not hard to find. You can get there through the grand hall. The kitchen is connected. If no one is in the dining room, knock on the kitchen door and ask Brigit for something to eat. Just make sure to knock even if the door is open. She's quite particular about her kitchen. I would walk you down there myself, but Imogen and I are having a bit of a breakthrough, aren't we, Imogen?"

"I sang to a staircase in Tunisia." Imogen grinned her strange, half-witted grin, made all the more unsightly by several missing teeth on both sides of her mouth, as she rubbed at the ball in the banister post like it was crystal, and Caroline clenched her own teeth on a swallow, trying not to let her misgivings show.

If this was a breakthrough, they were all in trouble.

"Most of the women here are completely sane. At least, they have nothing to warrant them being in an institution," Lei had told her the night before, in murmured asides, as she introduced Caroline around the room, and it did seem true. The majority of the women Caroline met at the party were bright and good-natured, calm and charming.

There were a few, though, that certainly begged some question, who spoke strangely or were far too enthusiastic to meet Caroline.

Then, there was Imogen, who required no deliberation. There was clearly something off about her. Singing the same song over and over, as the talent-impaired pianist switched melodies to try and match her tune, she had a sort of frantic energy about her that simply didn't exist in sane people over the age of five.

"What about her?" Caroline had asked Lei, and Lei's gaze followed her own, soft smile coming to her lips as she watched Imogen dance to the piano's tune, completely off-beat and in her own lyrical world.

"She's a little bit crazy," Lei said, seemingly delighted with the fact as she looked back to Caroline. "It doesn't mean she shouldn't get any cake."

"Will you sing with me?" Imogen asked Caroline now, and, glancing to Dr. Todson, Caroline waited for her to intervene, to keep things normal and civilized in her institution. But Dr. Todson said nothing. Did nothing. She simply watched Caroline, watched them both, waiting to see what Caroline might do. Determining something about her, perhaps, by what she did do.

"All right." Caroline didn't see what a song could possibly hurt. Aside from, perhaps, her bladder, which had been desperate for relief since the moment she climbed out of bed.

"Yay!" Imogen clapped her hands and launched into her song. Which, as far as Caroline could tell, was no song at all. It was more a series of observations. About the hallway. About Caroline. About Dr. Todson's fancy blue jacket and the morning's meal. This left Caroline in the unfortunate position of trying to echo and anticipate Imogen's words, a task much easier said than done, since they made very little sense on their own, let alone when all strung together.

"Those aren't the words." Imogen stopped cold, leaving her hanging on a note that sounded painfully off-key. "She did a terrible job. They never know the words."

"I know," Dr. Todson said as she took Imogen by the arms and captured her crystal gray eyes. "But Caroline did the best she could. That was kind of her."

"Thank you for trying." Imogen cast a pitiful, pouting look Caroline's way.

Like a child, it occurred to Caroline then. Imogen truly was just like a child. Not only with her boisterous voice and her frantic energy, but in every possible way. The woman had to be at least thirty years older than Caroline, but she was thirty years younger in her mentality.

"You're welcome." Caroline couldn't help but be struck by the sadness of that. What happened to her? she wondered. How did someone end up that way?

"Is it all right if we talk today?" As Imogen returned her attention to the ball on the banister post, Dr. Todson returned hers to Caroline. "If the weather holds, we could take a walk in the gardens after lunch."

"Yes, all right," Caroline agreed, tensing even as she did. Sun already blanching the walls of the hallway, she feared the gardens almost as much as she feared Dr. Todson. What did Dr. Todson want with her? What if she was still looking for whatever was wrong with Caroline? What if there *was* something wrong with her? What if she ended up like Imogen, a child stuck in an old woman's body whose only desire was to make strangers sing?

"Is there something else?" Dr. Todson's gaze was keen upon her, examining already.

"I just need to use the water closet," Caroline said.

"Yes, of course. Do you know where it is?"

"Yes. I used it last night."

"All right then." Turning back to Imogen, Dr. Todson let Caroline make her way down the hall on her own, and, out of their sight, Caroline stopped for a breath, for a moment's contemplation, reminding herself that she didn't need to know everything going on in that house right at that very moment. For now, she was safe and she was uncaged, which was more than she could have expected.

Chapter 4

Eirinn

1862

Chelsea was the perfect place for a museum, bohemian as it was. Artists had been pouring in since the middle of the century when the Pre-Raphaelites started taking up space on Cheyne Walk. Papa had already made inquiries to followers of the movement in nearby houses, hoping to build relationships and procure any new works once the museum was done.

Though, Pre-Raphaelite paintings were fewer and far less controversial than they once had been. A decade before, Pre-Raphaelite painter John Everett Millais nearly stopped Polite Britain's collective heart with his *Christ in the House of His Parents* - a painting so universally reviled even beloved son Charles Dickens got in on its criticism.

Elizbeth Gaskell, whose stories and novels Eirinn had pulled from her parents' bookshelves and devoured in her youth, was born in Chelsea some fifty years before. George Eliot, recently exposed in the papers as being a woman living in flagrante delicto with a married man, resided there currently.

All in all, the borough was a haven of culture and curiosity, where the nature of propriety shifted, decency took on its own meaning, and Eirinn felt freed from the confines of greater society whenever she was there.

"Come now. Don't hold back. Do tell me what you think."

Normally Eirinn felt freed from the confines of greater society. Gazing down the long red corridor of her father's current passion project, she couldn't even hear Chelsea outside its walls, and felt much as if she had been lured into a trap, Papa standing bright and expectant waiting for her opinion, and she didn't have one really. It was a hallway, to be sure.

"It's a beautiful color," Mama said, and Papa seemed as dissatisfied by the compliment as Mama seemed desperate to find one.

"In here." Refocusing his enthusiasm, Papa led them through a beveled doorway into an adjoining room, its walls purple instead of red, and each one every bit as empty as the one that came before.

"I love the ceiling," Mama said, and Eirinn glanced up.

It was a nice ceiling, truly it was, the coffered molding impressive with its baroque carvings and gilded paint. It was also entirely uniform, each sunken square an exact replica of the one beside it. When you had seen one twisted arrow around the stem of an ornamental flower, you had seen them all, and that was really all there was to see.

"Follow me." Sighing, Papa marched onward on an apparent mission. Or, perhaps, it had become a pilgrimage now.

Passing through numerous spaces with finished floors and painted walls, it was easy to see the hard work that had gone into them. When Papa first bought the building, it was no more than crumbling stone and dilapidated fixtures. Now, the towering rooms and corridors were filled with color and detail. Realizing what wasn't particularly exciting for her had to have taken a lot of dedicated effort on the part of Papa and the men and women he hired to do the restorations, Eirinn vowed to find something glowing to say when they came to their next stop.

"All right." Papa clearly wasn't going to make it easy for her. Leading them through the long, untouched great hall of the museum, with its dust and strange smell, to a Y-shaped staircase that stood at its far end, he held his arms wide with triumph. "How about this?"

Something nice to say. Something nice to say. Eirinn did vow to find one.

"It's... fascinating." Mama's skillful use of vocabulary met the challenge first, employing one of her great gifts, managing to be kind without telling a lie.

It *was* fascinating, Eirinn agreed, fascinating why Papa brought them there of all places when the room wasn't even partially restored like the others.

"Picture this." Framing his hands like a photograph, Papa set the scene. "Green walls. Dark green. The color of pine. The staircase." Running two steps up, he waved a hand toward his feet, and Eirinn half expected the small movement to send him careening through the rotting boards to the floor below. "Fully restored in all its glory. Deep blue carpet, green and pink trimmed, running up to this very spot. And here, right here..." Skipping the last of the missing stairs to the landing, Papa held his hands against the wall as if sizing up some great treasure. "Is where we will put *Government House In Winter With Sleigh* once we acquire it."

Bravo, Papa. Glancing over at Mama, Eirinn watched her expression change. The soft smile that lit Mama's face. The sheer affection that shone in her eyes. The trouble with an empty museum, even lovingly half-restored, was that only those on the working side of the final design could truly picture it in its final form. But Eirinn knew Mama was picturing it now, seeing it exactly as Papa saw it. Sharing one mind.

It gives me an overwhelming sense of peace, Mama had once said of the painting by C.L. Daly. *I don't know why. It's not the most striking, but it's softer somehow. Beautiful, without the need to fill every available space.*

"We'll put a bench here." Papa bounded back down the hazardous stairs to indicate a spot several long strides away from the bottom step. "So, what do you think?"

"It's stunning," Mama said, in all sincerity, which pleased Papa to no end.

"It really is lovely, Papa," Eirinn agreed.

"Thank you, Eir. Though, I have to say, you two did make me work for it." Walking back to them, Papa gave Eirinn's shoulders a firm squeeze as he slid his arm around Mama's waist, practically glowing when Mama pressed a lingering kiss against his stubbled cheek. "But we're not done yet," he said, casting a mischievous glance Eirinn's way. "I have something for you too."

The path to Eirinn's surprise proved even more treacherous. They had to step over the missing boards in the dusty old staircase and several splintered planks in the unfinished shell of the museum's upper floors to reach it.

"Don't worry. It's sound. Just be careful where you put your feet, so you don't twist an ankle," Papa said as they followed the balcony along the edge of the great hall back toward the front of the expansive building, at last entering a large room where no one needed to be told where to look first.

The picture window by far its most stunning feature, even from the far side of the room and through dirty glass, Eirinn could see patches of the Thames where it ran between buildings and beneath bridges.

"Go have a look," Papa told her, so Eirinn did, minding the floorboards that were turned up and broken, until at last she stood gazing out onto the streets of Chelsea below.

"It's incredible, Papa." Life buzzed about those streets. She could feel their energy even from two stories up.

28

"Look closer." Suddenly at her side, Papa produced a spyglass from out of his jacket, pulling it to length, and Eirinn did as she was told, placing the leather cup against her eye and staring down its long brass tube.

Streets brought immediately before her, the distinctive marks of Chelsea became even more apparent. The casual, colorful daywear. The men in their loosened scarves and half-buttoned shirts, sleeves rolled to their elbows. The women in their trousers and billowy tops, often unbuttoned nearly as far as the men's. Women who winked at Eirinn when they caught her eye in the street, as if they could sense that she, like them, would have to break the bonds of propriety if she wanted to suck the marrow out of life.

Eirinn didn't know what she was looking for exactly. Chelsea was Chelsea, special in its own right. Just a window onto its thoroughfares was a precious gift. What could be so much more interesting that her father would have her searching through a spyglass like a pirate or a -

Strange, gangly leaf entering the sphere of her vision, she ripped the spyglass away from her face, breaths coming in rapid shallow bursts as she looked for the garden by the river with her own two eyes, certain she could not have just seen what she thought she just saw.

Chelsea was full of greenery. Gardens abounded in its squares and along its waterfront, all with most of the same flowers and trees - sycamore, horse chestnut, wisteria, bluebells, roses, lilies, tulips, daffodils. Eirinn was well-versed in what London's gardens had on display, and never, not once in her life, had she ever seen a plant like that in one.

"Is that?" Raising the spyglass back to her eye, she searched for the garden once more, for the formidable black iron gate with the words molded right into it, marking it as private property and warning curious trespassers away.

"The Apothecaries' Garden." Papa couldn't wait for her to find it for herself, but Eirinn did, just one second later, catching sight of the black twisty letters of the gate's design through the long scope –

Apothecaries' Garden
1673

Heart skittering off at a gallop, Eirinn could scarcely breathe, scarcely think as she jerked the scope's aim back beyond the gate, gazing into the trove of treasures and secrets, seeing plants that could barely be seen from the street as if she was standing right next to them, an arm's reach away from leaves and buds she had never encountered outside the pages of a book.

"I thought we would have a telescope in here," Papa said. "*Window over Chelsea*. Visitors can look out at the river and Battersea Park and see whatever else they happen to see."

With some difficulty, Eirinn pried the spyglass away from her face to look to Papa in the dusty, unfinished room, half afraid the garden might disappear if she took her eyes off it for too long.

"They might lock it up like a fortress. But it won't stop you from knowing what's in there."

"Papa." Spinning his way, Eirinn threw her arms around his neck.

"That's more like it." The soft sound of Papa's laughter entered her ear as he gave her waist a gentle squeeze. "All right. Now that you've seen everything, let's get to that tea. I've had hardly any lunch and I'm going to eat both your sandwiches and mine."

Eirinn felt like she was floating, like she was walking five inches above the thoroughfare.

When they left the museum, they passed a man drawing in chalks on the stoop of a building - *I've passed him my information*, Papa told them - and heard a woman practicing opera through an open window so beautifully she could only be a singer for the Royal Opera House.

Make your mark, the people of Chelsea seemed to be uniting to tell her. *Let your voice be heard.*

"Here we are."

When they reached the door of the tearoom, it was a struggle to come back down to Earth to go through the door Papa held open for them.

Brushing his hair, which had gone without a cut ever since he started spending such long hours at the museum, out of his eyes, Papa looked pleased when his vision adjusted to the lower light of the room and he spotted someone at a nearby table. "That's Louis Arnold." He leaned in closer to tell them. "He's a professor up North, in London to meet with his editor about an educational text. English Literature." He knew that would be of interest to them.

"Mr. Arnold." Following Papa as he moved to the man's table, Eirinn watched Louis Arnold stand in greeting. Tailored brown suit, perfectly trimmed mustache, he didn't look like a man with a great love of literature. The writers on the streets outside were buttoned-down and open to life. Eirinn wasn't sure she had ever seen a man quite as buttoned-up as Mr. Arnold. "Simon Todson."

"Yes, I remember," Mr. Arnold said as he shook Papa's hand.

"I hope you don't mind us disturbing your tea. I just wanted to introduce you to my wife, Corinne, and my daughter, Eirinn."

"It's very nice to meet you both." Mr. Arnold bowed his head, polite enough about being interrupted.

"Corinne is my muse and the brains of the museum, and Eirinn..." Placing a hand on her shoulder, Papa give it a proud squeeze as he grinned her way. "She's been sitting in on lectures at University College. Her professor says she's the brightest in his class."

"Is that right?" Mr. Arnold glanced her way too, small smile twisting his face that didn't reach Eirinn like a smile at all. It reached her like a threat, cruel and sinister. She couldn't explain it, the odd sensation that crawled across her skin as Mr. Arnold looked at her. Not until it divulged itself in Mr. Arnold's very next breath. "If she were a son, you'd really have something to be proud of."

Air sucked from the room, the atmosphere changed so quickly it was almost staggering, leaving the people around them gasping for breath.

But nothing changed as quickly as Papa. So few times in her life had she seen it, it took Eirinn a second too long to recognize Papa's temper. His anger. A second too long to stop his arm from swinging forward and catching Mr. Arnold square in the jaw, his fist thudding hard enough against it to send the man careening backward onto the floor.

Skirting around the table's edge, Papa grabbed Mr. Arnold by his shirtfront and hit him again and again, and, no one else rising to stop him, Eirinn had no choice but to rush forward with Mama and grab one of Papa's arms to keep him from beating a man out of his senses. Or to death. Whichever came first.

"There's that street rat!" someone cried out. It wasn't Mr. Arnold. Mr. Arnold didn't know Papa well enough to know anything about his history, that much was clear. But somewhere in the shadows someone had just been waiting for his chance to say it, and Papa looked for him too as Eirinn struggled with Mama to haul him toward the door.

Back outside the tearoom, King's Road looked less sunny than it had a minute before - Chelsea colder and less colorful - and it grew even gloomier as they pulled Papa around the corner of a building into a lane where the sun didn't reach at all.

Letting go of his arm, Eirinn watched him take deep, heaving breaths, the anger on his face slowly dissipating, sense returning, and, with it, the shame. Not for what he had done - Papa would never be ashamed of fighting for her honor - but that they were with him when he had to do it. Papa was the gentlest man Eirinn knew, but there was always a scrappy street kid inside of him who felt like an impostor in his own life.

And she didn't know what to say to him. How to comfort him. How to thank him. Papa had given her the world and a forbidden garden, and she didn't even know how to make him meet her eyes when he wouldn't stop staring at the stone walk.

It was laughter, fluttery and unexpected, that at last drew both their gazes, and Eirinn watched Mama try to stifle it with the back of a gloved hand.

"I'm sorry." Tears shone like small diamonds in the corners of her blue eyes as she laughed, making them appear even brighter than normal. "There is just something so immensely satisfying about seeing someone who deserves it get punched in the face."

Guilt near-instantly abating, Papa looked relieved. Grateful. Then, he too started to laugh, less enthusiastically, but just as genuinely, and, watching them, Eirinn couldn't help but laugh along, despite how uneasy the laughter felt inside her chest.

"Do you think you'll get into trouble?"

"Oh, I'm sure of it," Papa said. "But not to worry. It will be no more than a fine."

Pretty convinced on the matter, he pushed his unruly locks back and straightened his jacket, and Eirinn just had to trust he knew the punishments gentlemen could expect for quarreling with each other better than she did.

"It won't be nearly as much as he'd be willing to pay to punch him a fourth time," Mama said.

"And a fifth and a sixth," Papa agreed.

Both of them so at ease, Eirinn felt the concern ooze out of her. But, in its place, she was left hollow. Stinging. She didn't know Mr. Arnold, only knew now that she had no desire to know him, but that didn't make his words any less callous. Or effective. She had long ago given up concern over what other people thought of her, but, every once in a while, their scorn could still take her by surprise. Not so much their thinking of it, but the fact that they felt so comfortable voicing it aloud.

"It was crowded in there anyway," Papa said as Mama slid her arm around Eirinn's shoulders. "I would much rather be alone with my two favorite ladies. There's an amusement fair two streets over. Should we go and see if we can find an oliebol?"

"Yes, please." Papa's ploy to distract her worked like a charm, replacing some of the sting with the thrill of the hunt.

Eirinn had tasted her first oliebol at The Great Exhibition when she was just nine years old. It was brought across the ocean from Holland, and she was positively mad for its deep-fried goodness. Every once in a while since The Exhibition, it appeared at fun fairs across London, but it was still rare, so a sweet surprise to find one each time. As they found it that day.

Papa was also right. The punishment for his altercation in the tearoom was nothing more than a fine. Sent by post. Not even a policeman came to their door. Papa paid his five pounds, easily affordable to him now, and the matter was quickly forgotten.

Or so they thought.

But resentment was a powerful motivator.

Kept alive, it grew and it festered, bubbling with infection years after the cut which first created it.

Apparently, Louis Arnold was far more insulted by Papa's public disciplining of him than any of them could have known, they would discover years later, along with the true extent of the man's spite.

Mama's favorite painting was *Government House In Winter With Sleigh*. Papa had been inquiring about its status amongst his society friends for months, certain someone could help him obtain it for the museum's collection. He had discussed the matter with his business partners, and they put what seemed a safe sum of money away for its procurement.

Everyone knew why Papa wanted the painting.

He was not shy about his reasons.

Then, in 1865, *Government House In Winter With Sleigh* went up for auction, and Louis Arnold dug into the depths of his fortune to outbid Papa, besting him at every raise to an utterly preposterous price, and hid the painting away in his home where no one could see it but him.

Chapter 5

CAROLINE

1886

The sun held, much to her great dismay. All day, or rather in the abbreviated time she had been awake, Caroline could see its determined light shining through the windows, glinting off brass key plates and glaring against the floors, so it was in as bright and sunny an afternoon as England ever got that she found herself walking alongside Dr. Todson in the gardens.

"Is this still considered Surrey?" Not sure what else to say once Dr. Todson stopped pointing out the features they passed - specific trees, herbs, early-season vegetable plants, the small pond situated in a square of easterly hedges - she thought knowing where she was in the world would prove the most comforting.

"Yes, it is. We're closest to Mickleham," Dr. Todson told her, and, nodding, Caroline took a slow, deliberate breath, amazed at the ease with which it passed through her throat and into her chest, even as she grew alarmed by its competing scents. Grass and pollen. Rose and lilac. Horror and misery.

It wasn't that she didn't care for the natural world - indeed, she was rather quite fond of its colors and fragrances - it was that the natural world didn't have much compassion for her. Every flower that tickled her nose, every breeze that cast pollen and feathers into the air, went straight to her head, threatening her with hours of potential convalescence.

"How are you settling in?"

"Very well. Thank you."

It had long been the sun, though, which had proven Caroline's greatest nemesis. Her true Goliath. Two minutes in battle, and she was almost assured of being stricken down. The clap could hit her so swiftly, so severely, she was convinced it was where writers got their descriptions of being smote by the gods. Most certainly, it was why Thomas had waited for a series of cloudless days for their trip out to the countryside. It made more sense to travel on dry ground than on sopping paths, but that was just a ready excuse. Taking her out in a sun-drenched day all but assured Thomas she would reach for her medication and, therefore, be more pliant and docile when they arrived at their true destination.

Just not pliant and docile enough to spare his face.

"Sincerely, Caroline..." Dr. Todson stopped and turned her way, and Caroline glanced out from beneath the wide brim of her sun hat, which had been left alone - unseized and unhidden - along with the rest of her clothes, as if she was a guest in this house instead of its prisoner. Not that she needed it. Leading her out the French doors and onto the terrace, Dr. Todson took her along an almost entirely shaded path, walking her through a canopy of fig trees that had been vertically trained to where they now stood beneath a seemingly endless pergola practically roofed by wisteria. "How are you handling all of this?"

Sun casting its radiant glow onto the leaves and blooms, it lifted the colors off their surfaces, sending them dancing on the air, like a prism or a rainbow illusion of serenity.

Graveyards have flowers too, Caroline reminded herself.

"How should I be handling it?" she asked.

"That depends," Dr. Todson said.

"On what?"

"On what came before."

A bit vague, Caroline thought. That could refer to any number of things. The immediate "before" she was dropped off here. The decade before when she was suffering her repeat failures and becoming a disappointment as a woman. During her childhood. In another lifetime. Over the past year, which was fabricated of pain and sapped most of her will to live.

"For some women." Blessedly, Dr. Todson didn't make her come to a conclusion on her own. "This is the best thing that could happen to them. If they are being hurt or used at home, terrorized, this can feel like an escape."

"Well, that isn't me," Caroline was quick to say, not sure why it felt like an accusation. She was many things back in London - fruitless, burdensome - but she was no victim.

"I'm glad to hear it." Dr. Todson's eyes moved over her, searching for signs of subterfuge, or, perhaps, the aforementioned abuse, and

Caroline squirmed in the rainbow prism, wishing she would just take her word for it. "Still, for other women, it is only their spirits that have been trampled, and they don't even realize it until they are free."

Statement a whip lashing against her skin, Caroline flinched. Or felt as if she did. Inside. She wasn't sure she actually moved at all, other than to start to tremble. On a common English spring day, with its built-in chill and rain in the air, she would have had a logical explanation for it. An excuse. But, today, she revealed herself, both to herself and to Dr. Todson. Pulse fluttering in her throat, she raised a hand to chase a gnat away from her forehead, glancing to the wisteria, marveling at the tightly-wound growth that forced all sunlight to filter through the purple, pink and white petals.

"Is that what I am here? Free?" What absolute bunkum.

"Yes."

"So, I can leave? Right now? I can walk straight through the grounds and out the gate and no one is going to stop me?"

"If you'd like."

Not the response she expected - not even remotely close to it - Caroline stood dumb for a moment. Trembling harder. Further confused.

But, then, why wouldn't Dr. Todson say that? They were miles out in the Surrey Hills. Caroline knew the name of the nearest town, but not the direction to walk to get to it. She was trapped here as surely as if there were poison-tipped bars around the gardens.

"Would you like a ride?" Dr. Todson asked her, and her heart battered excruciatingly against the wall of her chest. How was she to come to any conclusions if Dr. Todson kept opening new lines of inquiry?

"Are you really a doctor?" Caroline thought it only fair to turn the questions around on her. And it was a rather good one, she thought. Appearing from a vault in the night, leaving patients to roam about her institution at all hours, Dr. Todson didn't act like a doctor, at least not any Caroline had ever heard about or met.

"Yes, I am. I studied under Dr. Elizbeth Garrett Anderson and was licensed at the London School of Medicine for Women."

Just when she thought she was the one on the attack, Caroline went wordless once more, stared once more, not sure why it affected her so, but unable to pretend she was unaffected. She expected Dr. Todson to be a fraud, she realized, as illusory as everything else that day and night before had been. As phony as Rand. She was aware, vaguely, of universities issuing degrees to women, but from her bed in Lexham Gardens, it seemed such a distant, impossible thing.

"Are you all right?" Taking a step closer to her, Dr. Todson looked concerned.

"Yes, I..." Caroline lost her voice, her words, all thoughts and emotions ceding to something akin to wonder. "I've just never met a woman doctor before."

"Yes." Dr. Todson didn't seem at all bothered by her admission. If anything, she was mildly amused by it, a slight, sympathetic smile curving her lips. "I suppose to many people we are rather mythological."

And courageous, Caroline's mind instantly supplied. Trying to imagine what Dr. Todson must have gone through to reach such a position in a realm of men, she couldn't even begin, before she realized what she was doing and shook herself free of the thought. She didn't need to admire Dr. Todson. She hadn't even decided whether she was in danger or not.

"Do you know why your husband brought you here?" Dr. Todson asked her, and that question definitely felt dangerous.

Thomas didn't think she behaved like a woman of her means and status should. And her parents had thought it before him. *There is something disturbed in her*, she could imagine Thomas saying. *She lives like a hermit and sees no need for the niceties of society.*

It was true enough. Headaches more and more frequent the older she got, Caroline had long ago given up on visits and most social gatherings. She never really enjoyed them anyway and saw no point in keeping up pretenses just for the sake of it. But that wasn't why she was here. She knew very well why she had been brought out to the country - now - after all these years of Thomas and everyone else enduring her eccentricities just fine.

"I suppose he thinks I'm ill," was all she said.

"I know you were angry." Dr. Todson dangled the topic like a carrot, trying to entice her to take a hearty chomp. "Rand was quite descriptive of your anger."

Flushing hotly, Caroline dropped her gaze to the grassy path, watching a piece of orange rind drift through the blades seemingly of its own accord, the ant that carried it completely concealed somewhere underneath. So much weight on its back.

It was truly spectacular, Rand had recounted to Caroline and Lei after Dr. Todson left the party the night before. *I wish I was a better artist, but I did try to sketch it out for you. You had to see it from the outside to truly appreciate it.* Slipping a piece of paper out of his pocket, he presented it to Caroline, and Caroline could only give passing glance to his crude artistic rendering of her fit of temper and attack on Thomas in the reception room. *I let it go on as long as I could. I hope you were able to exorcise some of your anger.*

When he and Lei both laughed, Caroline laughed along, painfully embarrassed, but not nearly as embarrassed as she would have been had she been in a clearer state of mind.

"It was shameful," she uttered to Dr. Todson now.

"Your husband put you in an institution knowing damn well there is not a thing wrong with you, and your actions were shameful?" Dr. Todson raised her voice for the first time, and Caroline glanced up into equally heated light brown eyes. She felt tisked. Scolded. Yet... better somehow? Exonerated almost. Had she attacked Thomas anywhere else,

37

she could only imagine the sort of disgust that would have met her actions.

"I've been doing this for some time, Caroline." Moment passed, Dr. Todson shook back a loose tendril of blonde hair, her voice tranquil once more. "In my experience, women end up here for one of three reasons: they are inconvenient, they are uncompromising, or they are incorrigible. Which one are you?"

Trying to imagine what Thomas would say if asked the same question, Caroline accepted, with a hapless sigh, if those were the preconditions to her commitment, she had stood no chance. "All three, I suppose."

Dr. Todson's lips instantly quirked, soft glimmer coming to her eyes Caroline couldn't begin to interpret. "Good."

Good? Dear God. Who was this woman? A doctor or a charlatan? The answer to her prayers or a harbinger of torment?

"Why are you doing this?"

"Doing what?" Dr. Todson asked.

"This." Caroline raised her arms to the tunnel in all its spectacular, but unnecessary beauty. To the grounds. The house. The absurd reality at large. "All of this. Any of this."

"I know it sounds trite, but I always wanted to heal people," Dr. Todson said. "Like my mentor, Dr. Anderson, I thought women should have access to a physician of their own sex. What I discovered, over the course of my work, is that physical ailments are so few of our problems as women. I believe it almost a cruelty to heal a person's body if she is broken everyplace else."

Gasp seized, stolen, ripped from her body by one soft declaration, Caroline felt, with horror, the press of tears she absolutely refused to cry.

"Here." Doctor or charlatan, trick or not, Dr. Todson did her the kindness of pretending she didn't see. "I had Rand prepare these for you."

"What are they?"

"This one is laudanum..."

At once, Caroline lurched, not quite a convulsion, but a definite, visible jolt, forward and toward, barely biting back the moan that tempted her lips.

"For your headaches," Dr. Todson went on. "I hope the fresh air and regular meals and exercise might help some with those, and I would certainly prefer to spare you the addiction, but I also don't want you to be in pain."

Desperate to get her hands on the brown bottle, Caroline swallowed repeatedly as saliva coated her tongue, fighting to keep her arms down by her sides lest she look too eager.

"This one is a tincture that combines the two tonics Rand gave you last night - the sleeping draught and the restorative formula. You might have noticed you do not have a headache now." Staring into her eyes, Dr.

38

Todson forced the point clear, and Caroline blinked, trying to make sense of her words.

She had noticed, of course, that she was doing quite well today, but she hadn't considered the possibility there was a reason for it beyond good luck and the extra hours of sleep. Could Dr. Todson be telling her the truth? Could yesterday's injection combined with last night's shot of medication be the reason she was outside in a blooming garden on a sunny day with no imminent signs of consequence?

"You will only need to take this once a day, and you may find it prevents your headaches entirely. It will make you somewhat groggy, so I recommend taking it before you go to bed, but it won't make you nearly as groggy as the laudanum and should otherwise have no ill effects. But, as I understand you have no cause to believe that, I thought I would provide you with both to use as you see fit."

Dr. Todson holding the bottles out to her, Caroline snatched the brown one at once, feeling the pulse of her heart against the glass as she came away with it alone, before getting a hold of herself and going back for the green tincture bottle as well. Mostly because Dr. Todson was watching her, but also because it might be the only medication she would get and it was better to have something uncertain than nothing at all.

"Rand has written everything that's in the tincture on the bottle, so you'll know."

"Thank you." Caroline tried to stop the shake of her hands as she slid the bottles into the flapped pocket of her dress.

"I would like to talk to you about your headaches at some point," Dr. Todson said. "When you feel ready. I imagine your personal physician hasn't been particularly receptive to what you've told him about them."

"He did provide the laudanum."

"Which, I'll grant, is more than a lot of women get. That doesn't mean it's the best thing for you. Research indicates megrim is considerably more common amongst women than amongst men. For obvious reason, that makes many physicians consider it less of a problem. While I don't profess to know what you feel, I've been fortunate in that regard, I do understand how debilitating the pain can be."

That word - *debilitating* - God, how she despised it. It was so pitying, so enfeebling. Caroline looked for the creeping orange rind as shame flushed her cheeks.

"You are not weak, Caroline," Dr. Todson declared as if she could read her very thoughts. "You just need someone to listen to you."

Head shaking, it wasn't in denial of the statement, but of the tactic. Did Dr. Todson prey on all her wards' vulnerabilities like this?

"The things you say are all very right."

"Mmm," Dr. Todson softly hummed. "And that makes you wonder whether they're a lie."

Anger, white hot, flooded Caroline in an instant. Dr. Todson did not know her, had no right to make statements that should have been questions. And, yet... she was eerily accurate a disturbing amount of the time.

"One day, Caroline, you will accept that life can surprise you in good ways too."

All the right things, Caroline reminded herself, blinking rapidly to force back the tears.

"Right. Now, do you have any questions for me?" Dr. Todson asked her, and, unraveled, unsteady, Caroline couldn't think of a single one. When Dr. Todson had left the party the night before, there were so many questions in her head, but she felt utterly incapable of recalling any of them. Until a whoop from the garden captured her ears and served as reminder.

"What will my job be?"

"What do you mean?"

"I see the women working. In the house. On the grounds."

Soft puzzlement coming to her face, it took several seconds for Dr. Todson to work out what Caroline was asking her, and her head gave a small tilt of comprehension when she did. "This isn't a workhouse, Caroline. You are not required to do anything."

With some bafflement of her own, Caroline glanced back toward the gardens they had just passed through, where several residents had been hard at work, watering plants, pruning hedges, on their knees in work clothes ripping out weeds.

"The women who live here choose to work in the gardens," Dr. Todson said. "This is their home, and they want it to be beautiful and fruitful. Plus, days can feel endless when you do nothing at all."

Confronted, once more, with an intimately familiar truth, Caroline wondered if there was anything about her life Dr. Todson didn't already know, that she couldn't, in some small way, leverage against her.

"But they don't have to do anything. You don't have to do anything. You can do whatever you like."

Chapter 6

EIRINN

1866

Stench wafting from the half-opened basement windows of 69 Seymour Place enough to immobilize a bull, Eirinn stared at the three-story brick façade, wondering what sort of life she was so desperate to get herself into.

Until that moment, it had all been theory and observation. She was familiar with the more volatile aspects of human anatomy, the messy symptoms of disease, the dangers of the work. She had witnessed the dissection of multiple dead bodies, sticking her fingers into viscous wounds and decaying organs whenever she was permitted. But those things were wildly divergent from the realities of illness.

Illness was present and it was immediate. It was sights and smells any sensible person would try to avoid. Mostly, though, it was demanding. It required steady, competent hands. It did not require cowards. Reminding herself of the fact, Eirinn set her shoulders against the putrid wall of smell and marched up the stone steps, Rand following uneagerly behind her because they simply couldn't be sure what they might find inside the first dispensary for women and children in London actually headed by a female doctor.

The odor lessening, but not dissipating, as they stepped through the door, what they did find was a waiting room full of women, most with children in their arms or crawling about their legs or feet. Sick, almost all, the babies and several older children howled, while their mothers looked as if they might feel better if they could do the same.

Cholera was taking its toll on London once again with an outbreak in the city's East End, and it was leaving a trail of misery, dead bodies, and queasy doctors in its wake.

"Hello, I'm looking for Dr. Anderson." This created an opportunity for Eirinn. Though, she hated to think it in this room where so many people were so clearly suffering, it was an indisputable fact women had always been more likely to find work where men didn't seek it.

"Ain't everyone?" The woman at the reception desk pushed a logbook their way. "Put your name on the list and she'll get to you when she gets to you. There's no jumping line here. Rich ladies don't go first."

"No, I'm not ill. I'm..."

Slight sound - like a gasp or a sigh - drawing her attention, Eirinn turned back to the clamor of the room. It was strange enough the sound should reach her through the cacophony. Even stranger that she immediately spotted the woman with dirty light brown hair and a baby in her arms slumping slowly forward in her seat.

"Rand," she scarcely had the chance to say as she swept back through the maze of bodies, her long dress, even without its petticoats and crinoline, doing her no favors in the matter. Still, she made it to the fainting woman in time, catching her as she crumpled and holding the baby safely against her chest as they cleared a space for her on the floor.

"Get Dr. Anderson," Eirinn called out to the gatekeeper.

"She's busy."

"Get her now."

If you're going to walk into a place you're not sure you belong, always act as if you have the authority to be there, Papa reminded her that morning, and, apparently, it was solid advice. Solid enough, at least, to make the gatekeeper get up in a huff and shuffle out of the room. Whether or not the woman had actually gone to fetch Dr. Anderson was yet to be determined.

"Here, Rand. Hold the baby."

"Ah." Rand made a sound of general protest as Eirinn took the infant from its mother's chest and pressed it into his arms. "Fragile bitty things. I always feel like they're gonna break just from touchin' 'em."

"You'll both be fine," Eirinn said, lowering her head to the unconscious woman's chest and listening for a heartbeat against the din of crying and newly concerned whispers.

"What happened?"

Rising back up, her own heart leapt and sputtered as she tumbled into childlike awe watching the formidable figure that was Dr. Elizabeth Garrett Anderson walk into the room. She had heard plenty about the woman who procured her license from the Society of Apothecaries by using their own charter against them - a charter that was quickly amended to ensure no other woman could follow in her footsteps - but it was still unbelievable somehow. Like watching a goddess appear in one's midst. A myth come to flesh-and-blood life.

Then, Dr. Anderson was dropping down before her, amazingly corporeal, pressing her fingers to the same pulse point Eirinn had just checked, and Eirinn remembered she was there for a reason - with purpose - and her chance to make a good impression was fast fleeting.

"She fainted. Her pulse is weak and her heartbeat is arrhythmic."

Pausing in her examination, Dr. Anderson glanced up, one eyebrow sitting slightly higher on her forehead than the other as she looked to Eirinn. "Thank you for your assessment, Whoever You Are. Suanne, fetch John to help me carry her back."

"I'm Eirinn... Eirinn Todson, and I can help you," Eirinn rushed to say.

"With what?" Dr. Anderson returned.

"Anything. Everything. You must need help." Glancing to the women and children crushed into the room, yet another mother dragging a belligerent boy through the door at that very moment, Eirinn endeavored to keep calm and on point. "You look rather overrun."

Whatever happens, don't beg, Papa said. People can never un-see that. Show them who you are, but don't let them take it from you.

"Do you have a strong stomach?" Dr. Anderson asked.

"Very," Eirinn said.

"Do you take direction well?"

"It depends on who gives it."

Dr. Anderson went still, stunned, it seemed, by the admission, before a small grin slipped onto her visibly exhausted, but stoic face. "Are you a fast learner, Eirinn Todson?"

"My professors and instructors say that I am. You won't have to teach me everything. I've sat in on lectures and attended surgeries and dissections at University College. I'll only ask you what I don't know."

"Well..." A man who must have been John coming through a door, Dr. Anderson seized the unconscious woman by the shoulders. "Sounds like an offer I'd be stupid to refuse. Take that fancy dress off. You'll find suitable clothing in the back. And the pay won't be much."

"I didn't..." Eirinn didn't expect to get paid at all. She had come there to volunteer, to gain experience, to learn from the mythical Dr. Anderson in her first-of-its-kind medical facility. But she wasn't going to turn down her first paid medical post either. "I'm sure whatever it is will be fine."

"Whoa, wait! What do I do with this?" Rand looked positively panic-stricken as Eirinn glanced back, and she realized, in her overwhelming excitement, she had forgotten about him. And the baby he still held.

"The child is hers?" Dr. Anderson asked him, and Rand vehemently nodded. "Bring it back." Hauling the woman away with her assistant, Dr.

Anderson stopped and glanced to Rand again as they started through the door. "What about you?"

"What about me?" Rand said.

"Strong stomach? Good at taking direction?"

"Yeah, I suppose I am."

"Do you want to work? We're down a nurse and two assistants. We really could use the extra hands."

Glancing to Eirinn, Rand posed the silent question - All right? Not because he needed her permission. Not as her employee. Rand never needed permission from her. They had come to that agreement years ago. But he still sought it as her friend. This was Eirinn's passion - her dream - and Rand truly was loyal to her. He would never get in the way if he thought she didn't want him there.

With a swell of affection for him, Eirinn nodded her encouragement.

"Yeah, all right," Rand agreed.

"Good," Dr. Anderson said. "John's had to help me with patients, so the chamber pots in the basement haven't been emptied all day."

Look of revulsion coming to his face, Rand might have been reconsidering, before, with a sigh and a grimace, he accepted the job had to be done by someone and it might as well be him.

Chapter 7

CAROLINE

1886

Whatever she liked. It was exactly the sort of directive Caroline would have hoped to be given had she been so optimistic as to hope.

She hadn't, but she did take it immediately to heart.

Leaving the garden as soon as Dr. Todson was finished with her, she headed straight for the room in which she had slept, clutching the glass bottles through the fabric of her dress when they clanked dangerously together.

In the halls, she encountered no one, but could hear their voices whispering through the foyer, an eerie mosaic of disembodied conversation that seemed to grow in volume as she climbed the stairs.

Is one of them Lei?

She didn't let the thought distract her for long, continuing instead down the hall and into the bedroom, glancing to the four corners to ensure it was empty before she pressed the door closed behind her.

What's the gambit?

Pulling the bottles out of her pocket, Caroline lifted the green one to inspect it. HEADACHE ELIXIR, the label read in surprisingly crisp, black handwritten letters, and, on the back, just as Dr. Todson said there would be, was a list of ingredients, nearly all of which Caroline had seen or heard of in some form before. It seemed harmless enough. If any of it was true.

She set the bottle aside.

Grasping the dropper of the brown bottle, she twisted it up and open, sobbing pleasure as the pungent odor engulfed her senses and she watched the russet liquid drip from the dropper's tip back into the bottle's opening.

Laudanum, just as Dr. Todson had told her.

Laudanum. Caroline's heart beat triple and her stomach clenched with anticipation. Whatever pain she had, whatever its source, laudanum would ease it. In a high enough dosage, it could eliminate it entirely.

I'm not in pain. The thought came on a gust of awareness in the time it took another drop to fall.

It made no sense. She hadn't slept on schedule. She hadn't eaten on schedule. She walked through a maze of flowers out in the sun. Normally, any one of those things would have led to grave misery.

I feel fine, Caroline baffled herself again. Fair, not perfect. Her hands on the bottle trembled and her stomach lurched as if demanding to be satiated. But her head, as far as it went, felt strangely uneventful. No stabs. No triangles floating behind her eyelids. No unbearable vertigo that made her feel as if she was clinging upside down to the skirts of a whirling dervish.

What she did feel, watching another drop of laudanum form at the dropper's tip and fall just out of line to roll along the bottle's rim, was curiosity, almost as piquant and searing as her sudden craving.

This place is not normal.

At least, nothing about it had been thus far. All terrible expectations aside, there were no apparent rules. No structure. One could hardly tell who was in charge from one moment to the next.

The woman who was in charge scarcely seemed to know she was in charge.

What sort of doctor gives a patient a bottle of laudanum to use as she sees fit?

Not sure where her thoughts were leading her, Caroline did know what would happen if she took a half a dropper of laudanum. She would feel warm, serene, but powerless. The world would go hazy and every desire to know what was happening around her would disperse into a million prickles of welcome apathy.

It was tempting, too tempting, and, with a whimper of conviction and a resolute twist, Caroline tightened the dropper back onto the laudanum bottle, hands shaking as she scooped up the headache elixir along with it and shoved both bottles into a low drawer in the room's single dresser, next to clothes that weren't hers, where they would surely be discovered if anyone so chose to look, but they were at least out of immediate sight.

Smoothing her hands down the front of her dress, she felt flushed. Entirely discombobulated. Nothing at all had changed. She hadn't taken laudanum since she had been there, and she didn't take it now. The only distinction was in her knowledge she could.

I won't take it. Not yet. I can't, Caroline commanded herself. If she took laudanum, it would be like giving in, surrendering helplessly to whatever her fate might be behind these walls.

And they might take it away, the thought occurred to her too. Just because she was given laudanum now didn't mean there would be more to come. It could be a test, a tease. Dr. Todson had already proven herself more than adept at manipulating her emotions.

No. Not yet. Cold settling deep into her flesh, Caroline shivered. But she had to stay vigilant. Curious. Before she could relax by any means, shape, or fashion, she needed to find out just how many lies she'd been told.

Outside the door of the bedroom, the most prominent voices came from above, and Caroline followed their echoes up the vacant stairwell, glancing around the bright, expansive landing as she reached the upper floor.

Able to pinpoint the origin of the voices at once, it was only as she grew nearer the open pocket doors that she could make out what sounded like the recitation of a prayer, in French, and only when she was almost standing in the spilled light of the doorway that a word sailed out to nearly knock her off her feet.

Dazed - no, edging up on horrified - Caroline couldn't say she spoke the language with any real fluency, but given it was exactly the same in English as it was in French, with only slightly altered pronunciation, she did quite recognize the word "Lucifer."

"Entend nous Satan Lucifer alors que nous..."

There. There it was again. Lucifer. And Satan? *Did they just say Satan?*

Sort of thing probably best not found out, Caroline thought to go, to lift one foot and let it carry her back the way she came, down the stairs toward the safety of her appointed room. But intention only half-decided, her foot carried her forward instead, easing her closer to the sacrilege instead of away from it. There was a reason Lord Byron called curiosity "that low vice."

"Avec une luxure sans entraves..."

French oration covering the sound of her approach, Caroline closed her ears against it - not terribly difficult, given she only understood about every fourth word - as she drew up to the door, peering around its frame with anxious eyes, stupefied as she at last saw into the room.

She was looking for people, the women she heard praying, in some number, to the anti-Christ below, but what she saw first were books. Volumes and volumes of them, stretching from floor to ceiling on rounded wooden bookshelves that jutted out from the walls in half circles, one right after the next, so they created a sort of mirror illusion of infinite number.

Boggled by the sheer quantity - there had to be tens of thousands of books on those shelves - Caroline gravitated toward it, realizing she had drifted into view only when her gaze fell to the woman who stood before three other seated women in the library and found the woman already staring back.

"Bonjour." A crisp white smile appeared against the woman's dark skin. "C'est Caroline, non?"

Petrified, in the truest, most scientific sense of the word, Caroline turned instantly to stone.

God fashioned hell for the inquisitive. Saint Augustine had warned her too.

"Yes," Caroline husked.

"I'm Blanca," the dark-skinned woman reminded her.

Caroline had seen them, the women in the room, earlier that day when the household gathered for lunch not long after she had her breakfast and, before that, the night before when she met them at the party.

She had met most of the women who lived in the house the previous night. Lei introduced each by name - names Caroline would never recall given to her all at once - and she had noted then what an unusual mélange of people they were.

"This is Hazel, Amber and Nancy."

"Hello," the three women greeted Caroline in chorus.

"Hello," Caroline said in return.

She was used to a mélange of people on the streets of London, in the households and estates of acquaintances to some degree, but she had never seen so many varieties in a single room. At least not at the same apparent status. Even now, there were three colors amongst the four of them. Three amongst five, if she counted herself.

But why would she count herself? She wasn't part of any of this.

"Did you want to come in?" Blanca asked.

"No." Caroline whipped her head in far too fervent of denial, and Blanca's gaze narrowed, bewildered, it seemed, that she had no interest in joining their worship circle. Or coven. Whatever term it was they put to their sect. "I'll just -"

"Caroline."

Not sure whether to flee or to obey, Caroline assumed any spells or curses sent her way were just as likely to hit her in the back as the front and turned to face Blanca once more.

"We're reading from Le Grand Grimoire," Blanca said, but Caroline would really rather not know the details. She had learned her lesson about curiosity. Saint Augustine would be delighted. "I'm teaching them French. We read the spells for a laugh. We don't actually believe them. Although, we do leave out the occasional word... just in case."

Blanca looking somewhat abashed by the confession, Caroline felt a thread of embarrassment wind its way through her as well, tying the fragments she had witnessed together into one absurd misunderstanding. "Right. Of course."

"Please, do come in."

Relieved, though still somewhat dubious - witches were probably impeccable liars, after all - Caroline stepped across the bronzed threshold of the library, gaze drawn at once to the frescoed, sculpted ceiling above.

"It's brilliant, isn't it?" Blanca asked her.

"I've never seen anything like it," Caroline admitted.

The frescoes gentle in color - a wash of blues, whites, and pinks - they were similar to others Caroline had seen before. Multiple figures floating through them. Entering the images at all different angles. Angels and demons. Living and dead. But there was something distinctly different about them too. The faces in the paintings were softer. The bodies, softer. There was less anger and more compassion.

"Look long enough, you'll find yourself," one woman said, but beyond the fact it wasn't Blanca, Caroline couldn't say who.

Her eyes busy roaming the gates of Heaven, it wasn't even clear what the declaration meant until, blanching, staggered, she realized why the frescoes struck her as so abnormally merciful. All of the figures in them, from devil to divinity, were women. Just when she'd accepted these people weren't the worshippers of Satan she momentarily believed them to be, she was certain plenty of holy men would find blasphemy in that.

And in her. For her unfettered feelings. *Perhaps, I'm the witch*, the thought flitted through Caroline's mind. Because, beyond her shock, rose a strange sort of giddiness, a wicked delight that wanted to cackle out loud, but made it to her lips as no more than a smirk and a subdued sound of pleasure.

A universe entirely devoid of men? Created and ruled solely by women? Could she even imagine such a place? Yes, Caroline realized, she could. Quite easily and with immense satisfaction. She imagined it as she dragged her eyes away from the divine mother, as she looked to the ivy that chased its own tail around the fresco's edges and the skylights that cut across the slanted ceiling, allowing light to pass through to the heart of the room, while leaving its edges in shadow to maintain the integrity of the books.

Those leather-bound volumes all nestled snugly together on the shelves, a narrow balcony ran through their middle, splitting the bookcases into upper and lower halves. And, to access that balcony, at the far end of the room, stood a staircase - in the shape of a 'Y' - its first set of stairs rising to a landing before continuing upward in either direction, the carpet that lined the stairs thick and deep blue, edges trimmed in pink and a deep, forest green.

A lovely display in its own right, the whole scheme seemed designed to match the painting that hung on the landing wall. Every touch in the room, in fact, seemed to complement that painting - a winter scene with a large house and a sleigh. It was quite simple really, the artwork, especially when compared with the impeccable detail of the frescoes, but altogether quixotic. As if the sleigh might carry Caroline away to a place of serenity at any moment.

"It was Eir's mother's favorite painting."

"Eir?" Caroline glanced to Blanca.

"For Eirinn," Blanca explained. "That's Dr. Todson's given name."

"And she allows you to call her that?"

"Yes, of course. It's her name." Statement punctuated by a laugh, it grated Caroline's already frayed nerves.

No rules. No hierarchy. No way to wrap her mind around the strange world in which she found herself or determine how she fit into it.

"The library is modeled after one in Switzerland. I've never been, but I'll take Eir's word for it. Do you like to read?" Blanca asked.

"Yes, I do. Very much."

"Well, a boon for you then."

It was. Truly, it was.

Caroline's father had a large library by common standards, but it was nothing at all like this. His shelves were filled with books on trade and wars and the words of ancient men who lasted into the present due to the perceived brilliance of their thoughts. And that was all which filled them. Her father's books. Her father's interests. Why on Earth should his shelves contain anything else when, due to the vulnerability of their minds, women ought not to be reading and, aside from him, only women resided in his household?

"There are books on any subject you can imagine."

"I believe it."

"For learning or for pleasure. Whichever you prefer. Or both. We all have a bit of the profound and the frivolous in us, don't you think?"

"I know I do," Caroline said, and Blanca laughed. Hazel, Amber and Nancy laughed. Kindly. Without malice. "May I look?"

"Yes, of course. This is your home."

Statement jarring, conflict erupted in Caroline's chest. In her head. Happiness - no, not happiness - gratitude that Blanca would try to make her feel so welcome warring with steadfast defiance. This wasn't her home. She already had a home. Back in London. A household full of people she already knew. A nephew...

Oliver.

Room going aslant, Caroline wobbled on her feet.

"Are you all right?"

"Fine." Forcing a smile, she turned to the bookshelf beside her, blinking back tears and scanning the spines through their blur, glad when the other women returned to their conversation - in English and unimportant.

Whether there were truly books on every subject was impossible to tell from a single shelf's offerings, but the collection of literature was more than enough to impress. Picking up one familiar title, Caroline turned the hefty tome over in her hands, taken by the softness of its leather, before lifting a finger to run along the cover of the other books in the same row, reveling in the rugged, sensuous feel.

No simple paper or cloth covers here, every volume was bound the same - leather hard-formed but soft to the touch, titles pressed into their spines in neat, silver letters - as if they were all brand new and printed by the same shop. But, leafing through the pages of *Don Quixote*, Caroline could see the wear to its ink and its edges.

"Find something you like?"

Called from her observation, she glanced back, finding Blanca smiling her way. But she could tell that Blanca was worried. As Dr. Todson in the garden worried. As Lei had worried the night before.

"Have all of these been re-bound?" Caroline asked, and, with a glance, Blanca deferred to the woman she had introduced as Nancy.

"Yeah, they have. Me and some of the other girls do it," Nancy said.

"You did this?" Caroline uttered in shock.

"Let me see?"

Walking the book over to her, Caroline placed the copy of *Don Quixote* into Nancy's hands, waiting for her to inspect it.

"No, not this one." Nancy pressed the back cover open, pointing with one long, stained finger to the initials scratched inside. "That's Stella. See, it has her initials here. You keep looking, you'll find one with mine. NB."

"They're all beautiful." Caroline didn't need to find one specific book. They were all practically uniform and equally impressive.

"Thank you," Nancy said as she returned *Don Quixote* to Caroline's hands, and Caroline stared at the woman's weathered, wrinkled face. Astonished. Humbled.

She didn't know anyone, let alone any woman, with those types of skills. The skills of artisans. Valuable hands-on skills. The working men in Caroline's life made plans and dictated them. Why would they ever learn to do something when they could pay to have it done for them? Wealth attracted wealth. It spurned competence.

"I should leave you to your lesson." Feeling increasingly inadequate standing amongst the woman who provided French instruction and the one who could bind books, Caroline decided she had bothered them long enough.

"All right," Blanca gently dismissed her. "Do you speak French?"

"No. Not well," Caroline answered. She had learned it, of course, like every other lady in London society. But, like all things she had learned but had very little occasion to use, her memory of the language had faded with time, so she now scarcely remembered even basic conversation.

"We have our lessons every Tuesday and Friday after lunch, if you'd like to learn."

"All right. Thank you," Caroline said with an uncertain nod, gaze dropping to the book still cradled against her chest, sudden swell of attachment rising up to grip her. "Is it all right if I take this with me?"

"If you can lug it," Blanca teased her, and, laughing weakly, Caroline acknowledged the absurdity of choosing what had to be one of the bulkiest novels in the room, so thick and so heavy it must contain both halves of the story. "You're home, Caroline. You needn't ask for permission."

I'm not home. Sentiment looming once more, Caroline rejected it outright.

She may not know the truth of this house, whether it was what it claimed to be or all just a clever illusion, but she did know she already had a home. At Lexham Gardens in London. A nephew - Oliver. A life that might not be significant or triumphant, but was hers. And she wasn't giving it up without a fight.

Chapter 8

EIRINN

1866

Hours at the dispensary passed by like minutes. There were never enough in a day to tend to all those who needed tending, which was why Dr. Anderson had a system she adhered to religiously. The door locked at the time displayed on the plate next to it - 6.00 p.m. - precisely, no one got in after unless they were gushing fluids in the street, and everyone stayed until those inside had been treated.

"Think you can handle that, Novitiate?" Dr. Anderson asked Eirinn that very first night, and Eirinn assured her she could, though she glanced to the clock more and more frequently the closer it ticked to seven and when she got home it was the first time in her life her parents had ever started dinner without her.

"Let me get you a plate." Already on fruit and meringue by the time she made it to the dining room from washing up and changing her clothes, Papa darted to the kitchen to fetch her main course, and Eirinn answered her parents' questions with bittersweet delight.

That was the thing about change, as she had come to accept it. There was always some sense of loss to it, even when it was something one desperately wanted.

Over the next several days, Eirinn and Rand arrived at the dispensary early and stayed late. Sometimes it took only an hour to get through the patients who remained inside, sometimes longer, but it always went by at an expedient clip. Eirinn would take each patient's blood pressure, feel her or his pulse, and if Dr. Anderson found the patient well enough to convalesce at home after a series of questions and prods at their abdomens, she would provide them with physic and send them on their ways.

The good thing about a cholera epidemic, if one could be found, was there was very little need for diagnostic question. The symptoms were particularly pronounced, and ninety-five percent of the women and children who entered their lobby suffered the same. It was only those patients who suffered differently, the ones whose symptoms veered from the obvious tack or who were too sick to be sent home, who were brought upstairs to the makeshift infirmary.

After her first two days, Eirinn had already noticed a troubling trend. Poor women were far more likely to require a bed. They were sicker than the women of means who came in and had more secondary symptoms as well, like a cough that made one woman choke whenever she would vomit, far worse dehydration, or, in the case of Cerise, the woman who fainted in the waiting room the day of Eirinn's arrival, a nutrient-deficiency that rendered her nearly too weak to move.

It's because they wait so long, Dr. Anderson explained once it became clear the trend had made itself known. *Women of means see a doctor when they feel unwell. Poor women see a doctor when they feel that they may die. Or that their little ones might. Even then sometimes they wait too long.*

That might well have been the case for Cerise. How she had made it to 69 Seymour Place from the East Side with her baby in her arms was anyone's guess, and a near miraculous feat, because after she fainted in the waiting room she stayed that way for two days, moaning every so often before Dr. Anderson administered more physic and she fell back into a too-still sleep.

She didn't come here because she was sick, Dr. Anderson speculated before the mother had a chance to wake and speak for herself. *She came when her baby started showing symptoms.*

That baby, Little Lulu, for her part, was mostly lethargic when Dr. Anderson ran her tests. She didn't look when Dr. Anderson moved back and forth in front of her. She didn't smile or babble. She hardly cried. Probably a deficiency in the milk where Cerise was so terribly undernourished, Dr. Anderson diagnosed, because, blessedly, Little Lulu had been spared the ravages of cholera and came quickly around once nutrients were added back into her diet.

Still, her mother's milk was the best thing for her, especially in a time of rampant disease, so for the first day and a half, one of Eirinn's jobs was to prop Cerise up every three hours and hold her nursing daughter against her chest. It was a strange task, to say the least, and, of all those she had taken on since walking through the door of the dispensary, the most unexpected.

Perhaps the most unexpected part was that Dr. Anderson allowed two patients to occupy so much of Eirinn's time. There was a general consensus amongst those in the medical community, at least in the academic circles Eirinn had been in, that the more quickly one moved through patients the more patients one could treat. Especially when an epidemic was afoot.

But can they treat them well? Dr. Anderson asked when Eirinn gave voice to the matter, and it caught Eirinn quite far afield. *There will always be one more patient, one more person who needs your help. That is why we lock the door at the end of the day. It does no good to treat more people than you can treat with dignity and compassion. It does no good to focus on the task alone and wear yourself thin. There will always be more patients. Only treat those you can treat well, while taking care of yourself at the same time.*

Yes, Doctor, Eirinn said with a stunned sort of comprehension. Of course, that was the only way to treat a patient, well and with dignity and compassion. So why, in the multiple classes and seminars she had been in, was it the first time she had been given such a lesson?

"Hello, Baby Girl." Nearly one o'clock on another busy day at the dispensary, Eirinn excused herself from taking pulses in the waiting room to make way to the temporary nursery set up on the first floor, finding Little Lulu already standing in her crib, hands on its top rung as if she was plotting an escape. "Look at you."

Lulu gave a small bounce and a big smile when she saw her, and Eirinn's heart swelled and uncoiled, breaths coming easier in the relative silence of the nursery.

Working at the dispensary was taxing - as taxing as Eirinn expected when she first made her case for the job - but it had its perks too. Many of the women who came in were delightful and happy to talk, even in poor health. Most were excited to be treated by a woman doctor, even if, and in some cases especially if, it made their husbands uneasy.

"You are such a strong girl. Yes, you are." Then, there was Little Lulu, the tiny spitfire who still provided Eirinn respite from the influx of patients every few hours. "You want to see Mummy?"

Chubby arms reaching out, Eirinn caught Lulu before she fell backward in the crib, pulling her onto her hip, and Lulu batted excitedly at her in return, catching a stray curl that had loosed itself from her chignon so Eirinn had to pry eager fingers away with one hand as they made their way from the room.

"Let's go see Mummy."

Lulu batted harder, but she wasn't the only one anxious to see how Cerise was faring. The relief, on the third day, when Cerise woke up was shared by everyone. Until then, they didn't even know her name - she had entered the register with a single initial only - or that of her daughter. They had an anonymous woman and her infant, and what they would have to do with that infant if the mother didn't survive was a haunting thought that left the whole place in limbo.

"Look who it is." Stepping through the infirmary door, Eirinn was glad to see Cerise sitting up in bed. "I've got someone who misses you."

Warm smile coming to her face, Cerise held out her arms, and Eirinn transferred Lulu into them, watching Cerise's smile melt into a sigh as Lulu gave a hiccup of pure joy, small hands reaching out to pat her mother's cheeks with hearty abandon.

"Is she still okay?"

"She's perfect," Eirinn said. "She's been perfect the entire time."

Five days. Five days, they had kept Little Lulu - Lourdes, in their official medical records - separate from her choleric mother. For hours at a time and all through the night. *Just until we're sure she's no longer contagious*, Dr. Anderson said. But, sometime over the past day, they seemed to have passed that critical juncture. Not only was Cerise sitting up and smiling, she looked much, much improved. If Eirinn hadn't been there throughout her recovery, she didn't think she would recognize the same sunken woman who passed out on the waiting room floor.

"How are you feeling?"

"So much better."

"Good. I'm glad."

Glad didn't do justice for how Eirinn felt. Cerise and Lulu were her first two patients at the dispensary, and the only two who had given her extended cause for concern. Everyone else they had brought upstairs took no more than a single night to recover enough to go home. There was always some treatment or physic to set them right.

Cerise's survival was Eirinn's first true triumph. She was a living, breathing testament to the power of medicine and proper care. Plus, there was simply a certain bond that developed when one cradled a mother's baby to her breast, when one held a woman's limp, enfeebled body and felt the life slowly return to it. A transcendent friendship of sorts. So, it was only knowing what came next that put the small lump in Eirinn's throat as she watched Lulu grasp the front of her mother's cream-colored sleeping gown and tug.

"Are you hungry?" Cerise clutched the top of the gown with a laugh when it nearly fell open, and Eirinn felt the warmth rush to her cheeks as she laughed along.

It was hard to believe it still possible, that she could still blush after all she had seen and done. But, awake, Cerise was a different person. When she was unconscious, she was just a patient, important, of course, as important as every woman who walked through the door, but still a patient, a woman on the verge of death who needed to be cleaned and maneuvered and undressed as part of her treatment.

Awake, Cerise was awash with personality. She was kind and she was charming. She was smart and she was fierce. Eirinn had watched her get better over the past few days out of sheer strength of will. Her daughter needed her alive, and Cerise was determined to stay that way for her.

"Dr. Anderson said she could try applesauce today, if you'd like."

"Applesauce?" Cerise's gaze lifted, soft glimmer in her eye that sent a tingle over Eirinn's skin. "She's never had it before."

"I thought maybe, so..." Eirinn produced the small canning jar from out of her pocket. "I figured you would want to feed it to her."

"Will you stay with us?" Shimmying over, Cerise made room next to her hip as Eirinn popped the lid and handed her the applesauce with a spoon, and Eirinn knew she shouldn't, knew she should get back to work and start the painful process of weaning herself away. Knew, even as sat down on the edge of the bed, quite at home in the intimate space. And quite like a visitor. That was how she needed to think of herself, like a visitor in Cerise and Lulu's lives. Or they in hers. "I guess she likes it."

Spoon to her lips, Lulu's eyes went as round as scones, toothless, satisfied grin coming to her face and small specks flying through the air as she gummed the applesauce.

"I guess so. That is a happy girl." Eirinn reached for one pudgy hand, smiling as Lulu seized her finger.

But her eyes rose back to Cerise. To the light lashes that lay, long and thick, against her pale skin. To the curve of Cerise's nose where it sloped toward full, slightly white-chapped lips.

Sitting there, beaming down at her delighted daughter, Cerise looked the picture of health and vitality. As if she were sitting for a portrait instead of in an infirmary bed. The only shadows on her face were sunlit curls. The only palpitating heart, as far as Eirinn could tell, was her own.

"I heard you ate all of your breakfast too."

"I did. It was so nice to eat without feeling sick."

"I imagine. No problems then?"

"No. No problems."

Nodding, swallowing, Eirinn failed to clear the lump that lingered in her throat, feeling instead it pulsate and grow, reaching acidic limbs down into her stomach. It was a good pain, she reminded herself. Bittersweet. Change, but good change. Good for Cerise. Good for Lulu. "That's wonderful to hear. You're doing so well, Dr. Anderson thinks you might be able to go home today."

Happy news, she was determined to deliver it with a smile, and she did, embracing the positive aspects of it. Cerise and Lulu were both well. She couldn't be more grateful for that.

"Cerise?" But at the fall in Cerise's expression, her put-on joy wavered. "Are you all right?"

Falling further inward, Cerise said nothing. She just continued to feed Lulu, shoveling small spoonfuls of applesauce up to her daughter's lips, stopping only when a tear rolled down her face and dripped into the fabric of Lulu's gown and Lulu grew discontent in her lap.

Taking the applesauce jar and spoon out of Cerise's hands, Eirinn set them aside and pulled Lulu into her own lap, calming her without thought.

"Cerise?" Nothing else working, she cupped her hand beneath Cerise's chin and pulled her head up, and the fear and pain in hazel eyes ravaged her good sense. "What is it? It's all right. You can tell me."

"My husband."

Words not unexpected - Cerise had mentioned her husband before - they were still disconcerting in the moment and Eirinn tried to prepare herself.

"What about him?"

"He doesn't know where we are."

"I know. You said." Though it wasn't entirely true, Eirinn knew Cerise believed it.

"I was sick for days before I came here." Hand sliding over Eirinn's, Cerise lowered their joined hands to her lap, fingertips, still rough from the dehydration that had ravaged her body for days, scratching against Eirinn's skin and sending prickles of sensation up into her arm. "So was Henry. He went to the clinic. He had to, so he could get back to work. But me... it was just extra money for us to spend. Money we don't have."

My husba... He's gon be so angry.

It wasn't the first time Eirinn had heard something in this regard. Cerise's husband, Henry, had been Cerise's first concern upon waking up, when she was still feverish and out of sorts.

We nee... go. We hava get home.

You're too weak to go anywhere, Dr. Anderson had told her then, and Cerise proved the point quite dramatically, by falling immediately back into unconsciousness.

When she woke more fully and Dr. Anderson could explain to her the severity of her condition and why it had started to affect her daughter, Cerise stopped insisting they leave and preferred not to mention Henry at all.

"But then Lulu started to act so strangely, and I couldn't..."

"I know." Cerise didn't have to. The possibilities had been a constant source of torment in Eirinn's mind for days. What if Lulu *had* contracted cholera? Could her tiny, malnourished body have survived that? What if she hadn't shown any symptoms? Would Cerise have just let herself get sicker and weaker, until one day her helpless body couldn't rise to cross the city and she faded slowly to her own demise?

"You did the right thing, bringing her here. And yourself." Eirinn was certain she had to know that.

"He won't think so," Cerise said, and Eirinn's heart didn't know which cadence to beat to - the fear, the wonder, or the fury. Cerise's hand still clutching tightly to hers, all three jerked and jockeyed for position inside her chest. "No one has been there to keep his house or make his meals. I took money for the cable car and the appointment. He probably thinks we ran off. He's going to be furious when he finds out where we've been. And it truly was stupid. I spent money to get well just so he can kill me when I get home."

"You don't really think he would -?"

Cerise blinked up, a vacancy in her gaze that agitated Eirinn's spine. Like walking past an abandoned building that had seen far too much torture and death. It was clear Cerise really did think that, that she feared her husband and what he would do when he saw her again.

"You were taking care of your daughter. Of yourself."

"Yes, well... we've never been much of a priority for him."

Then, why the hell would you stay with him? Question raging to mind, Eirinn bit her tongue until it hurt, knowing she couldn't ask it. Her father didn't tell her much about the harsher aspects of his childhood - the way he talked about it, he made being poor sound almost quaint and mythical - but she knew it wasn't. She knew choices made in poverty were not the same as choices made in means. And, if she hadn't known it before, her short time at the dispensary would have provided the lesson. In poverty, one didn't weigh the good and the bad and choose the best option. There might only be one option, and "best" might just mean the least atrocious.

"Isn't there anyplace else you can go?" The question felt slightly less callous, but still utterly hopeless when Cerise's head instantly began to shake. "No friends? No other family?"

"I have a brother. Acton." A small smile flickered onto Cerise's face, almost out of place, the microcosm of affection amidst the sinister background of her world. "He would never allow this. He has always been very protective of me, and Henry knows to be scared of him. That was why he waited until Acton was gone to... But he's in Manchester now. He moved there two years ago. He was supposed to send word once he got settled, but I never saw it."

"He didn't worry when you didn't write back?"

"I'm sure Henry replied for me."

"Right. Of course." Eirinn felt so stupid. So agonizingly out of her depth. With no husband of her own, and men in her life who would never dream of stealing her voice, she could only empathize to a certain degree. She had power for a woman. Freedom. Not as much as she wanted, and not to do entirely as she liked, but it was so much more than most women had. So many women had boots on their throats, or the threats of them if they made too big of missteps. They had fear that was immediate and proved out.

Gaze drawn to the pink scar that ran along the ridge of Cerise's collarbone, just inside the opening of her sleeping gown, Eirinn saw it anew. There were marks like that all over Cerise - scars and burns, fading yellow bruises. They could have been accidents, the signs of someone who lived and worked a much harder life than her own - Papa had many a strange and inexplicable scar too - but Eirinn wondered now how that pink line ended up on Cerise, shuddering at the notion anyone could have put it there on purpose.

59

"I can find your brother." She didn't know where the words came from. One second, she was wondering what sort of monster a man had to be to hurt someone like Cerise. What sort of twisted, inhumane brute. Then, the words were just there, emanating from beyond her brain, instinctive and fully decisive.

"You can?"

"I should be able to find him," Eirinn amended, fearing her first declaration sounded too much like a promise. "My father has contacts in Manchester. He worked the rails, so he has contacts almost everywhere. As long as your brother is still in Britain, we should be able to locate him."

Hope flickering, like a stubborn candle, it lit Cerise's face for a moment, before the reality of her situation cruelly snuffed it out. "That will take days. I may not have days."

The statement oozed like raw sewage, sweeping the divergent emotions that ran through Eirinn up into a singular, sticky rivulet of desperation.

She couldn't imagine it, being afraid to go home. Literally could not imagine. What a terrible feeling that had to be. "Then, I guess you'll have to come home with me."

"What?"

"Well, you can't stay here." Dr. Anderson might allow it - she probably would, were the situation explained to her - but the longer Cerise and Lulu stayed at the infirmary, the greater Cerise's risk for re-infection or that either one of them might catch something far worse. That was the rational, scientific reason Eirinn grasped onto. "And I can't let you go home."

"What if you don't find Acton?" Cerise asked.

"We'll deal with that if it comes to pass." Mind already set, Eirinn moved onto what she would say to her parents when she showed up that night with a woman and child in tow. It shouldn't be all that hard to explain, and it was only temporary. But when she looked to Cerise again she realized Cerise looked torn, and it occurred to her, with a sickening sense of helplessness, it wasn't her decision to make. "Only if you want."

"I do," Cerise was quick to say. "I'm just... I'm worried. I'm sure Henry is looking for us. I'm afraid of what he'll do if he finds us. Not just to us, but to you."

Her concern was perfectly valid. More valid than Cerise even knew. Because Henry wasn't just looking for Cerise and Lulu, he had already found them. A woman from their housing block had seen them at the dispensary - not a particular surprise given most of their patients at the moment were from the same geographic area - and Henry had come around asking about them. He encountered Rand first, assessing the priority of patients in the lobby sometime while Eirinn was upstairs, and Rand told him he didn't know if they had treated his wife and child, but it was a dispensary, not a clinic, and patients didn't stay there overnight.

It was the right answer, Dr. Anderson praised his quick-thinking. And, technically, supposed to be true. 69 Seymour Place *was* only a dispensary as far as the city's records were concerned, and no one was supposed to be sleeping there.

"He won't find you," Eirinn assured Cerise, more worried Henry might find them if they stayed. "We'll all be all right."

"Why would you do that for us?"

"Why shouldn't I do it for you?" Eirinn tried not to think too hard about her reasons. There were plenty of valid ones. Anything else she could push down and ignore. "You need someplace safe, and that's with me. With my family. In my parents' home. But only if you want to go there."

"I do," Cerise said.

"All right." Now that she had her agreement, a sense of uncertainty set in. Was this the right thing? What else was she going to do? Send Cerise and Lulu home and let the consequences fall where they may? No. There was no possible way she could do that. "I'll tell Dr. Anderson you're staying until Rand and I leave so we can see you home. I don't know how she'll feel about all of this." She would probably give Eirinn a lecture about keeping her work and personal lives separate, and, perhaps, it was just the lecture Eirinn needed. "But it doesn't matter. This has nothing to do with her. We're friends, aren't we?"

"Yes." Soft smile coming to her lips, Cerise made it very hard to think beyond just the three of them. "We're friends."

Chapter 9

CAROLINE

1886

Don Quixote was no substitute for true familiarity. Knowing how one story ended told Caroline nothing of the outcome of her own, and, without guidance, beyond the walls of the library she felt adrift.

Around her, the air stood still, but for the resumed appeals to Lucifer out of the bookstacks. She could hear the levity in them now. The occasional sniggered word. The laughter which followed. If Blanca and the others were lying about their allegiances, they were doing so with gusto, and if they truly did worship the devil they had a considerably better sense of humor about it than any of the Christians Caroline knew.

Blasphemous. Caroline provided her own scolding, acknowledging the thought as profane before it even reached her mind. But still it came, vulgar and fully formed.

She had always had a problem with such thoughts. Scandalous, un-ladylike musings. They would bound with some frequency out of her subconscious, overriding any appropriate thought she was trying to produce. Less often, but far more dangerously, they came as darts off the tongue, shooting out into the world. Dead giveaways to the fault in her nature.

Always an anomaly. Even Caroline couldn't know when and where a notion might meet with action. She could masquerade as a perfect lady for months at a time, nary so much as a missed cue. Then, there were moments, moments when her thoughts and temper converged into a beast, swallowing up all sense and decorum, like a starving tiger just burst from its cage.

One such episode might well have set the tone for her life - *episodes*, that was how her parents and Dr. Allen always referred to them - occurring as it did during her introduction to society at Harrington Estate when a particularly pompous dance partner explained to her the headache she was developing was, in fact, all in her head - mental, not physical, he was sure to enunciate - and the impulse to show him just how much it truly, physically hurt possessed Caroline's lower half, morphing her leg into a post maul strong enough to pound his foot down into the floor.

Everything in the room stopped in that moment. First, the dancers nearest them who had witnessed the incident first-hand. *Did you see that? She stomped him.* Mouths hanging open. Stares disbelieving.

Then, the whispers spread to the four corners of the room - *Did you see what that girl just did? Did she kick him? Who is it? Can you see her?* - until even the musicians ceased to play and every gaze that wasn't already glued to Caroline found its way.

Her dance partner might have even called her mad that night, once he was done bowing over and clutching at his injured foot. Caroline couldn't possibly recall one accusation from the next, because, though she couldn't hear the specific words being spoken around and about her, she knew everyone was saying *something*. None of it good.

She had forfeited every good husband in attendance that night by her parents' estimation.

Yet another episode had occurred in church, one Sunday as Vicar Brown was reaching rapturous exuberance about how, ever since Eve, women had been challenging the moral integrity of men.

The night before, Thomas had come home stumbling drunk from a night of poker several houses down, and instead of going into his own bedroom had come into hers. Caroline was awakened by the jostle of her bed and a callous hand pawing at her in the darkness. No interest in being the conquest of a vicious, slobbering brute, she managed to kick away and escape her own room and Thomas hadn't the will or strength to follow.

Sitting next to her, he still boasted the black rings under his eyes and the sour smell of liquor on his breath. His breath. His liquor. So, despite the fact it was nothing she hadn't heard in church many a Sunday before, that morning Caroline couldn't just sit there listening to Vicar Brown blame women for the ills of the world when men were doing a sensational job of destroying it without any input at all from her. Gathering her skirts, she elbowed Thomas hard in the chest and pushed past the other parishioners in their row.

She might have played it off as fleeing in illness if not for the raw animus on her face that drew gasps from the members of the congregation she passed. Caroline knew that was what they saw, because she could taste it, every wicked, mouthwatering morsel. In that moment, she hated Thomas, Vicar Brown, the church, and every person in it. She could have set the nave aflame and walked out grinning. She was an adult then, no youthful feralness to be blamed. It actually wasn't long ago at all. Scarcely more than a year. That was the moment she lost God to her side, she would assume, if she had to pick just one.

Thought bounding her back to the present, Caroline clutched *Don Quixote* more tightly to her chest, the weight of its words keeping her grounded as she made her way around the upper level of the house.

Much like the floor below, the top floor felt lived in, but carried an air of only nightly use. The residents, it seemed, spent most of their waking hours on the ground floor or outside, saving the higher floors for sleep or for learning. Or for reading maps or tending plants, Caroline amended as she crept between rooms, finding each one unlocked and unoccupied.

Even the bedrooms, of which only a small number were situated on the top floor, were left open. Caroline could tell at once which was Dr. Todson's, not because it was bigger or more fanciful than the others - it wasn't - but because it had a certain air about it, a distinction, as the woman herself did, a sense of style and purpose that was easy to place even having known her only a short time.

A stethoscope hung over the back of a chair. A pile of books balanced precariously on the floor next to the bed, though the bed itself was crisply made. A dress hung outside the wardrobe that Caroline could imagine no one else in the house wearing, at least not with so much flair.

But there were oddities too. On the far bedside table lay a singular book, worn and tattered, most likely a journal, on top of which sat some sort of small, half-carved wooden sculpture. A pair of heavy leather boots rested next to a chair, deep pockets sewn into their outer sides, as if they were made to hold something, a tool or a weapon. A red, orange, and turquoise mandala looped around part of the design in the beautifully ornate blackened wood headboard.

Caroline didn't know that Dr. Todson wasn't superstitious, or that she had no need for weapon-wielding footwear from time to time, but if she were to be presumptive - and, really, what else did she have to do? - she would presume two people slept in that bedroom, despite no previous signs to that effect. Even if Rand's feet fit those notably small boots, Dr. Todson had introduced him as her dearest friend, nothing more, and all the other men who worked the grounds were kept at a prudent distance as far as she could tell. All of this, Caroline observed and thought from the doorway. There was a fine line between looking and snooping, and that line for her was, apparently, the threshold of the door.

It was only when she came upon Rand's room a few doors down that she was absolutely convinced he wasn't Dr. Todson's nightly companion. Like Dr. Todson's room, Rand's room was easy to identify. Potted plants and vials littered every surface. Several sets of mortars and pestles lay scattered about, most with cracks on their bowls or chips in their bases. A microscope sat buried beneath a pile of braces and belts on the dresser.

Aside from two other bedrooms with no identifying characteristics - at least, none Caroline would recognize - the remainder of the rooms on the top floor were novel in their purposes. Next to Rand's room, an atrium with slanted glass walls bathed potted plants inside in a warm yellow glow. It had to be Rand's winter garden, for those things he put into his potions couldn't possibly grow outside all year in England.

Two small reading rooms with couches and lamps and fireplaces, each adjacent to a room with a desk, and four water closets - two for bathing and two for toileting - rounded out the upstairs' offerings.

Each room had a purpose. Each purpose was clear. All except for one.

Across the landing from the tall pocket doors of the library, a matching set of pocket doors led into a narrower, but just as elongated room. A massive table dominating its space, twelve chairs tucked neatly around it, bookshelves and worktables piled high with books and papers at the room's edges, enough maps and plans visible from the door it might have been an explorer's private study. Only, like everything else, the room was unlocked, free for Caroline to walk right in and nose around at her leisure. Hardly private.

In her quest to find answers, it seemed a good place to start, between the parchments in a room that felt oddly out of place. But, it occurred to her, she no longer wanted answers. Not at that very moment. Not badly enough to go digging through books in a cluttered room all by herself.

She wanted to sit for a while and observe.

She wanted to see what happened if she did nothing.

She wanted to hear the sound of voices once more, because as she had lingered the last few minutes at Dr. Todson's bedroom door and in Rand's winter garden, Blanca and the others finished with their lesson and retired down the stairs, leaving her entirely alone on the upper floor, where the space was giving her mind far too much room to echo.

Minutes later, *Don Quixote* abandoned on a side table as she made her way through the foyer, Caroline stood outside the front door.

Outside.

Not a soul there to stop her.

Not a bell to toll in warning.

She simply walked out, free as if in her own home.

Freer, perhaps.

Sun still shining, she looked to the sprawling front gardens and wooded grounds beyond, unable to see the fence or gate that surrounded the property. If she started to walk, there was some distance she could go before anything at all got in her way. But then what? Hop the fence?

Walk through the front gate? To where? Her life so wrapped up in Thomas's, what was left for her outside these walls? Where could she run that would be safer than where she now stood? How could she care for herself when she had no means and no skills?

She couldn't.

Instead of setting her free, the truth held her captive, and Caroline sank somewhat at her reality. Not only did she have no place to go, she had no motivation to go there. The only thing she had left was her curiosity and her senses, and she followed both around the side of the house to the back gardens, where she located nearly the entirety of the household. Or a fair portion of it. Half a dozen women lounging in the shade just where she could see, she didn't know who she was looking for exactly until she saw her nowhere amongst them.

"Hello." Approaching two women who sat side-by-side on a wicker swing suspended from one sturdy tree branch, Caroline made the effort to smile.

"Hello," the women greeted her in return.

"Caroline," Caroline reminded them.

"Francie," one of the women said.

"Stella," the other told her.

"Stella." Recalling the name from her very recent upstairs' conversation, Caroline felt slightly more at ease as she realized they had at least one thing in common. "I just borrowed some of your work from the library."

"Is that right?" Stella asked. "And what did you think?"

"It's beautiful."

"Thank you very much." Stella looked pleased, and it seemed enough of an opening to press for some friendly information.

"Have either of you seen Lei?"

"Not since right after lunch," Francie said, and, nodding, disappointed, Caroline wished that it helped, but that was when she had last seen Lei herself. Right after she discovered how the women ate, all together, not at long tables spooning slopped up gruel off of metal plates, but like at a dinner party, passing around appetizing recipes in fine serving dishes. "But I'm sure she's in her workshop, like always."

"Her workshop?" Caroline let hope dawn. Left to her own devices, she didn't even know how to begin to look for Lei. The house was manageable enough, but the grounds were immense. It would take all day to search them, and, in the meantime, she and Lei could easily pass each other by acres.

"You've been down to the cellar, yeah?" Francie asked.

"I have." Caroline's hope faltered.

"It's down there. Once you get to that level, veer left and you'll find it. Just follow the sounds of clattering and profanity."

Stella laughing a raucous laugh, Francie laughed at herself, but Caroline's amusement felt stilted as she glanced back toward the house.

"Thank you," she half-lied.

The path down was every bit as uninviting as Caroline remembered. The dimly-lit stairwell. The cold stone walls. Hints of her former expectations crawling through the cracks and the damp.

She had never liked being below ground. It always made her think about death in the basest of terms. Even as a young girl. It was all those terrible turns of phrase - *six feet under, pushing daisies, back to the earth*. They connected death to the ground in a tangible, fixed way that was neither real nor imagined.

Death *was* earth. Earth was where one ended up once she ceased to be. Humans in boxes or ashes, animals decomposing back into the soil. Assuming they didn't get picked off by vultures or other scavengers first.

But death also wasn't earth. It was poison and bodies lying prone on a kitchen floor. It was a list of things to do and responsibilities one never thought to have. It was shock and it was grief. It was pain so intense, one beckoned it next to her door. A downward spiral into numbness and lethargy.

Downward. It seemed everything bad waited at the bottom of a descent. Even religious mythology situated Heaven above and Hell below.

Yet, even with all of that, Caroline had followed Lei down the same set of stairs she looked to with apprehension now. She didn't want to - the same clutch of fear she always felt when she looked to a basement stairway strangled her throat and pressed the air from her lungs - but she did it anyway. In search of salvation. What she searched for now, aside from Lei, she was less certain, but it was enough to make her take the first stair and then the next even as she questioned her own judgment. And Lei's. Who would choose to be down here in such bleak emptiness when there were so many beautiful places to inhabit on the floors above?

The answer to that question, that was what she was seeking, Caroline told herself as she forced her legs onward and downward. Despite the chill that puckered her skin. Despite the foreboding that battered at her breastbone.

When she reached the bottom of the stairs, she stopped to listen. A scurry the first sound she heard, it melted her will. That connected death to the earth too - its rats and its insects - those carriers of disease that spread the Black Death in waves of human suffering.

Maybe I'll just wait for Lei to come back upstairs, she contemplated for the dozenth time before another noise, a clang just as she had been told to expect, resounded through the dead space ahead.

Clang. The sound came again, metallic and ringing. Trailing off in a series of repetitive thumps, Caroline followed the rhythm down a long, narrow corridor - there were multiple ways she could go - hoping her ears weren't deceiving her in the labyrinthine space.

Several closed doors greeting her along the way, she tried her best to ignore them and thoughts of what might be behind them, standing at last before the door from which the sounds seemed to emanate. Unmarked, like all the rest, it looked stark and unwelcoming, but at another clang

67

from within, she raised a hesitant hand to knock, waiting for reply. Then again, louder, when none came.

Unsure what to do next, not sure she wanted to know what was inside that room if it *wasn't* Lei, she moved her hand to the handle, hesitating for a moment before giving it a small press and pushing the door slightly ajar. At least, that was her every intention. Door heavier and more stubborn than anticipated, it stuck for a moment before giving way, dragging her into the room on a resounding creak.

Sharp flash of light assaulting her vision, Caroline didn't have time to consider whether it hurt or not as the more acute pain shot across her thigh and, with a startled cry, she staggered unseeing into the room.

"Oh! No! Oh no! Caroline! Oh my God! Are you all right?!"

Lei. At least she had found her. Although, Caroline certainly couldn't see Lei to prove it. White light clearing, she saw nothing in fact. Nothing but vacuous space with no end and no edges.

"Are you all right?"

Let me consider, she mused, Lei's raw panic - unseen, but certainly felt - having a strangely calming effect.

What do I feel? Lei's hands upon her, suddenly, one on her side, the other resting gently beneath one elbow. Soothing. Pain, scorching, ravaging the front of her right thigh. Caroline imagined it had to be what livestock felt when they were branded.

What can I see? Nothing. Nothing at all. The world, in its entirety, was a dark, empty chasm.

Other than that? She felt fine. A bit dizzy perhaps from her sudden loss of vision, and Lei's hands, which were disorienting and distracting where they touched her without visual warning.

"Can you see?" Lei only seemed to realize why she was acting so strangely.

"No." And it was only as she spoke the word that Caroline felt her first trace of raw fear.

"Here, sit down."

Lei urging her forward, Caroline could do nothing but trust her intentions, hobbling along for several agonizing steps to be sat down on something that felt solid, if not particularly comfortable.

"Did it hit you?" Lei asked her, but her hands were already seeking, moving through the folds of Caroline's skirts.

"Just on the thigh," Caroline said at the same time Lei seemed to find evidence of her own.

"Oh God," Lei breathed, but Caroline didn't know what would happen next until she felt the chilled air enwrap her ankles, then her calves, then her cheeks flush hotly as she realized Lei was pulling her skirts up.

"I'm fine. Really." Pressing the fabric back down, she tried to maintain some level of decorum.

"You're bleeding."

"I am?"

"God. Hold on. Just stay here."

Faint as the length of her dress gathered in her lap and air rushed into the wound on her thigh like a jab with a needle, Caroline didn't know where Lei thought she was going to go. Without her sight. With no idea where in the room she was or how to get back to the door. With pain. So, so much pain.

"Don't worry. Your vision will come back."

"Good to know." Caroline couldn't even tell where Lei was in the room, despite her efforts to track her movements. Sounds reaching her from multiple directions, it was clear Lei was searching for something, and her voice seemed to come from nowhere and everywhere at the same time.

"I've done it to myself. It shouldn't cause any permanent damage."

That was comforting. All except the "shouldn't" part. It was far more comforting when, seconds later, light began to flicker in at the edges of her vision, and Caroline could at last make out the outer walls of the room. Though, center still dark, she couldn't find Lei and assumed she had to be somewhere directly in front of her.

A moment later, she heard Lei's footsteps and felt her presence, coming closer and lowering down, much as it had the night before as she lay half-conscious on the fainting couch.

"This is going to sting," Lei warned her, waiting for her slight head bob of acceptance before pressing a wet cloth against the wound, and, preface wholly inadequate, Caroline pitched forward, reaching out on reflex to grab Lei's shoulder, strong and sturdy before her. "Sorry."

The wound soaking up the burn in the liquid, Caroline felt as if she had been set on fire, like her thigh was kindling and she was standing at the stake. Until, several torturous seconds later, the flesh began to cool, liquid in the cloth sieving away the pain and leaving a sizzling tingle in its wake.

Her vision trickling clearer too, little by little, spot by spot, she jolted as she saw a great pair of green bug eyes staring her straight in the face. Before more of Lei materialized and she recognized the eyes as goggles, pushed up on Lei's forehead, and saw Lei's real eyes were still there, staring up at her, as dark as ever and blatantly concerned.

"I can see you," Caroline told her, and Lei huffed a weak breath, shoulder rising and falling beneath Caroline's hand.

"Good."

The panic starting to subside, along with the pain, Caroline became aware of the contrasting sensations in her leg. The cool crackle of the solution against the warmth of Lei's hand where it held the cloth to her skin. Drop of liquid squeezing loose to roll down the inside of her thigh, she bit her lip to withhold a gasp, or a moan, as the sensation tingled upwards toward her torso and accelerated her breath.

"How about this? How is it feeling?"

Unexpected. If Caroline were to limit herself to a single word. Then, what could she have expected? She couldn't recall the last time someone else's hand was on her bare thigh. If she could ever recall one. She wasn't sure there had ever been. Not since she was in nappies. "Better." Reaching for the cloth, she wrenched if from Lei's hand. "I've got it."

And, relieved of her duty, Lei sat back, but it wasn't of particular relief when her hands came to rest on Caroline's exposed knees. "I am so sorry," she said. "I was working on a ricochet. The door startled me just as I was hitting the trigger and I shifted enough to change the trajectory. Did you knock?"

"I did."

"I had my ears plugged to hammer. I should have known better. I should have been listening for someone."

"I heard noises." Watching the guilt crawl across Lei's features, Caroline felt the incredible urge to chase it away and at least partly responsible for what had happened. "But I wasn't sure if they were you. I was told when I found you there would also be profanity."

The statement did the trick, disrupting Lei's vigil of self-chastisement, sparking first surprise, then indignation, then mild amusement on her face. "Who told you that?"

"Francie."

"Of course, she did. She isn't wrong. Is it terribly painful?" Lei asked, glancing to Caroline's hand where it held the cloth to the wound, and the wound oozed magma, up through Caroline's leg and into her lower abdomen. Renewed embarrassment, perhaps. Modesty making a belated, valiant stand. Caroline couldn't say exactly what it was she felt, but she did know she was oddly, achingly aware. Of Lei's gaze up her dress. Of the slight shift of Lei's hands on her knees whenever either of them moved or breathed.

"No, it isn't that bad." Each time she thought she was extinguished, no longer in danger of burning alive, another ember sparked.

"Honestly," Lei beseeched her. "I never would have done this to anyone on purpose, but now that I have... what did you feel when it hit you?"

"Are you researching me?" Distracted, it took Caroline several seconds to realize.

"Do you mind?"

"No... I suppose not." She did, however, suffer a moment's disbelief. Lei's contrition a few seconds before was genuine, the guilt that played over her face every bit as blatant as the curiosity that showed on it now.

But the curiosity was genuine too.

"So, what did you feel?"

And, evidently, most eager.

Dragging her eyes away from Lei in an effort to restore some of the function to her brain, Caroline tried to recall as she looked around the room, discovering it wasn't that difficult. The moment was seared into her memory almost as tangibly as the wound in her thigh. "It was an incredible shock," she said. "And immensely painful."

"More than a sting?"

"Much more than a sting."

Expression on Lei's face difficult to interpret, it might have been because it was such an amalgam of incompatible things. Caroline was certain she saw pride there, amidst Lei's acute interest, but it was darkly tinged with regret.

"And now?" Lei asked.

"Now?" Pulling the cloth away from the wound, Caroline felt it the only way to get a true account. She just didn't expect that account to be quite so ghastly. Stomach lurching at the sight of her own thigh, she pressed her lips together, swallowing down the surge that rose into her throat.

"It's bad," Lei warned her too late, clearly afraid Caroline was about to expel everything she felt. And Caroline couldn't promise she wouldn't.

Skin missing for several inches along the top and inside of her thigh, it looked as if a plow had rolled across it, or a ditch-digger, tilling up flesh in preparation for the laying of seeds or piping. It was a pit. A veritable trench of raw, pulverized meat. Grotesque as it looked, though, it proved a rather weak indicator of the pain, which returned with a bite like the teeth were still lodged inside her skin. With a hiss and a flinch, Caroline recovered the gnarly gash with the cloth, shocked by how much the liquid had been keeping the pain at bay.

"That painful?" Lei winced along with her.

"It actually is rather excruciating," Caroline confirmed, and there was no longer any vacillation. All pleasure at her chance experiment draining out of her, Lei looked positively shamefaced.

"Hold on. I can help with that." Rocking back on her heels, she set off in the direction of a large L-shaped workspace cluttered entirely with parts and machinery. "I always keep some of Rand's tonics down here just in case. Which one is it? Here. This one." Searching through a cabinet on the wall, she came away with a small jar.

"It's all right. I can handle a lot of pain," Caroline said.

"Why, when you don't have to?" Lei looked softly baffled as she came back her way, and Caroline had no answer for that. She *could* handle a lot of pain. Many days of her life, she had no choice. But why would she appeal for it? Was she looking for punishment, or an excuse? Because, as the pain in her leg reared its ugly truth, she couldn't deny how quickly her mind had jumped to the laudanum in the upstairs' drawer.

"It's only a balm," Lei assured her. "It's very much like the serum in the cloth. It will relieve the pain and help the wound to heal. With any luck, you won't even have a scar. Well, you'll have a smaller one at least." Lei seemed to accept, as Caroline had accepted, there was no conceivable way there wasn't going to be some sign of this incident left behind. From the size and depth of the wound, Caroline was just surprised there wasn't a puddle of blood by her feet and she wasn't unconscious on the floor.

"It was a ray, not a projectile," Lei explained as she handed her a dry cloth, and Caroline removed the serum-drenched compress with thrumming fear, knowing now just how quickly the pain would come chomping back. "I know it looks bad, but it's clean. It won't get infected."

"Is that why there's so little blood?"

"Yes. It creates a sort of seal. It's heat. It closed itself. May I?" Jar of balm cradled like an offering in her hands, it was clear what Lei was asking, and why she was asking it. Though, it seemed strange for her to seek permission at this point. She had spent the last several minutes under Caroline's skirts. What were a few more? If Lei needed to atone, Caroline would let her. That, and Caroline didn't think she could bear the sight of her own leg long enough to put the balm on herself.

"All right."

Sinking down before her, Lei pressed her dress further up as she situated between her knees, and Caroline held the fabric higher on her hips, all awkwardness overshadowed by her surge of dread. Wound already searing, she knew it was going to hurt, she knew it was going to hurt quite a lot, and she was right. The first brush of Lei's fingers nearly intolerable, a strangled cry reverberated in her throat and she gripped the edge of the wooden crate with her free hand to keep from shoving Lei bodily away.

"I am so sorry," Lei said again, and Caroline accepted the apology with a clenched jaw and a nod, feeling the tears press behind her tightly shut eyelids.

It took time, several mercilessly long seconds, for the balm to do anything but add to the onslaught, to the injury, but when it did finally start to soak into her damaged flesh, it found the bite and conquered it quite handily. Teeth dislodged, warmth starting to cool, Caroline opened her eyes, looking to Lei crouched down before her.

"Any better?" Lei hands came to rest back on her knees, and Caroline felt dizzy. Exhausted. At the whim of her body, its pangs of both pain and pleasure.

"Much. That is amazing."

"I know, isn't it? Rand does know his physic." Clean swath of fabric brandished in her hands, Lei draped it across the wound, wrapping the ends gently, but securely, around Caroline's thigh, front to back, then back to front. "You should still let Dr. Todson look at it," she said as she secured it in a small knot at the side. "She'll know better than I do how to tend to it."

"All right," Caroline returned, not entirely sure she was ready to let another woman under her skirts any time soon, even if she did have Dr. in front of her name.

"I truly am sorry."

Lei looked so defeated, regret so raw and unforgiving on her face, Caroline suffered another unexpected pang. Of sympathy. Bordering on affection. Fingers twitching, she wanted to reach out, to ease the distress that crinkled Lei's brow, but it would be wildly inappropriate. She couldn't just touch Lei as if they were on such intimate terms. Even if

Lei's hands still rested on her knees like they had every right of possession.

"It truly is all right. You said it was a beam that hit me?" Realizing Lei would have no place to put her hands if she weren't still so utterly exposed to her, Caroline eased her dress down her legs, giving Lei no choice but to rise to her feet or tumble backward onto the floor.

"Yes." Lei chose the more graceful former option. "It's a light. An energy."

"Will you show me?" Caroline asked, and Lei's head gave a small tilt. "Can you stand?"

It was a fair and most considerate question. One Caroline couldn't possibly answer until she made the attempt. Glancing down at the wooden crate, she sought a sturdy handhold, detecting Lei's hand as it drifted into her sightline and accepting it as the most sensible solution.

Pain still present - she couldn't pretend it wasn't - as she rose to her feet, it faded to an afterthought, a distant echo of what it had been only moments before. She could even walk with only the hint of a limp, and that limp abated as they crossed the room, as if Rand's balm was still seeking out the enemy and deploying new regiments to its cause.

"This is it." Lei laid her hand atop a tall metal contraption on the L-shaped workbench when they reached it.

"All right. How does it work?"

"It amplifies light."

"How?"

"It's all about the atoms." Clearly waiting to be asked, Lei grew increasingly animated, flipping open a panel on the front of the machine and pointing out the cylinder within. "This tube is fitted with a diamond core. Energy stirs up the atoms inside the diamond and as the atoms return to their original state, they release particles of light. Mirrors bounce the light particles back and forth and as those particles collide they create even more light particles, multiplying at an exponential rate until there is a build-up of light energy of the same wavelength. When the shutter - here - opens, it shoots out, acting as... as an arrow of sorts. It's powerful enough to cut through many materials. Paper, wood, stone."

"Flesh." Caroline grinned to assure Lei it was only in jest when Lei looked abashedly her way. "Where did you learn all of this?"

"Archimedes."

"Archimedes? Really? I never would have guessed you for two thousand years old."

"From his works." Lei softly laughed. "Do you know about his death ray?"

"Mirrors redirecting the sun's light to set fire to Roman ships?"

Lei looked pleased. Marginally impressed, even. Thankfully, that was all that it took, because Caroline had officially exhausted her knowledge on the subject.

"It makes logical sense," Lei said. "Redirect the energy of the sun into a single point and the heat is thousands of times greater than the heat of that light dispersed. It's easily testable with a magnifying glass and a blade of grass."

"So, you're recreating the energy of the sun?"

"Not the sun exactly, but the amplification process."

"And you built this machine by yourself?"

"I had extra hands when I needed them, but the design is mine."

"It's big."

"Yes." Lei's dark eyes moved over the imposing contraption. "It looks impressive, but it's often easier to build something large before you build it small. It has limited purpose in this form. I'll figure it out, though. Smaller and stronger. It will just take time."

Voice brimming with fervor, calculations working behind her eyes, Lei's enthusiasm was intoxicating. Infectious. Caroline felt the draw of it, the enchantment tugging her into Lei's orbit.

"Is that why you're here?" It was also dangerous. *Light energy. Death rays. Archimedes.* Where Lei had gathered her knowledge was of little consequence compared with how many people would prefer she not have it. Both Lei's interests and her passion were exactly the sorts of things that got a woman put into a place like this if anyone found out about them.

"Not exactly." Lei's excitement didn't extinguish, but it did dim. "I chose to come here."

"Why? Why would you choose to come here?" Caroline asked.

"Is it really all that bad?"

"No." Question fully considered, Caroline couldn't say that it was. But she had only been there a day and spent much of that time unconscious. She knew very little of what happened inside these walls or how real any of her experiences that day had been. "But this isn't your home."

"According to whom?"

"Don't you have a family somewhere? A house?"

"Yes. Here." Glancing her way, Lei's eyes carried a hint of warning, as if Caroline was treading on sacred ground and should think long and hard before taking another step in the same direction.

"I'm sorry. I didn't mean to offend you."

"You didn't."

No, Caroline realized as Lei looked away. Offense would have been kinder. She had wounded Lei, much as Lei had wounded her. Unexpectedly, and entirely by accident.

"Would you like to see how it works?"

"Yes." Caroline would like to do anything to extricate them from their current failure of conversation.

"Here. Put these on." Lei handed her a pair of goggles, green-lensed, like those still perched atop her own head, and Caroline struggled to situate them, at last finding a strap to fix them more securely to her face as Lei pulled on her own. "Are you ready?"

"I think so."

"Don't worry. I promise not to shoot you again." Sparing her another glance, a small grin played over Lei's lips, and, statement relaxing her shoulders, Caroline was relieved to hear it.

"This switch redirects the steam." The next few minutes were a lesson in science as, machine whirring in the background, Lei explained what was happening from the start of the process to the end, pointing out the steam that rose from the water heater beneath the table and explaining how it excited the atoms inside the tube. "Do you want to press the trigger?" she asked after looking through the scope atop the machine and locking it on target - a large block of wood clamped in front of a metal-sheathed wall across the room.

"Yes." Absolutely, Caroline wanted to press the trigger. What sane person wouldn't?

"This one." Lei pointed out the big green button, and, squaring up to it, Caroline recalled the pain she had felt as the beam crossed her thigh and imagined Thomas's face in its crosshairs. His wooden block head, smirking, so proud of what he had done. Smashing the button with her hand, she sent the light - bright green through the lenses of the goggles - shooting across the room to hit him right between the eyes.

As the glow fell away, she couldn't tell at first anything had happened, beyond the streak of light itself. Then, she saw it, the small hole in the wooden block. Glancing to Lei to make sure it was safe, she peeled her goggles over her head as Lei pushed hers up, drifting to the end of the workbench to squint through the clean-cut tunnel she could see even from a distance.

"No. Light, really? Is it really just light?"

"It is really just light," Lei told her, and Caroline caught her enthusiasm.

"Can we do it again?"

"Of course." Smile tilting her lips, Lei tugged her goggles back on.

For some time after that, they did damage with the light ray, and, in that time, Thomas had taken all sorts of pains. To his face. To his manhood. To his black, black heart. It was so immensely satisfying watching the beam pass through whatever material Lei put in front of it, at some point, Caroline forgot where she was. She could have been in a university or a business research laboratory or in the stately home of an eccentric friend.

Light is the most powerful force in the universe, Lei said when Caroline questioned the very nature of what she was seeing, and, turning her attention to the other devices in the room, Caroline felt the pulse of wonder in her wrists and her throat. If one machine did this, what might all the others around them do?

"Is there anything else in here we can play with?"

"Oh, there are loads of toys in here," Lei said, but, much to Caroline's disappointment, she was already easing her goggles over her head and settling them onto the workbench. "But not right now." Shutting the light amplifier down, her eyes flicked to the wooden device in the center of the wall that Caroline had conjectured was some sort of clock, despite it having no hands, nor numbers for that matter. "Right now, it's almost teatime."

Chapter 10

EIRINN

1866

Eirinn wasn't sure who was more surprised when they at last made it to the house - Cerise, whose eyes went wide, mouth falling slightly agape as the brougham stopped out front, and again when they stepped into the foyer, or Mama and Papa, who were still in the dining room and sat with gently inquisitorial expressions as Eirinn introduced Cerise and Lulu to them.

Despite the gravity of those questions, Mama and Papa didn't put them into words, not while Eirinn and Cerise were eating their dinner, Mama perfectly delighted to hold and entertain Lulu so her mother could feed herself. They had to know where Cerise and Lulu came from - it wasn't as if Eirinn and Rand were out gallivanting about the city when they were gone during the day - but they accepted Eirinn's explanation that Cerise and Lulu needed to stay with them for a few days without immediate debate.

It was a temporary reprieve, Eirinn knew, a kindness afforded to Cerise and Lulu, not to her. She owed her parents more information - it was, after all, their house - so, after setting Cerise up in a real bath, much to her great pleasure, with Lulu in a makeshift pen on the bathroom floor and Bally just outside in case they needed any help, Eirinn made the expedition back down the stairs to meet her parents' remarkably patient curiosity in the parlor.

"Of course, we'll look for her brother and get her a train ticket if we get a favorable reply," Papa said in response to her request, which came complete with explanation.

Papa looked angry then, in hearing why Cerise and Lulu needed their help, the tensing of his jaw visible even in the low light of the fire, and Mama shook her head, pulling her shawl tighter about her shoulders as if she would never quite get used to the coldness of the world.

But Cerise and Lulu's situation wasn't the only thing troubling her parents' expressions. Eyes cast toward his brandy, Papa ran his finger around its rim, and Mama looked to the fire, pensive as she stared into its flames.

"All right, what is it?" Hard as she tried, Eirinn couldn't ignore both of them, and, question on the air, Mama and Papa exchanged a long, opinion-laden look.

"Are you certain you can trust her?" Papa asked at last, and Eirinn felt jostled. As if she had just taken an unexpected knock from an unruly crowd, she skewed slightly on her feet. And, just like with a knock from an unruly crowd, it took only a split-instant for that surprise to warp into indignation.

"Of all the people to ask me that? Papa, I thought you would -"

"It's not because she is poor, Eirinn." Papa obliterated her looming tirade with his calm and steady tone. "It's because of you."

"Me? What did I do?"

"You have an incredible heart. You respond naturally to those in need."

Nice as the sentiment sounded, it felt like an accusation, an unfair one at that, and Eirinn cast equally accusatory eyes Mama's way.

"Yes, you get it honestly," Papa conceded. "And it happens to be one of your finest qualities. But some people *will* take advantage of that."

"He's right, Sweetheart." Given that she was the source of the aforementioned problem, Eirinn thought Mama could at least have held out a few more seconds before agreeing. "We know very well how smart and how capable you are, but you are also incredibly sensitive, and you have little experience with how people might use someone of your nature. Your father isn't criticizing or doubting you. He is asking you."

Put like that, it sounded entirely reasonable. Loving, even. Of course, it was loving. What else would it be? Her parents had never been anything but to her.

"Yes," Eirinn said. "I am certain I can trust her."

"Very well." Papa seemed content with that. "But there is nothing I can do tonight. I'll reach out to my contacts in Manchester first thing tomorrow. If her brother is there, we'll find him."

"Thank you, Papa," Eirinn said, and Papa nodded, lips still pressed tight with concern.

"You know we'll do anything we can to help you. And your friends. Just be careful, Eir. There is always some danger in messing with the order of things."

"And a tender heart is easily bruised," Mama added. Which sounded ominous. Like a curse almost. Until a smirk curved her lips. "No matter how bold and scrappy its exterior."

"You make me sound like a determined puppy."

"Yes, I know." Raising her teacup, Mama hid her smile behind its rim, but Papa's laugh resonated, deep and mirthful, as he reached for his brandy to take a drink.

By the time Eirinn made it back upstairs, Cerise was out of her bath and Bally was waiting in Eirinn's bedroom, keeping an eye on their guests in the adjoining chamber. Considerably smaller than Eirinn's room, the chamber was originally built as a companion's suite, but it hadn't been used for that purpose for as long as they had lived in the house. Bally and Rand were the only two employees who had ever resided with them, and they took their rooms at the other end of the hall as to have a modicum of privacy, so the companion's suite was only ever put to use when Eirinn's friends or cousins stayed the night.

That had been some years ago, though, and those friends and cousins were younger and smaller, without babies in toe. It wasn't an ideal space, and Cerise had been offered better. She could have had her choice of the guest rooms down the hall, but had opted to stay in the room nearest to Eirinn. It had to be frightening for her, Eirinn imagined, being there in a strange house amongst nearly all strangers. Cerise and Lulu had gone from the unfamiliar accommodation of the dispensary to the unfamiliar accommodation of the Todson house, and Eirinn hated to think they might feel equally uncomfortable in either place.

"Are they all right?" Eirinn asked Bally in a whisper, and Bally smiled, tired, Eirinn could tell, from her day, but still willing to do her this one last service. As a favor, not as a duty.

"They're clean and they're warm." Little knowing Cerise and Lulu, it was the best assessment Bally could make. "That little one is a dream."

"Yes, she truly is." Eirinn glanced through the door of the companion's suite, gaze alighting on Cerise where she stood alongside the crib that Rand had dug out and dusted off from storage. Cerise's hair still damp from her bath, it looked a shade darker than usual where it fell against the soft blue paisley pattern of her borrowed wrapper, and appreciation seized Eirinn. It couldn't help but seize her. She did, after all, share her mother's love of beautiful things.

"Don't be getting too attached now." Bally gave her arm a gentle squeeze. Everyone seemed to be warning her. She should probably pay heed to that. "It'll just make it harder when they go."

"I know." Ache already pressing, it was the same one Eirinn had felt since she thought Cerise and Lulu would be leaving the dispensary, and had only grown more pronounced when she realized the safest place for them might be two hundred miles away from London. "I don't think I fully considered how easy it would be to become attached when you take care of someone."

"You could have just asked me, Dear," Bally said, and Eirinn smiled as she glanced over at her, hand sliding over Bally's where it rested on her arm.

"Goodnight." Bally pressed a kiss to her cheek.

"Goodnight, Bally," Eirinn returned, watching her go out the bedroom door and nodding when Bally looked wordlessly back to see if she wanted it closed.

Left alone in her bedroom with Cerise and Lulu, Eirinn barely glanced through the door of the companion's suite before she was drawn through it. "Is she asleep?"

Cerise nodding without looking up, Eirinn dropped her gaze to the crib, finding Lulu in a deep, steady slumber on her stomach, her tiny blanketed back moving up and down with comforting consistency.

"She's beautiful, isn't she?" Cerise asked.

"Yes, she is." For once, Eirinn didn't have to exaggerate for the mother's sake. She had told many a white lie regarding the loveliness of people's children since she started work at the dispensary, but, dark hair feathering against the side of her head, cherubic cheeks tinged pink with sleep, Lulu truly was one of the most beautiful babies Eirinn had ever seen. Which made perfect sense. "Just like her mother."

At last, Cerise looked to her, small smile softening her face, but tears shimmering in her eyes. Along with the other thing, the pressing one, the one that had Eirinn teetering precariously on edge and Cerise leaning more freely against her in the brougham on the way to the house. A casual understanding that the same rules no longer applied. Freed from the dispensary, they were no longer a doctor's apprentice and her patient with a certain expectation of decorum and distance. They were two women who yearned for something more than the moments that had passed between them. Eirinn could see it in Cerise's gaze as distinctly as she felt it through her own body.

"Are you all right?" she asked.

"Yes." Glancing back to the crib, Cerise's eyes roamed Lulu's sleeping face. "I've just never seen her sleep like this. There's always too much noise. It's too cold. She sleeps, but it's restless, like everyone else there. She looks so peaceful here."

Tears rushing to her eyes, Eirinn shook them away, struggling to breathe through the tightness in her chest as the admission seared into her. It was painful to think about, two people she had come to care so much for in such a short amount of time living such a difficult life. She couldn't fix it. She certainly couldn't undo their past. She could only be there for them now, and, reaching out, she laid her hand against the warm curve of Cerise's neck, thumb stroking the contours of her jaw before coming to rest on the strong, steady pulse that, just days before, had been terrifyingly sluggish.

"You didn't have to do this for us." Cerise turned to face her, and that pulse jumped and quickened.

"Yes, I did." It was as close to an admission as it felt safe to get, and the ethereal fantasy orbited around them, pressing them closer, dreamlike and intangible until they decided to make it real.

So many women Eirinn knew were confused or ignorant of their own feelings. They thought it a proper, feminine trait, their ignorance, because it was inappropriate for ladies to speak of such things. But Eirinn knew exactly what she felt. Mama had always been very candid with her about what she would one day feel, *should* one day feel, about the emotions another person could stir.

Don't listen to other women when they talk about intimate relations, she told Eirinn just days after she turned thirteen. *They will tell you sexual relations are the temptations of men. That they are something women have to endure. They will tell you to find other things to think about. It is the most worthless, dangerous advice I have ever heard young women given, and, as you know, that is saying something. If you have to send your mind somewhere else, your body is in the wrong place. That's a good rule in most things, but especially in this. Being intimate with someone should feel good. Always. Beyond good if you're doing it right.*

Mama smiled then in a way that was absolutely traumatizing at the time. But, in the years since, her guidance had saved Eirinn from many a potential mistake. Plenty of men had tried to convince her she wanted what they wanted, from their physical advances to marriage, and Eirinn was quite resolute in the fact she did not. She couldn't have understood it at the time, but in being honest with her Mama had given her two things most women were never given - the freedom to feel her true, unfettered feelings and the freedom to refuse.

There was great power in knowing what one desired and what one didn't. There was great power in feeling equally desired in return.

"Is this okay?"

When Cerise's hand slid onto her chest, Eirinn felt both - desire and desired - Cerise's gaze whispering something that couldn't be put into words. Or, if it could, not with the same eloquence.

At a loss for words herself, Eirinn found they weren't particularly needed as she slid her hand beneath the wet fall of Cerise's hair, and took a forward step, the warm press of Cerise's body against her own like an affirmation as Cerise's lips met hers.

Far from chaste, the kiss was still utterly tender, questioning and exploratory. Yet, Eirinn's skin and veins responded as if it was a full-body assault. Even before Cerise kissed her harder with more abandon, moan humming in her throat that weakened Eirinn's knees and nearly sent them toppling into Lulu's crib.

Many soft, pulsating minutes later, Eirinn felt the mark of Cerise's lips across her cheek and down her throat, and, senses misfiring in all directions, she marveled at her own astonishing stupidity. She thought she knew a lot about the human body, but a dozen lectures on anatomy couldn't possibly have prepared her for this. Even her mother's words of wisdom felt wildly insufficient. Or maybe there was no logic or explanation that could encompass something so personal. So intimate. So visceral and of the flesh, yet so utterly mystical.

"Wait." Sense and reason slipping rapidly away as Cerise's hands worked against her chest and chilled air slipped through the newly unbuttoned fabric of her dress, Eirinn glanced to the crib and Lulu sleeping within in it.

"She'll be fine," Cerise said, and Eirinn looked back to her, realizing, with a flush of surprise, she was nervous. Incredibly, tremulously so. She had walked into so many places where insults greeted her at the door and eyes pierced her back, yet she had never been more nervous than she was right now. In this moment. In her own home. With a woman who looked at her with so much affection it was almost reverent.

"You don't owe me anything." Eirinn had to be clear for her own sake. When this was over, all she would have was the memory, and she didn't want it tainted with uncertainty.

"Good thing." The statement brought a gently bemused smile to Cerise's lips. "Because I'm not that good at this."

"Well, I've never done it before at all. So, I guess we'll be not that good at it together."

Smile flickering, fading, Cerise's eyes flashed slightly wide, and Eirinn worried. Worried she had ruined everything. Worried she had broken the spell that had been cast between them. She knew how she came across to people. Confident. Unassailable. As if she had seen and done it all. She had to come across that way or she would be picked apart piece by piece. For the most part, the cloak was real, sewn together from scraps of past skirmishes with threads of determination. She *was* confident. She *was* hard to penetrate. But not impenetrable. And, at twenty-four years old, there were still plenty of things she hadn't done.

"We'll figure it out." Cerise's gaze held her own. "And I promise to be gentle."

Eirinn's legs failing her completely, Cerise's surprisingly sturdy arms were there to hold her up, to ease her fear and lead her through the door of her bedroom and into her bed, where they discovered, some hours later, much to both of their delights, they were quite a lot better at it than either of them thought.

Chapter 11

CAROLINE

1886

Teatime in the Ajax household was an informal affair. Thomas was never home in the afternoons, and, due to her precarious health, people rarely stopped in, never knowing whether the lady of the house would want to or be able to greet them.

When she did take tea, Caroline almost always took it alone, sitting in her bedroom or the parlor. Occasionally, one of the staff would join her if she made a powerful enough bid, but most often they made their excuses, too afraid of what would happen if Thomas found out. It simply wasn't worth the risk to their livelihoods to drink tea with their reclusive mistress.

But that had all changed over the past year when Oliver came to live with them. Oliver adored teatime. Or, rather, he adored the cakes and biscuits teatime brought to his table. He loved it so much and looked so forward to it each day that Caroline endeavored to get herself up out of bed at four o'clock and make it to the parlor to partake with him. Sometimes it required an extra dropper of laudanum. Sometimes Oliver would take one look at her and know he needed to speak in a whisper. It was a heavy thing for a young boy to have to know, but he was there, and she was there, and they were making it through together, one dessert-filled afternoon at a time.

When Lei told her it was teatime, Caroline's heart clenched. She had thought of Oliver many times over the past two days, with desperate helplessness and a sort of sinking numbness that prevented her from dissolving into tears. What would happen to him while she was away? Who would find him when he got lost inside himself, as he so often did? Was he having tea now? Who would remember? Thomas's cousin Mary? Yes. Mary would recall that Oliver needed cakes and sandwiches at four o'clock and would sit with him as he ate them, even if no one else in the house would have the nerve. Mary knew Thomas favored her, whether she knew the nature of his favor or not, and she wasn't afraid of him. It was why Caroline had liked the woman from the moment she arrived at their house in London, despite Thomas's best efforts to pit them into competition for his affections. Mary could have Thomas if she wanted him, and all the misery that came along with him. She just couldn't have him in Caroline's home with her nephew serving as their surrogate son.

"Hello, Caroline. Lei."

Caroline couldn't have imagined teatime, however, as Lei meant it, in the most formal sense of the word. Walking into the grand hall, she was surprised to see the tables set with such care - elegant tablecloths draped across them, linen napkins folded into swans where they set atop the plates, cutlery properly arranged. The display had little in common with the simple teas she and Oliver took in their parlor, and it was a strange transition coming up from the dark, curious world of Lei's workshop into such a bright, lavish presentation of English custom.

"I see you found her," Francie said as she approached with Blanca and Stella, and, nodding, Caroline was about to thank her for her help in the matter when Francie charged on. "And that she already roped you into something, if those ferret eyes are any indication."

Lifting a hand to her face, Caroline touched the cheek where Francie looked, rash of embarrassment warming the skin beneath her fingertips when she found the indentations the goggles had left behind. She had noticed them on Lei, but they were negligible, scarcely a line along the outsides of Lei's cheeks. Her own lines felt cavernous, like moats dug deep into her skin to keep enemy invaders from storming her eye sockets.

"Lei." Blanca was the next to laugh, gaze finding the black singe on Caroline's dress. "What did you do to her?"

Glancing down at the blemish, it looked darker and more ominous in the white light of the grand hall, and Caroline considered the image she had to present. Dress scorched, face marked, she was a right disaster on a beautiful affair. Fitting really, given her history as such. If someone asked her parents, they would probably say they expected nothing more.

"It wasn't her fault." Flustered though she was, she couldn't leave Lei to suffer the blame all on her own. "It was an accident."

"I shot her with the light ray," Lei said, and Blanca's humor dissipated. All at once. Flying from her face so quickly Caroline could only assume she had witnessed the light amplifier and its functionality before.

"Holy Christ and the queen. Are you hurt?" Stella asked.

"It's only a flesh wound," Caroline hedged.

"I practically took the top of her leg off," Lei amended.

"Well, I'm glad she didn't kill you at least." Blanca looked wide-eyed at Lei in a way that concurred with Caroline's own estimation that, just a few inches higher, and her stay at Dr. Todson's Home for Women might have been a remarkably short one. "Will you sit with us?"

"Only if *someone* doesn't eat all the clotted cream," Lei said.

"Listen. I'm gonna do what I'm gonna do." Francie's expression set in stone.

"I'll make sure we get extra." Blanca was back to laughing, and a small smile tugged at Caroline's own lips. She might be out of place and look a sight, but at least she liked these women as far as she had gotten to know them and they were pleasant to her.

"We'll be right over," Lei said to the others, apparently attuned to the fact Caroline needed an extra moment to get her bearings, to adjust to the light and clamor all around them. Every person in the house streaming into the grand hall, the room bustled as it had for the party the night before, and she wasn't sure she was ready for such sensory invasion. She had been loath to go into the basement in search of Lei's workshop, but, once she was down there and her vision returned, she actually found it rather agreeable, the calm and quiet below the house. "I'm sorry."

Caught inspecting the char mark on her dress, Caroline felt twinges of so many things she couldn't identify them all as she swallowed and cleared her throat. "It's just a dress."

"It's not just a dress. It's your only dress."

So, Lei could follow the terrible progression of her thoughts.

First, Caroline was merely uncomfortable - self-conscious - to be making such a shabby appearance at such a formal affair. No one was elegantly outfitted - Lei wore the same trousers and loose top she'd been wearing all day, Imogen may well have been in a well-tied bedsheet - but no one else wore soiled and singed clothing either.

Then, it occurred to her, with the drop of reality into her stomach, that she couldn't simply go upstairs and change. She had been left there with only the dress on her back, quite literally, and now that dress and her leg both had holes through them. At this point, she was just glad she wore enough layers the blood hadn't seeped through.

"I'll find a way to repair it." The dress, Caroline assumed Lei meant, distracted from her darkening thoughts as Lei reached for her arm to give it a reassuring squeeze. "And get you more clothes in the meantime. There's plenty of fabric and a sewing machine in storage if you like to make your own. And, if not, Livvie will be happy to make you something. She's so good with a pattern, she can sew a dress in a day. Not so good with her fittings, though, or she just really likes poking me with needles."

Lei's attempt to brighten her mood was so valiant, so kind, Caroline couldn't help but be somewhat brightened. "Would Livvie appreciate you volunteering her like this?"

"Absolutely. She loves it." It sounded like something that could only be a lie. Caroline had met the woman who was the formal housekeeper in passing the night before, before Livvie and Brigit the Cook, like Dr. Todson and Rand, retired early from the party, and not once did the woman plead to make clothes for her. "She truly does enjoy it. She plans to have her own dress shop one day."

"All right then. I trust she'll make something better than I -"

"Will you sing with me?!"

Sudden shout startling her forward, Caroline put one hand to her heart, feeling the rapid, unsteady beat beneath her palm, and glanced to where Imogen was soliciting Blanca, Francie and Stella at their table.

"I will," Stella said. "But you know I won't know the words, so don't be gettin' up in a ruckus when I muck 'em up."

"I won't," Imogen promised, and they launched into a cacophonous duet, the awful clash of which drew the attention of the women at the other tables and gave them something to snigger along to.

"What's wrong with her?"

They were well-intentioned, the words Stella chose, meant to make the others, and certainly even Imogen, laugh at their bawdiness.

"It put a tingle in his dingle..."

Caroline felt her own face flush.

But watching Imogen grow more and more frustrated by Stella's inability to harmonize, it wasn't laughter, or even embarrassment, that stirred Caroline's stomach. It was pity. She could only feel sorry for Imogen. She was a hypocrite for it, she knew. She hated people feeling sorry for her. But it had to be lonely, having songs in one's head no one else could follow. Like speaking a foreign language no one understood.

"Some sort of psychosis," Lei said. "She used to be a performer. But one day her mind just stopped working right. Now, she has some coherent moments, but mostly she stays like this."

"Her mind just stopped working?" Caroline uttered.

"Yes. That's what Eir... Dr. Todson said."

"That's it? Her mind just stopped working? Just one day?" Pulse thrumming, body trembling, Caroline wasn't sure why the statement bothered her as it did, but it did. It simply didn't seem fitting, Lei's tone. She was far too calm, far too stoic, as if that was simply a thing that happened, someone's mind ceasing to work, that demanded no fury. "That doesn't sound right. Something must have happened to her."

"Yes, it must have. And I'm sure Dr. Todson knows what that is. But she's not going to tell us."

Dr. Todson. There she was again. Name bantered about as if they needn't be afraid to speak it.

"What about the others?" Looking around at the unusual array of faces, they all seemed well enough. Content enough. Happy maybe even, in this place. They were also a mystery to Caroline. None of the women she had met that day were anything at all alike. Pieces of the puzzle revealed to her one by one, they seemed to fit together less and less. "Are they like Imogen or like you?"

"Crazy or not crazy, you mean?"

"No, I -" Caroline rushed to deny it, but Lei already smirking at her, she realized it was exactly what she was asking. "Well?"

"A combination of the two. Sometimes all in the same person."

Riddle or confession? Turning to Lei, Caroline studied her face for clues, gaze coming to rest on the small grin that still teased full lips.

"You said you chose to come here. Why?"

"Because I was alone on the streets and I was invited," Lei answered, and Caroline stilled. Swallowed. Sensation like dread prickling her skin, she looked more carefully at Lei. More anxiously. She thought it was the answer she sought, why Lei was there if she didn't have to be, but it only opened so many more questions.

Lei alone on the streets? Why? How?

No wonder she was so hurt when Caroline suggested this house couldn't possibly be a home.

"Besides, look at this place. Why wouldn't I choose to be here? It's a palace."

"It's a madhouse." The words came without consideration. Without conviction. Perhaps without merit, it occurred to Caroline now. It was simply reflex, to say the thing she thought she knew yesterday she was certain at the time to be true.

"Is it?" Lei asked her, and she had no answer to that. Thoughts tumbling about her, Caroline struggled just to maintain her form at the moment, like a brolly taking a battering by the rain. "We should get to our table."

Lei's hand soft at her elbow, she led her to the empty chairs at Blanca, Francie, and Stella's table, and four things happened in succession -

One, applause broke out across the room. Caroline followed the gazes of the women to see Brigit the Cook, a full head above most of the residents, enter the grand hall, Livvie the Housekeeper, smaller and less prominent, walking alongside her.

Two, Brigit raised a hand to the women as Livvie curtsied with both hands on her skirt, greetings easily accomplished since neither of them was carrying even a single tea or scone.

Three, *Sit down. Sit down.* Brigit good-naturedly ordered them all, taking her own seat next to Livvie at what could only be described as the head table, situated prominently as it was.

Four, the rest of the room began to settle too, Caroline sinking into her chair next to Lei with increasing puzzlement. If Brigit and Livvie, who together made up the sum total of the household staff, were already seated, who was bringing the tea?

It was a deliberation that lasted mere seconds before Dr. Todson swept into the room, a paradoxical image in her fine dress with a silver tea service clutched in her hands.

Rand walking behind her, he carried a tower of delightful-looking delicacies, and two of the house's residents came after, hands empty, but bright smiles on each of their faces.

When they reached the head table where Brigit and Livvie sat, Dr. Todson placed the tea service before them and took a step back, waiting for Rand to bestow his tower of treats, and then the whole lot of them - Dr. Todson, Rand, and their two supporting residents - bowed or curtsied to Brigit and Livvie.

"This looks perfect. Thank you," Brigit accepted their offering with a smile.

"Yes. Thank you," Livvie agreed, and Dr. Todson returned to the table to pour the tea, distributing cups first to Brigit and Livvie and then outward to the women who sat alongside them.

"Bon appétit." The entire troop, led by Dr. Todson, curtsied and bowed once more before retreating from the grand hall, only to return seconds later with more towers and tea services in their hands. The two residents helping with the carrying now, the group was able to serve two tables at a time, doing so in an expeditious fashion, so, within minutes, Dr. Todson and her aiding resident were at the table where Caroline sat.

"Thank you, Eir. Thank you, Jean." The general refrain went round as the tea and treats were delivered, and Caroline could not stop staring - marveling - not even when Dr. Todson's gaze met hers and she was caught out doing it.

"Bon appétit." Dr. Todson gave Blanca's shoulder a small squeeze before she walked off, and, regaining control of her eyes only when Dr. Todson disappeared back through the dining room door, Caroline turned to watch Stella pour tea into their cups as if nothing of particular interest had happened.

"Is it a special occasion?" Reeling several seconds inside her own head, she at last found a question that made sense.

"No," Lei said, turning softly her way, knee brushing Caroline's where they met beneath the table. "Dr. Todson believes being in constant service to others can be difficult on a person's humanity, so, once a day - at teatime - we honor Brigit and Livvie, and Dr. Todson does the serving."

"I see." Caroline did. Had just witnessed the event with her very own eyes. But she couldn't say she understood it. And seeing wasn't entirely believing.

Dr. Todson had no cause to serve these people. She paid them for their services, or was paid to keep them. Her name was on the building. Admittedly, Caroline hadn't seen a lot in her years on the planet, but she had seen plenty of rich people with their servants and not once had she seen any of them swap places just for the sake of it. Or the decency. Certainly not for the humility.

88

Reminded suddenly of a parable, she knew it would be absolute sacrilege to anyone outside these walls, but, watching Dr. Todson serve the house's residents, she couldn't help but think of Jesus washing His disciples' feet.

Chapter 12

EIRINN

1866

The days and nights Cerise stayed at the house were overflowing and insufficient.

Eirinn couldn't abandon her obligations to the dispensary - she didn't want to - so Cerise was left at the house with Mama and Bally during the day, a pleasure for them all Eirinn could tell, and she and Cerise had what time there was left in the nights, stretching them as long as they could while still maintaining a tenuous grip on reality.

As expected, it took little time for Papa to locate Cerise's brother, Acton, and, as Cerise knew, Acton was quite keen to have her and his niece transferred to his care in satisfactory condition. He was in a favorable financial place for it, he said, without elaborating further in the limited medium. And furious, if the tone of his reply was any indication. He told them he would come by train on Saturday so Cerise and Lulu wouldn't have to travel from London to Manchester alone, but Cerise was insistent she and Lulu would be perfectly safe on a daytime train in a fully-booked carriage.

If your brother wants to come for you, I think we should let him, Papa said. *I'm a bit uneasy about putting you on a train without seeing there is someone to pick you up on the other end. We'll cover his passage and he can stay here with us. It will be no trouble at all.*

I'm afraid Acton will kill Henry if he comes back here, Cerise confessed her true worries to Eirinn later that night. *He's a good man, but he does have a temper about certain things. He's gotten on the wrong side of the law before. If he's doing well, the last thing I want is for him to get tangled up again.*

We'll keep him well-occupied, Eirinn promised, secretly grateful for Papa and Acton's intervention in the matter. She didn't want to put Cerise and Lulu on the first train out to Manchester either. Incidents were far too frequent against women who traveled the rails alone. That was more than enough reason to wait for an escort.

But it wasn't the only one.

If they waited for Acton, Cerise and Lulu would be at the house several more nights. Eirinn wanted those nights, and all that came with them, like she wanted the air to breathe. They occupied her thoughts at the dispensary and whispered her awake in the mornings. She always thought she knew exactly what, and all that, she wanted out of life, but every morning she looked over to see Cerise's soft hair spilled across the pillow next to her she was shaken by the realization of how much more there could be.

No matter how she dreaded it, Saturday was bound to come, and that afternoon found Eirinn waiting with Cerise and Lulu on a platform at Euston Station for Cerise's brother to roll in on the 1:30 train. Rand commanding the carriage to the station as usual, he gave them their space when Eirinn asked, waiting out front with the brougham so she could walk with Cerise and Lulu to the platform alone.

"Has it been the whole two years since you last saw Acton?" Eirinn asked, so she wouldn't be aware of each second that passed on the clock. And so she could hear Cerise's voice. As much as possible. Before she was gone.

"More than," Cerise said.

"So, he hasn't even met Lulu?"

"I don't even know if he knew I had a child until we sent the last telegram."

"Hm." Contempt flaring, Eirinn swallowed the upswell of flames and thought it best to say nothing. She could never imagine hating another person, truly, deeply hating a person, she had never laid eyes on until these past few days with Cerise. Every scar she uncovered on Cerise's body, every halting story Cerise chose to share, had added blight to her image of Cerise's husband until he appeared a veritable monster in her mind's eye. She could hate a monster, it turned out, quite easily, sight unseen. "Are you excited?"

"Yes, of course I am," Cerise said, but the expression she wore was contradictory. Half-false, just as Eirinn's was.

It was good, Eirinn reminded herself. Good for Cerise. Good for Lulu. They would be with their family. They would be well-treated and protected. Cerise had every faith in her brother. And what other option did they have? They couldn't just keep Cerise and Lulu hidden away in the Todson house forever.

"Ce-RISE!" Yell cutting through the platform like a steam engine, Eirinn's softly simmering blood turned instantly cold, congealing inside her veins, as she whirled to see a man marching straight for them. No more than thirty, he had dusty brown hair and not half the blight Eirinn imagined. He might have even been handsome if he didn't look so bloody vicious, dressed in his filthy clothes, stalking their way like a werewolf. Shoulders hunched. Teeth bared.

"Henry." Cerise shrank next to her. Though, he really needed no introduction. Who else would this right devil of a man calling Cerise's name into the crowd and boring down upon them be?

"Did you think I wouldn't find ya? Huh?"

Glancing around, Eirinn wasn't sure what she was waiting for until she saw no signs of it. Where were the men to intervene? These gentlemen in their top hats and waistcoats with their chivalric temperaments and impeccable reputations? The people closer to Henry's size to get in his way and stop a madman from barreling straight into them and unleashing the savage notions so prevalent on his face?

"What? You think I'd just go back to work and not worry about where you'd gotten off to? Huh?"

If anything, the throng actually parted for Henry, not wanting to be the ones in the path of his fury or his filth. Seeing him coming, several well-dressed ladies whisked their dresses back against their legs, worried he might dirty their hems.

"Where you goin', huh, ya dumb bitch? I knew ya'd show up here. I knew if I just stuck around long enough…"

It took Henry getting within two body lengths of them and Cerise's rapid breaths in her ear for Eirinn to accept the fact no one was coming to their aid, just as they hadn't four years ago when Papa was beating Louis Arnold in the tea shop, and to step in front of Cerise and Lulu, scorched throat painfully dry, heart pounding like a war drum inside her chest.

Much to her surprise, the move drew Henry to a stop. Eirinn was certain it was more out of shock than any real fear of her. An assumption proven correct when a bitter grin settled onto Henry's face and he closed the distance between them, stopping before her with a short, hiccupping laugh and an exhalation of cheap gin.

"Afternoon, My Lady." Henry doffed a nonexistent cap. "But would ya mind gettin' out of my way? I got a matter of some importance to discuss with my wife."

"Yes, I would mind."

Eirinn's answer seemed to flummox him, confound him into silence for several gaping seconds. Then, to infuriate him. Malice flashing in light blue eyes, Henry's cheeks hardened, hand gripping the waistband of his pants in a fist that turned his knuckles white.

"Well, ya see that there is my wife and child, so you ain't got no bloody business with it."

"No, but this isn't business."

Henry might not know it, even fathom the possibility, but Eirinn had some anger to draw on too, an abundance of venom built up from Cerise's scars and stories. And, thanks to her tendency to push her way into places people felt she didn't belong, she had ample experience in dealing with bullies. She was scared of him, she wouldn't pretend she wasn't, but it was because he was drunk and raging, not because he was a man claiming his place and telling her what to do. She'd grown tired of that song and dance years ago.

"Cerise, come here." Quickly growing tired of her as well, Henry looked past her.

And, feeling the press of Cerise and Lulu against her back, Eirinn reached for them, finding Cerise's hip with her hand and trying to provide comfort. "She's not going anywhere with you."

"Is that right?"

"Just go, Henry," Cerise begged him. "Acton is on his way. His train will be here in a few minutes. You don't want to be here when he gets here."

Cerise was the one terrified Henry would still be there when her brother arrived. Eirinn could feel the worry that churned through her shaking form, could sense her looking back every few seconds, panicked the train was going to pull in and Acton was going to come barreling out the door straight into a murder charge.

"I knew ya'd go cryin' to your brother. After ya stole money off of me and ran away. How else ya think I'm here? Only one station with trains out to Manchester." Henry tapped the side of his head.

Yes, yes, it was surprisingly well thought out, Eirinn gave credit where it was due as she tried in vain to think herself.

It might have even been a touching gesture, a husband waiting around a train station for days for his wife and daughter. If there was any affection in it at all. Any contrition. Any apology. But Eirinn could see who this man was, even without Cerise's account of him. He was an angry brute who had searched for his family out of spite, as lost possessions he was determined to have returned to him. There wasn't an ounce of love in him. Not for his wife. Not for his daughter. It was an egregious injustice in an unjust world. What sort of twisted universe gave so little to two people who deserved so much?

"Just go home, Henry. Please," Cerise pleaded with him again.

"Now yer askin' me?" Henry said. "Whatever you think yer gonna do, ya go right on ahead and do it, but that's my baby and I ain't leavin' here without her."

Cerise sobbed, gasping helplessly behind Eirinn. Henry had hit upon her other fear, her greatest one, the one that kept her up at night. And he knew he was on it if the malicious grin on his face was testament.

"Well, you're not leaving here with her."

Two minutes. Eirinn glanced to the platform clock, wondering if she could just stall long enough for the train from Manchester to arrive. She understood Cerise's concern, but if the choice was between Acton getting his knuckles bloodied or Cerise and Lulu leaving the station with this barbarian, she had no split loyalties.

"And just who the fuck are you?"

"It doesn't matter who I am."

"Ya know what? Yer right."

In the future, Eirinn would recognize such words as warning. Realize when someone agreed you didn't matter it could only signal worse things to come. But, in the moment, it didn't even occur to her that Henry was so drunk, so delirious with his rage, that he would strike a total stranger in the middle of Euston Station.

Thud of his hand against her cheek, the surprise spun her around and knocked her off her feet as much as the blow. Meeting the platform with a sprawl that pained both elbows and knees, Eirinn looked back as Cerise cried out to see Henry grabbing hold of her arm and dragging her and Lulu away down the platform.

"Are you all right, Miss?" Useless when needed, at least three people rushed to Eirinn's side. To check on *her* condition. To see that *she* was tended. To help her back to her feet. But no one, not even one amongst them, went to help Cerise and Lulu. Clearing Henry's path, they just let him go, march off with them, regardless of the fact both Cerise and Lulu were crying, that they were clearly being taken against their wills, and, of all the things prodding her fury at the moment, it was that which incited Eirinn most of all.

"No!" Pushing off the bogus Samaritans, she saw only Cerise and Lulu and Henry ahead as, hearing the race of her footsteps coming behind them, Henry turned to defend himself.

No idea how to fight a man, or anyone for that matter, Eirinn simply lashed out, driving her hands into Henry's chest and barely nudging him backward before unleashing a wild swinging of fists upon him, getting in a few good hits - they felt good, at least - before Henry sent her flying backward onto the floor again.

"No! No! Please, no!"

Cerise's screams were her only warning before Henry was beside her, his heavy boot swinging back to deliver a sharp kick to her side that Eirinn felt all the way through her torso, making even her lungs quiver in protest.

"No! Stop! Please, stop!" Rushing up to him, Cerise grabbed Henry's arm to drag him away. "We'll come with you! Please! Just stop! Don't hurt her! Please."

Henry looked as if he would like to do more than hurt Eirinn. He looked as if he would quite happily kill her given the opportunity. But Cerise's relentless tugging and Acton's impending arrival didn't afford it to him, so he turned his anger back on Cerise, grabbing her by the neck and dragging her and Lulu away once more.

Watching them disappear, Cerise and Lulu both crying, no one in their path raising a finger to help them, the strangest, most unexpected thing happened. Station still buzzing around her, everything in Eirinn went suddenly, eerily still. Deathly still. If fury was a storm, she was in the eye of it, and the winds were twice as strong on the other side.

"No!" Surging back to her feet, she ran at Henry again, and though Henry let go of Cerise and turned to make his stand, his foundation wasn't nearly solid enough. She felt the bulk of his chest against her shoulder and they went down in a heap on the platform.

Fists flying through the air, Eirinn felt hatred like she had never felt before and the power to equal it. She could be ripped and torn, bruised and bloody, and she was still going to end this man's tyranny. She would be the last time he ever laid his hands on Cerise like that or dared to underestimate a woman he didn't know.

As he had the first time, Henry tried to easily flick her off, but this time Eirinn held on, taking a hit to the side of her face that hurt and stunned her, but only digging her fingers deeper into Henry's chest. She didn't have to win. She had no illusion she could. She only needed to hold out long enough for Cerise's brother to get to the station and off the train.

"Eir!" But it wasn't Acton who made it to them first. Looking up, Eirinn saw Rand sprinting down the platform, shoving people out of his way as he came.

Distraction enough for Henry to thrust her off of him, he staggered to his feet, glancing to Rand coming at his back and Cerise and Lulu crying by Eirinn's side.

"Keep 'em." His only choice to stay and fight a fair fight or to flee, Henry tried to make a good show of it. "I'm tired of payin' on 'em anyway." Spitting on the skirts of Eirinn's dress, he took off through the crowd as Rand made it up to them.

"Eir, are you all right?" Rand dropped to his knee beside her, struggling to catch his breath as much as Eirinn, and, adrenaline abandoning her, Eirinn felt pain. A lot of it. All at once, in a piercing screech.

"I'm fine." She wasn't. It was hard to breathe, hard to speak. But she would be. Fingers moving over her ribs, she could feel nothing had moved or twisted. Swollen and certainly bruised - her entire body was likely to be one big bruise come morning - a rib or two might well be cracked, but not to the point of immediate danger. She would just have to take it easy for the next several days. Hopefully, Dr. Anderson wouldn't take one look at her Monday morning and send her home. Taking pulses and feeling foreheads didn't require a fully functional ribcage, just working fingers and a decent place to sit.

"People came out talking about a fight. I really hoped you weren't in the middle of it, but somehow I knew you would be."

Eirinn heard what Rand had said, but she was more concerned with the soft touch at the corner of her mouth as, handkerchief in hand, Cerise tried to wipe the blood from her lip. Covering Cerise's hand with her own,

Eirinn watched the tears flow down her cheeks, wishing they were alone so she could comfort her as she wanted to.

"Help me up," she said, and Rand did, Cerise aiding as much as she could with Lulu still whimpering and sniffling in one arm.

"Where were you?" Eirinn heard someone demand in the next instant, and it was quite the impressive feat, given she was looking directly at Cerise and Rand and neither of them had opened their mouths. Glancing around, she spotted a gray-haired woman dressed from head to ankle in furs, looking absolutely aghast at Rand.

"She asked me to wait in front of the -"

"You're her man. It's your job. You should have known better than to send her in here alone."

"She told me -"

"*Look* at her! What do you think her people are going to say when they see her like this?"

Her people. *Her people.* Eirinn thought she was depleted, thought she didn't have an ounce of energy left for anger, but rage crackled inside her, heart thrumming a dangerous warning. *Her people.* As if this woman could possibly know who *her people* were. As if Rand and Cerise and Lulu couldn't possibly be *her people*, because they were the *wrong kind* of people. People like Eirinn's father. People like Eirinn herself in a million ways this woman couldn't begin to imagine with her tiny pea brain in her big, fat, overly-coiffed head.

"You should be ashamed of your -"

"Oh, shut your bloody mouth, you stupid shrew!" Eirinn felt the tweak to her ribs as she glared with all her might, and the fur-clad woman gasped, small "humph" falling from her lips as she went back to her own business. As she should have done in the first place.

"I'm all right." Looking back to Cerise and Rand, Eirinn didn't need a mirror to know just how bad she looked. She could see it in the reflections of their faces.

"You don't look all right," Rand said. "You look like you just stopped a crow with your face."

"It was more of pigeon. Spread out. Knuckles first."

Rand huffing a laugh, Cerise sobbed. One thing truly seeming to lead to the other, Rand's humor petered out, terrible look of guilt coming to his face. "Hey, hey," he said, reaching awkwardly out to pat Cerise's shoulder.

"I am so sorry." Cerise sobbed again, and Eirinn felt a hazy sort of exhaustion. Storm passed, the damage remained. The ground was muck, the shutters battered. She was quite tired, she realized, of being apologized to for things that didn't require apology and never for the things which did.

"Don't be sorry." It was the people around them who should be making amends, falling to their knees and begging for forgiveness. She did hope they at least made their confessions to God for being so worthless all day. "Not for this. Never for this."

Taking Cerise's face in her hands, Eirinn stared into her stormy eyes, trying to make her see how very worth it she was, before the urge overtook her and she kissed the corner of Cerise's mouth and pulled her into her arms, one hand sinking into her thick hair, the other finding its way around Lulu to embrace them both, not sure how intimate it looked and not giving one single damn in the moment.

Spectacle over, no one seemed all that interested in them anymore anyway.

Except for Rand.

Face sliding into view over Cerise's shoulder, Rand wore an agog look of inquiry, followed by a raised eyebrow of dawning comprehension, and then a grin so impish Eirinn preferred not to know what he was thinking.

Two minutes later, the 1:30 train rolled in out of Manchester.

The next day, it would roll out again, carrying Cerise and Lulu off to a new and better life.

Cerise didn't want to leave. Eirinn didn't want them to leave. But it was the right thing. For all of them.

Eirinn would never regret the time they spent together, she would wish it longer and less filled with pain, but she had known from the very start it was never going to be forever.

Chapter 13

CAROLINE

1886

Her belief there was no structure, no hierarchy, at Dr. Todson's Home for Women was a misperception. It just wasn't the schedule of torture and slop-feedings Caroline expected when she first arrived, and so deft, so skillfully light-handed, as to be almost imperceptible.

Breakfast, lunch, teatime, and dinner came at the same times each day. Though, Caroline had yet to see that last meal served on time. The residents started to gather at the top of the hour, but they waited until everyone made it to the dining room to eat. It didn't matter who was last to arrive.

That was the structure. That was the schedule. That was the cadence and rhythm of the days. Like most households, life revolved around mealtimes, and the hours between one had to fill on her own.

In those hours, Caroline found refuge in the last place she would have expected.

"It's safe," Lei called out to her on her third afternoon at the house when she found her way back down to the door in the basement and wisely remembered to knock.

"Is it all right if I come in?" Caroline asked from the doorway.

"Yes, of course," Lei said, and Caroline stepped into the workshop, breaths coming easier the instant she was through the heavy wood door. "Come to play with something else?"

"No," Caroline answered at once, wanting to assure Lei she wasn't there to be a nuisance or distract her. She could tell Lei was involved in something, could hear her tinkering before she even knocked. "I don't want to interrupt you. I was just hoping I could read down here."

"There are far more comfortable places in this house to read." A slight grin teased Lei's lips, but Caroline's relief waned.

Where would she go if Lei wouldn't have her? There was no dearth of things to do inside or outside the house. She could go to the gardens, even in the foulish weather. Being it was England and bad weather was to be embraced or forever shaken a fist at, multiple structures had been erected to enjoy the gardens regardless of rain or dreary gray skies. She could read in the library or work at a project of her own. If she could think one up. Or take lessons in a subject one of the women knew well enough to teach.

"Not that I wouldn't love your company." Lei spared her the effort of figuring out where else she might find comfort. "I just don't want you to be miserable."

"I won't," Caroline promised.

"Well, in that case, my workshop is your reading dungeon." Lei waved a welcoming hand, and, smiling, grateful, Caroline went to the bench mounted in a cubby on the wall she had spotted the day before once her vision came back and she was able to take in the dark, curious fixtures of the workshop.

"Just warn me when you're about to blast blinding light, so I can close my eyes and protect my organs."

Glancing up in the gentle husk of Lei's laughter, Caroline settled into her book, and Lei returned to her work, a hum of noise that was surprisingly conducive to Caroline's peace of mind.

Five days later, Caroline's name appeared with Lei's on the schedule for teatime, indicating her attachment to Lei's heel hadn't gone entirely unnoticed by the others in the house.

"Could you tell Eir I'll just be a few minutes?" Lei asked when the strange numberless clock above her trilled its reminder.

"All right," Caroline agreed, though she would really prefer not to. Since she had started spending her days in the workshop, she was rarely without Lei by her side - she was comfortable, she found, with Lei there - and she hadn't been in the intimate company of Dr. Todson since their walk through the gardens.

Since she witnessed Dr. Todson serve tea.

Since she learned Dr. Todson was a real doctor, in the truest sense of the word. Not just as she told Caroline she was, in the official, abstract way, or to Imogen, who so clearly needed intervention of some sort, but to most of the women in the house. Caroline was surprised by how many of the residents took appointments with her, even those she could never imagine having need for them.

Twice a week every week, Blanca disclosed when Caroline couldn't hide her surprise at Blanca's mentioned session with Dr. Todson in the hour after teatime. *You'd be amazed how it helps.*

But that was abstract too - Blanca's testimonial - an extolled remedy for an undisclosed problem. For all Caroline knew, Blanca simply had gangly toenails and Dr. Todson was excellent with a pair of clippers.

So while, admittedly, her curiosity about Dr. Todson had only grown in the days she had been there, with every piece of information gathered about her from the house and its residents, Caroline felt weak at the thought of encountering her alone. "Five minutes?" she encouraged Lei to a time limit.

"Yeah. That should do it," Lei said, distracted by trying to wedge a metal pin that seemed quite unwilling to fit into the device in her hands as Caroline got up. Unsteadily. Unhurriedly. Hoping Lei would make the pin work in her contraption within the next few seconds and be ready to head upstairs with her after all.

When she didn't, Caroline set her book in the pile of cushions Lei had outfitted the bench with by her third day in the workshop - *I've already maimed your leg. I can't be responsible for the slow destruction of your back as well.* - and walked to the door. With all Lei had done for her over the past week, not the least of which was allowing her to occupy her space and company without complaint, she knew she owed her at least one favor. What was more surprising was her realization she didn't want to disappoint Dr. Todson by showing up late.

"Hello, Caroline." Dr. Todson was wrists-deep in dough when Caroline tapped the open door and stepped into the restricted domain of Brigit's sacred kitchen. "How are you?"

Stunned, Caroline stood for a moment, not entirely certain how to answer. How was she? Baffled. Hallucinating, perhaps. Feverish? Slowly, she blinked. "I'm well. How are you?"

She didn't know what she thought happened there, in the hour before teatime. Why she thought they had to arrive early. So Dr. Todson could crack a whip over them, hustling them through the preparations? So they could do all the real work with Brigit and Livvie, and Dr. Todson could float in just before four o'clock to put on her performance of service?

"I'm very well. Thank you." Dr. Todson gave the dough a last few firm presses and patted it into a rectangle as she glanced toward the door. "Were you down in the workshop with Lei?"

"I was," Caroline said.

"I take it she needs a few minutes?"

"Yes." Nodding uncomfortably, Caroline tried to come up with a noble excuse for Lei's delay. Not that Lei didn't have a noble excuse. Caroline was certain whatever Lei was working on was extremely important. Urgent. Important and urgent enough to take precedence over coming up the stairs with her at precisely three o'clock and saving her from the anxiety of this conversation.

"She'll make up for it in the clean-up. She always does. Can't disrupt a great mind when it's fixed on a task. We can manage for now. Do you mind making sandwiches?"

"What kind?" Caroline took a tentative step toward the ingredients lined up on the opposite side of the enormous wooden prep table from Dr. Todson.

"Whatever kind you like. I'm sure you've had a quality tea sandwich at some point in your life," Dr. Todson said, glancing around her immediate area, locating a rolling pin close by, and taking it to her dough in a series of solid thwacks before rolling it out in steady, rapid movements.

"How have you been feeling?" she asked as she worked, and Caroline picked up the large knife from the cutting board, marveling at the sheer size of it and wondering if all the women in the house were allowed unrestricted access to such large instruments of destruction. Imogen seemed harmless enough for the most part, but the way she flitted about, Caroline could imagine her turning into a right menace with such a massive blade in her hands. "Any headaches?"

"No. Not really." Not sure how to tackle the brown loaf of bread roughly the size of her torso, Caroline was so focused on the task she didn't notice the small pause to Dr. Todson's efforts.

"Not really means some?" Dr. Todson asked her, and, glancing up, Caroline realized, as preoccupied as she seemed, Dr. Todson was actually paying quite careful attention to her.

"I've had a few pinches." The fact made her exceedingly nervous. "But only at night when I get tired. Not all the time and nothing at all like before."

"Good." Without further pressing, Dr. Todson returned to her task. She didn't even ask Caroline which medication she was taking to produce such extraordinary results. Extraordinary for Caroline, at least. Caroline was certain Dr. Todson had every expectation of the outcome and knew exactly which medication would produce it. "And your leg? How is it healing?"

"Very well." Better than well, if Caroline were to tell the full truth of it. By far the worst wound she had ever had, it was also healing the most effectively. Dr. Todson looked at it only once, on Lei's insistence, the evening after it happened, prescribing a salve from Rand and telling Caroline to change the wrappings once a day unless she noticed any leakage. But the wound didn't leak. And it twinged on only the rarest of occasion. With Livvie able to repair Caroline's dress to practically new, it was almost as though the incident with the light ray never happened.

101

Except, of course, for the permanent cleft left in the front of Caroline's right thigh.

"Good. Very good." Dr. Todson sliced the dough into strips, and Caroline tried to focus on the ingredients in front of her, pairing them into agreeable combinations in her head. It should have been easy, a quick and mindless task, but her eyes kept being drawn back to Dr. Todson. As they might be drawn to a starry sky or moonlight on the ocean, something undeniably real, but still a fantastical source of wonder.

Dark blue jacket left hanging on a hook in the dining room - Caroline knew, because she had passed it on her way in - Dr. Todson wore an apron atop her ruffled and lace-trimmed blouse, which she had rolled to the elbows, loose tendrils of blonde hair, with only the slightest hints of gray, tumbling around her face as she leaned over the table, patch of flour dashed across her forehead.

Even there, in Brigit's kitchen, she looked entirely in her element. It was almost a parlor trick, Dr. Todson's ability to assimilate, to be wherever she was and make the impression she was exactly where she was meant to be. That was why Caroline had thought there was no hierarchy in the house. She didn't recognize it, because it looked nothing like any governance she had ever seen before.

Dr. Todson didn't dictate or hold court. She didn't punish or demand. She led artfully from the inside out, by integrating wherever she was and actually caring about what she was doing in any given moment. She didn't cut dough into precise, careful strips to make a show out of doing it. She did it because it mattered to her as much as checking on the state of Caroline's health or seeing to the household's concerns.

That was what Caroline had noticed the most over the days she had been there. The women in the house respected Dr. Todson for a reason. They trusted her for a reason. They accepted her guidance and told her their secrets because they had every faith in her. For a reason. Dr. Todson held sovereignty on the basis of their respect and admiration alone, and it felt like a heady presence to stand in. A presence that encouraged and inspired without actually doing anything at all.

Even now, Caroline realized, she didn't want to simply make tea sandwiches. She wanted to make exceptional tea sandwiches, superb tea sandwiches, the best tea sandwiches she had ever made. They were only sandwiches, yet she wanted to impress Dr. Todson as a child might aim to impress its mother. Reaching for the salmon, she was certain she knew at least how to impress Brigit's Swedish palate. But before she could make her first cut, her body betrayed her, ambushing and jolting her as it so often did, with pain and instability, a reminder of her defects at the most inopportune of times.

"Caroline."

Impossible not to react, Caroline saw Dr. Todson's movement out of the corner of her eye as she gasped and reached for the table's edge, holding herself on a knife's point as the pain went through her, from just below her sternum all the way through to her spine. But she couldn't look at Dr. Todson. Or breathe too deeply. As always, when these twinges came, she had to be still, as still as humanly possible. If she wasn't, the pain would come again, shrieking with an intensity that would take her to her knees.

"Are you in pain?" Dr. Todson seemed to recognize the precariousness of the situation. Though she came to Caroline's side, hovering close at hand in case she was needed, she didn't try to touch her. Not until Caroline could pull herself back up to near standing on her own, hint of danger still lingering in her chest, but momentarily unafflicted.

"No. Not at this moment."

"But you were just one moment ago. Will you tell me what kind?" Dr. Todson asked, and Caroline turned, slowly, gingerly, entire body trembling just enough to be annoying, the spasm in her back causing her shoulder to tic like the spout cap on a kettle about to whistle.

Why this? Eyes drifting past Dr. Todson's shoulder, she felt the shame, like hot tar, pour through her. *Why now?* Of all of her afflictions, she knew this was the one that made her look the most frightful. Like a lady possessed. And, indeed, in her youth, her parents had consulted as many priests as doctors about the condition. Luckily, the stabs came on such rare occasion, they were easy to conceal, and Caroline had learned to conceal them whenever she could, playing them off as common stitches when she couldn't.

Feeling Dr. Todson's gaze on her shoulder that simply would not stop twitching, her impulse now was to do the same, to tell Dr. Todson it was only a stitch, nothing more, to say she would go sit in the dining room until it passed and would be sure to catch up on the sandwiches when she came back in.

Words hovering at her lips, they felt like a lie. They never had before. They always just felt like self-preservation. Kindness even, telling people what they wanted to hear so they wouldn't have to worry about her.

But the women in the house trusted Dr. Todson - with their health, with their secrets - and it was impossible not to be swayed by that.

"It's a shooting sort of pain. I get them sometimes through my chest."

"Are you still feeling it now?"

"No. Not exactly. A tightness remains. A... quaver of sorts. The pain tends to come back if I move too much."

"Where in your chest?" Dr. Todson asked her.

"Here." Placing her fingers just inside the curve of her left breast, Caroline knew it only gave cause for greater concern as Dr. Todson stepped back to take a clean glass off the rack of dishes next to the sink.

"If I touch you, will it hurt?"

"I don't know," Caroline hedged. She had no possible way of knowing. Whenever the pains came, most people were too afraid to touch her, lest they too become afflicted. "I don't think so."

Nodding, Dr. Todson was as careful as she could be as she placed the rim of the glass against her chest, just above her heart, and her ear to its base.

Looking silently toward the door, Caroline felt exposed. And somewhat silly. It was absurd really, Dr. Todson with her crude tool in the middle of the kitchen, and Caroline expected Lei to walk in at any moment and have a good solid laugh at her expense. *First the workshop, now the kitchen. Do you take all of your medical care in the strangest of places?* she imagined Lei teasing, and it helped her to relax. To breathe. To remain calm under Dr. Todson's close examination.

"Your heartbeat sounds strong, so that's good." Dr. Todson took the glass away and straightened back up, studying Caroline with a concerned and meticulous eye. "Have you always gotten these pains?"

"For as long as I can remember," Caroline admitted.

"May I try something?" Setting the glass down at the prep table's edge, Dr. Todson waited for her approval, and, still shuddering, Caroline gave it with a nod. The worst Dr. Todson could do was make the pain come back, and just taking too deep of a breath had the potential to do that.

If she could breathe at all. Because for a moment when Dr. Todson first placed her hand on her shoulder, thumb sliding along the top of her clavicle to press into the indentation at the base of her throat, it felt frighteningly as if she might be trying to strangle her.

"I'm going to press with my thumb."

That brought no comfort to the matter.

"It will probably hurt quite a lot. You'll feel it up into your head and down into your arm and torso. And, while I do it, I want you to hum."

"Hum?"

"Yes. Mmmmm." Dr. Todson demonstrated.

"I know how to hum," Caroline responded. Almost a snap. Which she didn't intend. It just sounded ludicrous, like absolute quackery. But, then, what about the last few moments hadn't been entirely queer? In for a penny, in for her entire self-worth, she supposed, and closing her eyes, because she simply couldn't imagine following the directive with them open, she began to hum.

As Dr. Todson pressed.

First eruption of pain altogether shocking, Caroline gasped and opened her eyes.

"Breathe through it," Dr. Todson said. "Breathe in when you need to. Keep humming when you breathe out."

When she breathed in.

When she breathed out.

Good luck to her doing any of that.

Pain almost as bad as the original jab itself, only far more rampant, it ran from the base of her skull all the way down into her chest and back, and Caroline struggled to breathe at all. If someone wanted to torture her, she could imagine no greater method of doing it. But, still, she did as

Dr. Todson instructed, humming and convulsing under the pressure of Dr. Todson's hand for several agonizing seconds, before at last the pain started to recede, to let up, muscles in her back and chest releasing one by one and reducing the quake through her.

Each breath coming a little easier than the one before, it took Caroline a moment to realize the pain hadn't just left her body, so had the tension which produced it. Shoulders falling, neck looser upon them, she felt almost... limp. And it was somewhat disconcerting. She couldn't recall the last time she had felt so relaxed without also feeling lethargic, laudanum never providing one without the other.

"Better?" Dr. Todson asked, and, opening her eyes again, Caroline was confounded. Amazed.

"Yes." Was that really it? A press and a hum and she was right back to normal? Better than normal. A pain like that back in London, she would have been in bed for hours, trying to prevent it from coming again and making sure no one saw it if it did.

"My mother used to get headaches," Dr. Todson said.

"She did?" Caroline returned, surprised Dr. Todson would share such personal information with her.

"Mm. Peculiar pains with no obvious cause. Not like yours. Not so frequent. But when she did get them, they could be quite terrible. Sometimes it was hard to distinguish them from something far worse." Eyes drifting off for a moment, darkness permeated Dr. Todson's gaze. Loss, Caroline recognized the echo at once. From seeing it so many times in the mirror over the past year. And on Oliver. Before Dr. Todson forced a smile and looked to her again. "They were as likely to be brought on by distress as by anything physical. Emotions manifest in the body, you know. Certain feelings - sorrow, grief, betrayal - they show up in very real ways. Heartache isn't just a poetic turn of phrase, it's a physical condition. If you're unhappy, your body will know it."

"I'm not unhappy." Caroline wasn't sure why she felt the need to tell Dr. Todson that. Or when she had even decided it herself. But, words leaving her lips, she realized they were true. "I am... hurt." She should be unhappy, she thought. She had been driven out to the country and left in a house full of strangers. "I am... angry." Her life in London wasn't perfect - far from it - but it was the life she had made and it had been taken from her abruptly and against her will. "But I'm not unhappy. I'm just... I... I don't know how I feel."

"That's all right too."

Tears clouding her vision, Caroline looked to the kitchen door. What was it about this woman? Just the sound of her voice made her want to fall to her knees and weep at her feet.

"I can't give you anything to take this pain away, Caroline. Nothing I haven't given you already. Rand's tonic is the best thing for you. But you may talk to me whenever you like, and perhaps it will start to lessen."

Standing there in her immediate presence, Dr. Todson's eyes and voice consoling her, Caroline almost understood. Was this why Blanca and the others took time with Dr. Todson on their own? Why they heeded her advice and told her their troubles? Why Caroline had listened to her, even when Dr. Todson hadn't been particularly forceful? Because Caroline *had* listened to her. She *did* heed the recommendation in Dr. Todson's words. Every night, she had a choice, and every night she chose to take Rand's tonic instead of the laudanum.

It wasn't easy. Those first few nights, her flesh crawled inside her skin. She craved the warm, bitter relief and the familiarity. But she couldn't ignore how she had felt under Rand's tonic. The clarity she had. The absence of discomfort. And it gave her the strength to think. Part of her thought, if the tonic proved ineffective, she could always take the laudanum after, double up on her medication, consequences be damned. But within minutes of lying in bed, she didn't need it, the tonic easing the agitation in her body so she had no desire to get up and collect the laudanum from out of the dresser drawer.

If she were perfectly honest with herself, she had been under Dr. Todson's care the entire time she had been there.

"But I would also like to listen to your heart with an actual stethoscope after tea, just in case."

"Yes. All right," Caroline agreed, and, satisfied, Dr. Todson skirted back around the prep table's edge.

"But right now, if I don't get these tarts in the oven, we will be left to live on sandwiches alone, and I would prefer to prevent a riot if at all possible."

Huffing a laugh, Caroline realized she should actually get back to those sandwiches too or they would be left to live on tea alone, and for the next several minutes they worked in silence, Caroline reaching and stretching for ingredients with lingering apprehension, but nary a pain.

"Sorry I'm late." Sometime later, Lei hurried through the door, apology plain on her face.

"Breakthrough?" Dr. Todson asked.

"Followed by an unmitigated disaster. Remarkable how one always seems to follow the other, isn't it? Or is that just me?"

Glancing to Caroline, Lei winked and grinned, and Caroline felt the very truth of what she had just said to Dr. Todson. She wasn't unhappy. She should be. But she wasn't. She had no explanation, but no one was asking her for one. It was the first time in a very long time, she realized, she felt no need to justify her existence.

Uncompromising

Chapter 14

EIRINN

1872

Room carrying a hint of rain as she drifted out of sleep, Eirinn shivered in bed, trying to conjure the will to move as she looked to the weak traces of dawn light leaking in around the shutters.

It would be a gray day in Paris, she could tell it already. Many a day in the city started out with overcast skies that gave way to white clouds and sunshine by the afternoons. But not this day. This day, the gloom was going to cling, hanging like garland over the buildings, sinking like dew into the parks and the carriages. As a Londoner, one got a sense for such things, and came to appreciate them in a nostalgic sort of way. The occasional gray sky kept Eirinn from getting too homesick. When she awoke to such dreary light, she could almost imagine she was waking in London, but a changed London on the precipice of the future.

It was a lovely fantasy for as long as it lasted.

Had she and Rand actually gotten a flat together in London, it would have been a scandal of unimaginable proportions. She could hear the good church ladies blessing each other with the salacious Sunday gossip - *Moved in with her servant, did you hear? Can you imagine? What must her parents be thinking?* - getting their danders up over nothing at all of concern to them and further besmirching the already controversial Todson name.

When she and Rand moved into the Montparnasse borough of Paris, residents scarcely blinked an eye. And the eyes that did blink blinked due more to the fact they were English than unmarried young people letting a flat together.

There was a feeling there, in Montparnasse, in Paris as a whole really, an eagerness toward the future. Toward possibility. Times were changing and antiquated customs were being pressed to change along with them. It was early still, something not quite set in stone, but already poured into the movement's foundation. Free love. Free life. Spreading in every country - even Victoria's England - it was most pronounced in Montparnasse and Montmartre. The basic tenet in the simplest of terms: no one cared what other people were doing in their own homes.

It made quite the delightful change from London where, just before they left, Eirinn was accosted by a society acquaintance of her mother's, a woman who knew very well why she was headed off to Paris with Rand, who placed a hand on her cheek with genuine sorrow in her eyes and a small tsk-tsk shake of her head and said, "Such a waste of a pretty face."

Her own face full of riotous laughter was definitely not what Lady Milton expected in return, but it was what she got, and she walked off with a disturbed expression, as if she thought Eirinn had gone completely mad with knowledge-lust. And, perhaps, Eirinn had. The future was so close now, everything she had worked and wanted so long to have waiting just outside her front door.

But first she had to brave the chill and get out of bed.

Light insufficient, as always it was this time of morning, Eirinn cinched her wrapper more tightly about her waist, stopping to stoke the fire in her bedroom hearth and catch a wick and carrying it into the main room to light the oil lamps and see to the stove.

On the other side of the kitchen and small sitting area, Rand's door was pressed closed, assuring her he had made it back to the flat before dawn. He didn't always. Paris wasn't just a window to the future, it was also a haven of current, radical delights, and Rand was determined to experience every one before his time there was through.

Eirinn couldn't imagine her parents, or Bally for that matter, being too keen on their arrangement - Rand taking a hedonic tour through Paris's burlesques and music halls half the nights of the week, Eirinn occasionally joining him, but otherwise left alone in the flat - but Eirinn was grateful Rand had found a way to occupy himself and for the silence he left behind. She didn't know how she was expected to study with his pouting face always lurking about, bored stiff and earning pay with nowhere to spend it.

Paris meant freedom for Rand too. He had worked in small ways for Eirinn's family ever since he was a boy and had never lived his adult life without some sort of constraints upon him. But, in their own flat with no parents to wring hands over them, they could live as they liked, and that was independently... together.

Last lamp in the room lit, a soft yellow glow brightened the small space as Eirinn added more wood to the stove, the warm, familiar aroma of cedar rising up to tickle her nose as she tossed the log in with the hickory and turned to the small window above the kitchen sink, flicking the latch to pull open the shutters and startling as a knock came almost immediately at the door.

It was early, too early, for anyone, friend or foe, to have business at the flat, and she and Rand hadn't made a lot of friends in Paris. Well, Rand hadn't made a lot of friends. Eirinn had made exactly none. Spending her time in circles of men, many of whom would prefer she not be there, wasn't exactly conducive to cultivating friendships. She was willing, but most of the men she encountered didn't know how to make anything but a wife or a mother of a woman, and she wasn't about to get herself tangled up in that snare.

When the next knock came at the door, Eirinn realized she hadn't imagined the first and went to the double doors of the balcony, pulling one side open and unlatching the exterior shutters to push them slightly ajar. Nothing immediately visible in the dark street below, she thought it might have been an echo, not imagined, but a knock on another door along the street that reverberated between buildings and sounded as if it was on theirs.

Then, the illusory visitor came into view, stepping back from the cover of the entryway to glance up toward the flat. Calf-length black coat and large, frameless hat concealing the person almost completely, it inspired little confidence as to the caller's purpose there, and Eirinn's heart skittered to a halt when the obscure figure caught sight of her peering through the crack in the shutters. Before she could close and re-secure them, the caller pulled off the flopping hat, slinking back into the light of a gas streetlamp and revealed herself.

Herself. As a woman.

Hat raised in greeting with one hand, the lady caller pulled open her coat with her other, and, though it was dark, nearly too dark to see, Eirinn recognized the stain of blood on her white blouse on instinct.

"Rand!" Turning from the balcony doors, she didn't wait for his reply as she rushed back through the sitting area and around their small table to the stairwell door.

Only the lamplight from the kitchen and dreary gray glow through the window above the entry door to light her way, the stairs down to street level were perilous, but Eirinn navigated them without incident, arriving at the entry door and unlocking it to pull it wide, realizing it was imprudent only when she was already standing in the open doorway.

Or, rather, when the fact was pointed out to her.

"Did you come down here alone?"

Fixed by the caller's dark gaze and low rasping tone, Eirinn was struck mute, dumb, feeling rather helpless to respond. The caller quite possibly the most beautiful woman she had ever seen, she felt rather helpless to do anything before she checked her already well-secured wrapper and comprehended what the woman just said.

"Why?" Dragging her eyes away from dark eyes and high cheekbones, she looked to the twilight behind her for potential conspirators. "Is this a ruse? Are you not really hurt?"

"No, I am. I definitely am." Leaned in her doorway, the woman pulled open her long coat, showing Eirinn the blot of blood that marred her abdomen, which looked far larger and wetter up close. "But this is a wealthy neighborhood and you..." Dark eyes trailing her from head to toe, Eirinn felt like she was standing naked in her entryway. Minus the chill. "...would be a desirable target for a lot of things, I imagine. You really shouldn't be opening your door to strangers in your robe."

"Thank you for the advice." Pulling the tie tighter on her wrapper, Eirinn suppressed an aggrieved growl. She could say the same for the caller, and she was the one out walking the streets alone at dawn.

Of course, there was some sense to what the woman said as well. The stranger might be gorgeous - a desirable target for a lot of things, if Eirinn were to use her crass choice of words - but she was dressed so neutrally in her long jacket and hat, she could easily be taken for a slight man with just a glance.

Beneath the coat and hat, though, there was no question. Hint of curl in shiny dark hair where it was braided to rest against one shoulder, pin-striped trousers cropped to her calves and ending in lace cuffs where they met tall brown boots, stained blouse she wore beneath her open vest ornately needle-worked, breasts straining against its fabric as if they were part of the design. No. Once beneath her outer layers, this woman definitely could not be mistaken for a man.

"Sorry." Grin spreading slowly across her face, the caller looked sincerely contrite. And sincerely humored. "I was just trying to hel..."

Crumpling forward on a groan, she stumbled off the doorframe, hat falling from her hand, and Eirinn caught her, laboring beneath the sudden weight before she got her knees set and their balance secured. Closer up, she could see the paleness of the woman's skin wasn't even remotely her natural complexion, could feel the cold clamminess of the caller's wrist as her hand closed around it.

"Dammit," the caller said, and Eirinn could hear the deficiency in her breaths, feel the tremble that went through her as she slid her arm around her waist to hold her up. "I had a whole... patter worked out. It was going... it was going to end in common... humble pleading. But I thought... a little... precursory banter -"

"Save it," Eirinn said, referring both to the woman's words and to her breath, which was obviously in dangerously short supply, as, kicking the door closed, she turned for the stairs. "Rand! Can you make it up the stairs?"

"If I can find them.

"I know. It's dark." Eirinn made the hopeful assumption that was the only reason the woman struggled to see at the moment. "There are eighteen total. The first one is right in front of your foot, and there's a pair of boots on the third. Are you ready? Let's try it."

Despite the effort it took getting started, they made it up the stairs in a relatively expedient go, the caller leaning equally on Eirinn and the wall and taking dutiful steps, until they made it through the entry door and into the soft light of the kitchen.

"Rand!" Turning to her bedroom, Eirinn didn't stop until they were at the side of her bed. Trusting the caller could hold herself up once they were no longer in motion, she eased her arm from around her waist, grabbing the black jacket at the shoulders and sliding it and the vest the woman wore beneath it off in the semi-darkness, finding exactly what she feared she would find below, a blood stain on the back of the fancy blouse too.

"Rand!" Hand sliding down the black jacket, Eirinn paused as she encountered crusty fabric, indicating the blood had seeped all the way through at some point and dried. "When did this happen?" Tossing the jacket and vest aside, she turned the caller toward her, urging her to sit on the edge of the bed, wondering, with rising dread, just how much blood she had left to lose.

"Last night."

"What time last night?"

"Eleven-thirty? Midnight?"

"Midnight?!" So much for bedside manner, Eirinn's panic coursed through her, jittering her nerves and sharpening her tone. "Where were you? Versailles?"

"Just in Auteuil. I waited... outside... until you were awake."

Words and words about the sheer stupidity of that filling her throat, Eirinn didn't know why she thought she had the right to say them or wanted to so badly. "You shouldn't have done that," she meekly managed.

"I was already asking... a stranger for a favor. I thought she would be... a lot more... accommodating... if I didn't also... wake her up."

"Lie down."

"Don't you want... to put... something...?"

"Just get on your back."

"Yes, Ma'am."

Where she found the will to keep on smiling, Eirinn hadn't a clue, but delirium did wondrous things for a person, and the caller lay back with an amused grin as if they were engaging in a casual repartee over tea.

"Hey. What is it?" Rand at last appeared, disheveled and only half-buttoned in his one-piece long underwear. "Ah, hell," he said when Eirinn moved aside so he could see the state of affairs for himself.

"I need your help."

"Yeah, yeah." Shaking free of his early morning shock, he ambled a few steps into the room. "What do you need?"

"Water, a clean towel, and whatever you have for the pain. And please button yourself up."

"Yeah, I could see how *all of this* might be distracting." Running a hand down his exposed torso, Rand winked as he turned through the door, and Eirinn probably would have been irritated at him for wasting time if he wasn't trying to make their patient feel better. And if it didn't work. Producing a small laugh, the caller broke off in a ghastly struggle for breath, series of choking coughs swallowing her inhalations until she at last lay very, very still, every effort focused on drawing in air and pushing it back out again.

"In the briefest possible terms." Eirinn tried not to let the weak, gurgling sounds distract her as she unbuttoned the bottom buttons of the woman's shirt. "What happened to you?"

It was a courtesy. Pulling up the shirt's ends to inspect the deep, dark line that cut through russet-stained skin, she could see very well what sort of wound this was.

"Would you... believe me... if I told you... I was attacked... by a violent pigeon?"

"That is not the briefest possible terms." Eirinn tried to maintain some humor, but it was evaporating quickly in the face of what she saw. "And, generally speaking? Probably. But, given that I am looking at the wound and you chose to come here instead of going to a hospital, I assume you weren't. Who stabbed you?"

Sudden clattering in the kitchen making both of them jump, Eirinn settled the caller with a hand on her stomach, glaring in the direction of the door.

"Damn! Just a minute!" A whisper of conversation, a voice Eirinn didn't recognize, and Rand appeared back in the doorway, still unbuttoned and disheveled. "Sorry, I let a... friend... stay over last night. He's just going now. The water's almost warm."

Explanation rendered, he rushed out again, and Eirinn took a deep, calming breath, wondering just how little sleep he had gotten, something about Rand being so *Rand* giving her some comfort in the moment. It wasn't his fault a visitor had showed up bleeding and wounded at their door before the day could even begin. "I know it doesn't seem like it, but he really is incredibly competent."

Languid gaze drifting back to Eirinn's, the caller huffed a weak smile, knowing better than to laugh again. Or too weak to.

"What's your name?" Eirinn asked her, question tremulous on her lips, because she was asking it now for a reason.

She could feel it. Death. Close at hand. Not quite in the room with them, but hovering in the gray just beyond the window. She could hear it in the caller's breaths and the distant trill of Notre Dame waking up - six rings that sounded slower and more somber than usual.

"Aya," the caller said.

"Do you have a last name, Aya?"

"Dauphine. That's what I go by here. But my real name is Kobzari."

"Is Aya your real first name?"

"Yes." Recognition, soft and tinged with sorrow, floated in Aya's gaze. Eirinn wondered if she could hear it too - the city's mournful lament.

"Do you have any family?"

"I have a sister. Still alive... I think. Feliza. But I don't know where... she ended up. I last saw her... in Alexandria, but when I went back for her... she wasn't there. That was some years ago."

Confirming the statement with a nod, it was a decent amount of actionable information to have, and Eirinn filed it away with Aya's full name and alias as her gaze swept over her. From Aya's forehead specked with perspiration. To the dark arch of her eyebrows. To her slender nose and deathly pale lips. To the hideous wound that made collecting such information imperative.

"Are you going to tell me who did this to you?"

"Don't worry. It was a stranger."

"Why would that not worry me? Why would a stranger do this to you?"

Aya glanced away, unable or unwilling to meet her eyes. It didn't surprise Eirinn. Many of the people who knocked on their door didn't tell the truth about how they had ended up injured. At least Aya chose to keep quiet rather than to lie to her. That meant something and mattered, though Eirinn couldn't say what it meant or why exactly as she noticed Aya's stomach still felt warm beneath her hand.

A sure sign of life.

Or a sure sign of infection.

"Were you stabbed with a carving knife?"

"It was a sword."

"A sword?" Tone so sharp, it practically sliced Eirinn's tongue.

"Yes. I wasn't exactly expecting it either."

"Jesus Christ." Looking to the wound with enlightened eyes, it seemed a thousand times worse. No wonder it went all the way through Aya.

But it wasn't just the depth of the cut that gave Eirinn such cause for concern. It was the sheer size of it from end to end. Blade big enough on its own, at some point it had also jerked downward, it was clear by the rips to the skin, dragging through flesh and God only knew what else.

"Can you roll onto your side?" Helping Aya to shift, Eirinn tugged the back of her shirt up, looking to the exit wound. Closer to Aya's side than the entry wound, it indicated the blade had gone in at an angle. Given the trajectory, it was possible it missed all of Aya's vital organs. Not likely, but there was always some miracle of fate.

"I'm going to go wash my hands. Can you unbutton your shirt for me?"

"I can. But is this... really the time... to be flirting with me?"

Caught unexpecting, to say the least, Eirinn stumbled over her own feet as she stood. Never mind Aya's ability to be so casual given the amount of pain she had to be in. What was more perplexing was how a woman covered in so much blood with a giant, gaping hole through her could still be so undeniably seductive. Eirinn felt the lusty overture in Aya's gaze sweep over her, confusing her entire body as to what it should feel.

"Unbutton your shirt." Skin on fire, she marched to the wardrobe, finding a clean linen and pulling it out. "Here. You can use this to cover up." Unfolding the fabric enough to provide ample coverage, she left it on the bed next to Aya, praying Aya made use of it as she escaped to the kitchen.

"I was just about to bring it in." Rand turned with a half-full pan of water and a white ball of fabric in his hands. "I couldn't find a clean towel, so I got one of my undershirts. It's clean, I swear," he tacked on when Eirinn gave him a look.

"Could you pour some water into a bowl for me?" Taking the bar of soap off the kitchen window, Eirinn scrubbed it beneath her fingernails, lathering up in the water Rand poured out. "Did you clean everything?"

"Come on now," Rand groaned. Which was fair. He had worked for Dr. Anderson as long as she had - a temporary post that turned into several years' gainful employment - and was as interested as Eirinn in the medical developments of the day. Germs, and the way they spread infection, were still theoretical, but it didn't hurt to adhere to theory when it took little time, couldn't hurt, and might well be proven true.

"I also got you these." Rand held out two small vials. "Oral for the pain. Topical to numb the wound. Do you want a poultice?"

"I will. Two of them. But I'll need your help first."

"All right. I'll wash up again too."

"Just give us a few minutes before you come in," Eirinn said, grabbing the pan, undershirt, and vials, and going back into the bedroom, looking to Aya where she lay in her bed, linen draped casually but effectively across her.

"I could unbutton it, but I couldn't get it off."

"All right." Eirinn had no expectation Aya could. She honestly didn't know how Aya was moving at all. Taking her arm to help her lean slightly forward, she stared at the empty space next to Aya's head as she pushed the blouse carefully from her shoulders, tossing it in the direction of Aya's bloodied jacket and vest.

"Hey. Careful. That's my good shirt," Aya quipped, and Eirinn felt a small smile pull at her lips as she laid Aya back against the pillow and situated the linen over her, leaving the wound exposed between its bottom edge and the waistband of Aya's pants.

"This will help with the pain." Removing the yellow stopper from Rand's vial, Eirinn handed it to Aya, and Aya swallowed its contents rabidly, the first sign she was in the sort of pain she should have been in. "It should kick in fast. This will still burn, though," Eirinn warned before dripping the topical serum along the gash, watching the pain seize Aya's features, though Aya did little more than tense up and clutch the edge of the mattress in response.

"So…" Looking to the door, Aya swallowed a shaky, deliberate swallow, and Eirinn just hoped she could keep Rand's tonic down long enough for it to prove effective. "What are you… and your brother… doing in Paris? Aside from… studying medicine and… tending to the broken?"

"Rand isn't my brother," Eirinn uttered.

"You act like he's your brother."

"His mother works for my parents. We grew up together."

"Same thing," Aya said, and Eirinn agreed that it was. She just wasn't used to others recognizing the fact. But it was something else in what Aya had said that required her immediate attention.

"How did you know I'm studying medicine? Who told you to come here?"

Normally, Eirinn did this sort of vetting at the door. Before she let a person inside. It was risky, what she was doing, a threat to her future that had started out innocently enough. A child on the street with a cough that worried her so much she offered the parents one of Rand's tonics. An old neighbor with a bad case of gout who refused to call for a doctor, but whose son - an acquaintance of Rand's - was worried.

"It's a well-spread secret. If you don't want it getting out, you probably shouldn't be doing it," Aya declared. And she was right. On both counts. Eirinn didn't know how knowledge of her clandestine treatments was getting out to the citizens of Montparnasse and Greater Paris, but it was obvious it was, and she shouldn't be doing it. If she was caught, she would be kicked out of the country before she ever got her license, assuming she wasn't arrested instead. It should have made her far leerier of every person who came to the flat seeking her help.

But when a beautiful woman showed up bleeding on her doorstep, it was hard to say no to her.

"Hey. Are you ready for me?" Knock coming at the door, Eirinn tucked the linen more tightly around Aya's side.

"Yes, Rand. Come in."

Aside from still wearing his sleeper, Rand looked almost presentable as he stepped into the room. Buttoned up. Clean enough. His hair had even settled somewhat from its chaotic morning state as he waited for the water to warm.

"Hey there again," he greeted Aya.

"Hello," Aya drawled softly in return.

"How are you feeling?" Eirinn asked her.

"Warm."

"Good. But this is still probably going to hurt quite a lot."

"Yes. I assumed."

Dismal acceptance whispering through the words, Eirinn couldn't let that dissuade or delay her. They needed to get to this - it should have been done hours ago - and dipping Rand's undershirt into the pan of water, she wrung it out and lifted it to Aya's wound.

Her first few strokes exploratory, just removing the outer stain and making the size and shape of the cut more discernible, after that there was nowhere to go but the wound itself. At the first touch of the cloth against its outer edge, Aya cried out and arched off the bed, but Rand was there, pressing her back down by the shoulders.

"Sorry," he said, but Aya couldn't speak. Tears streaming from her eyes into her hairline, she just stared up at the ceiling, sobs and whimpers joining her weak exhalations in a terrible chorus.

Eirinn glanced up only briefly, the guilt clutching and gnawing at her even as she knew these were the necessary steps to save Aya's life. Aya might have walked there on her own, she might have been beautiful and funny and flirtatious, but her wound was deep, it was definitely infected, and she would die if they just closed it up and allowed nature to run its course.

"Thank... you."

Last thing she expected to hear, Eirinn looked to Aya again, into dark eyes that were somehow completely, steadily focused upon her. And now it was she who couldn't speak. What would she say? It might well be Aya was thanking her for failing. For being too late and too unskilled. For killing her. At a loss, she returned her attention to the wound, but before she could make her next sweep, Aya reached out and caught her hand.

"I just... I want you to know..."

The sounds of Aya's distress, her labored breathing, the gurgle once again at the back of her throat, seized and enfolded Eirinn until Aya's sounds and gaze were the only things she could distinguish in the room. The bed, the wall, Rand all dissolving into shapeless blurs at the periphery, it was as if Aya had stopped time, altering the fabric of reality between them so that Eirinn felt her everywhere. In her past. In her future.

"If this... is the end... for me... I'm glad... You... were the last thing... I got to see."

Words winding through and around her, they might have been tangible - vines or serpents - and Eirinn felt herself falling nowhere. If a portal opened behind Aya's eyes and sucked her in, she wouldn't have been the least bit surprised to emerge on the other side of it.

Before those eyes drifted closed, and Aya's head fell to the side, all opportunity abandoning them.

"She's unconscious."

Warping instantly back to fear, Eirinn sucked in a breath, anxiety seizing and convulsing her hand. "Good." She tossed Rand's shirt into the pan of water, light-headed, not entirely convinced she hadn't been bewitched as she wiped her dry hand across her forehead and contemplated her options.

"Is something wrong?" Rand asked her.

118

Something? Everything. Everything was wrong. Aya had just suspended her in some sort of celestial fantasy realm with her bloody words and eyes alone and now she was going to die in her bed.

"I don't think I can handle this," she confessed.

"What? Of course, you can. You're Almost Dr. Todson."

"No, Rand. I... I... I-I'm serious," Eirinn stuttered. On her panic. Her fear. More than she should have felt. More than she could explain. "Look at her. I have never seen this much blood in my entire life. She was stabbed with a sword. A sword! If it hit anything at all important, she is going to die, and I cannot be responsible for that."

Sitting back, Rand stared across Aya's still form, stunned, confounded, maybe recognizing the extent of Eirinn's discomposure, probably not. How could he?

Then, his gaze went to Aya, shifting from her face to her wound, which, even somewhat cleaned up, looked beyond brutal. "Well, I hate to be the one to say it, but if she dies I don't think it's gonna be because of anything you do or don't do."

Closing her eyes, that was exactly what Eirinn feared. That it was a lost cause. That there was no hope. That Aya had come into her care - into her life - only to die within hours.

"Whatever you want to do, Eir," Rand said. "But I don't think you've got a lot of time to decide."

No time. No time. The words pounded in Eirinn's head. No time to dawdle. No time to call in another doctor. Not that she would trust another doctor with Aya's condition. She had met too many surgeons who would take one look at Aya and pronounce her a waste of their time and resources, who would ply her with opium to keep her comfortable until the inevitable end and go back to their patients who were easier to save.

"I need my bag, and I'm going to need a lot more light in here."

"I'm on it." Rand was up in a flash, and Eirinn tried to steady her hands. Her heart. She did know how to do this. She knew at least what needed to be done, the best way to go about doing it, and how to do the least amount of damage in the process.

And the one thing she could say without doubt, even if she could make no sense or reason of it at all, was that no one would care more whether Aya lived or died.

Chapter 15

CAROLINE

1886

When she first saw Dr. Todson's Home for Women, she thought it wore a mask. It donned its yellow paint and white casements the way she had been taught to brush rouge over her sallow complexion and layer petticoats to cover her too-thin frame. Trickery to conceal broad, fundamental flaws in nature.

More and more, the house revealed the bright, gentle colors of a country retreat to be its true face. If Mr. Hyde was waiting in the unused rooms of the basement or the far hedges of the fields, he had yet to make an appearance.

Days of reading and occasional demonstrations down in Lei's workshop fueled by decadent meals that required many an after-meal walk gave way to pleasant nights of frivolity and conversation. Card games. Impromptu musical performances. The occasional dance if anyone had energy left by day's end to indulge Imogen.

In those nights, Caroline learned a lot about the women who lived alongside her.

Stella had once worked for the circus.

"Hoops of fire," she told Caroline when Caroline's eyes went wide at such an unusual prospect. "It's an act more popular under the big top than on the streets, and much easier when you're young. Set yourself on fire once and people think you're crazy."

And so ended the mystery of how Stella ended up at Dr. Todson's Home for Women.

Francie did "every job a woman could do," as she put it. "And don't think I'm leavin' out the ones you think I'm leavin' out. My favorite was being governess. Free food. Free lodgin'. Just messin' about paintin' pictures with two sweet girls all day. Until the lady of the house realized I couldn't paint or play an instrument or read myself. You'd be amazed how long you can get away with it. Kids are too stupid to know they ain't learnt anything. I think I bunked up with 'em six months before they got wise to me. Had to leave at a gallop when they did, though."

Laughing, astonished, Caroline couldn't decide if she thought Francie quite terrible for doing such a thing, or quite genius for it. It was wrong, of course, to lie so boldly, to take pay for work one couldn't actually do. She might argue Francie's job those six months was really more as swindler than as governess. But having received her own education from a series of stern, straight-laced spinsters who would rather have been married with children of their own - much of what they taught her forgotten, nearly all of it useless - Caroline imagined she would have learned quite a lot from someone like Francie during a six-month apprenticeship. Things that mattered and stuck. Francie probably did those girls more good than anyone who came before or after her.

"Of course, it's a laugh 'cause I got off without any real trouble. Hardly right when others are only doin' good and take the abuse."

When Francie glanced to Blanca, Blanca looked back at her with a soft, merciful smile, and Caroline waited on edge. For Blanca to look her way next. For her to offer some explanation. When Blanca didn't, the disquiet spread like mites beneath Caroline's skin, making it itch and crawl.

"Is that what happened to you?" She knew she shouldn't ask, had no business asking when she would prefer not to answer questions herself, but how could she not ask after such a statement? It was a horrible thing to have hanging out there without knowing.

"Yes," Blanca said. "I worked household at an estate and got caught up in the cataclysm of the day. It was bound to happen eventually. There was always one brewing in the caldron. The master and mistress were perpetually bored and always looking for some drama or other to befall them so they would have something to do with themselves."

"They hurt you?" Caroline asked.

"Only within the bounds of legality." Blanca pinned her with a stare, and Caroline sharply inhaled, feeling the prick of air inside her chest. "They hurt my prospects far more. Vowed to make sure I would never find domestic work in London again and they managed it quite well."

"Why would they do that to you?"

"I understood too much."

"Under...? What?" Caroline was at a loss, truly, head-scratchingly baffled. "Isn't that a good thing?"

"When I was brought on as housekeeper, I didn't speak any French," Blanca explained. "That was all the Altiers spoke at home. They didn't think I could possibly pick it up, savage as I was. But I've always had an ear for languages. I absorb them quite readily. I speak perfect British, don't you think?"

"English isn't your native language?"

"English, yah... nah de Queen's English."

Caroline jolted. Same face, same words, but suddenly Blanca sounded like a completely different person.

"I grow up in Barbadus. Cum tuh England when I did bout twelf."

Sounds tinkling, unfamiliar and delightful, to her ears, Caroline practically swayed to their rhythm. She could understand what Blanca said, with just a little extra effort, but it sounded like music. "Is that your native dialect? It's lovely."

"Ah. Tank yuh, Luv. I like yuh voice too."

"What the hell is she sayin'?" Batting her eyes at Blanca, Francie turned a scrunched face toward Stella.

"It don't matter. She ain't talkin' to you."

"But I find it easiest to talk to drunks in their native tongue," Blanca leaned into Caroline's confidence to impart, and Caroline spit laughter, making the effort, but failing, to stifle her residual giggles as Francie glared their way. Humor fading just as quickly when she recalled what Blanca had been saying just before they went slightly off-course.

"So, that's it. You understood their language, and they dismissed you for it?"

"Well, they did say a lot of things best left unheard," Blanca said, and that was certainly grounds for a future conversation. "They thought I should have told them the second I started to make sense of it. I don't know what I did that day." Head giving a small, absent-minded shake, Blanca looked lost in the memory. "It must have been a glance, or the way I pulled my mouth. Something small gave me away. I could have lied, of course, pled in English I didn't understand a word of French. But to what end? So they could find some other excuse months on, and we could act out their melodrama all over again? Rich people don't need a reason to find you expendable. They do as they like."

Wincing, Caroline looked to the table, embarrassment rising up around her neck to warm her cheeks.

Blanca didn't mean her. She knew she didn't. She was speaking in generalized terms, and, generally speaking, Caroline knew that it was true. Her parents had let go of many an employee without sufficient explanation. And in her married home, Thomas was often angry, just on the edge of senseless rage. About everything. It was because of her, her failure to run the household to his liking, but since he couldn't direct it toward her, he took it out on the others. Yelling. Glaring. Threatening lost wages or employment. He had never struck any of the people who worked for them, not that Caroline knew of, but she was so often confined to her bedroom, and if they thought it might cost them their positions, would they have told her if he had?

"I'm sorry that happened to you." Filled, suddenly, with concern for the employees left behind in London, Caroline wondered what Thomas might do with them while she was away. For days, it had been only Oliver in her worries. The staff was paid to be there and were all adults. They could take care of themselves, she had thought. But what if Thomas decided to seek out his drama? To mistreat or discharge them in her absence? Where would they go? Would Thomas purposely try to bar them from future employment? Would he tell lies about them just out of spite? Caroline had no comfort he wouldn't.

"It wasn't your doing." Head dipping to capture her gaze, a soft smile curved Blanca's lips, and Caroline felt marginally better. What would worrying do? As first to be exiled, there was hardly anything she could do about it now. "And it worked out all right. Better than. It turned out, my penchant for language could be transferred to ink. I make quite a good living off of shilling shockers and articles for the papers. More than I ever made as a domestic. The Altiers' heads would probably explode if they knew how much better off I am without them."

"You write shilling shockers?" One thing that could distract her from all else for a moment, Caroline grinned. "I love shilling shockers."

"Well-bred girl like you? That does come as a surprise."

"Well, Thomas… That's my husband, Thomas." She couldn't recall if she had told Blanca before. "He would be absolutely appalled if he knew. My parents too. But Thomas's cousin, Mary, she came to live with us a while back." *Almost a year. After…* the thought formed, but dissipated in Caroline's mind. "She picked them up on her days off and always lent them to me when she was done. I find them quite good fun."

"They are good fun," Blanca agreed.

"So, what have you written? Could I have read one?"

"Possibly. *Girls of Whitehall*? *The Gothic Lane*?"

"No." Caroline was disappointed. She did hope she could tell Blanca she had read one of her stories and thoroughly enjoyed it.

"Well, it's not too late. There are copies up in the library. You can read them now whenever you like."

When Blanca smiled again, Caroline smiled back, feeling quite let in on her friendship. Embraced by it, as she had been embraced by all of the women in the house. And increasingly guilty for safeguarding her own secrets when the others had been so open with her.

But what of interest did she have to tell them? They had all done such compelling things, had lived such full, singular lives. What had she done? Spent the last ten years confined to her home. Practically to her bed. These days and nights in Surrey were some of the most living she had ever done. But it had to be so mundane for them, Stella and Francie and Blanca, to be stuck amongst the hills and the trees where there were no hoops of fire to jump through or swindles to pull off. Books to be written, but no urgent need to write them.

A life of luxurious domesticity. Almost boring in its ease.

Indeed, the crisp evening eleven days after Caroline's arrival, the environment was almost sedative as the women of Dr. Todson's gathered in the parlor.

Wind howling outside, it pushed firmly against the shutters. But sitting at the games table next to Lei, closer than was necessary or even physically prudent, Caroline felt perfectly secure, uncommonly relaxed, most of her at least, as she watched Blanca deal cards to the only players left in the game - Lei and Stella - trying to make out whether Lei had anything worth having and still trying to grasp the rules. Perhaps, grasping only how to lose by them if Lei's series of curses and frustrated brow furrows told the story.

"Come on, Mad Scientist. Don't you have some calculations you can use? I feel bad you're making it so easy on me," Stella heckled, and Lei glared across the table, minor irritation tensing her jaw.

"You can't calculate luck."

"Eh, you just think it's luck because you're terrible at it."

"It is luck," Lei grumbled below her breath, and Caroline slid her hand onto Lei's leg under the table, giving it a gently encouraging squeeze, satisfied as Lei took a deep, steadying breath and her shoulders fell slack. "Give me three."

Plunking the unwanted cards down, Lei settled back and Caroline felt the shivery calm settle into her. Paradoxical by its very nature, she was still getting her thoughts around it, and the feel of it all under her control.

Like most of London society, she had been raised with the belief touch was generally unwanted, often unseemly, and almost always unnecessary. It should be reserved for those dearest to you, and even then, when in doubt, it was best to keep one's hands firmly to herself.

But that simply wasn't how the women at Dr. Todson's got on.

Francie was always poking her at the table. "Too skinny," she always said at first, unaware Caroline had long been sensitive of the subject. Headache days, it was difficult to keep food down, if she felt like eating at all, and since so many days were headache days back in London, she had done a lot of unintentional fasting in her life, never keeping weight on the way she should and always looking quite emaciated as a result.

Then, "Glad to see you're fattening up. You wasn't gonna make much of a meal if we had to roast you on the spit," Francie said to her just one night before, noticing the weight Caroline had started to gain and maintain to the point she was thinking about asking Livvie to let her dress out very soon, and Stella had cackled in response.

Blanca was the first to kiss Caroline's cheek, when she was pecking all the other women before heading off to bed early one night, and

Caroline was so unaccustomed to it, it felt like an attack, skittering her mind and sending her senses misfiring in every direction.

Poor breeding. Practically harlots, she could imagine her mother clucking if she saw the way the women at Dr. Todson's embraced for the sake of embracing, pushing each other's shoulders in jest, slapping hands when they thought someone was hiding a card, kissing each other's cheeks in the mornings or at night.

But Caroline found her own breeding fell quickly by the wayside in the face of the spontaneous affections.

"That is a lot of cards to need," Stella heckled Lei again. "Do you want to just push the pot over here instead?"

Leaned into Lei's shoulder, Caroline watched the three cards Blanca dealt turn up in Lei's hand, trying to keep her expression blank, which, as far as she could tell, was ninety percent of the skill involved in the game, and felt the muscle tense in Lei's thigh. Good or bad, she wasn't entirely sure, but she suspected all of those side-by-side jacks in Lei's hand couldn't be a terrible thing and knew Lei conveyed something.

"Come on. Watcha gonna do, Mad Scientist?"

"What's the minimum raise?" Sliding her hand face-down on the table, Lei stretched her free arm across the back of Caroline's chair, and Caroline felt the usual eruption of conflict inside of her.

Of all the touch freely given at Dr. Todson's, it was still Lei who touched her the most. Almost unconsciously, it often seemed. She would reach out and take Caroline's hand when it was time to go upstairs or push her hair from her face so it didn't fall into her plate. Each time she did, delight stirred Caroline's stomach, a warm, reflexive sensation that didn't quite know how to feel. Caroline felt calm *and* wonder, familiarity *and* something new and altogether exhilarating, the response so addictive, she had started to touch Lei back. Whenever she could. Whenever it made logical sense. Whenever she was just sitting next to Lei at a table and had nowhere better to put her hand.

Most touch *was* unnecessary, she had come to realize. Which was exactly what made it so incredibly appealing. Having someone choose to reach out to her, to draw her attention or show her affection, was that what her life had been missing before? Why she had been so miserable in her home in London with Thomas? Would she have been happier in a house full of handsy harlots? Caroline nearly laughed herself silly three nights before when the thought occurred to her in bed.

"One-nine was the call," Blanca said.

"Nearly two shillings." Lei shook her head as she made a show of counting her dwindling stacks of pennies, threepennies, and sixpence. "Well, I've only got six shillings, six pence left, so... I guess I'll just raise all of it."

Trying not to react, Caroline cast her eyes across the table, watching the suspicion that came to Stella's face, one eye narrowing, the other arching, bit of a frown tugging at the corner of her lips as she looked between them - Lei to Caroline, Caroline to Lei - trying to find a clue in either of their faces.

"You're bluffing."

"Maybe I am," Lei said.

It was a duel. A right stare-down across the dusty wasteland of chips and cards. And one of the few instances in which Caroline's stoic upbringing actually proved beneficial. She was quite good at going blank of face, and that was what she did, staring emptily ahead as Stella tried to glean something from their silence and a resident nicknamed Pidge continued to play a fair approximation of real music on the upright piano across the room.

"I stole a burlesque star's short pants once."

Statement so abrupt, so jarring, it fractured her composure, and Caroline jerked her eyes to where Francie lounged behind Stella on the sofa, wondering if she might be trying to help her friend cheat by distraction. A notion immediately quashed when Stella turned fully around in her chair to look at Francie, so irritated as she turned back to the table one would have thought Francie announced the contents of her hand to the room.

"No, she didn't. She's lying."

"I'm not lyin'. It's true."

"If that had happened, you would have told us long before now. No way in eight Hades you could have kept yer trap shut about it this long."

"I forgot," Francie said. "It literally just came into my head. I think I've always wondered if it was real or a dream, but I recall it quite vividly now."

"Sure, you do. Yer mind is obviously clear as a bell."

"How did you forget you stole a burlesque star's short pants?" Blanca gave Francie slightly more benefit of the doubt, and Francie set up straighter on the sofa, scratching her hair and catching herself on the back of Stella's chair when she teetered.

"Well, I was a tad bit intoxicated."

"Now, there's yer surprise," Stella said.

"When I did the actual stealin' and for several days after. I s'pose it fickled with my memory."

"Everything fickles with yer memory."

"I remember meetin' you, that sour look on your face like ya'd just eaten spoilt mutton. Yep, tha's the one right there."

Without looking back, Stella tossed bits of leftover scone over her shoulder, hitting Francie square, but it barely phased Francie, who just picked the biggest crumbs off of her wrapper and popped them into her mouth before brushing the remainder onto the sofa and floor.

"Ah, don't worry, France. Stella thinks everyone is bluffing tonight." Lei smirked. And, then, since she could tell how much it was irritating Stella - "Now, tell us about these short pants."

"Well, they was short, short." Given a lick of encouragement, Francie couldn't wait to breeze on. "Right up to my tuzzymuzzy. And they

126

was fringed. I wore 'em around for days, 'cause I liked the way they tickled me on my thighs."

"Dear God. Not a soul wants to hear about your thighs," Stella complained, and, flushing furiously, Caroline felt the ripple of laughter through Lei's body most acutely in her fingertips. Suddenly aware of just where her hand rested on Lei's leg, she edged it downward slightly toward her knee.

"I'll have you know my thighs have been the topic of many an enthusiastory conversation."

"At the local butcher's shop, no doubt. All right, Mad Scientist." Stella didn't even pause for her well-deserved laughter before pushing her chips into the pot. "You got 'em, let's see 'em."

Bet formally called, Lei let herself indulge in a small smile. But, before she could reveal her hand, a low chug penetrated the room. Unexpected. Unusual. Like a train rolling past at quite some distance. It diverted Lei's attention for a moment, pausing her hand before she at last turned her cards up for all to see. "Triple jacks."

"Well, I s'pose you gotta get lucky every once in a while." Stella accepted defeat by tossing her cards face-down on the table and rose from her chair with a stretch.

"I thought it wasn't luck," Lei said as she raked in her massive pile of winnings, but left the coins in disarray as the rumbling outside grew closer and louder and even Pidge's music at the piano tinkled to a stop.

"Who is it?" Caroline felt a touch of unease when Lei stood too.

No one looked worried, but it was an unsettling feeling, someone arriving at the house so late. It was well past time for visitors, if any ever came there. The only people Caroline had known to ride up to the house since she'd been in it were those who first left it.

"It's all right." Holding out a hand to her, Lei beckoned her to come and see, and Caroline found some solace as she took it, leaning into Lei as they joined the processional through the parlor and entry hall and out the front door.

Curious vehicle rounding the drive as they spilled onto the stone stoop, it looked much like a bicycle, but with fatter tubing and large cylinders on its back and sides, steam pouring from the tall curved spout at its rear like from the chimney of a steam engine.

Coming on at near impossible speeds to pedal, the person atop the contraption didn't appear to be doing any pedaling. Instead, the rider's feet were planted on stationary platforms at the bicyclar vehicle's base, not moving at all until it rolled to a stop at the bottom of the steps and one boot-clad foot came down to kick out a stand and brace it upright.

"Did you make that?" Caroline asked Lei.

"Modified. But, yeah, that was me," Lei said as the rider swung off the bike, pulling up the heavy goggles and unbuckling the strange black leather cap, and dark hair, nearly as dark as Lei's, tumbled around the rider's shoulders in a cascade that caught the light spilling out of the doorway and streaked it in shades of amber.

"Hey, Ladies," the rider said.

"Hey, Aya," the women greeted her in return.

"That's Aya?" Caroline asked.

But before Lei could answer, she was pressed flush against Caroline, softness of her breast yielding against Caroline's own, breath warm against Caroline's neck, as the residents made a path and a streak of purple burst from the house like an arrow off a taut bow.

Recognizing the streak as Dr. Todson only when it was halfway down the steps, Caroline realized it was because she had never seen Dr. Todson like this, so casual, so... *normal*, dressed as she was in her wrapper instead of one of her usual fancy dresses, house shoes on her feet, tendrils of damp hair clinging to her neck as if she had vaulted straight out of a bath.

Luminous smile appearing on Aya's face, she tossed the leather cap carelessly aside so it missed the strange bicycle's seat and skidded through the dirt, striding forward to meet Dr. Todson at the bottom of the steps, and Dr. Todson fell instantly into her arms, kissing Aya in a way Caroline had never seen two people kiss before in her life. The sort of kissing people wrote about in books and did in the privacy of their own bedrooms. Caroline assumed. She had never once kissed Thomas like that. Nor anyone for that matter.

Her shock at the sight manifesting in an invasive flush, it threatened to burn her brain and sent searing lines down into her stomach. But, chorus of whistles and catcalls going up around her, no one else seemed at all surprised by the scandalous display. No one else's mouth hung agape, inviting the night air and gnats in. Realizing it, Caroline snapped hers closed, watching Dr. Todson and Aya separate with heaving breaths, arms still wrapped around each other, eyes locked like they were the only two people there.

"Hey, Darlin'. Did you miss me?" Aya murmured, but the night air and stone seemed to amplify the words so they might as well have been whispered into Caroline's own ear.

And, in lieu of answer, Dr. Todson kissed Aya again, softly, lingeringly on her lips, and laid her head on Aya's shoulder, and what was incredible about the situation changed. Caroline had never seen Dr. Todson look at all vulnerable either. Until that moment, she hadn't even imagined she could.

"Come on. Let's get inside. A lovely spring evening, this is not." Aya glanced back toward the gardens as a gust of wind snapped a branch in a distant tree and started up the stone steps, Dr. Todson clinging to her side like a barnacle as most of the residents headed back through the doors.

But not Lei, so not Caroline. Not sure what to do, Caroline did know she didn't want to be without Lei by her side, so she stayed where she stood, knees rickety, face aflame.

"Hey, Lei."

"Hey, Aya."

Caroline had heard Aya's name, time and time again in the house. Aya appeared in so many of the women's stories, it was clear she was a major part of life at Dr. Todson's when she was there. But no one had bothered to mention she was Dr. Todson's... consort?

"Safe and successful?" Lei asked as Dr. Todson and Aya made it to the top of the steps.

"Indeed. I have been both." Aya's eyes alighted on Caroline. "Hello."

"Hello." Caroline didn't realize her throat had gone unusably dry until she tried to speak.

"I'm Aya."

"Caroline," Caroline barely managed.

"Caroline arrived here last week," Dr. Todson said to Aya, fingers toying with the clasps on Aya's leather riding jacket.

"Oh, right," Aya returned as if it was something that had been anticipated and discussed. "And? How are you liking it so far?"

"It's nothing at all like I expected," Caroline husked, answer even truer now. The things she had encountered at Dr. Todson's were things she couldn't have even thought to expect. They were beyond her realm of speculation, so exotic to her, she may as well have been dropped off on another planet.

"Well, that's a true descriptor if ever I've heard one. Welcome."

"Thank you."

"Who's hungry?" Through the door with Dr. Todson a moment later, Aya addressed her question to the rest of the residents, and there was a general chorus of response. "Come on. Let's go to the dining room. I'm starved."

In the next instant, the residents commenced their pilgrimage to satisfy Aya's stomach, but Caroline felt dead-legged where she stood, staring off the stone stoop into the dark gardens. Wind whipping at the bushes, she watched their branches bend this way and that, and it felt like a representation of her own internal state, thoughts pressing her all different directions.

"Are you all right?"

Glancing to where Lei still stood beside her, Caroline didn't think she could possibly get any more flustered, but the way Lei was looking at her, reflection of the lights gleaming in her eyes, soft lift to her cheeks, she might have been trying not to laugh.

"Of course, I am. Why wouldn't I be?"

"I don't know. I don't know what sort of moral piety you come saddled with."

Offended. Caroline was truly, furiously offended. "Dr. Todson has been nothing but kind to me."

"I'm glad you realize that."

Bristling more, Caroline crossed her arms, leg twitching in a near-stomp as she turned to face Lei. But Lei was completely unmoved by her tantrum. Eyes moving over her - gently, worriedly - it occurred to Caroline she might be overreacting. Lei didn't know her. Not well. Not deeply. Not yet. But she did know Dr. Todson and Aya. Well and deeply. She had every reason to try to protect them.

"I am not bothered by the nature of their relationship."

At that, Lei did laugh.

Sound accosting her, Caroline tucked her arms more tightly to protect herself. It did sound rather proper, she had to admit, hearing the words cross her lips. No wonder Lei thought she came burdened with some worrisome moral indignation. To be honest, she did. As much as anyone. It was simply a shocking thing to see.

"But you're not indifferent to it either."

"Well, it's not exactly something one sees every day."

"No." Lei shifted closer, breast brushing Caroline's again, and Caroline felt it differently. Even more acutely. Tinder stoked, she feared the flames would erupt within her, set her ablaze from the inside out and immolate her for a cause she never meant to promote. "Shame, isn't it?"

Leaving her words to linger, Lei took her soft breast and body heat through the front door, and Caroline was left alone in the chilled and gusty night, spinning through a kaleidoscope of conflicting emotions. Some new. Some familiar. Many she couldn't name. Most she hadn't the courage to try.

Chapter 16

EIRINN

1872

Three hours, she picked through Aya's wound, a tiny breadth at a time, cleaning flesh as she went.

Inside, Eirinn found much what she expected to find, a large slit through Aya's large intestine. There was no logical way such a deadly blade, so roughly handled, wasn't going to hit something of significance, but it was along the outer edge and the diagonal nature of the wound meant the intestine held largely together instead of breaking off or leaking too much of its contents into Aya's abdomen. Or so it appeared.

With little disturbance to already damaged tissue, Eirinn succeeded in stitching the intestine back up, as tightly as she could get the sutures together, and Rand laid a poultice inside Aya's skin as they turned Aya onto her side, repeating the same meticulous procedure on the wound in her back, before removing the poultices to close up her flesh.

It would take time. To see whether the poultices had been effective at drawing the infection out. To see whether Aya would get better or worse. So, the rest of the day was spent checking for fever or signs of a worsening condition every hour. Or every forty-five minutes. Or every ten.

"Don't you have class?" Rand asked only once when eleven o'clock ticked on, dropping the matter when Eirinn just looked blankly his way.

"Eir, want me to take over?" He didn't try talking to her again until the sun was fully set and the room had grown darker around them.

Ten hours before, Eirinn had dragged the most comfortable chair in the apartment to the side of her bed, reading a manual Dr. Anderson had given her first by daylight, then by lamplight, trying to look for anything she might have missed in her treatment of Aya. Anything more that might be done to aid in a more certain outcome.

"No. I don't want her to be alone when she wakes up."

"I can sit with her. You should rest."

"You rest. I might need your help at some point."

With what onerous task? That was the question that hung in the cool, damp air. What would their next responsibility be? How long should they wait before calling in a surgeon to check Eirinn's work? Would it really improve Aya's odds? There was a twenty-five percent surgical death rate in many London hospitals. Eirinn didn't know the rates in Paris, but couldn't imagine them being much better.

Thankfully, Aya's fever seemed to have largely broken by nightfall. As the sky had broken to let the rain that loomed over the city all day fall and gently pelt the windows of the flat. Only Aya's abdomen remained overly warm, where the flesh was inflamed both inside and out.

"All right." Realizing she wouldn't be moved, Rand came into the room, edging around the bed to squeeze Eirinn's shoulder, before going to one knee on the floor next to her. "You want in on this?" he asked, and, with an agitated sigh, Eirinn closed the book in her lap, leaning over it to clasp Rand's hand where it rested against Aya's hip not far below her wound. "Be strong. Be safe. Be well."

Not a prayer exactly, because Rand didn't pray - *Con men preaching to hypocrites*, he always grumbled behind his mother's back when she tried to get him through the doors of a church on Easter or Christmas - they had learned at the dispensary it felt better to say something. Many of the women who came in were scared and were worried. They were comforted by simpler words. It was one thing to know some unseen force in the heavens was looking out for you. It was another, perhaps more important, thing to know those standing right in front of you were sincerely invested in your recovery.

"Hang in there, Troublemaker." Rand offered the more personal words of comfort to Aya. "You too." He squeezed Eirinn's knee and stoked the fire on his way from the room, leaving the door open as to better hear if she called for him, and, reading already disrupted, Eirinn looked to Aya in the firelight.

The shadows of flames licking Aya's face, she appeared mystical and illusory where she lay in the bed. As if she was on the other side of some ghostly veil. Eirinn wanted so much to reach through it, to run her fingers along Aya's dark brow and down her too-pale cheek, to assure herself Aya was still there amongst the living. But it felt wrong to do it when Aya wouldn't know and it had nothing to do with her care. So, she settled for raising the back of her hand to Aya's cheek instead, finding it both warm and cool to the touch, Aya's scant fever warring with the chill of the room.

It was dangerous, she knew, to indulge herself even this much. To let her hand linger too long. To stare too hard. To study the contours of Aya's face.

Not that she had to look at Aya to see her.

Or touch Aya to know how she felt.

Aya's image swimming in the medical text, Aya's skin on her fingers where they rested against the pages, Eirinn accepted, without argument or comprehension, that Aya had been seared into her memory the instant she staggered through her door.

It was sometime later she woke to the press of Aya's hand.

No idea what time it was, Eirinn knew she had fallen asleep some hours before by the pain in her back and her hips, which felt tight and out of alignment where they slumped haphazardly in the chair.

"Aya?" Lucid in a moment as Aya squirmed and whimpered in discomfort, Eirinn did allow herself a touch then. Just the brush of her thumb against Aya's temple. "Shh, Aya. Try not to move."

Either the whisper or caress was enough to soothe her, and Aya settled into slow, steady breaths, each one most certainly paining her to a dreadful degree. They could have given her more for the pain, kept her sedate and largely unaware throughout the healing process, but Eirinn was afraid to ply Aya with anything that might prolong her waking. Whether or not Aya opened her eyes over the next few hours had become her sole determining factor as to whether or not Aya would survive this, and it might be selfish, almost certainly was, but she would rather see Aya's eyes open and clouded with pain than not open again at all.

"Hey." A few seconds later, Aya's eyes did open, and Eirinn slid forward in her chair, squinting to see in the failing firelight. "Do you want some water?"

Taking her a moment to adjust, to remember where she was, to recognize Eirinn, if she did recognize her, Aya scarcely nodded, and Eirinn took the half-full glass from the bedside table.

"Easy," she said when Aya tried to take the glass and raise up on her own. "Let me." Hand sliding behind Aya's upper back, she helped her off the pillow, just high enough to safely drink, holding onto the glass with her other hand as Aya tilted it to her lips. "Just a little. I know you feel thirsty, but it's the blood loss. Unfortunately, this won't help."

Aya took another small sip, and another - surely, she felt like downing the entire thing - before handing the glass reluctantly back, and Eirinn set it aside, lowering her back down to the pillow and resituating the covers higher on her chest.

"How do you feel?" Reaching for Aya's hand, Eirinn cradled it between her own, glad to feel it dry and unfevered, but Aya only stared, eyes dark and hooded as if she might drift off again at any second.

"Aya?" Eirinn worried. She had pinned all of her expectations on Aya waking up, but, now that Aya had, she realized she needed to hear her speak, to know she wasn't just alive, but she was intact. That she was the same woman who walked through her door hours before.

"Curious." At last, Aya spoke, her voice low and rough, and Eirinn couldn't entirely ignore the shiver that nudged her senses. Even now. Even as relief dominated her emotions.

"Curious how?" she asked.

"That I'm still here. I didn't think I was going to wake up."

Ill-prepared for such brutal honesty, Eirinn flinched, trying to steel herself as she sucked in a tight breath, but she couldn't stop the tears that permeated her vision. She had thought it herself, but it was worse knowing Aya had thought it. Right up until the moment she lost consciousness, Aya was nothing but gallant and steadfast of spirit. She had to have been far more frightened than she let them know.

"Why?"

"Because you looked so worried," Aya murmured. And grinned. A slow, beguiling grin that returned the strength to Eirinn's chest and eased her anxiety.

"Oh." Eirinn laughed. Shortly. Weakly. "Perhaps, I could use some work on my bedside manner."

"No," Aya uttered, and Eirinn met her gaze. Or, rather, she fell helplessly, headlong into it, swallowed up like a speck in the vast universe. "Don't change anything."

Aya's dark eyes glittering with flecks of light like the midnight sky, the room blurred in a torrential storm to match the storm that still pressed against the windows outside and Eirinn's heart thundered in time. She was just waiting for a bolt of lightning to strike the bed in an actual sign from the heavens.

Desire clutching her harder, she lifted her hand to Aya's face, smoothing her fingers along Aya's dark brow and down her cheek as she longed to do before, and Aya reached for her hand, eyes closing as she pulled it tenderly to her lips.

Electrified, Eirinn didn't know if she would swoon or soar. If she was more firmly grounded in the world or being carried away from it. It was barely a brush, barely a breath - barely a kiss - but, current surging through her and charging the air around them, it may as well have been lightning.

Chapter 17

CAROLINE

1886

Lightning. It was always lightning.

For days, the storm would rumble, swirling and foreboding in the atmosphere, but in the end it was always a sudden flash which unleashed the tempest, swallowing her up in an invisible melee and battering her until she could hardly stand.

"I don't feel well," Caroline excused herself after dinner as Lei and the other residents relocated to the parlor, retreating up the stairs and to her room and barely getting the door closed behind her before the deluge came, pouring over her, out of her, bowing her to the floor and leaving her gasping for breath in the rising floods.

Why are you crying, Caroline?

I don't know.

People don't just cry for no reason.

I know. But she did. She always had. At least, for reasons she couldn't put into words or pick out into pieces.

Because it was never just one thing. A single event. A single reason. It was everything. It was the holding herself up when she wanted to lie still. The getting through the day when she just wished for the days to end. The very act of not crying. Storm clouds ever-hovering, a shift in the wind and they broke.

It's not real, your comfort here. These people don't even know you. How can they be your friends?

It's temporary. When they find out who you really are, they'll abandon you too.

You're a failure, Caroline. You're weak. You're a burden on everyone around you.

Fingers thrust into her hair, Caroline tried to block out the voices from her own mind.

From the past? How often she had heard those same words before.

Or the present? Was this what the others were thinking?

She was just empty. Empty.

And too full.

Depleted. And overwhelmed.

She thought about escaping, but by what form?

Worthless.

If she ran from it all, from her life, where would she go?

Alone.

If she downed the entire bottle of laudanum or jumped out the window, where would she go?

Wicked.

Would anyone notice if she just disappeared?

Sarah.

Sarah would have.

But Sarah was gone. Sarah was dead. Sarah was dead and gone, and it was all because of her.

If only she had been better-natured, she wouldn't have ended up with the dregs in Thomas.

If only she'd had a child, an heir, he would have had no reason to...

It was her fault.

Her fault.

She was sick.

Sick.

Worthless.

Empty.

Alo -

Knock coming at the door, Caroline's thoughts fragmented and scattered, scurrying like insects across the wooden floor.

"Caroline?"

Blinking blearily upward, she felt that floor beneath her, the cold, hard press of its boards. Heart pounding. Head swimming. From the darkness of its reflections or the surprise of the interruption, she wasn't sure.

"It's Lei. Is it all right if I come in?"

Oh.

No.

Caroline looked wildly around her. At her position, in a heap next to the bed. At her mess, skirts askew where they spread out around her on the floor.

No one could see her like this. No one.

Especially not Lei.

Suddenly aware of the bed frame where it dug into her back, now she felt stupid. Stupid for crying when she had no reason to cry. Stupid for getting caught at it. Stupid because she couldn't entirely halt the gasping breaths or instant humiliation that made her want to start all over again as she dragged to her feet, fighting numerous spasms of discomfort to brush the floor debris off of her dress.

"Caroline?" Lei called to her through the door as Caroline endeavored to right herself, to wipe away the tears, knowing she couldn't possibly hide their traces, contemplating whether she should just tell Lei to leave.

I'm fine, Lei. Please go. Rehearsing the words in her head, she stifled a sob even as she thought them. She didn't want that, for Lei to leave, to be alone again, but she could hardly encourage Lei to stay. Looking down at herself, she felt entirely disoriented, dress still twisted in her mind's eye even as it appeared perfectly straight and smooth.

"Caroline?"

She couldn't let Lei see her like this. So messy. So... broken.

"I know you're in there. I heard you."

Crying. If Lei heard her, she heard her crying.

Eyes shuttering at the realization, Caroline felt the pulse of pain behind them, the tension in her neck that sent waves of discomfort up into her head, and her thoughts drifted to the laudanum in the bottom drawer of the dresser. At some point, she would have ended up there, once she found the will to get up off the floor or the desperation to crawl. Just a drop, and she would stop crying. Stop feeling. She would calm down enough to have a perfectly pleasant conversation.

"Caroline?"

But she wasn't sure she wanted Lei to see her like that either.

"Caroline, please..."

Hearing the defeat in Lei's voice, her resignation, Caroline's eyes welled again. How was she supposed to tell her to leave now, or say nothing? How could she continue to keep Lei waiting when Lei had been so good to her? So uncommonly kind?

"Yes, Lei. Come in." She didn't want it, for Lei to see her. But she didn't want her to leave. And what was the point of keeping her out if she already knew?

At the turn of the door handle, Caroline searched around her for something she could right or hide, but there was nothing embarrassing or revealing. Nothing but herself. As usual, she was her own most damning testimonial.

"Hey," Lei softly breathed as she pressed the door open, standing for a moment in its shadow, hesitant, it seemed, to come all the way inside.

137

Caroline was used to having such an effect on people. Her family thought her incapable of any sort of societal influence, but she did know how to bring down the mood of an entire room.

"Hot cocoa," Lei explained of the mugs she wielded precariously in one hand so she could press the door shut behind her with her other. "Don't tell Livvie. She insists chocolate is impossible to get out of the linens. It isn't. You just have to give it a really good scrub before she sees it and she never knows it was there."

"Or we just won't spill it," Caroline meekly suggested.

"An even better idea." Lei grinned as she drew near enough to hand Caroline a mug, and the ache in Caroline's chest roared and receded. Full. Empty. "It's cold in here. Aren't you cold?"

"I didn't notice." Caroline followed Lei's gaze to the hearth that sat dormant and colorless on the far side of the room. Though, it made sense she should be. The hearths in Dr. Todson's Home didn't light themselves. They just almost did.

It works like a flintlock, Lei explained the first time she showed Caroline how to get one going. *Press the trigger and it generates a spark. As long as the kindling and logs are in place, of course. It can't burn empty air.*

Caroline wouldn't be surprised if Lei invented a hearth that *could* burn empty air, but, for now, the trigger mechanisms were just how the hearths in Dr. Todson's Home worked. Tinder situated against a steel strike plate, logs piled atop it, all one had to do was press a button on the wall and the flames would catch. No need for matches or the risk of burned fingers. Just flint and steel and Lei's ingenuity put to real-world use.

"Let me get it."

"I'll do it," Caroline said, but, before she made it two steps, Lei's hand brushed her arm and she flinched, nearly tossing the cocoa she had just vowed not to spill.

"Let me," Lei gently requested, and the tears pressed, just out of sight, despite the fact there was nothing new to cry about. "For now, why don't you crawl under the quilt?"

Figuring Lei had a better grip on good decision-making than she did at the moment, Caroline nodded, grateful for the guidance. But it was only once she was settled in the bed, quilt over her, warm mug in hand, that she realized just how cold she had let herself become as her legs began to thaw, sensation trickling back in with small, uncomfortable tremors.

"May I?" Back at the bedside a few seconds later, Lei looked to her with an expectant expression, and Caroline sat bewildered, unblinking, scarcely comprehending the request. She didn't know why. It wasn't as if she had never shared a bed with a friend before.

"Yes, of course."

Lei pulled back the edge of the quilt and kicked off her shoes, and Caroline scooted to make room for her.

"I brought it from downstairs. It shouldn't be too hot now. Hopefully, it's still warm enough," Lei said as she retrieved her cocoa from the bedside table.

Watching her take a small sip, Caroline mimicked the movement, worried she wouldn't be able to swallow through the tight stinging in her throat. But, much to her relief, the sweet warm chocolate slid down easily, soothing raw flesh and warming her deep into her chest.

"It's good." She breathed a small sigh of appreciation and took another sip, hoping she had said the right words. She always felt muddled after a crying storm. Vacant. Like a weighty shroud had fallen over her. Protective, she always assumed it was, meant to keep her from thinking terrible thoughts by hampering her ability to think at all. "Did you go into Brigit's kitchen without her permission?"

"Shh. I won't tell if you won't." Lei flashed her a bright grin, but, trying to return it, Caroline's tears only weighed heavier when it felt disingenuous. Dropping her gaze to the mug, she swirled the cocoa inside, rich smell of chocolate wafting up as she raised it for another shaky sip, resisting the urge to hold it to her head when the pain throbbed behind her temple. "Are you all right?"

"I'm fine." Her heart lurched a hard, quaverous beat.

"You don't look fine."

Teeth catching and gnawing at her lower lip, Caroline fought the surge of shame. Of discomfort. She knew she didn't look fine. And she knew just how terrible she had to look. Not just now, in this immediate moment, but for hours to come. As long and as hard as she cried, she could feel what she would see when she looked in a mirror. Puffy eyes that wouldn't go entirely down by morning. Telltale webs of red on her cheeks that would belie her excuse it was just sensitivity to the pollen or the dust in the house.

"Did I do something?" Lei asked.

"No." Guilt piling atop her embarrassment, Caroline glanced to Lei with apologetic eyes. She couldn't let her think that. Not even for a second. If anything, Lei had been the one thing holding her together in all of this. She had been so kind, so gracious. Maybe too gracious. Caroline hadn't learned to survive in this house without her.

"You didn't come down to the workshop today," Lei said, and Caroline tried to think up a plausible excuse, an alibi, that would make it sound simple. Silly. Like a capricious whim. But whatever she came up with was bound to be a hard sell with her state of mind so blatantly on display. "Is it Aya?"

Sucking in air, Caroline didn't know how to respond to that. Or really want to.

It wasn't *not* Aya.

The morning after Aya's arrival, when Caroline went down to the dining room for breakfast, Dr. Todson was still there, an event that had never once occurred in her time at the house, and Aya was sitting beside her, picking from a pastry with sticky fingers.

"Here, Caroline." Lei saved her a seat. Which was always nice, comforting, knowing Lei didn't mind her company day after day and would go to the effort to ensure they could sit together. But now Lei's thoughtfulness put Caroline in the line of scrutiny, directly across the table from Dr. Todson and Aya. They could observe her, she could observe them, which made breakfast feel more formal, and less relaxed, than it normally did.

Only for Caroline, of course. Everyone else seemed quite used to the circumstance of Aya's existence.

"Hello again, Caroline." Aya had even troubled to engage her. "I was hoping you would make it down here. I feel like we barely got a chance to meet last night."

"No, we didn't," Caroline replied. Though, that was hardly through any fault of her own. Aya had taken only the time to eat a plate of scones and honey, engaging in insignificant chitchat with the other residents, before announcing, "My goodness, it's late. We should really get to bed," with a look and leer directed toward Dr. Todson that indicated sleep wasn't at all what she had in mind.

"So, where are you from?" Aya asked her.

"London," Caroline said.

"Which part?"

"South Kensington."

"South Kensington. Interesting."

Caroline didn't know why it was so interesting to Aya that she was from South Kensington, and she didn't ask her. She didn't want to ask anything that might prolong the conversation any more than was necessary. It was ill-mannered, petulant even, perhaps, but she wanted things back the way they were, before Aya, when she had Lei largely to herself and didn't have to answer questions first thing in the morning.

She had already had her night disrupted. Occupied by thoughts and impressions etched onto her brain.

Every time she closed her eyes, she would see Dr. Todson and Aya kissing. Feel the same sweep of sensations she'd felt as she stood watching them from the stoop. This was why people kept these things behind closed doors. Bringing them out into the open invited others into their intimacy. Even Rand's tonic couldn't stop the replay of images through Caroline's mind.

Or her mind from further invention.

Beyond the stoop, she envisioned Dr. Todson and Aya in their bedroom, kissing the way they had kissed outside, which could only lead to other, more carnal things. And, much to her agitated surprise, Caroline could imagine those too. In quite graphic detail. Aya tugging off and tossing her boots on the way through the door. Dr. Todson slipping out of her purple wrapper. The two of them knocking over Dr. Todson's pile of books next to the bed. Dr. Todson and Aya *in* their bed.

Sitting at the table, she flushed just remembering remembering it, and it was nothing compared to what she had felt in the night.

"So, who exiled you here?"

Aya clearly did not get the announcement Caroline preferred peace with her morning meal. Or any innate decorum, apparently.

"My husband," Caroline said.

"Ah... typical," Aya returned as casually as though Caroline had said it rained in England, but when Caroline glanced up, Aya's gaze was darker and more thoughtful than her tone let on. "I'm sorry he did that to you."

She sounded sincere. She looked sincere. But Caroline didn't know how she could possibly, truly empathize. Aya obviously didn't have to worry about a husband looking for a means to dispose of her. She was with Dr. Todson, which, as far as Caroline could tell in her short time in the house, might have been the safest, most compassionate place any woman could be.

"Thank you." It crossed her mind that she might be being unfair to Aya, and most certainly rude. Aya lived in that house and had just gotten home from wherever it was she had been for at least the last eleven days. She had the right to linger over her breakfast. Her lover had the right to linger with her.

It was only one meal. Caroline could have her routine disrupted for a single meal.

If it was only a single meal.

Then, Aya invaded the workshop.

It was fine that first morning. After breakfast, Caroline and Lei retreated to the basement and settled into their usual places, Lei working on the same contraption that had occupied her attention all week and Caroline trying to develop a better understanding of fulcrums and velocity on her reading bench nearby.

"Archimedes?" Lei had asked a few days before after Caroline stopped by the library for the change in reading material.

"If I'm going to be down here, I thought I should at least have a basis," Caroline said, and Lei smiled a near-ecstatic smile, light dancing like stars in her eyes, before her gaze turned deadly serious.

"Everyone should," she stated, and they shared a small laugh. Just one of the many light, intimate moments between them that had made Caroline like Lei more and more over the days they had spent together. That made her *want* to make Lei laugh. Make Lei smile. Make Lei speak.

But that was before Aya. Before she followed them down the stairs after lunch. Before she kept following them, being there, loitering about the workshop. It seemed every time they retreated to the basement, Aya was either already down there or appeared soon enough. So, instead of the clatter and hum of Lei working on her devices, Caroline was besieged by Aya's voice, which was intermittent and always directed toward Lei, but somehow sounded as if it never stopped yapping right in her ear.

"You see. When the energy gets too high, it breaches the circuit and flares. I've had to replace a dozen of these so far," Lei told Aya that first afternoon.

"Have you tried the granite?" Aya asked her in return.

"The granite. The alabaster. The limestone. It's just so irritating. The principles are right, I think, but the materials... I don't know what it is."

Listening from across the room, Caroline heard traces of things Lei had told her before. She knew Lei was struggling with her device, a miniature version of her light ray. It either failed to produce a sufficient beam or broke apart from the energy before it could fire at all. But, in all their conversations, Lei had never sounded so frustrated by it. She always sounded calm, certain, as if she knew it was only a matter of time before she solved the mystery and overcame physics.

Now, in Aya's presence, it occurred to Caroline perhaps Lei didn't trust her with her frustration, because Lei hardly knew her. She had grabbed onto Lei as her routine, as her anchor, in this new and uncertain world, but that didn't mean Lei felt the same sort of attachment to her. Lei might just be being generous because Caroline was new and she thought her delicate.

At any rate, Lei didn't need her. Aya's presence had made that fact painfully clear. Lei already had friends at Dr. Todson's, people she trusted and confided in. And, watching them from her reading bench, hearing the way Lei and Aya talked and joked with each other, Caroline realized she was the one out of her element. She was the one who was invasive and in the way. She was the outsider, angling to find a toehold in a place she didn't belong.

"Why would it be Aya?" Sitting in her bedroom with Lei and hot cocoa, Caroline couldn't quite confess.

But Lei smiled. A soft, knowing smile. "I know she can be a bit... much," she said. "She has a tendency to take over any room she's in. It's not an altogether bad thing. She's an amazing leader. She likes the workshop, and a lot of the things I work on are of most interest to her, but... I'm sorry. I know it's not the same."

Not expecting apology, in no position to receive one - she was the one intruding upon them, wasn't she? - Caroline felt overcome by it. By Lei noticing something was wrong with her. By Lei showing up at her door with hot cocoa and her usual attentive kindness. By Lei. Just by Lei.

Tears threatening the levee which held them back, she glanced quickly away. "It's fine."

"Caroline?" Lei's hand slid onto her shoulder, coaxing her gaze back around, and Caroline was caught by the concern in dark eyes. By the tenderness in Lei's fingers where they brushed against her neck.

"I'm sorry." Levee failing, she looked to her mug as the first tears fell.

"Don't be sorry. Just tell me what's wrong. Please."

But it was a thing easier asked than answered. It wasn't even Aya. Not really. Aya had just been the catalyst. Not even the catalyst. She had just been... a reminder. Nothing had changed since Caroline first came to Surrey. Not really. Not in any true, substantial way. She was in the same place with mostly the same people. Her schedule was the same. Her days were the same. And none of it was hers. Not this house. Not this life. Certainly not Lei. Caroline knew, had known, but she had somehow convinced herself otherwise. She just didn't realize how delicate her illusion was until Aya stuck a toe in it and the entire thing rippled apart.

"I think..." She knew she needed to answer Lei, that Lei deserved an answer, but she struggled to get the words past the tears and the lump in her throat. "I think I just feel a little lost."

Slow as she was to respond, Lei was equally quick, taking the mug from her hand and setting it on the bedside table with her own. Turning back, she wrapped her arms around Caroline, pulling her into a tight embrace, and Caroline went rigid on instinct. She was used to the touching now, for the most part, but it always came with some warning. She couldn't recall the last time someone other than Oliver had seized her like this, without precursor, in a very unreserved and unabashed way. Arms closing around Lei's shoulders, almost a reflex, she felt dazed. Vulnerable. Uncertain. And better, she realized, after several seconds in Lei's arms, as the tension in her body didn't dissolve exactly, but transmuted, re-shaped, releasing its negative properties to become something else entirely.

"I'm sorry you feel that way," Lei said, and the purr of her voice against her ear raised goosebumps down Caroline's neck. "But you are not lost. You're here. With us. I know it's not what you wanted, but I, for one, am grateful you are."

Words stealing her breath, her tears, Caroline hadn't realized how much she needed to hear them. Wanted to hear them. And not just from anyone. From Lei.

In the next instant, the smell of Lei's hair - bergamot and lemon - engulfed her senses, and Caroline turned into it, more aware of Lei's hand where it moved up and down her back. Of the mold of Lei's upper body against her own, unmistakable even through the layers of their clothing.

She wanted Lei to kiss her, she realized when Lei pulled back, brushing the hair from her face and gazing into her eyes. She wanted Lei to more than kiss her. It was a thought she wouldn't have had a few days before. Or maybe she would have and would have been unable to place exactly what she felt. Now, Caroline couldn't mistake her feelings, and what she felt most was need, acute and aching, and so overpowering it pushed all other thoughts and worries out of her mind. At least, for the moment.

But Lei was oblivious. Or pretended to be. Turning back to their mugs, she took them off the bedside table, handing Caroline's back to her before taking a drink from her own. "We've never talked about your family," she said, softly, carefully, some seconds later. As if there was a reason she had been so delicate in broaching the subject.

"We've never talked about your family," Caroline returned, taking her own jittery sip.

"You never asked."

"Well, I figured I shouldn't ask if I wasn't ready to be asked."

"Are you not ready to be asked?" Lei posed, and, glancing to her, fleetingly, worried she would outright stare if she looked too long, Caroline wasn't sure what she was ready for anymore, but she did know she was more ready with Lei than with anyone.

"What do you want to know?" she husked.

"Are your parents still alive? Are they royalty?" Lei asked her, and, even distracted, Caroline laughed.

"Yes, my parents are still living. No, they're not royalty. What about yours? Are they royals? Brilliant scientists, maybe?"

"Both my parents are dead."

Statement wiping out all lingering preoccupation, Caroline felt even more ashamed to have been blubbering away as she was before. "I'm sorry."

"It's all right." Leaning in, Lei gave her shoulder a gentle nudge with her own, and Caroline closed her eyes as the touch spread everywhere. "They died a long time ago. My father, before I was born. There was an outbreak of typhus on the passenger vessel that brought them here. He never made it off the ship."

"And your mother?"

"She died when I was nine."

Nine. Caroline swallowed, trying not to look too troubled by the revelation, worried it would only upset Lei, but she couldn't stop the small frown that worried her jaw and tugged at her lips. That was a terribly young age to be without either of one's parents. Oliver was a year older than Lei when both his parents died, and Caroline saw the weight he carried each day. The fear. The disorientation. As if he didn't know who he would be now, or where he would go, because his guides had been ripped out of his world and carried off to another.

"Did you have any other family?"

"I did. But they were all back in China."

China. Caroline nodded. She knew that was where Lei's parents were from.

And Lei's soft, shiny black hair.

And her midnight eyes.

Her full lips.

Her mesmerizingly perfect cheekbones.

"Did anyone try to contact them for you?" Shaking free of her study, she realized she had ended up staring after all.

144

"No," Lei said. "But I never asked anyone to. When my parents came here, it was a time of great unrest in China. There was a civil war. My parents fled for a reason. I couldn't imagine it would be better to go back there. Plus, England was the only place I had ever known."

"That seems a heavy thing for a young girl to have to reconcile."

"It was," Lei admitted with a slight, sad smile, and Caroline frowned again as she considered it - Lei just nine years old, both parents dead and her all alone. Tears pressing harder, she blinked them away, at least satisfied this time they had a real cause.

"So, what happened to you?"

"I was sent to a workhouse."

Withholding her gasp, just barely, Caroline likewise held her breath, not entirely sure what would happen when she released it. She knew about workhouses, of course. Of their existence. Their essence. At least as portrayed in the pages of *Oliver Twist*.

Utter nonsense. Of all the books her father disapproved of her reading, it might have been the one that infuriated him the most. *The poor always seek sympathy for their positions rather than ways to improve them. It is why they remain poor. They should be glad the places exist. Where would they go without them?*

It might have been an argument one could make - and often did make in society, regardless of its hypocrisy - if not for the fact it wasn't merely a book that told the stories of those places. Everyone Caroline knew was terrified of them. They pretended they weren't, but then used them as cautionary tales and insults. "You're gonna end up in the poorhouse" was a common refrain amongst members of the upper classes when someone made a financial gamble and lost big. They scorned the poor for protesting their appalling conditions, but feared falling into those same conditions more than Hell itself.

"How long were you there?" she hesitantly asked Lei.

"Four years," Lei said.

"Four years." Caroline simply couldn't fathom it, stomach it, the thought of Lei in the care of strangers, being fed a deficient diet, slept too many to a room, put to work at the will of her guardians. For a moment, she almost wished she hadn't read *Oliver Twist* herself. "What was it like?"

"Unpleasant." Lei kept her voice light, but it was all there in the single word. The sorrow. The wretchedness. The fear. Caroline was certain she heard them. "Though, not a total loss. I did get my first formal schooling there. They even taught girls arithmetic. And while there were no science lessons of which to speak, not even for the boys, it's amazing what one can learn when she knows how to pick a lock and to read."

Grin coming to her face, she glanced Caroline's way, and Caroline nearly swooned with relief. Delight. She might have expected Lei to be no less than absolutely clever and rebellious, regardless of her surroundings. But four years in the workhouse also meant Lei was only thirteen years old when she left it. If she left the workhouse at thirteen, where did she go? How did she survive on her own?

"But beyond my parents, no," Lei went on before Caroline could ask her. "No great lineage. I do like to fancy I'm Wang Zhenyi's very great granddaughter. I'm not. But I do like to fancy it."

"Who's Wang Zhenyi?" Caroline asked, and the question softened Lei's expression, bringing a dream-like quality to her smile that made Caroline yearn toward her even more.

It's made to believe, women are the same as men. Are you not convinced, daughters can also be heroic?"

"She was a writer?"

"A poet," Lei returned. "She was also a scientist. Self-educated, of course. My mother told me about her in bedtime stories before I could even hold a rattle properly in my hand."

"She could see who you were from a young age."

"Or urged me along the path. Are we here to be discovered or to be molded? Who knows why we become who we become?"

It was a fitting question. One Caroline couldn't possibly answer. She was struggling to recognize who she even was at the moment as her gaze fell to the small mole just above Lei's lip. Sighing, she fantasized about reaching out, brushing her finger against it. To see how it felt, if it felt like anything. What would Lei do, she wondered, if she did?

"But this isn't a philosophical discussion. And I am not so easily distracted. Your parents are still alive."

"Yes." It was a great privilege, Caroline realized, sitting there with Lei. As to whether she had parents who would actually claim her at this point was more difficult to say. Caroline could only guess what her mother and father were thinking, because she had heard nothing from them. Did they even know she was here? Did they care?

"What are they like?"

They hate me. The thought came unbidden, tightening her throat and making her eyes ache as she forced back the tears. "Distant. Conventional." Though, they mustn't have always. She could recall moments from her childhood when her mother doted upon her and her father found amusement in her antics. When her natural disposition went from simple oddity to terrible embarrassment to them she wasn't entirely sure, but it must have been sometime around puberty, when they hoped she would just instinctively incline toward marriage and sociability.

When she didn't, Caroline couldn't miss her fall from her parents' graces. They had done the raising, yet somehow she ended up wrong. Defective. In so many ways. Thank God there were governesses around on whom they could place the blame, and Sarah, who turned out just right to spare them total humiliation.

"Do you have any siblings?"

Yes, Sarah. Thank God for Sarah. Not just for her parents' sakes, but for Caroline's own. She suspected she would have resented her sister, and how well she turned out by comparison, if Sarah hadn't always been her best and most loyal friend and ally.

"I had a sister. She died with her husband last year."

"I'm sorry," Lei said.

Nodding, Caroline didn't dare try to say anything more. Taking a drink of the nearly-cold cocoa, she forced herself to swallow it, absolutely determined not to start weeping again.

"What happened to them?" Lei cautiously asked, and Caroline looked to the quilt, finding a snag she could pick at, room seeming darker somehow, Lei more lost to its shadows beside her.

"They were poisoned."

"Poisoned?"

"Yes. The authorities said one of them must have done it."

That was what the authorities said - *one of them* - because Caroline's parents had wealth and influence and that made it prudent to spread the blame around. The insinuation, of course, was that a woman left alone with her husband must have done the cooking, and none of it mattered because Sarah was dead, not by her own hand and not by Nathaniel's.

"The household staff was gone. Sarah and Nathaniel always gave them the same week's holiday each year, the week of their wedding anniversary. They liked to celebrate their freedom from chaperones, they said."

Despite the dark path that led them there, Lei gently laughed, resituating next to Caroline on the bed so Caroline could feel the weight of her thigh more prominently against her own.

"That's nice."

"Yes." It was nice that Sarah and Nathaniel actually liked each other. It had always given Caroline some measure of peace, some sliver of hope in the rightness of the universe, to know her sister was in a happy marriage when her own was so desperately unfulfilling. But now Sarah and Nathaniel were dead. So, perhaps, the universe was kind to no one.

"It hardly sounds like two people who would kill each other."

Hair sparking, skin prickling, Caroline lifted her gaze, glancing to Lei in the light of the hearth. Lei didn't know it, but she was creeping dangerously close to an even darker path, casting light haphazardly its way.

"Do you believe that?" Lei asked her directly, and Caroline felt cornered in her own brain, notions buzzing around her she knew she couldn't speak aloud. Not even here. Not even to Lei.

"No," she said. But she didn't merely doubt the official account of Sarah's and Nathaniel's deaths. She knew, without a doubt, it could not possibly be true. She knew her sister. She knew Nathaniel well enough. "Sarah would never have left Oliver, and Nathaniel would never have hurt her."

"Who's Oliver?"

"Their son."

"You have a nephew," Lei said, and Caroline nodded.

"He was with us when Sarah and Nathaniel died, and, after, he came to live with us permanently, Thomas and I."

"Does Oliver have any... cousins... at your house?" Lei cleverly broached a topic she had bumped up against on several occasions, but had never outright asked.

No one had asked Caroline whether or not she had children. They had asked around it, talked about their own, given her the chance to contribute to conversation. But Caroline never did. At some point, she just assumed they all knew.

"No. I never had children. I couldn't."

"How old is he? Your nephew?"

"Eleven."

"Almost a man." Lei smiled, trying to ease the weight of the conversation, but it only yanked at the knot in Caroline's chest.

Lei had no way of knowing it, but Oliver's age was one of her biggest worries. Eleven meant he was old enough to be away at school, and Thomas had been trying to ship him off to Eton ever since he came to live in their house. But Oliver wasn't ready. Age was just a number, a meaningless marker that lied about what one could endure. Oliver had always been quite slight for his age, gentle and overly sensitive, and now he was grieving, stunted by his tragedy. Thomas kept insisting he be a man when he was just a little boy constantly reaching for someone to hold his hand.

"Almost." Worry creeping and clawing at her, it was displacing all the good feelings Caroline had amassed since Lei came into her room, and she didn't want to squander them entirely. "So, how did you come here? To this house? You say you chose to, but you couldn't have known about this place on your own."

"No." Lei seemed to understand her need for the sudden change in subject. "I met Aya in London a few years back. I was on my own, and she asked me if I wanted to come and live here."

"That was it?" Caroline returned. "She just found you in London and asked you that?"

"Well, there was slightly more to it," Lei acknowledged. "But, for the most part, yes, it really was that simple. She saw a struggling, lonely young woman and offered her security. Family."

Hearing Lei say it, it occurred to Caroline again how much she must have hurt Lei when she dismissed this house as a proper home. But she had learned a lot about the world inside these walls in the days since. Had she known then what she knew now, she never would have made such a boorish mistake.

It was also possible, she considered, much to her great chagrin, that she may need to rethink Aya.

"Are you done with your cocoa?" Lei suddenly asked her, and panic flooded Caroline's veins.

"Yes." Looking to her mug, she was troubled to see she was, in fact, at the bottom silt, and, taking it from her hand, Lei set the mug on the bedside table along with her own, before turning back.

"Is it all right if I sleep in here?"

Caught off-guard, Caroline blinked, and blinked again.

"Sometimes I just prefer not to be alone in the dark," Lei said, but Caroline knew the request had nothing to do with Lei or any previously undisclosed fears of hers. It was Caroline the dark waited for tonight.

"Yes. You can always sleep here," she whispered, instantly grateful, marginally nervous, and momentarily confused when Lei paradoxically rose from her bed.

Reaching for the hem of her blouse, Lei pulled it over her head, and, where seconds before she had been abnormally blinky, Caroline could no longer close her eyes at all, drawn as they were to the outline of Lei's body through the thin layer of her chemise, mesmerized by the shadows of curves beneath cream fabric.

Wrenching her gaze away, it occurred to her, if they were going to sleep, she too should probably be somewhat appropriately dressed, and moving to the edge of the bed, she pinched the top of her dress together, loosing the hooks from the eyes with trembling hands, stealing a glance back as the bed dipped to see Lei crawl beneath the sheets in nothing but her combination chemise.

Her own sleeping gown left hanging in the wardrobe, Caroline thought about rising to get it, about taking it behind the dressing screen and changing properly. But if Lei could sleep in only her undergarments, so could she, and, standing up, she let her dress slip downward, easing it over her hips when it hung and laid it on the trunk at the end of the bed next to Lei's clothes.

Lei waiting with a soft smile as she crawled between the silken sheets, her hand rose to Caroline's neck. For a brief, glimmering moment, Caroline thought Lei *would* kiss her. Then, Lei's lips pressed against her cheek, as always they did.

Turning just enough, Caroline felt the ghost of them against the corner of her mouth, and it amplified her senses, needling out all painful thoughts, as Lei settled down next to her as if it was the most natural thing in the world.

Maybe it was.

In the warm cocoon of the covers some minutes later, Caroline's pulse still danced. Her body still hummed. She could feel Lei there, hear her, the soft rise and fall of Lei's breaths amidst the occasional pop of a log in the hearth.

Assuming Lei had to be asleep by now, she turned onto her side as carefully and quietly as she could, resituating her cheek on the pillow so she could stare at Lei's profile in the firelight. Every bone and muscle in her body longing to be closer to Lei, she wondered what would happen if she just did what she felt, wrapped herself fully around Lei, pressed her lips to the side of Lei's neck so delicately and temptingly exposed to her.

A moment later, Lei's eyes opened, head turning on her pillow, and Caroline was caught thinking it. Though, curiously, she was unbothered. Unafraid. The late hour and semi-darkness bulwarks against the insecurities and modesties of the day.

Lei must have felt the same, because she turned on her side too, black hair slipping back over her shoulder as she settled her cheek onto the pillow, eyes staring into Caroline's through the flickering firelight, blinks slow and heavy.

She walks in beauty, like the night...

Caroline wasn't sure when she fell asleep, or if she did so before or after Lei. She only knew one moment she was lost in the depths of Lei's gaze, words of great poets swirling deliriously through her head, and the next she was waking up next to her, dreams nothing but sweet, morning bashful and giddy, and knew she would never be exactly the same.

Chapter 18

EIRINN

1872

It was difficult treating a woman who was such an insatiable, unapologetic flirt.

It was difficult denying a woman she so fiercely wanted to permit.

Warring factions meeting, Eirinn spent her days in a state of near perpetual arousal, attuned to each brush of Aya's hand, to every provocative word Aya murmured when they were standing close, and Aya seemed to find it amusing, Eirinn's resolve that they could do nothing to move forward in their relationship, in any form, until she was healed and no longer under her care.

This is what I get for seeking out a saint, Aya loved to quip when Eirinn was forced to remind her of the rule. Several times a day.

Of course, it was easy for Aya to find humor with the situation when she didn't know everything Eirinn knew, when she thought all her secrets safe, and that the obvious was the only reason Eirinn had for postponing.

Eirinn wished it was her only reason.

"How does it feel?"

First things first, Aya just needed to be able to walk across a room without pain.

"Better than before, I think. I can only imagine the new positions my body will be able to twist and turn in now. Was that always your intention?"

Making it to the window, a wicked grin came to Aya's face as she glanced back, and Eirinn smiled in kind. She might not be able to act on them. Not yet. That didn't mean she couldn't enjoy Aya's attentions.

"If you had any infection left, we would know it by now. I think we got it cleaned and closed in time. Properly even."

"You really shouldn't sound so surprised when you say that," Aya said, in such good humor Eirinn suffered the levity as she stepped up to the window beside her, hand sliding onto its ledge, the feel of the wood and activity on the street below grounding her in time and place when Aya's presence felt so surreal and ephemeral. "So... how long should this care and healing last?" Aya's fingers tapped an anxious cadence next to Eirinn's own.

"That's hard to say. You say you're in only nominal pain, which is a good sign. But, still, the internal, it could take two, three weeks to be -"

"Three weeks." Aya's hand went from tapping to clutching at the window's ledge as she exhaled in unmistakable misery.

"Are you all right?" Eirinn asked, her own hand flying from the window to Aya's side, worried Aya might collapse or be sick.

Instead, Aya smirked - of course, she did - turning beneath her hand so they stood face to face in the soft afternoon sunlight.

"You know, there are other types of physical suffering," she uttered. "Deep, terrible pangs. Incessant aches. Throbbing. Shouldn't you check on those too?"

"Those won't kill you," Eirinn said.

"Are you so sure of that? Because you're here and I'm here, and it honestly feels like I'm about to die of thirst."

Heart thudding against her breastbone, the dam splintered and broke, and Eirinn felt the desire flood her body. Again. And ignored it. Again. It was almost easy now, Aya had given her so much practice.

"You won't." Stopping the progression of Aya's hand as it tried to sneak around her waist, she used it to pull Aya away from the window, providing sufficient room. "Bend for me."

"And here you are giving me scolding stares. That is positively vulgar," Aya teased. But, still, she went through the movements Eirinn needed her to do from memory. To one side. Then, the other. Back as far as she could go. Then, forward to touch her toes. With an emphasis on style. Eirinn swore to God, the way Aya moved, she could be trying out for a burlesque show and easily make the bill.

"Any pain?" she asked when Aya was done showing off.

"No. None at all."

Eirinn tugged at the hem of Aya's shirt, eyes determined to stay on target. The skin beneath Aya's front stitches still perfectly intact, she didn't need to touch them to know for certain, but she touched them anyway, thumb sliding along the delicate ridge of Aya's wound, gratified as Aya's skin turned to gooseflesh beneath her hand.

"You're cruel," Aya husked when Eirinn skirted around her to check the stiches in her back, and it was difficult not to abandon all sense. Not to press herself up against Aya, slide her hands up under Aya's shirt, attach her lips to her neck and suckle her skin.

Dropping her shirttail instead, Eirinn took a substantial step backward, but it little mattered when Aya turned and repossessed the space between them, her sheer proximity leaving little room for Eirinn to ignore the blood that rushed through her veins.

"Bread?" Eirinn asked, almost a shout, and Aya looked instantly confused, which was better than her being absolutely intent on seduction, Eirinn supposed.

"I am unfamiliar with that particular euphemism, but I'm willing to give anything a try."

Dear. God.

"It's not a euphemism. It's actual bread. You can have some today, if you want."

"Bread? My," Aya purred. "Now, don't go getting too gourmet on me. I'll never leave. Do I get butter with that?"

"No. No butter."

"Is this a metaphor?" Aya asked her, and it was Eirinn's turn to be confused. Not that it mattered. Aya's dark eyes on her, Aya's breath whispering against her face, she probably would have stood there forever letting Aya confound the hell out of her. "Plenty of substance. None of the good stuff?"

Ah. A small, helpless grin curved Eirinn's lips. "You'll get to the good stuff eventually," she said, but smile already fading, she wavered slightly as she hoped it was true.

"All right." Amazingly enough, Aya conceded. Eirinn wasn't sure if she was grateful or disappointed as she moved away from her toward the door. Though, not without the small dalliance of running her finger down her arm and over the back of her hand on her way past.

Following her out into the kitchen, Eirinn rushed to help Aya pull out a chair at the table and situate the pillow at her back in an almost certainly overbearing way. If Aya could touch her toes, she could handle a chair and pillow.

"No crust?" Aya pouted when Eirinn pulled back the linen over the bread board to reveal the soft brown loaf underneath.

"This is crust." Eirinn tapped the top of the loaf with her bread knife.

"Barely."

"Crust is too hard," Eirinn said as she cut a reasonable-sized slice and looked around for a plate on which to put it. "This is good, I promise. I had some this morning."

"Can I have jam? It is just soft fruit."

"I didn't say anything about jam." Plate finally acquired, Eirinn tipped the slice onto it, setting it down before Aya, and Aya's gaze was softly imploring as she looked up at her, her long, dark lashes working even harder than usual.

"It really is just soft fruit," she said again, and Eirinn sighed.

"Don't use a lot." Sliding the jar of peach jam down the table, she handed Aya a spoon. "And drink this."

Aya looked far giddier than she should have considering the meager offering as Eirinn poured her a glass of water from the pitcher on the table, but it was the first solid food she had been allowed in the full week she had been there.

"Do you want tea?"

"Of course. I'm no monster."

Returning to the counter, Eirinn tested the kettle, grateful to discover Rand had refilled it from the tap before he left, and faltered as the folded newspaper that sat tucked behind a stack of jars in the corner rustled into view.

Or, perhaps, she was looking for it.

Kettle placed on the cooktop, she glanced to the black and white menace, story hidden within its folds reaching out to grip her about the shoulders and hunch them in defense.

She needed to do it, mention the article to Aya and see what Aya had to say for herself - it had been an albatross around her neck for days - but how did she start a conversation she so desperately didn't want to have? And did she really have to have it? Couldn't she just let Aya heal, return to her own home, wherever that might be because she was evasive whenever Eirinn asked, and wait for things to evolve from there?

Perhaps Aya would tell her on her own, somewhere down the road, when she was in prime health and Eirinn had earned her trust.

But what if she didn't?

What if Aya had no intention of telling her anything?

What if weeks went by? Months? Years? And the secret between them remained a secret? Where would they be then?

Eirinn couldn't bear the thought of it, that she would get closer to Aya, *feel* closer to her than she already did, only for Aya to never tell her the truth. It would be like walking deliberately into a fool's paradise, hoping somehow it might be made real.

"Can I ask you something?" Words ghosting past her lips, they barely had the volume to rise above the small sounds Aya made at the table.

"Of course. It's your flat."

Eirinn turned against the counter, leaning heavily upon it, needing its support even more when she saw how gleefully Aya was chewing her food. How gorgeous she was performing that mundane of an act.

For a moment, it muzzled her, Aya's beauty - her joy - made her silence her own questions. Everything in her wanted Aya there, wanted the flirtation and the banter and everything that came with and after them. But they couldn't build anything solid on a foundation riddled with pockmarks. What Eirinn didn't know and what Aya didn't know she knew could hurt them both. It felt like a lie between them. Eirinn just couldn't say who was lying to who.

"How did you get stabbed?"

Smile on Aya's face instantly fading, it occurred to Eirinn she was a right heel for choosing this of all moments to ask. Even more so when Aya dropped the bread back onto the plate and stared ahead of her down the table. She could have asked at any time, confirmed Aya's constant expectation of news.

No one who's healing needs news, Eirinn told her instead, but, worthwhile as the sentiment was, it wasn't why Aya had been banned from newspapers.

Eir, you're going to want to see this. Rand found the story the same day Aya arrived at the flat - printed in the afternoon edition - and watched as Eirinn consumed the details over a dinner he forced her to eat.

A burglar broke into the home of a banker. His intention? To rob, officials assumed. The banker heard the intruder as he snuck into his bedroom. A former Navy officer, the man slept with his service weapon - a silver sabre - next to his bed. When the intruder approached, the banker attacked with the sword, driving it through the intruder's midsection. *He might have gotten away, but there's no way he survived that wound*, the banker proudly proclaimed his victory in print.

This says the thief was a large man. Eirinn looked for any proof the story couldn't possibly be about Aya, and Rand just raised a helpless hand, because, regardless of what it might have gotten wrong, the rest of the story was impossible to dismiss. It wasn't as if people got run through with swords in the middle of Paris each day.

"Here." Aya taking too long to answer her, Eirinn grabbed the crumpled paper from its hiding place and opened it on the table. She didn't want to give Aya time to decide not to tell her, or, worse, to invent a lie that would ensure she would never be able to trust her. "Is this how you got hurt?"

Aya pulled the newspaper closer, skimming its contents, and released a small huff of laughter, despite the fact none of this was funny. "They always say I'm a man. And a large one at that. I suppose they don't like the story a small woman might be out to do them personal harm."

Eyes drifting shut, it was exactly what Eirinn didn't want to hear. She didn't want Aya to lie to her, but she *did* want Aya to deny it. She wanted Aya to deny it, and for that to be the truth.

"What were you doing in his house?" she asked, breaths fluttering in her throat, in her chest, as she waited for Aya to say something. To explain. Surely, Aya had a perfectly logical explanation that would clear this up and let them move past the whole thing.

"I should go." Aya rose to her feet instead.

"Wait. What?" Startled from her fragile composure, Eirinn lurched off the counter. Toward Aya. As Aya drifted toward the bedroom door.

"It will be better for you."

Better for her? Aya leaving? Better? Eirinn would much prefer to be the decider of that. "So, you're just going to leave me?" She didn't intend the "me" part, to think or to say it, but there it was, out loud and painfully earnest.

"I should have left already."

"Then, why didn't you?" Panic strengthening her hand, her grip, Eirinn seized Aya's arm harder than she meant, pulling her around and gasping at the tears that shined in dark eyes. She wanted to undo it, to stop them from forming, to assure Aya it didn't matter to her, she just didn't want any secrets between them, but she deliberated a moment too long.

Aya closing the distance between them first, she seized Eirinn's lips in a kiss that was, at once, tender and punishing, as if all the pent-up feelings between them converged into a single point - lightning - and all the strength Eirinn had in the instant before leaked out of her. Legs going feeble, body pliant, she reached out for Aya, finding the front of Aya's borrowed shirt and holding on with dwindling awareness.

Aya's lips, and the way they felt against her own, the only absolute truths in her universe, she didn't even realize she was moving again until her backside hit the edge of the kitchen table and she was hoisted up onto it.

No, that shouldn't happen. The thought scarcely blipped Eirinn's mind as Aya's lips moved along her jaw and down her throat, stealing her capacity for further reason.

"Oh, God."

Aya's fingers were as nimble as a seamstress as they located every button and hook on her dress, and Eirinn felt the fabric melt away, slackening at her chest and falling back against the table. Wearing only her sleeveless silk chemise underneath, she suffered Aya's hands like flat irons where they smoothed against her sides through the translucent fabric, setting the whole of her deliriously aflame.

Thud.

Winding her hands into Aya's hair, Eirinn tugged Aya's mouth back to hers, tracing its curves with her tongue, as Aya's hands stroked over her, down her, skimming the skirts of her dress to the hem and sliding back up beneath it, over the legs of her pantalettes toward the furious, pulsating need between her legs.

Thud.

Noise entering her addled brain, it was followed by several more, in a series, drawing closer and louder, until at last they broke through the haze of desire enough for Eirinn to recognize the sounds and pull away from Aya's lips on panting, frenzied breaths.

"Rand?"

"Yeah?" Rand's voice came from the top of the stairs, just beyond the closed door of the entryway.

"Don't come in here!"

Momentary silence falling in response, Eirinn could hear Aya's ragged breathing, could feel her own heart, and several other parts of herself, pounding in time.

"Why? Are you naked?" Rand asked, and Eirinn tried to think of another reasonable response, a less revealing response, as to why Rand couldn't come into his own home. But, given Aya had officially annihilated her sense, she had nothing, and her most immediate concern was that he didn't get nosy and try to see for himself.

"Yes," she confessed. "Somewhat."

"Is Aya naked with you?"

"Not yet," Aya returned, and Rand burst out in a hearty guffaw, his gasping laughter echoing up and down the stairwell as though there were three of him and it was the funniest thing any of the Rands had ever heard.

"Yeah, all right. I've got to go pick up some... ah, hell. I'll just go." Sniggering once more for good measure, he tromped down the stairs, the thumps and thuds of him taking off his boots reversing as he pulled them on and went back out the door.

"You shouldn't be doing this." Frustrated at the disruption, Eirinn was also grateful for it. It gave her a chance to think, to collect herself, to have a coherent, vital thought. "You're not healed enough."

"I think I am."

"No." Eirinn shook her head. Aya shouldn't be on her feet. She shouldn't be bending and twisting to put warm, wet lips to her exposed skin. She sure as hell shouldn't have lifted Eirinn onto the table. "You should be in bed."

"All right. Let's go then."

Eirinn breathed a weak laugh. For mercy. It was difficult enough to do the right thing when she wasn't half-dressed with Aya's hands up her skirts. But she could. She had to. As long as Aya was still there, as long as the possibility existed between them, they could wait.

"How about we just take it slow and easy?" Aya disagreed. Hand slipping inward, her thumb found the slit in Eirinn's pantalettes with amazing precision, and Eirinn bucked beneath her touch as it stroked her most intimate flesh. "Isn't that the best way anyway?"

Oh, bloody hell.

At the next deliberate stroke of Aya's fingers, Eirinn seized her forearm. "Bedroom." Again, not the word she intended, it was the word that left her lips, and Aya looked immensely satisfied with herself as she withdrew her hands from her skirts and pulled Eirinn from the table.

"Wait." Eirinn pulled back.

They were going to do this. They were going to do it now. It was sort of an inevitability at this point. But the disruption hadn't just given Eirinn the chance to recall Aya was injured, that they needed to be more careful, it had given her the chance to recall the words Aya had said just before she consumed her, before lust and sensation overtook her brain and made her forget how much they had hurt.

"Promise me you're going to stay." She tried to sound strong, tried to sound resolute, but she only sounded scared. She *was* scared. Minutes before, Aya was ready to walk out her door, to leave her without any explanation because it was the easier thing to do. That would have been devastating enough. She had no interest in making the pain more acute or prolonging her agony.

"I promise," Aya said.

Chapter 19

CAROLINE

1886

If this was how courting was meant to feel, Caroline understood now why people made such a fuss about it. Why poetry was written. Music inspired.

That night in her bedroom changed nothing - she still felt the same blush of elation when Lei looked at her, the same quiver of excitement through her stomach each time they touched - but it revealed the truth of everything, and it occurred to Caroline, much to her surprise and great intrigue, that she may be experiencing her first real rush of attraction. Her first mutual affection that wanted more, that wasn't quite enough.

Could such a thing happen to a woman her age? She had been led to believe a woman nearly past the age of childbearing should have no need for such desires. She had been led to assume her inability to carry a child to term explained her lack of sexual interest entirely.

It was cloaked in less vulgar words of course. No one in her former life would dare say such a thing aloud, but it was always there, the insinuation - *If you could produce a child, you would feel much more compelled to copulate. And, honestly, since you can't, there's no need.*

But Caroline felt need.

Insistent, unambiguous need.

Whenever Lei touched her. Whenever she touched Lei. She yearned. She longed. She imagined Lei's touch deeper, in the places that burned hottest, and could scarcely walk or form a thought for the inferno that threatened to raze her into cinders.

It should terrify her, she thought in her more lucid moments, give her some pause or anxiety. Feel as if it came out of nowhere. Was illogical. Sinful. But she suffered no such tragic emotions. She *was* surprised. She *was* confused. But instead of feeling as if it came out of nowhere, it seemed to come from everywhere, as if it had always been there, inside her, tamped down and waterlogged, her capacity to feel more than life had given her cause to feel, and she knew, just knew, if Lei would kiss her the way Dr. Todson kissed Aya, the rest would come quite naturally to her and her jumbled feelings would sort themselves out.

"I'm not going down to the workshop." As fate would cruelly have it, Caroline clued into the true nature of her swirling, leaping desire for Lei just as Lei found more to occupy her time in the house. "Do you want to go outside or find a card game and I'll see you at teatime?"

"Yes, all right." Caroline felt somewhat dazed by the lunchtime announcement. Not that Lei was doing something other than retreating to her lair - she did so with some regularity - but that it was fairly obvious she, Caroline, wasn't invited. Lei changed her routine, but not once had she done so with the insinuation Caroline couldn't come.

"I'm sorry. I might be a little busier over the next few weeks." Lei at least felt guilty about the fact as she fiddled with her napkin and licked at her lips.

Watching her tongue disappear, slow and wet, back between them, Caroline swayed, biting down on her own lip, engulfed in a wave of sheer lust. She didn't try to pretend it was anything purer than that. Not at that moment.

"You're welcome to go down to the workshop on your own if you'd like."

"No." Caroline realized she still had no desire to be below ground if Lei wasn't with her.

"I truly am sorry." Lei's hand slid over hers on the table, and Caroline grew instantly more acquiescent. Is this what courtship would do to her? Would she be made simple and docile with a single touch? "I'll see you at tea. All right?"

"All right." Caroline really didn't know what choice she had in the matter.

In the next instant, Lei kissed her cheek, and that might have been the end of it. She might have swooned into complacency.

If it was only Lei. And if it was only time and walls which came between them.

160

Secrecy was another thing. A treacherous, sinister thing that moved like a serpent and felt like a monster clawing its way around the shadows and gardens of the house.

The map room, that long, narrow room that looked dark and chaotic when Caroline first explored the upper floor, was where they met - Lei, Dr. Todson, Aya, Blanca, Francie, Stella, and the other members of the crew. "The crew," that was what another resident had called them when Caroline went looking for Blanca, Stella, and Francie, and found they too were occupied elsewhere.

"It's for the house. Just general upkeep. It's really not that interesting." Lei was evasive at tea, Blanca, Francie and Stella deferred to Lei, and the secrecy flourished, taking root and sprouting up everywhere, so that Lei and Aya would stop talking when Caroline entered the workshop or Lei and Blanca would exchange glances when she asked too direct a question.

Secrets, it could be said, were what Dr. Todson's home ran on. They were the coal that fed the engine, the oil that kept the lamps burning inside. Dr. Todson kept most of them herself. Even Lei didn't know Caroline had no children until Caroline chose to disclose the fact, though Dr. Todson had to have known it from the start.

Caroline suspected the men who guarded the front gate and Mr. Poke, who came onto the grounds or into the house for odd jobs and deliveries, had only limited knowledge of the true nature of the place. And Thomas certainly didn't know what went on behind this house's walls, or he never would have left Caroline in its clutches. What those on the outside didn't know, and couldn't possibly guess, was Dr. Todson's Home's greatest asset and safeguard.

But those secrets all had noble purpose. They protected the women who lived there. This secret was being kept from them. Or, perhaps, only from Caroline, because no one else seemed bothered by the always-open doors that were suddenly closed to them or the people who went missing for hours at a time.

So, it wasn't so much simple curiosity as true apprehension, with a trace of her former fear, that drew Caroline more and more often to the third floor. To the opulence of the library. To stand in the doorway if no one was there and stare across the landing toward the map room door.

They would stay in there for two, three hours at a time - the crew - door closed, sometimes meeting in the mornings, sometimes the afternoons. Only Dr. Todson would retreat for any extended period. To see to an appointment with a resident or prepare for teatime, Caroline assumed, depending on the time.

She felt safe making such assumptions because she had been watching the door for days, getting a feel for its activity. There was a rise and fall to it, like the tides, a rhythm that was inexact, but had notable peaks and valleys. If Dr. Todson left, it was always some time before she returned. Half an hour or more. If any of the other members of the crew left, it was always for a much shorter period. Then, when any one of them came back, the door stayed closed for at least twenty minutes. These were the lulls that tempted, the times Caroline stared at the door the longest and hardest, trying to will herself the goddess-like power to hear what was being said inside.

Power never manifesting, all she had was reconnaissance, so she reconnoitered, and a week after the meetings in the map room began, she stood once again in the library doorway, awaiting a sign of the tides.

It was an hour, maybe more, before the door to the map room opened, giving the same resounding creak it always did, and Caroline side-stepped behind the library wall. Over the past few days, she had perfected her technique. From her position on the far side of the pocket doors, away from the stairs, she could see who was coming and going without being seen herself. Today, it was Lei, slipping out the open door of the map room and down the stairs toward the first floor.

Somewhat compelled to follow her, to steal a moment alone with her in the halls, Caroline forced herself to remain where she was, listening for what she could hear with her normal ears across the landing in Lei's absence. But it was a useless endeavor. Instead of clues and revelations, the conversation turned to small talk, the occasional bark of laughter refracting upward toward the ceiling, giving her nothing at all of use before Lei returned, carrying a large case and pulling the creaking door shut once more.

What are they doing in there? Sliding into the open doorway, Caroline's fingers thrummed the ornate wooden framework. *What sort of normal upkeep project takes eight women seven days of meetings to plan? What's in that case Lei carried? Why are they keeping secrets from me?*

That was the question that troubled her most. Terrified her, if she were honest. The one that finally lured her across the landing, tiptoeing her atop the runner that ran from the library to the map room door. Standing just outside it, Caroline could hear Lei's voice. Though, wood inches thick, it was no more than an indistinguishable murmur. They could be planning her demise right on the other side of it and she would never know. Not until it was too late.

It was a ridiculous notion, of course, one she knew better than by now, but it did give her the justification to move closer, to listen harder, to press her ear as near to the door as she could get without touching it, because she had watched long enough to know the creak that resounded each time the map room door opened didn't live in its hinges, it lived in the wood itself. Which made the operation all the more precarious. She had to listen closely *and* to balance. Be attentive to the words on the other side *and* to her feet.

"Do you want to sing with me?!?"

Attention occupied with those two things, Caroline didn't see or hear Imogen until Imogen was all but upon her and startled forcefully.

Headfirst. Directly into the map room door. Wood groaning as if it too was in physical pain, she bit back a cry, freezing solid, except for the hand she held up to Imogen, praying it would keep her from speaking again, knowing more movement could only make the matter worse.

Then, she heard the footsteps.

Turning to flee, her foot tangled in the edge of the runner and she lurched as the map room door creaked open behind her.

"Caroline?"

Caught mid-stumble, she stalled where she stood, half-bent, face flushed, wishing the floor would open and swallow her whole.

"Are you all right?"

"I'm fine." Putting on her most innocent of expressions, Caroline endeavored to right herself, to convince herself, before she turned back around and swept a casual hand in the direction of her feet. "I was just passing through, and I tripped on the runner."

In the next instant, Lei's eyes moved over and around her, taking in the scene, adding up clues, and a hint of a grin tugged at her lips as she looked to what had to be the very red, very telling mark on Caroline's forehead where it collided with the map room door. "Runners can be dangerous. Everything all right, Imogen?"

"Yes!" Imogen sounded positively chipper to be asked. "I came to listen to the records, and I saw Caroline listening at the door!"

So much for denial. Shuttering her eyes, Caroline felt the flush grow on her face. She didn't even have any anger to temper the humiliation. Imogen wasn't snitching. Not intentionally. She was just stating a fact, no idea how absolutely mortifying it would be for Caroline.

"I'll just go." Unable to look at Lei, Caroline trudged toward the stairs, shoulders slumping as much in defeat as in shame. All those days of surveillance made fruitless because she had acted on impulse. She couldn't stay in the library after this without them knowing what she was doing there. She had banished herself to ignorance. Now, she would never know what they were doing in that room. Not unless someone suddenly decided to tell her.

"Caroline." Unexpectedly, it was Dr. Todson's voice which called her back.

Turning to find her standing with Lei in the map room door, Caroline expected a scolding, a due admonishment about boundaries and spying on people in their own home.

"You can come in," Dr. Todson offered instead. "If you'd like."

"Yes." Caroline would like. It was all she would have liked to do for days. She just wished she knew if Lei wanted her there. Because, as Dr. Todson said it, Lei glanced to her with wide eyes, lips slightly parted as if she wanted to say something - argue the point, perhaps - before they pressed tightly back together, curling inward until they disappeared in a thin line.

"Hello, Caroline. Fancy finding you standing right outside the door," Aya just had to announce as Caroline stepped into the room.

Face already burning, Caroline chose to ignore her. She found ignoring Aya's presence a preferable way of engaging with her much of the time.

"Lei was about to show us a device she's just finished," Dr. Todson said after sending Imogen off to her records in the library and pushing the door closed once more, and Caroline felt it like a slap, wounded eyes swinging instantly to Lei.

If that was what this was about, all the hiding and the secrecy, it hurt far more. She hadn't seen everything in Lei's workshop, hadn't even asked to see everything Lei had made. But she would have thought if Lei finished something new and exciting she would choose to share it with her. She wanted Lei to show *her* the things she invented. She wanted Lei to want to show her first.

"I have goggles. These will protect you from the effects of the ray," Lei went on as if Caroline wasn't standing, waiting and bruised, beside her. "But I do need one of you to volunteer."

"I'll do it. I've lived the longest," Francie said.

"You're not going to die," Lei uttered.

"Quote that on my tombstone, will you?" Francie glanced to Stella, and the room erupted into laughter. Lei's. Dr. Todson's. Blanca's. All of the people Caroline felt closest to in the house.

"Caroline." Handing her a pair of goggles, Lei paused to hold her eyes for a moment, giving her arm a small squeeze, and comforted by the fleeting touch, Caroline felt foolish and obvious, face flushing even hotter as she sat down in the nearest empty chair and made sure the goggles were well-molded to her face.

"All right. Where's this going to hurt?" Francie asked.

"It's not going to hurt," Lei said.

"Is that right, Caroline? No pain when Lei shot you with her light ray?"

"I told you, it's been modified. All the light, less heat. That's the purpose. It incapacitates without leaving a mark."

"Yeah, we'll see." Francie sounded unconvinced.

"And I'm going to shoot you right between the eyes."

"Right between the eyes." Stella snorted. "That's going on her tombstone too."

This time when the other women laughed, Caroline felt like laughing along, still nervous, but lighter in their presence than she had been all week, as everyone but Francie checked their goggles and waited for Lei to pull something that looked remarkably like a gun from out of the case Caroline had seen her carry from downstairs. Its center barrel flanked on both sides by enclosed cylinders - metal tubes of sorts - the device wasn't long, no way near the length of a rifle or a bayonet, but it still had two handles, and Lei gripped both as she took the contraption in hand.

"What can I expect? Am I gonna get knocked on my ass or what?" Francie asked as she moved to the table's far end.

"By light?"

"Listen here, you little..."

"You're not going to feel anything," Lei said, but Francie just sighed, only half believing her. "All right. Is everyone ready?"

Caroline wasn't sure "ready" was quite the word for it. She felt both mesmerized and horrified. She knew Lei would never do anything to hurt Francie or any of the other women in the house on purpose, but just the anticipation sent a phantom pain through her maimed thigh. She was pretty sure she wouldn't have survived that same shot right between the eyes.

"Three, two..." Green light bursting from the gun, it hit Francie. Square, for sure. Right between the eyes or not was harder to tell. Though the goggles seemed to do the trick at protecting her from temporary blindness, the ray was still bright enough to light the whole room and fill Caroline's vision with spots as the blast cleared.

"Holy Hell! Mother of all scallywags! God knows your name!"

The map room was also considerably warmer in an instant, heat dripping around the edges of Caroline's goggles and rolling between her breasts.

"Uh oh. Sounds like you've killed her." Stella sniggered again.

"Well, did it hurt?" Blanca asked.

"No, it didn't hurt!" Francie seemed rather madder about the fact than if it had hurt. "But I can't see a damned thing and it feels like the world is spinning me sideways."

Wincing, Caroline empathized with that too. Even with the pain to contend with, the disorientation was the worst part. One second, she felt perfectly normal. The next, she was topsy-turvy. Sightless and helpless. Unbalanced and flailing through an empty void.

"Someone get me a chair."

"Here, France. Sit down." Blanca stood and helped Francie into her seat, and watching Lei put down the light gun and remove her goggles, Caroline figured it was safe to do the same.

"How long will it last?" Francie asked.

"Fifteen... twenty minutes."

"Fifteen minutes? Uh, God. I'm gonna puke. Why didn't I take a brandy before this? Stella!"

Rising from her chair with a smirk, Stella went to the bookshelf, pulling off a small globe and glass from behind it, and Caroline was surprised to see the globe was also a bottle as Stella popped a cork up near Greenland, pouring a long shot and putting it into Francie's hand.

"Aw. Sweet stupor," Francie said as she put the glass to her lips.

"It's brilliant, as usual, Lei." Dr. Todson seemed both pleased and amused as she wiped around her eyes with a handkerchief.

"Don't be too sure yet," Lei said. "Let's see if her sight comes back first."

"See. There it is." Francie threw up a hand, meant to be in Lei's general direction, Caroline could only assume, because her aim was truly, amusingly off.

"How does it work?" Blanca asked.

"Just like the ray downstairs," Lei said. "The crystal and chambers are smaller, so there's less energy, but still enough to create a blinding blast. The prism diffuses the light, which is how the flash filled the room and why Francie doesn't have a third eye right now."

"I will see again," Francie warned.

"And how long to reset?" Aya asked Lei next.

"Two seconds. Give or take. The oil stored in the grips wicks into the bulb as soon as the charge clears. Practically by the time the flash fades, it's ready to fire again and will continue to fire as long as there's fuel. With the double wells, maybe an hour total fire time."

"Well, that's... useful." Sitting back, Aya looked duly impressed.

Everyone looked impressed. Understandably so. But also strangely satisfied. Which left Caroline on the outside and alone in her ignorance once again, because no one was asking the most obvious question.

"What's it for?"

Delight falling from Lei's face, Caroline suffered immediate regret. She didn't want to upset Lei or the delicate mood of the room, but it was clear she had done just that. Looking around, no one seemed particularly anxious to look at or talk to her, and the monster in the house scratched at its walls.

"Caroline," Dr. Todson murmured at last. Gently. Haltingly. "A house like this doesn't just come to be. It certainly doesn't pay for itself. And, as you might expect, institutionalized women aren't exactly a priority when it comes to people's charity."

"Charity? Isn't my husband paying you?"

"Yes, *your* husband is," Dr. Todson said, and it made sense if Caroline thought about it. It was clear from the start the women who lived in the house weren't all of the same financial means. Her conversations with them only verified the fact. "But most of the women here didn't end up here as you did, and they all deserve a beautiful home with every comfort they can have. Providing that requires some ingenuity."

"All right." Caroline wasn't going to argue the point. She was in perfect agreement. It still didn't answer her question. "So, what? Lei's making weapons?" She was on the pulse of it, could see the confirmation on Dr. Todson's face. "For who? The Army?"

Aya scoffing a laugh, Caroline looked irritatedly her way.

"So some British colonel can take credit and make a name for himself?"

"Well, what else would it be for?" Caroline shot back. She might be completely obtuse, a brainless, clueless moron in Aya's estimation, but she was only asking a question. And it was reasonable enough to assume. Who else would have use for such a thing?

Looking to Dr. Todson, Caroline waited for her to tell her. But Dr. Todson was lost in thought. Lei was lost in thought. Only Aya was impatient, opening her mouth again when Caroline would rather hear from literally anyone else in the room. "We use Lei's devices."

"Okay. For what?" Caroline asked.

"To liberate funds from those who hold them hostage and let them roam free here." Aya slid her hand onto Dr. Todson's thigh, as if to remind Caroline she had far more right to be in the room than she did, and Caroline was confounded, first by working out what Aya was saying and then by determining whether or not she was lying to her. If Aya was telling the truth, only one interpretation of her words made sense, but who would admit to such a thing so freely? And... *No. Aya couldn't possibly mean...*

"You're using them to steal?" Eyes going back to Dr. Todson, Caroline gave her the chance to correct her, to laugh and shake her head at the obvious misunderstanding. But Dr. Todson only gazed back, expression tinged with sympathy, but no denial forthcoming. "You're thieves?"

"I suppose that's one way of putting it," Dr. Todson said, and Caroline lost her breath. Not so much at the response, but at how blasé Dr. Todson sounded when she said it. At how easily she confessed to thievery and criminality without shame or apology. "I know this seems... simple to you, Caroline."

What happened to the Christ-like figure Caroline had watched knead dough and serve tea? The woman who seemed to have an almost divine ability to see what was truly hurting her and alleviate it with a word?

"Everything you've been taught tells you that stealing is wrong. Both criminal and immoral."

"Well, isn't it?"

"You're a smart woman. I am certain you know how many men in this world have made their fortunes through nefarious, often unforgivable means, exploiting the desperation of others and giving nothing in return."

"What does that have to do with anything?"

"Quite a lot, I hope."

Weak.

Weak.

Lightheaded.

This was it, Caroline realized, watching Dr. Todson through glassy eyes. All this time, she had wondered what was wrong with this house, what darkness lurk behind its charming facade. Now, she knew. It wasn't a house of mad women, it was a den of thieves.

"There are men who deserve to lose their fortunes."

And Dr. Todson was one of them.

Lei was one of them.

"You get to decide that?"

"Why not?"

So many reasons, Caroline could only assume the question was meant to be rhetorical. But she didn't want to swap rhetoric with Dr. Todson. She wanted Dr. Todson to take it back, to tell her she was in on Aya's joke and for them all to laugh about it. Dr. Todson's refusal to do so, to relieve her of her scattered thoughts and tie her back to the Earth, sent waves of fury through Caroline. How could Dr. Todson have lied to her about this? How could Lei have lied to her? How could they let her believe they were better than this? Not just better. Near perfect.

"I was wrong about you. All of you." The words and breaths fluttered in her chest as she looked from Dr. Todson to Lei, the full, brutal winds of their betrayal whipping about her. "No wonder you didn't want me to see this. You're criminals and you're liars."

Tears coming quickly on, she jumped out of her chair, brushing past Lei on her way to the door, but, path suddenly blocked, she stumbled backward, gazing blurry-eyed at Aya where she stood before her.

"Don't you dare talk to them like that." Aya's stance was unyielding. Her eyes fire.

"It's all right, Aya. She can say what she likes."

"No." Glancing past her to Dr. Todson, Aya's furious eyes returned to Caroline, and Caroline felt... not threatened exactly, though it seemed as if she should. She felt... ashamed, she realized. Withered. Just that quickly. The way Aya looked at her made her feel as if she was the one who had done the lying and the betraying. As if she was the criminal in the room. "You can *think* what you like, but you will not stand in this house and talk to them that way. Lei has been nothing but good to you since you got here, and Eir... Eir is the kindest, most compassionate person you will meet in your life. I am certain she has done more for you already than half the people who made you promises."

Flinching, gasping, Caroline couldn't deny it. Dr. Todson *had* done more for her than just about anyone. The moment Dr. Todson truly listened to her, she handed her back so much of her humanity. But it wasn't just that. She had also done what Caroline thought impossible. She had relieved her of her headaches, with Rand's help and a magic serum. Or, perhaps, it was the house itself, which felt less cold and oppressive than anywhere Caroline lived before it.

And Lei... Lei changed everything. For years, Caroline barely felt the world. Her emotions were dull echoes dying slowly inside of her, only ever rising in anger or in grief. From the moment Lei shot her with the light ray, she felt boundlessly. Things she hadn't felt for a very long time. Things she had never felt before.

Dr. Todson healed her. Lei revived her. But they did it under false pretenses. They were lying to her. Weren't they?

"If anyone was wrong about anyone, it was Eir. She was obviously wrong about you. Now, get out."

Walloped by the hard fist of truth, Caroline felt winded, further withered, wobbly on her feet and in her conviction, as Aya walked around her, leaving her stunned in place, and, all she wanted to do a moment before, she struggled to leave. She had wanted in. She had wanted out. Now, she didn't know what she wanted, and, tottering, she turned around, feeling raw and beaten, and as if she might be sick when Lei refused to look at her.

Clap of thunder in her head pounding into her temples, she raced for the door, struggling to wrench it open in her weakened state, and staggered into the hall and down the stairs, pain blinding her like Lei's light as she felt her way to her room. To the dresser. To the drawer which held the laudanum.

One hand on the bottle, she twisted it open, watching one viscous drop fall before squirting the rest beneath her tongue. The warmth sliding instantly, rapidly through her, she sank back against the drawers, bottle clutched to her chest, not realizing how hard she was crying until the tears dripped from her chin and onto her hand.

Before, mercifully, the fog started to descend. The calm. And, in the next moment, like a curtain rising on a stage, she watched figures appear through the miasma.

She saw herself.

She saw Dr. Todson.

They were in the garden the day Dr. Todson gave her the laudanum along with Rand's serum.

On Dr. Todson's face - concern. Caroline could see it. Feel it. The truth in it. She evoked Dr. Todson's expression in minutest detail.

She knew, the thought shimmered in a flimsy reflection. About her headaches, yes, but also that most of her headaches in recent years had come from the laudanum itself. Or, rather, the lack of it. She knew Caroline never went long enough between doses to know what other causes her headaches might have anymore.

Dr. Todson knew and she gave her the laudanum anyway. She gave her a solution and a choice. She knew and she didn't judge her or make the decision for her.

And Lei didn't know any of it, because she had never asked and Dr. Todson never told.

Caroline had her secrets too, and she had been allowed to keep them. Without pressure. Without ridicule. Without angry words or accusations of being someone she wasn't. Or, perhaps, even someone she was.

Somewhere between the soft dulling of her temper and the wash of apathetic bliss, it was a perfect moment of clarity. Five minutes too late.

Chapter 20

EIRINN

1872

It wasn't her intention to fall asleep. In fact, Eirinn had exactly the opposite intention, to stay fully awake, or at least reasonably cognizant, so she would know if Aya tried to escape. But Aya had thoroughly enervated her, and gently compelled her, falling asleep beside her first, giving her a sense of security. False? Eirinn certainly hoped it wasn't as she awoke alone in her bed.

Emptiness needling, she refused to get ahead of herself or the facts, and, sitting up, she listened, wishing she had left something of Aya's in plain sight instead of tucking everything away into the wardrobe.

The first voice she heard Rand's, Aya's laughter came in the instant after, followed by trailing words that brought Aya closer to the bedroom door, before she stepped inside, carrying a full plate and a glass of water.

"Hey. I was going to wake you." Smile on her face as she leaned against the door to push it shut, Aya moved toward the bed with a swagger that belied her recent near-death experience. "I figured you'd be upset if you couldn't get to sleep tonight and get up at that godforsaken hour of morning you so seem to enjoy." Coming to Eirinn's side of the bed, she bent one knee, tucking her foot up beneath her so she could sit facing her. "Sorry. I was starving. No butter." She showed Eirinn her bread with only jam for proof. "I do follow the rules... sometimes. Do you need anything?"

"No. Not yet," Eirinn husked - sighed - amazed, she realized, to see Aya still there as Aya balanced the plate in her lap, reaching beneath the quilt to find her thigh with one hand. "How are you feeling?"

"Oh. Were you looking for an evaluation of your lovemaking skills? They're top-notch, Darling. Your expertise on human anatomy well-noted. A bit tentative perhaps, but that was to be expected. When I'm well, I do hope you'll be slightly less gentle with me."

Spark flaring low in her belly - from Aya's gaze, from the warm rasping purr of her voice - Eirinn could not believe Aya was really trying to talk her back into bed when she was literally still naked in it.

"I meant how are your stitches?"

"Still stitched." Aya took a bite, and Eirinn would just have to take her word for it until Aya was back out of her borrowed wrapper and she could see matters for herself.

She had been gentle with Aya, but she hadn't been *that* gentle. The proof was in the deep red blood bruise left behind on Aya's collarbone. Who knew what other marks she had made on Aya? What damage she might have done? The next time Aya was unclothed, it had to be for a thorough medical assessment.

But that could wait. At least, until Aya finished eating. Which she did in short order, popping the last corner of bread into her mouth and chewing it thoroughly, before pressing a soft, lingering kiss to Eirinn's lips and crawling across her, soft, sweet exhalations stirring the air at Eirinn's neck as Aya propped her head up on her hand, gaze drifting across the room toward the window, free hand toying with the line of the sheet where it laid against Eirinn's chest.

"What do you think of the world?"

Question rather open-ended, Eirinn wondered if they had really gotten through all the simpler getting-to-know-you topics. They had talked a lot, hours each day, but had they really reached broad-sweeping life philosophies?

"In what terms? Geologically? Aesthetically?"

"Spiritually," Aya said. "Do you think it virtuous?"

Feeling the sputter to her pulse, for a moment Eirinn couldn't identify why. "I don't think it anything. It's neutral. Only people can have virtue or not."

"Do you think it just?"

"No, of course not." Eirinn wasn't in Paris because she wanted to study twice as hard, learning medical terms and reading textbooks in French. She was there because she wasn't permitted to study medicine in England. Not to any useful end. Her ambition had exiled her from her own country. As tyranny and inhumanity had exiled Aya from hers. Along with millions of others. "Do you?"

"I think it's beyond unjust," Aya unsurprisingly answered. "I think it's... enslaved."

That choice of word, however, new to Eirinn, it sent a small trickle of uncertainty down her neck.

"I think so few control so many by the very fact they are monstrous enough to do so. Those who would strike a man down to get at a shilling behind him, those are the men who rule the world. And it's by the very nature that decent people are so very different from them, that they cannot do the same harm, or even contemplate doing it, that they remain enslaved. That doesn't feel neutral to me. It feels as if evil is quite rewarded by this world."

It was a rather bleak prospect. Fatalistic really, in its thinking. And Eirinn would have loved to possess any proof at all to refute it. She didn't. Other than the way she felt at the moment. The way she hoped Aya felt. As if she had been rewarded. Given something most people never got the chance to feel.

"I assume this has something to do with how you ended up stabbed?"

"Smart girl," Aya murmured, and the same part of Eirinn that would have cringed at being called "girl" by anyone else found it flirty and endearing from Aya's lips. Bloody hell, what was wrong with her? "It's not a happy story. Do you still want to hear it?"

Confession hovering, Eirinn wasn't sure if she did want further context. She already knew what Aya had done, had read about it in the paper. Did she really need to know why Aya was there in the banker's house? In his bedroom? What her plans were beyond the breaking and entering already committed?

"What did he do to you?" she whispered.

"To me? Nothing." Aya gently stroked her arm, and Eirinn breathed considerably easier than in the moment before. "I mean, aside from the glorious scar I am sure to have. But to others... to others he's done far worse."

"What's far worse than almost killing someone?"

Aya wavered, deliberated, fingers tapping an off-beat rhythm against Eirinn's arm.

"He gives off-book loans to the poor," she answered at last. "Knowing they can never pay him back. With the agreement they will work for him instead. But the tasks he asks of them are not common labor. He tries to make them do... grotesque things. And, if they refuse, he has them arrested and sent to debtors' prison."

"What sorts of things?"

"Do you really want to know? I'll tell you if you do."

Blatant warning in Aya's eyes, Eirinn shook her head. One day she would ask again. One day she would feel sturdy enough to take some of the burden off of Aya's shoulders. But today was not that day.

"How do you know this?" she asked Aya instead.

"The same way people know to go to the banker for loans. Word gets around about a man offering such services. Word gets around about what he demands in return and the consequences if one doesn't comply."

"Why would anyone go to him for money if they know what he might make them do for it?" Eirinn was outraged, and slightly appalled, even without further detail.

Before Aya's gaze softened upon her, a sad, gentle smile coming to her lips. "They're that desperate, Eir. Why else?"

Tears rushing to her eyes, Eirinn blinked them away, realizing, at once, she had no right to cry them. She had never been in such a position. She had wanted plenty, more than was easily obtained, but she had never been desperate. Indeed, it was by the very fact she had all that she needed that she could long for bigger, more radical things. Fleetingly, she wondered whether her father had ever been so destitute, if he or his parents or his brothers and sisters had ever been so close to starvation, so deep in their own misery, they would have done anything to survive.

"So, why were you in his house?" Eirinn shook the thought away. "To rob him like the papers said?"

"Oh, I would have taken a few things on my way out to cover my living expenses for a while," Aya admitted. "But, no, that wasn't the main reason."

"What was the main reason?"

"I went there to hurt him," Aya said, and, though the insinuation had been there, in Aya's tone, in the dark glint in her eyes, Eirinn was still shocked to hear her say it out loud. So bluntly. So easily.

"How?"

"I hadn't decided that yet. That was my mistake. I always knew what I was going to do in advance. I was always quick and smart about it. It was usually easy. The punishment fit the crime. But I couldn't decide with him. He deserved so much suffering, and I knew I could never watch any of the things he had made others do. I had a satchel full of options, and I was distracted. I should have seen the sword by the bed. I should have known he was awake before I got close. My mind was somewhere else."

"You didn't have a satchel when you came here." No idea where else to begin with that, Eirinn opted for what felt like the least perilous path.

"I dropped it at the boarding house on the way. I thought it in poor taste to show up at someone's house of healing with a bag full of knives and vises."

Knives. Vises. "So, you do have a home."

"Something of one. Temporarily."

"And you've obviously done this before."

"Yes."

"How many times?"

"Two... three... dozen."

Well, that is... substantial, Eirinn considered. More than she could have expected. And quite the troubling range. Had Aya hurt twenty-four men or thirty-six? Was it usually as easy as she made it out to be or was it always harrowing?

"Have you ever killed anyone?"

"No," Aya answered at once. "I wanted them to suffer. There is no suffering in death."

"And how many times have you been stabbed?"

"Just the one."

Hand sliding up her arm, Aya's fingers brushed against her collarbone, and Eirinn tried to reconcile any of this with what she had learned about Aya over the past few days. With how safe she felt under Aya's hands. Even now. Despite knowing Aya was a vigilante of justice. Despite knowing Aya had a satchel full of presumed torture devices stashed in a rented room somewhere. "That's a very winning record," was all she could think to say, and Aya seemed to understand. It was going to take time, and more than a single conversation, to make sense of this.

"I can't imagine what you must be thinking."

Eirinn was certain Aya couldn't because she barely knew what she was thinking herself.

"I've done what I've done, and I can't undo it. I wouldn't if I could. These men deserved what I did to them. They deserved far more, but I did what I had the power in me to do."

Aya's voice soft, convicted, Eirinn listened. She heard Aya. She nodded along in acknowledgment, feeling ever more confused. "And how did you know you were the one meant for this task?"

Her gaze drifting back to the window, Aya stared out it for several long seconds before at last she sighed. "My entire life, my mother was the only person whose judgment mattered to me. If I had listened to any of the other voices around me, I would have hated myself."

Furious, instantly, Eirinn's teeth clenched as she ran her hand down Aya's forearm.

"When she died, no one's judgment mattered to me anymore. I could do whatever I wanted without any other voice in my ear. Only my own conscience. And that didn't work. Or maybe it did. I just couldn't stop thinking about these men who had gotten away with so much. How there was no retribution for the rich and the powerful. They could do whatever they wanted with complete impunity. Banish undesirable people from their cities and countries. Starve entire nations. So why not me? Why shouldn't I do the same? Good had long failed to abolish their evil. Maybe only more evil could do that."

Maybe, Eirinn's subconscious automatically supplied. It was a troublingly sound theory. One frequently tested throughout history in war after war. But, then, how often were wars truly waged against evil and how often was that merely an excuse? It seemed to her Aya had done something others only ever talked about.

"There's just one problem," she said.

"Just one? You must be even more of a saint than I thought."

"I don't think you're evil."

Aya's bravado wavered. Her mask slipped. Eyes tearing, in direct testament to Eirinn's point, she cleared her throat and looked away. And Eirinn realized why she couldn't reconcile the Aya of story with the Aya who hovered above her. Because they were already reconciled. They were already the same. Everything Aya just told her, and nothing about her had changed. She was exactly the same woman who walked through her door eight days ago. That woman was brash and headstrong and devilish in all the right ways. She was not even remotely evil.

"But..." There was something else, something Aya wasn't saying, but Eirinn could still see. Remorse. Aya said she had no regrets, and maybe she didn't. But she did have sorrow. She did suffer the things she had done. Or, perhaps, she just suffered having to tell Eirinn about them. "If it doesn't feel good... if something has changed... if there was something else that made you hesitate that night, that's all right too."

Tremble nearly imperceptible, Aya gave herself away. Confessed everything without saying a single word. Sliding down in the bed, she laid her head against Eirinn's chest, and Eirinn could feel the warm, wet flow of tears as she pressed her lips to Aya's head, breathing her in, fingers combing through near-black hair, absolutely certain everything Aya had done she had done with the noblest of intentions. Not sure why she was so certain, but believing it without question or doubt.

To the very extent of her soul.

Chapter 21

CAROLINE

1886

Aya was invading her dreams.

Of course, she was. Why wouldn't she be? She had invaded everyplace else. The house. The workshop. Caroline's relationship with Dr. Todson. With Lei. Why shouldn't she conquer Caroline's last bastion of self? Batter down the barricades of her subconscious and declare herself victor and queen?

"Caroline."

It wasn't as if Caroline's defenses weren't already in significant disrepair, every fortification she had built up in her entire adult life cracking and deteriorating since the moment Thomas dropped her off.

Dr. Todson with her intuitive kindness and concern, putting thoughts and sentiments into her head.

Lei with her big, dark eyes, clever words, and undeniable magnetism taking a firm hold on her heart. And other parts of her.

"Caroline, wake up."

I would love to do that, Aya. Really, truly, I would.

If it would stop her from having to hear Aya speak, Caroline would love to force her eyes to open, to have some measure of control over the semi-conscious state in which she, once again, found herself in this palace in the Surrey countryside.

"Hey!"

Voice irritating enough, it was Aya's presence that was the most vexing. Nearly impossible to ignore. Caroline could almost feel her there, hovering, like a mosquito or a mite threatening to sting or infest.

"Caroline!"

Eyes flying wide, Caroline squinted and stared at the space above her, recognizing the wall and ceiling of the bedroom as she blinked them into clear - well, relatively clear - view and followed the call through the lamplight, snarling as she saw Aya sitting, actually sitting, stern and solid, on a chair next to her bed. God, it was worse than she thought. Aya was in her dreams AND in her bedroom. Where did she have to go to be free of this woman?

"What are you doing in here?" Sitting quickly up, she realized it was too quickly when her stomach hiccupped and shifted and she wobbled in the bed.

"Eir got worried when you didn't come down for dinner. She found you unconscious and drooling on your floor. Your pulse and blood pressure were low, so she didn't want you left alone. Lei was worried you wouldn't want to see her, so I volunteered."

Losing energy with each word, like a music box in need of a good winding, Caroline fully depleted at the mention of Lei's name.

"Why? So you can kill me without witnesses?" Rest of it too painful to endure, she concentrated only on that which fueled her anger.

"Don't tempt me," Aya said as she rose to her feet, and, watching her cross the room to look out the darkened window, Caroline wished she could get up too. Rise to the occasion, so to speak. She felt rather unfairly matched, Aya fully clothed and in control of all her faculties, while she had somehow ended up in only her chemise in bed.

"Did you put me to bed?"

"Eir," Aya uttered, and Caroline wasn't sure if that was better or worse.

Unconscious. Drooling. Dragging herself to the bed's edge with some effort, shame clawed, rabid and biting, at her insides. Even after everything, regardless of what she had thought or said, she apparently cared a great deal about what Dr. Todson thought of her.

"There's a remedy on the nightstand, if you feel as bad as you look."

"I feel fine," Caroline said, even as the acid rose into her throat, scorching and choking, and it occurred to her, if she did look and feel at all comparable, she had to look pretty unsightly.

So, this was how she found herself. Doped up and clammy in her bed. Drowsy. Pathetic. She didn't even feel good from the laudanum. That was the most pitiful part.

Glancing to the tonic bottle left sitting next to a glass of water on the nightstand, Caroline closed her eyes as a halo danced around the reflection of the lamplight off the glass. She didn't have a headache, not a full one, not yet, but she did recognize the telltale signs. If she did nothing, she would almost certainly have a banger of one within the next few hours. Assuming she didn't take more laudanum, or whatever was in that vial, first.

"It's from Rand, not me, if that makes any difference to you."

It made all the difference. Caroline wouldn't trust a puppy out of Aya's hand. Especially now. Though, at this point, she wasn't entirely certain she could trust Rand either. He was, after all, Dr. Todson's best friend.

"If I take it, will you leave?"

"Don't be rude to me." Crossing her arms, Aya turned from the window. "I am trying to help you."

"How can you possibly help me?"

"Well, if you would stop being such a spoiled twat, I could provide you with some insight."

Mood tapering, drawing back in an instant, Caroline felt violently cocked. Like an arrow on the verge of fire. Never in her life had she been called something so hideously vulgar, and she wasn't about to start by letting Aya get away with it. Not after Aya was the one who came in and ruined everything. Who changed everything. Who took everything. God, she hated her. At that moment, Aya was the bane of her very existence, and Caroline wanted her to know it, wanted Aya to hear exactly what she thought of her. The words were like teeth sprouting on her tongue.

"Is this really where you are right now, Caroline?" Aya warned her, voice low and strangely disarming. "Are you in a position not to take the only hand reaching out to you?"

Quickly as it bloomed, Caroline's anger withered - Aya had a great talent for withering her, it seemed - and she shivered painfully.

Lost.

Cold.

Alone.

Why was Aya reaching out to her, that was the question? What possible reason had she given Aya to be standing in her bedroom offering her a hand of any sort?

"What sort of insight?" she asked.

"Take Rand's tonic and put those on." Aya gestured to a pile of clothes at the end of the bed as she moved back across the room. "It's raining. You're going to need a coat. Not too long of one. The pants will keep your legs dry."

"What time is it?"

"It's the middle of the night. Do you want insight or don't you?" Aya stopped, standing with impatience just inside the door. Because she didn't need Caroline's participation. If Caroline refused, Aya would just go up to bed with Dr. Todson. She would rise in the morning, eat her breakfast, and go down to the workshop with Lei. Her life would in no way change if Caroline said "no" to her. If anyone needed anyone, it was Caroline who needed her.

"Yes," Caroline said.

"I'll be in the foyer. Don't take too long." Aya went out the door, and, left alone in her bedroom, Caroline wound down completely, head drooping to her chest, body unwilling to move.

Did she really want to go with Aya? Out into the night and the rain? Did she want to get out of bed at all?

What other choice did she have?

Beams of pain reaching over the horizon to prod at her, she was in a right state. A precarious state. A familiar state. A state that could live or die equally and feel the same either way.

I don't want to die, the thought went through Caroline's head. And Caroline blinked - dazed - realizing it wasn't just a passing notion.

She had always had a symbiotic relationship with death. In its metaphysical sense. She embraced it as a satisfactory possibility and it consoled her on her worst of days. But there was always some reason to cling to the world. Sarah who loved her even when no one else did. Oliver who needed her after Sarah was gone.

Now - now Caroline felt as if she had finally lost everything. Everyone. She had been stripped down to her own skin and bones, and she wanted to live. To wake again tomorrow. To make the amends she needed to make. To find out what came next.

She wanted to live, and, for once in her life, it wasn't for anyone else.

Desire flickering, strange and iridescent, like a second heartbeat inside her, it was a rush, choosing life for the sake of it. Enough of a rush for her to toss off the shackles of laudanum and get out of bed.

Chapter 22

EIRINN

1872

Aya wasn't well enough to return to all normal activity, but she was well enough to take a walk outdoors, and Eirinn was glad to have something else to occupy her time. Stuck in the flat, Aya's entire occupation seemed to be trying to persuade Eirinn back into bed, and, while that wasn't a wholly unappealing prospect, it hadn't allowed either of them much chance for progress, Eirinn in her studies or Aya in her healing.

A walk in the sunshine would be good for both of them. It would bolster their constitutions, invigorate their airways, give them back some semblance of reason. Eirinn did hope. Because every second spent alone in the flat with Aya, her reasoning grew all the more tenuous, frayed by Aya's voice and her gaze and her hands. Whatever spell Aya had cast over her the night of her arrival had yet to break. Eirinn was entirely in her thrall, and at times scarcely recognized herself as the woman of science and intellect she always believed herself to be.

"Which do you like more?"

Even watching Aya approach through the busy thoroughfare of the marketplace released a sigh deep within her chest. She had never imagined it like this. Not for her. She always thought finding a companion, if she ever did find one aside from Rand, would be more of a business transaction, two strong-willed people agreeing to compromise on minor, quotidian things in pursuit of a mutual future.

"An orchid or a rose?"

"I don't know. Both." Even as she spoke, Eirinn heard the longing in her voice. "But the orchid, I suppose."

"Good answer." Pulling the stem of four tiger-striped purple blooms from behind her back, Aya presented it with a proud grin, and, matching expression coming to her own face, Eirinn felt calmer than expected. Righter with the nature of things. She wanted to be outside the flat with Aya, to walk arm in arm with her through the city streets and see how she felt. Now, she had been and she did. Her feelings for Aya might have developed in a vacuum, but they certainly didn't stay there. If anything, the light of day only cast them into starker light.

"Where did you get this?"

"I snatched it from a flower stall. The toss-away pile," Aya went on before Eirinn could call her penchant for thievery into question. "Some of the petals are ripped, see. But I figured that would only make you appreciate it more. Broken wings and all."

Holding one bloom up to her nose, Eirinn took a breath, intoxicated by the sweet, familiar fragrance. And by Aya, who produced a second flower, the aforementioned rose, which wilted in two vivid shades of orange, from behind her back. "Thank you."

"You're welcome. But you should know I didn't do it with entirely selfless intentions. I *am* trying to court you."

"I do know, and you're succeeding." Beyond succeeding, perhaps already successful, Eirinn was forced to admit to herself as Aya held out her arm and she slid her hand into its crook, as taken with this version of Aya - the gentle, whimsical woman who strolled and laughed with her through the farmers' market - as she was with the brooding seductress who first shadowed her doorway.

Showing up at the crack of dawn with a potentially lethal wound and a mysterious past, Aya had a darkness about her that simply couldn't be denied. But there was also a draw toward the light. She looked at people with an air of mistrust, of skepticism, but found faith in the smallest of things. A well-tended rock garden. A snail on a branch. Maybe it was due to the darkness that Aya appreciated those things far more. Current case in point, she had the money in her pocket to buy any flower she so desired from that flower stall, but chose to dig through the throwaways to see if there were any that might be saved.

"Ooh, plums. May I have a plum?" Vibrant, abundant fruit stall coming into view, expectation danced on Aya's face as she turned to Eirinn with beseeching eyes.

"Yes, of course. A small one." Eirinn only wished she knew nothing would go wrong as she watched Aya set off at a gallop.

Nothing had gone wrong. At least, not yet. Aya had no lingering pains. She was eating solid foods. There was nothing abnormal or enlarged when Eirinn pressed on her abdomen during their check-ups.

But, still, Eirinn worried. About the crudeness of her equipment. About her lack of specific training. About Aya's past and everything Aya had told her. There was so much uncertainty, every statement between them felt as if it came with a silent, looming question mark. Including her own feelings. What did she feel for Aya? What did she want from her?

As Aya took her time picking out her single plum from the stall's offerings, Eirinn took her time considering the question. She had never really thought about marriage, or long-term romantic relationships in general really. She'd had her dalliances, of course, occasional lovers since Cerise. Not many, granted, and they had all been the same, passing fancies that faded quickly in the face of reality. Anything more than casual relations simply didn't seem compatible with getting a medical license as a woman. The inequality of the system had set her back years behind her male counterparts, so she was already only months shy of thirty. Her spinster status was earned in the minds of society some years before, having since solidified into thornback.

Thornback. Imported from the colonies. A pejorative. Or it was meant to be. Women feared the classification without considering its origin - the thornback ray, which had extra spines for protection from its predators. *Its predators.* Which, Eirinn thought, really said more about the men who used the term than the women who were called it.

"Merci. Au revoir."

And now there was Aya. Aya. This sudden, wondrous circumstance. What was she supposed to do with her? Marriage? Not legally binding, and certainly hard to imagine. It was hard to imagine Aya in any sort of moored domesticity. She had been all over the world. She owned a satchel full of torture devices. Would she even be interested in something so old-fashioned? So... banal?

"Oh my God." Shining the chosen plum against her shirt, Aya took a bite as she reached Eirinn, jutting forward to let the juice dribble from her lip to the grass between them in an impressively quick and lithe display. She certainly didn't look or move as if she was still broken or unwell. But, then, Eirinn had already made that assessment. Up close and in the deepest of recesses.

"Good?"

"It's perfect. Here. Have a bite."

"No. You should eat it if it's making you moan like that."

"I moan over all sorts of good things. Doesn't mean I prefer to enjoy them alone," Aya said, and smirked. Because she knew. Knew how easily her words could stoke Eirinn into a frenzy. Knew how much power she had over her with a single look. "Please."

Inside or outside, day or night, Eirinn was helpless to resist her, so she didn't know why she bothered to try. Leaning forward, she took a bite of the plum in Aya's hand, endeavoring to escape the path of its dribble, but still ending up with a sticky line of it down her chin.

Aya's free hand rising at once to claim it, Aya sucked the juice off her thumb, and Eirinn could see multiple curious faces turn in her peripheral vision.

"You're drawing attention."

"And tons of envious ire, I imagine. Another bite?"

"No." Eirinn preferred not to have her senses whipped to a desperation point in public, and Aya finished the plum on her own, turning to toss its pit into a refuse sack up near the fruit stand.

"Do you know what you'd like for...?" When she glanced to Aya, Eirinn seized, portentous fear flaring deep inside her gut. "Aya?"

But Aya stood deathly still, her breaths the only things in her that moved, eyes frozen wide, and Eirinn followed her gaze across the fruit stall to see what she was staring at. Or, rather, who.

A rotund man staring back, his eyes were so venomous, Eirinn knew at once to worry. To embrace the fear. To breathe quicker and shallower, as if preparing for battle.

"Don't follow me." Taking a step away, Aya didn't look to her as the words left her lips.

"What?"

"Thief!" the large man bellowed before Aya could respond, and Aya dashed away, quick steps carrying her across the grassy thoroughfare faster than Eirinn could possibly follow.

"Aya!" Eirinn cried, pled, yearned to go after her, but Aya had told her not to, she knew she could never keep up, and that would only draw more attention, two women running through the market, one of them wearing a bright yellow dress.

Turning back to the banker - Eirinn assumed that was who the man had to be - she saw he was already in pursuit, laborious and panting, but pursuit nonetheless, and hollering up an army as he went.

"Stop that woman! She's a thief! She tried to rob me in my home!"

As he rounded the corner of the stall, her instinct to protect Aya kicked in and Eirinn got one narrow boot behind a stack of potato crates balanced haphazardly next to her, sending them toppling into the banker's path.

Hitting one rolling spud with his foot, the banker went down in a blaspheme of pain. But it didn't end his quest. A band of much younger men rushing to his aid, the banker pointed Aya out as they helped him back to his feet, and they took up the chase on his behalf, much swifter-footed than the banker, who limped and puffed behind them through the crowd of curious onlookers. A battered sheriff and his brigade of incited deputies with a crush of enthusiastic spectators to cheer them on.

"Merde! Quelle pagaille!" The vendor from the vegetable stall was suddenly before Eirinn, throwing up his hands and cursing his bruised and filthy lot.

"Here." Eirinn didn't know if the vendor knew it was her who had toppled his potato crates, but she put all the money she had in his hands anyway. To quiet him. And to appease karma. If something happened to

Aya, she didn't want it to be because she failed to make right with the universe. Yet another thought she never expected to have before Aya stumbled into her life.

And, as the vendor's excitement faded, so did the ruckus in the marketplace. The patrons put down their pitchforks and torches and returned to their shopping. The vendors grinned at the fleeting entertainment and returned to their sales.

Within seconds, everyone and everything was exactly as it had been before.

Except for Aya.

Aya was gone.

Chapter 23

CAROLINE

1886

Means of transport not entirely unanticipated, Caroline couldn't possibly anticipate the intimacy of it.

It was a strange feeling, holding so tightly to a woman she had sworn to dislike, whom she was equally certain didn't like her in return. But she had no choice in the matter. She had watched Aya ride up to the house on the steambike, had heard the chug-chug of its motor in the night, but even having seen and heard the bike in action, it was far faster than she could have guessed. On a straight stretch of road, the night sky went by in a disorienting blur, so they were on the outskirts of London in little more than an hour. The same route by carriage took a long, full day with a steady pace and rest breaks for the horses.

"Giddy-up." Aya hadn't missed her opportunity to harass her after she retrieved the steambike from the barn, pushing it Caroline's way with a small jerk of her head. "We've only got a few hours, and we've got a ways to walk before we can get on."

That ways was, in fact, a full, unforgiving mile from the house to the main gate of the property, and should have been foreseen, Caroline supposed, even as she grew quickly tired of trudging through the drizzle of rain in boots at least a size too big for her with only the small glow of the steambike's headlamp to illuminate their way.

"Heya, Johnny."

After what felt like half her life, and ankles already aching, they at last made it to the gate.

"Heya, Aya." The skinny watchman stepped out from the small guard shack to greet them, scratching at an itch behind one ear that drew Caroline's attention to just how big his ears truly were. *Gigantic* wouldn't have been an unreasonable descriptor. What better characteristic for a watchman? *All the better to hear you with.* Of course, if Johnny heard miles down the road, he had to hear what was going on *in* the house too. "Hello." He cast a small smile Caroline's way.

"Hello," Caroline said in return.

"Have you two met?"

"We haven't," the watchman said.

"Caroline, this is Johnny. Johnny, Caroline. I've got something for you." Aya wasted no time, pulling out a generous bottle from the satchel she wore draped across one shoulder. "Straight out of Spain."

"Ah. The good stuff," Johnny hummed as he took it. "Thanks, Aya. How long you gonna be?" Setting the bottle inside the safety of the guard shack, he pulled a large key ring off his belt, pressing the largest, most prominent protrusion into the substantial lock that secured the gate.

"Back before you leave, I hope. Now, don't be drinking that while you're on duty."

"I would never." Johnny, jokingly aggrieved, set them free, and it was a notable response. The grin on his face. The amusement in his tone. He seemed to truly like Aya, this skinny, big-eared Guard Johnny. Like seeing her. Like talking to her. Everyone seemed to like Aya. As far as Caroline could tell, in her pursuit of steadfast antipathy, she was an army of one. "Be good. Be smart."

"You know I'm not good at either of those things."

"Hell. Who is?" Johnny laughed as he pulled the gate behind them, and, hearing the scrape of the key in the lock, Caroline stalled suddenly, feet too heavy to move in her borrowed boots, knees giving way to a tremble, palpitant sensation invading her chest.

"Are you all right?" Aya turned back when she realized she was no longer beside her, or even trailing slightly behind as she had been for most of the walk.

"Yes, I'm fine," Caroline uttered.

"You're obviously not fine."

For a moment, they stood, Aya studying Caroline from beneath the wide brim of her hat almost as intensely as Dr. Todson liked to study her. Apparently, two people who had been together so long and actually still liked each other adopted each other's annoying quirks. "Do you want to go back?"

"No." Caroline did not want to go back. Had no intention of. She had come this far in too-big boots and the spitting rain, and she wanted to know whatever it was Aya was going to tell her. She wanted to get on that strange steambike and go wherever they were meant to go.

She just needed someone to tell that to her feet.

"I'm not going to hurt you, Caroline."

"That's not..." It wasn't... Caroline wasn't scared of Aya. Well, she was, somewhat, but not in the way Aya thought.

It was the path, the lane, that was gloomy and uninviting. Not the trees that lined it or the rolling hills, which looked fake and distant in the weak glow of the steambike. It was the end, specifically, where the path disappeared outside the scope of the light's beam. The unknown ahead.

"I'm coming." Caroline forced her feet to plod along anyway, to catch up to Aya, and Aya turned to push the steambike once more. Walking a half-step slower. Glancing toward the tree line every so often to ensure Caroline was still there.

"Not much further." She might have even been trying to comfort Caroline, and it worked in its way, Caroline hated to admit, that Aya would say anything to her she didn't have to say.

Grudgingly, it occurred to her it might actually help. To talk to Aya. To hear a voice that was known to her in the dark, rainy night, even if it was mostly known for being invasive and irritating.

"Do they know?" Glancing back toward the guard shack, Caroline shivered as she watched its outline slip into obscurity through the falling rain, which felt colder and seemed to blow even more sideways outside the gate.

"Know what?" Aya asked.

"About Dr. Todson?"

"What about her?"

"That she's a... she?"

"Yes, they do."

"How do you know you can trust them?"

Peering ahead of her down the lane, Aya seemed to be considering. Contemplating whether or not she could trust Caroline. "All the men who work here, with the exception of Rand, have served time in our queen's gaols," she said at last.

"Oh." Caroline faltered, not sure how that made them *more* trustworthy.

"For Offences Against the Person."

"Violence?"

"No, Dear. For buggery."

"Oh," Caroline said. Then - "OH!" Gaping freely, she watched the rain bounce off the path, knowing her extreme shock showed on her face, grateful for the fact Aya was looking ahead of them and the fog, which gave her some semblance of cover. "All of them?"

"Yes, all of them. Have you met Ben? The Titan?"

"The man who was at the gate when I first arrived?"

"Yes, I assume he would have been. He and Phileas... Mr. Poke who brings the wood and the coke fuel, they're all but married. They keep a lovely cottage just off the grounds."

"Really?" Caroline could hardly begin to imagine it. Not the two men keeping a house together. That part, she was somewhat surprised to discover, was rather easy to envisage. And somewhat nice. She liked Mr. Poke, in the limited contact she'd had with him, and it was good to know he wasn't alone in the world.

It was the rest she couldn't quite wrap her head around. She couldn't envision Ben, the Titan, with anyone really, man or woman, so unequal to him in size. What sort of embrace...? What sort of position...? Going suddenly warm in the frigid rain, Caroline realized she probably shouldn't be trying so hard.

"Mm. Phileas calls Ben 'The Minotaur.' You know, half man, half bull." Smirk coming to Aya's face, Caroline was certain now that she was intentionally trying to provoke her, to embarrass her, and was ashamed to acknowledge just how easily it had worked.

"Are they really even a couple?"

"Yes." Aya grinned. "They are."

So, that was it then. The missing piece. The glue that affixed everyone at Dr. Todson's together. The women who lived there and the men who worked the grounds were all vulnerable, some of them in the exact same ways. No man who had been imprisoned for sexual impropriety with other men would dare tell anyone Dr. Todson's Home was half-ruse, scarcely an institution at all, or that Rand wasn't a real doctor. The house was as much a refuge for them as for the women who lived inside its walls.

Absorbing the fact, Caroline felt full of questions. Questions she knew Aya could answer. Questions like -

What was the right way to engage in sexual congress with another woman?

Was it as intuitive as it seemed?

It wasn't as if Caroline had no idea where to start. She did know how to touch herself to bring pleasure, to bring... completion. Was it enough to imagine a mirror image? Could she satisfy a woman as she satisfied herself? A particular woman, perhaps? A particular woman with whom Aya was close friends and might put in a good word?

Blushing and huffing into the night, Caroline recognized she was deluding herself even as she thought it. She had done nothing to get Aya to put in a good word with Lei. If Aya was putting in any word, it was probably "Run." *Run very far, very fast. Get away from this one, because she's a mess and not the kind made from having too good a time.*

"All right. Hop on." Rolling to a stop, Aya dipped the steambike to make it easier for Caroline to climb aboard, and Caroline realized this was probably the least opportune time to be thinking any of this - immediately before she was about to straddle a vibrating machine and go down a road that would almost certainly have plenty of bumps and divots in it.

188

Fairly certain Aya would never stop laughing if she asked if there was a way she might ride sidesaddle, she swallowed her discomfort and threw one leg across the wide seat, realizing now why Aya had brought trousers to her room and grateful they were as baggy as they were.

"Put this on and shuffle back." Aya handed her a leather helmet from out of her satchel, and Caroline took down her hood to pull it on, fumbling with the buckle beneath her chin, as Aya replaced her own hat with a similar helmet, crumpling the hat into the satchel and attaching the satchel to the back of the steambike before climbing on in front of Caroline, not nearly far enough away.

"Are you all right?" she asked when Caroline scooted back to put a respectable amount of distance between them.

"Yes, I'm fine."

"Are you sure? It's not a short ride."

"I'm fine," Caroline said again.

"All right. But you're going to want to hold on." Reaching back, Aya pulled Caroline's arms around her waist, and, tug sliding her forward into Aya, Caroline choked back a cry of surprise. Of sensation. Of piquant arousal she had produced with her own thoughts and didn't want to feel while pressed against the back of her sworn enemy. "And don't lean too far away from me. The smokestack gets hot."

"Fantastic," Caroline grumbled, last syllable turning to a growl below her breath when she felt the soft rumble of Aya's laughter in response.

An hour later, signs of civilization cropping up on the landscape ahead, Caroline smelled London before she recognized her first landmark. The fog of soot that brought the sky low to nearly swallow up the city. The lye from the laundry houses along the Thames. The horses with their excrement. The factories with their chimneys. Until then it might have been any other city in the South - Croydon or Guildford, Crawley or Reading.

Somewhere on the other side of the Thames, Westminster stood. St. Paul's. The Tower. And Caroline's own home.

Where are we? she wanted to ask Aya to see if Aya would tell her. But she was equally afraid of what Aya might say.

Was Aya bringing her back? Bringing her home? Could Aya be that anxious to be rid of her? Could Lei and Dr. Todson be ready to be rid of her? Was this a plot hatched in the map room as she lay unconscious and drooling in her bed?

It terrified her, Caroline realized, contemplating the very thing she thought she wanted mere weeks before. To be back in her own city. In her own home. In her old life.

Dank wind blowing off the Thames as they turned to the east, Caroline saw the river in spurts and fragments, or rather she saw the dots of light along its embankment, the street lights like fireflies with their

auras of haze, and she kept waiting for the bridge to come -
Hammersmith, Chelsea, Vauxhall - but Aya never turned into the city.
Holding a straight line through the marshy south side of the river
instead, they moved past shanties, then tenements, each looking equally
likely to be knocked over by a stiff breeze as the next.

Watching them go by at a near-crawl - Aya had slowed a great deal
since they entered the city's outer reaches, bringing the noise of the
steambike down to a hum - Caroline recognized the unfolding world
around her from hearsay and newspaper pieces. She had never been to a
London slum, not even the ones north of the Thames. They were fabled
microcosms of the poor. Vile, depraved places where God punished
sinners and the lazy. At least, that was how they were spoken of in society
by those who believed in their existence at all.

"You can let go now."

Reek of rotting fish on the air, a soft vibration permeated the night,
dwarfing the chug of the steambike as they rolled into the shadows of a
dockyard. Several large ships blocking out the night sky and bobbing like
buoys in the harbor, Caroline looked to Aya, unable to see her face for the
helmet. Though, it took her several seconds longer to comprehend what
Aya just said.

Glancing to her arms, still locked rigidly around Aya's waist, she felt
instantly abashed. For someone who didn't want to be holding onto her,
she was clutching Aya quite vehemently, grip tightening with every
anxious thought that went through her mind. When she let her go, Aya
lithely dismounted and pulled off her helmet, tucking it into the satchel
she untied from the steambike.

"What are we doing here?" Reaching for the buckle of her own
helmet, Caroline considered she might feel safer with it on when Aya
looked wordlessly at her and walked away.

Hastening to get off the bike, she wasn't sure if she was safe at the
dockyard with Aya, but she knew she stood absolutely no chance without
her, so she hurried to keep Aya in her sights as she finally got the helmet
off, nearly plowing into her from behind when Aya rounded a corner and
stopped suddenly at the base of a towering scaffold that had been erected
against the side of a ship undergoing repairs.

Without warning, Aya grabbed the helmet from out of her hand,
adding it to her satchel as she stepped onto the first rung of the scaffold.
No desire at all to climb the side of a ship, Caroline just watched her for a
moment before accepting she had no choice but to follow. Aya could just
tell her whatever it was she was going to tell her. Could have done so back
in Surrey. Clearly, she was going to make her work for it, knowing damn
well the condition she had been in just an hour before. It was a test of
will, and Caroline had will - the will to strangle Aya with her bare hands.

"Careful." At least, Aya didn't make her climb all the way to the top.
Exiting the ladder two levels up, she waited beside it, helping Caroline
safely onto the platform when Caroline proved she had no natural
prowess at any of this, especially in boots too big, and led her to the edge

of the scaffold where it looked outward toward the only currently occupied dock in the shipyard.

The ship already powered up and wafting its steam into the air, it was the source of the vibration that drowned out the rest of the night and put a light tremble through the scaffold on which they now stood, half a dozen men milling about its deck and the docks below.

"What is this?"

Pulling something dark and metal from out of her satchel, Aya pulled it to length and offered it to Caroline. And, realizing it was a spyglass, Caroline ripped it from Aya's hand with growing impatience. This would be a whole lot easier if Aya would just tell her what she was supposed to be looking for, why they were there, what vital information she expected her to glean from this obvious life lesson.

Putting the spyglass up to her eye, it helped little when she had no idea what she was meant to see. Yes, those were men, she could now verify for a fact.

"Who are they?"

"Just wait."

Ah, yes. Another worthless directive. Caroline huffed over at Aya. But Aya wasn't at all bothered by her growing impatience. Indeed, she seemed to rather enjoy it as she leaned against a post in the scaffold in a dangerously casual fashion and pulled out a silver pocket watch to check the time.

"Any minute now." She returned the watch to her vest, revealing nothing, so Caroline turned her eyes back to the dock, keeping watch with her naked eye, waiting for something new to happen.

For some minutes, nothing did. The same drone filled the air. The same men puttered about the ship and the dock. But, then, a new group of men appeared, a dozen or so of them, moving in a creeping cluster, and Caroline raised the spyglass back to her eye.

One man leading the brigade, white hair jutted from beneath his black top hat, the crutch he carried moving like an extension of his arm and leg. With each right-sided step, the length of wood swung forward and provided support, giving the man's gait a pronounced jump on that side as, behind him, other men walked two by two. A dozen precisely, Caroline counted five sets of heads between the man with the crutch and the one who walked in the back, rather larger than the others and carrying a truncheon in one hand.

"What are they doing?"

"I don't know exactly." At last, Aya turned to watch with Caroline instead of watching Caroline. "The ship is a cargo vessel from the East Indies. The man with the cane, that's General Joffreys, dedicated veteran and vermin of the Poona Division, Bombay Army."

"How do you know him?"

"Did you notice his limp?"

"Yes." Caroline wasn't sure how Aya thought it possible not to notice it.

"I gave it to him," Aya said, and unease slid, like ice, down the back of Caroline's throat.

"How?"

"I wrapped a vise around his leg and crushed every bone in his calf and ankle."

Prickle erupting from the base of her skull, it reached up into Caroline's hair and trickled down her spine.

"Why?" Hand on the spyglass suddenly tremulous, she pulled it away from her eye, glancing over the tube toward the ship and the river, instantly more aware of how close she stood to the platform's edge. Of how close Aya stood beside her.

"I thought a permanent shackle a just reward for the shackling of thousands of others."

"He's a slaver?"

"He was. Still is, if the evidence adds up. Regardless of laws or debilitation, the will for wealth finds a way!" Aya announced as if she was giving a toast at a party. "Clearly, he's established a market somewhere."

It was wretched. Vile. Caroline couldn't pretend it wasn't. But it also provided a basis for rational argument.

"Slavery is illegal. If you know he's breaking the law, why don't you call the police?"

"Oh, Caroline." Aya laughed. "Don't pretend to be stupid."

That's it! Caroline took a deep, furious breath. Either she or Aya was definitely going off the side of this scaffold.

"Is this why you brought me here? To insult me and show me you're not just thieves, that you're also dangerous?"

"Eir and Lei would never hurt anyone. You know that," Aya said.

"But you would."

"If I have to." Capturing her gaze, Aya held it until Caroline at last gave in and looked away first. "But no. Not like that. Not anymore."

"Reformed?" It occurred to Caroline she probably shouldn't be quite so cheeky with someone who just admitted to being genuinely dangerous, and possibly slightly sadistic, but Aya did just call her stupid, so...

"Yes." She was surprised when Aya answered so simply. Surprised enough to glance to Aya again, to watch her look off toward the ship currently in the process of stocking humans with a slight squint. "When I met Eirinn, I was a different person. I saw the world exactly as it is. Unfair. Unjust. I saw rich men get away with literal murder. Kings and queens and rulers, far worse. The things I did I truly thought needed to be done."

"And now you don't?"

"I think there's a better way. A way that hurts them just as much, if not more, and helps others at the same time." Turning to look at her, Aya's expression softened as she let out a slow, steady exhalation. "Eir made me believe it wasn't my responsibility, that I didn't have to right others' wrongs or take on the burden of their cruelties. She made me feel worthy enough to choose myself. And I... I just wanted to be good enough for her."

It was a sensational confession, near mesmerizing in its honesty, given that Aya carried herself like someone who thought she was supreme at everything. That Aya had doubt, that Aya had weakness, it was like a bat admitting it sometimes feared the dark.

"Why are you telling me this?" Caroline asked.

"For Eir," Aya answered. Simply, once more. "And for Lei. You look at what we're doing, Caroline, and you see wrong - glaring immorality - and that's fine. We all see things as we choose to see them. But you think that we think we're right. We don't. We don't have to be right. We just need to do something. It might make little difference, it might just be a drop in the ocean, but at least it's a drop."

Caroline didn't know what to say to that. Trying to think of something, she realized she didn't really want to say anything. It might have been the first time Aya had said a word to her she didn't immediately desire to refute, to cast aspersions upon. Could it be it made some sense?

"I know you don't like me. It's all right," Aya went on when Caroline opened her mouth. For what purpose, she wondered. What was she going to do? Argue? "I realize I'm an acquired taste for many. But you do like Lei. And Eir... Eir is everything that is right with this world. She isn't like the rest of us. Be better to them. I do still have my vise."

Flinching, Caroline didn't have to wonder if Aya was serious.

"Come on if you're coming. I want to be home before Eir wakes up."

Spyglass seized from her hand, Caroline realized Aya meant that too. She wasn't going to drag her back down the ladder and onto the steambike. *If you're coming*... she had all but said as much. Standing there, above the dockyard, she could go anywhere. Down. Up. Out to sea. Back to her house in South Kensington.

Anywhere.

Cold river air piercing through her borrowed clothes and skin, all Caroline wanted was to be warm again, and when she thought of warmth she thought of only one place. She could go anywhere, and there was nowhere she wanted to be but back at Dr. Todson's. On Aya's bike and headed home.

Home. The word came as easily and with as much conviction as she had fought it only weeks before.

Home.

Gripped, bewildered, she staggered her way back across the platform, careful of her footing as she stepped onto the scaffold ladder and hurried down it after Aya, not doubting for one single instant Aya would quite happily leave her behind.

Chapter 24

EIRINN

1872

The sun that shined through the window above the kitchen sink cast a glimmer on the sitting room wallpaper so the leaves and vines it touched glittered and sparkled like choice harvest amongst those around them.

Even when the sun didn't shine, the spot was apparent, in the exact opposite manner. Years of sun damage had left a dull, lifeless streak in the otherwise still vibrant and healthy design, as if the swath had been struck by blight and was dying a quicker, less dignified death than the rest.

It was at this spot Eirinn stared over the next several hours.

Sun moving through the sky, slipping in and out from behind the clouds, the spot changed and changed again, glittering to drab, drab to glittering. Lively to dying. Dying to lively. It made quite the existential spectacle from her spot in the sitting room armchair.

"You have to eat, Eir."

Rand waiting with her, he was almost as stagnant, getting up only to stretch his back or bring fresh tea and food, but Eirinn had let most of the mugs go cold and hadn't eaten a thing. She knew he was right, could feel it, weak, ill, but every time she tried to take a bite her chest constricted and her throat burned with unshed tears. She would picture Aya running off, the band of men chasing after her. She imagined Aya being captured, mob closing in, hands grasping roughly at her delicate, not-entirely-healed body and feared she might choke on the vision alone.

"She'll be here soon," Rand tried to reassure her, or perhaps to convince himself, but neither of them believed him.

If Aya had gotten away clean, Eirinn was certain she would be there by now.

It was sometime in late afternoon when the knock came at their door.

Though Eirinn startled at the sudden, vehement intrusion, she didn't move. They had left the downstairs entry door unlocked, knowing Aya would use it freely, which meant there was no reason to be too eager, to let hope bloom, or to hasten too much to rise.

"Three men. I think they may be police." Rand looked to the street from the balcony door, and nausea bloomed in hope's place, unfurling like an octopus over the back of Eirinn's throat. "I'll go down."

Looking blearily toward Rand, Eirinn said nothing - could think of nothing purposeful to say - and Rand slipped through his bedroom door, coming out in a collared shirt that he buttoned and tucked as he crossed the room. No real desire to, Eirinn swayed to her feet to follow him, stopping on the other side of the wall at the top of the entry stairs and listening at the ajar door. Even in her despondence, it occurred to her it was probably best to know what was being said.

"Hello there, Gentlemen," Rand greeted the men cheerfully.

"Bonjour, Monsieur. Parlez-vouz français?" one of the men asked him.

"No. Not much and not well. Sorry," Rand said.

"I'll do my hardest."

So died Eirinn's hope that might be the end of it, that they would determine Rand a simple Englishman, or, at the very least, require the aid of an interpreter and be on their way for now.

"We are police with Petit-Montrouge ward. We are looking for a woman."

"Who isn't?" Rand quipped, and there was silence in return. "Sorry. English humor."

It wasn't. Not even remotely close. The punchline was too simple. It wasn't nearly droll or innuendoed enough. But it wasn't the words Rand was trying to sell, it was the attitude. This was not a man who had just been sitting upstairs in silence, worriedly watching his best friend turn into stone. This was a perfectly normal young English chap going about his perfectly normal day, bursting with energy and reveling in every second of his freewheeling lifestyle in Paris. It was an easy character for Rand to portray, because it was who he had been, right up until a few hours before when he turned both guardian and nursemaid, hovering over Eirinn like a sentinel and trying to coax her into healthy habits as his mother used to do.

"So, a woman you said." Rand cleared his throat.

"Yes - uh. This woman is black hair, light, uh... brown, but not too brown..."

"Tan?" Rand offered.

"Tan. Tan. Tan skin," the officer said. "Dark eyes. Very dark. Very beautiful."

The description of Aya - vague, but troublingly accurate - sent a rush of concern through Eirinn's entire being. Of longing. To see Aya for herself. To know that she was safe.

"She was seen at farmer market today. Some saw a woman with her."

"Well, only one woman lives here."

"She is light hair?"

"Blonde? Yes. My... sister, Eirinn."

"We can talk to her?"

"Yes, of course. Would you like to come in?"

Oh, for the love of all graces. Eirinn rested her head on the wall for a moment, trying to get her bearings, before walking gingerly back to the armchair, careful to avoid the floorboards that creaked the most - not that Rand and the policemen would hear with the racket they were making coming up the stairs - and made it back to her seat just as Rand stepped through the entry door.

"Eir, these men are police. They want to talk to you."

Wearing her best expression of surprise, of appropriate puzzlement, Eirinn slid the teacup and saucer she had picked up like a disguise back onto the side table and made an effort to rise, realizing she should have eaten as the room quaked and blurred and she had to steady herself on the back of the chair.

"Are you all right?"

"Just a little dizzy," she said, and Rand nodded, trying to will her strength from across the room.

It might have even played well for them, her visibly weakened condition. If they thought her too ill to leave the flat, the police might not bother with any questions at all. What could they ask of a woman who was infirm and house-bound?

"C'est elle."

It *might* have played well, if not for the third man who followed the policemen up the stairs. Face appearing just over their shoulders, inquisitive and slightly flushed, Eirinn recognized the vendor from the vegetable stall. And he recognized her.

"Were you at the market today?" the English-speaking officer asked.

"Yes, I was." So much for denying everything. "It was there that I took ill."

"And you were with a woman?"

"No." Furrowing her brow, Eirinn endeavored for palpable confusion. "I was there with Rand."

"This man saw you with a woman."

"A woman? Oh. The woman with dark hair?" Eirinn asked.

"Yes. Black hair. You saw her?"

"I did. She came to my aid. Rand was lingering at the spices table." Cued by her irritated glance, Rand gave a shrug of abashed confirmation. "I walked ahead. I started to feel dizzy, and the woman escorted me to a stand. Then, a man started to chase her and she ran off. Several other men started chasing the woman too. It was really quite strange. Many people saw it, the men chasing her. Are you looking for them too?" Eirinn couldn't entirely tamp the coolness in her stare.

"The man you saw is the one who called us," the English-speaking officer said. "The woman you were with tried to rob him in his home in Auteuil."

"What? Are you sure? She was quite slight. Could she really have done such a thing?" Sow doubt. It was all Eirinn's brain could come up with to do.

"He recalled her very well. We're sure there must have been a male accomplice."

"Unbelievable," Eirinn said. It was. Truly. Unbelievable the banker still insisted a man must have been in his house even after identifying Aya in the marketplace.

Still, if they found her, the police would know the truth. Aya had the wound to prove her part in the crime, and Eirinn had her bloodied coat stashed in the wardrobe in her bedroom. The bedroom toward which the English-speaking officer's thus-far-mute partner was steadily retreating, head turned, eyes already scanning the contents through the doorway.

"Can he look?" the English-speaking officer asked.

"Yes, of course," Rand said, and Eirinn reached for the back of the chair again, panic swirling her knees and unsteadying the floor beneath her feet as the vegetable vendor leaned over the English-speaking officer's shoulder, whispering something in French, and they both looked accusatorially her way.

"He says the crates fell in the man's way and you paid him for his ruined potatoes."

"Yes, I did." Though, had she known he would turn out to be a snitch, she might have reconsidered. "I assumed I must have fallen into them. I was quite unsteady on my feet. Lady troubles, you see. My monthlies have always been quite -"

"Oui. Oui."

Words translating, the English-speaking officer batted a hand to make them stop, and Eirinn took some satisfaction in his visible discomfort. The ultimate sparer of explanations, "lady troubles" was the one phrase that could make even overbearing husbands disappear from examination rooms when she needed to talk to their wives alone. Perhaps, it had the power to make the police disappear too.

"Ah. Merci." The officer relayed her explanation - the unsteadiness part only, not its stated cause - and the vendor seemed satisfied with that.

"It was the least I could do." Eirinn's voice faltered as she realized they were the truest words she had spoken since the men came up the stairs.

"He also says he's never seen you with the woman before."

"No. I told you, I only met her today." It burned, cramped, lie so excruciating, Eirinn toed up to the verge of confessing. Maybe she would feel better if she just told the truth. She couldn't possibly feel any worse.

When the nonspeaking officer emerged from her bedroom a moment later, Eirinn expected a big showing, a flourish of black - Aya's signature color - cut and bloodied from out of her wardrobe. A slew of new questions. Demands as to where Aya was hiding.

Eirinn wished she knew.

But the officer only strode past her, continuing on into Rand's bedroom.

"Sorry about the mess!" Rand called after him, catching Eirinn's eye and willing her to relax, or at least better pretend. This was why he had invited the police in, after all, to show them they had nothing - and no one - to hide. Now, the police could tell the banker they had done their jobs thoroughly and their search turned up nothing.

"Did the woman tell you her name?"

Her name? Aya. Her name was Aya. And losing sight of her in the marketplace felt like losing a piece of herself. "No. She never said."

"Elle n'est pas là."

So, they *were* just searching for Aya, the point was confirmed a moment later as the second policeman came out of Rand's room.

"The men who gave chase didn't catch the woman?" In her momentary relief, it occurred to Eirinn, though she had given them nothing but lies, the police could still give her something of use. "I'm surprised. They seemed to be keeping quite good pace with her."

"No. They lost her in the crowd," the English-speaking officer said. "That's when the banker called us. If they caught her, we would be looking for pieces."

That's what she got for asking, a strong, swift blow with an accompanying laugh and roil of bilious acid through her stomach.

"If you'd like, I can keep an eye out." Watching her fade, Rand tried to hasten the police and the vegetable vendor's departure. "Watch for her, you know," he added when the idiom didn't translate.

"Yes. Good," the English-speaking officer said.

"Is there anything else?"

"No. No." Seeming to realize they were now just loitering - they had asked their questions, they had poked around - the officer glanced to Eirinn. "Merci, Madame."

"Merci. Au revoir."

"Au revoir."

The officers and vendor turning for the stairs, they made an even noisier exit than they had an entrance as Rand saw them out, and Eirinn listened for the downstairs door to close behind them before sinking back down in the armchair, thoughts instantly devolving into Aya. Her eyes. Her smile. Her lying in bed in the middle of the night, moonbeams casting a golden halo around her shoulders.

"Eir?" Back up the stairs a few seconds later, Rand stopped to peer through the kitchen window to ensure the police had fully departed before coming to kneel next to her on the floor. "Are you all right?"

Question absurd, Eirinn didn't bother to answer it. Rand had been with her all day. He knew very well how she was.

"This is good news, Eir. Now you know no one has her."

"Yes." It was good news, Eirinn agreed. Especially since, if the men did have Aya, she would apparently be in pieces right now and the Paris police would find it amusing.

Aya, herself, would probably find it poetic justice, the vigilante done in by vigilantes.

But Eirinn didn't find it amusing or poetic. She found it barbarous. She found it debilitating. Even knowing Aya hadn't been caught, the officer's words would haunt her next several hours.

As would Aya's absence.

"So, where the bloody hell is she?"

Chapter 25

CAROLINE

1886

The ride back to Surrey was exactly the same as the ride into London. Same turns in the road. Same peaks and valleys. The same long country lane back to the gate.

But it seemed softened somehow. Scenery flying past, it blurred and it muted, allowing Caroline time to think. And no time at all. Before she knew it, the light on the steambike was catching the "Private Road" sign near the entrance of the estate and Aya was asking her to climb off the bike so she could push it the rest of the way.

"Hey. You made it." Johnny welcomed them back with a grin as he unlocked the gate, and Caroline smiled back, eyes closing like a prayer as the iron rattled and re-secured at her back.

Home. The word teased her mind again. But it didn't scare or mock her as it had before. It simply floated, like a dream, in the vastness of her mind, not quite real, but not entirely fantastical anymore either.

"Do you need me to roll you there too?" Aya did mock her. Of course, she did. What other pastime had she? But even that felt different than it did before. There was a certain gentleness to it, almost affectionate. Had it always been there? Caroline wondered now.

All the way to the house, she wondered, thoughts and questions bounding through her brain. As they had on the ride back. But she couldn't give voice to a single one until Aya told her she could go ahead inside while she put the steambike away, and she felt the opportunity slipping away.

"Do you think all fortunes are made through nefarious means?" she asked, watching Aya's eyes dart to the darkened windows, worried she wouldn't make it inside before Dr. Todson woke. But, still, she turned to Caroline, toeing the stand on the steambike down into the grass so she wouldn't have to continue to hold it up.

"I'm sure there are the odd few with wealth who have done no harm. Eir's father built their world from scratch. Eir's mother... well, her family history is not quite so exemplary."

"And mine?"

Aya's expression softly widened.

"Oh, come on now. South Kensington," Caroline said. "You were intrigued when I said I was from there. It's because it's wealthy, isn't it? You know I come from money. Are you telling me you haven't looked into how my family made it?"

Small smirk appearing on her face, Aya gave the slightest hint of admission, maybe even of being impressed by Caroline's skills for deduction. But any pleasure she felt faded quickly as she looked off toward the gardens.

"Your family got rich off of sugarcane in the islands. Do you think they did that work with their own hands?"

Much what Caroline expected, she still suffered it like a slap. It wasn't what her father did, not as his daily profession, but her father didn't do much of anything other than make investments. He had been born into wealth, just as she was. And the profits from those plantations still poured in, swelling the family coffers, no longer reaped through slave labor, but ever standing on its legacy.

"Why didn't you just tell me that?" Trying to meet Aya's gaze, she found she scarcely could. And wasn't that exactly what Aya wanted? For her to be humbled? "You had all the ammunition you needed to repudiate me right here. Why the theatrics? Why drag me off to London, make me trudge about the dockyards, climb a scaffold?"

"Are you saying you didn't have a good time?" Aya asked, and Caroline groaned. Annoyed. Or she wanted to be annoyed. She was less annoyed than expected. "I have no intention of repudiating you. Whatever wealth your family has, wherever it comes from, it wasn't your doing."

Caroline was surprised, frankly, Aya would make such a distinction. "Yes, but I've benefitted from it."

"Have you?" Aya held her gaze through the dark night, and, rain falling in a light mist between them, Caroline had no answer to that. She had spent her entire life in beautiful homes, never wanting for a single material comfort. But to what end? She had been dropped at an institution. Her sister was dead.

"Is that why you did this? Because you feel sorry for me?"

"No," Aya assured her with a rather convincing laugh. "You've gotten some bad breaks. I won't pretend I don't know that. But it doesn't give you the right to take it out on others."

Accepting her scolding with a nod, Caroline was glad for it in a way. Glad Aya was still angry with her. It was better than her pity.

"Thank you," she said, somewhat surprising herself. But Aya looked downright stunned, near fascinated as to what she might have done to garner anything resembling civility out of Caroline. "I know you didn't have to tell me this. That you have no reason to trust me."

"You're a woman in an institution, Caroline. Who's going to believe you?"

The soft turn of Aya's lips a moment later took some of the cruelty out of her words, and Caroline breathed a laugh, weak and delicate, but a laugh all the same.

"How do I make amends with her? Dr. Todson? Eirinn?" It sounded wrong. Disrespectful. Like referring to her parents by their first names. Or to a goddess without reverence.

"You don't," Aya uttered, and it was everything Caroline feared. That there could be no going back. No undoing. There was no penance strong enough for her sins. "You don't have to. Eir forgave you before you even walked out the door. I told you, she isn't like us."

"And when you say she isn't like us?"

Small grin flickering onto Aya's face, it spread like a wolf's in the fading light of the moon. "Well, she swears to me that she is of this Earth, but you did feel compelled to ask."

Kicking the stand on the steambike up, Aya rolled it off toward the barn, and Caroline stood for a moment watching her disappear around the side of the house before her eyes rose to the middle floor windows. All dark, as expected. Sunrise looming, it had yet to come, and she let the twilight carry her inside, warmth washing through her the instant she was through the front door.

Up the stairs to the first level, Caroline was too tired to think. Too tired to rationalize or overrule her own feelings. Door to her room ajar as she left it, she walked past it, stopping at the door to Lei's room, knocking at a volume she hoped was loud enough to rouse Lei, but quiet enough not to bother the women who slept in the rooms on either side of her.

"Caroline." Lei answered more readily than expected. As if she had just been waiting up for her. Or too worried to sleep. Maybe both. "What's wrong? Are you all right?"

Just seeing her, hearing her, the obvious concern in Lei's voice, Caroline breathed easier. Let all of the fear that Lei might hate her warp into the certainty she didn't. Let the anger at Lei and Dr. Todson, and what felt like betrayal, warp into what it truly was - hurt.

"What are you wearing? Are those Rand's clothes?" Lei asked her.

"I know you're a good person." Caroline heard the question, but she had only one concern at the moment. Lei. How she might have made Lei feel. It didn't matter whose clothes she was wearing, how cold and wet she was, or that it was the middle of the night. "A better person than me. I know it doesn't matter what I think, but I want you to know that. And I'm sorry. I take laudanum. I used to take laudanum. All the time. When I didn't feel well. When I did feel well. So I didn't even know how I felt anymore."

Now - now, Caroline felt too much. Numbed or overwhelmed, she never seemed capable of finding even.

"I have bizarre thoughts and terrible mood swings, and a host of strange, unpredictable physical ailments. I don't know anything." That was the point, she realized, in all of this verbal spewage. That she was no moral authority. How could she be when she was such a mess herself? "I am so tired of trying to know things."

Lei went slack against the doorframe, looking instantly depleted. As depleted as Caroline felt. As sad and as uncertain. And so, so beautiful, it almost hurt. "It's all right," she murmured. "You don't have to know anything."

Sobbing, Caroline smiled, unable to decide how to feel. A state not at all improved as Lei took a step off the doorframe, arms sliding around her waist, adding at least half a dozen colors to her already overflowing and messy palette.

"May I sleep in here?"

The question gave Lei pause.

Pulling away from her, there was an instant when she just looked at Caroline, eyes close and pensive - an instant in which Caroline wondered what would happen if she leaned the few inches forward to touch Lei's lips with her own - before at last Lei nodded, moving out of the doorway to let her inside.

Chapter 26

EIRINN

1872

Eirinn slept and she didn't sleep. Mind racing, but body lethargic, she fell into a fitful half-state, the terrors from her mind entering the real domain of her bedroom so specters hovered all around her, brushing her legs with their empty, icy touches, whispering horrors.

Somewhere, in her dream, a door opened, echoing both inside and outside her head. A hollow thud, a rustle of fabric, and she could almost recognize the sounds. They were the same ones Rand always made when he came in late in the night.

Jolting to semi-awareness, Eirinn didn't know if she was awake or sleepwalking as she tripped over her house shoes and padded barefoot across the floor.

It was only outside her bedroom door that she found some sense of place and normalcy. Rand awake too, he stumbled out of his room in his undershirt and drawers, tousled with sleep. Realizing he would only be awake if the noise she had heard had been real, Eirinn yanked open the entryway door, heart skittering to a stop at the sight of the shadowy figure standing at the bottom of the stairs.

"Hey, Darlin." Face turning upward, Aya looked pale and haunting in the darkness. "Did you miss me?" She grinned.

She grinned. She. Grinned. As if nothing tragic had happened. As if it wasn't the middle of the bloody night and Eirinn hadn't been waiting all day for her to appear.

Sob catching in her throat, Eirinn rushed down the stairs, something painful underfoot sending her sideways with a whimper, equally ready to be relieved or disappointed as she reached bottom. The instant Aya's hands touched her hips, she knew for certain Aya was there, that she was real, and she fell against her, sending Aya staggering backward into the door with a thud and a groan.

But that didn't stop Aya's lips from meeting hers or Aya's arms from coming around her, pulling her impossibly close until she couldn't tell whether she was feeling Aya's heartbeat or her own.

"I'll take that as a yes." Aya smiled as they parted, but Eirinn's breath shivered, tears and fury hovering just out of sight. How dare she walk back through her door so calm? So unrepentant?

"Where have you been? Do you have any idea how..." Terrified. Anguished. Despondent. "Worried I have been?"

No. Aya had no idea. It was clear from the wide-eyed, slack-jawed expression on her face, shock laced with guilt that melded into something that looked obnoxiously like satisfaction. "I mean, I did hope, but I didn't know it would manifest in such a physical way. You know, there are other means of relieving the tension."

Yanking her hands away from Aya, Eirinn clenched them into fists and crossed her arms, jaw and throat tight, tears pricking the corners of her eyes as she looked to the dark wall.

"Hey." Aya's hands came gingerly to her, rubbing slowly up and down her arms. "I'm sorry. I had to make sure no one was following me before I came back here. I couldn't risk leading anyone to you."

Hearing Aya say it, Eirinn realized she already knew. She knew the only reason Aya wouldn't have come back to the flat was in order to protect them. She also knew Aya would never come back if she thought that was what it would take to protect them. After her concerns for Aya's safety, it was what had terrified her the most. That Aya would make such a decision on her own. That she would just go, disappear from her life as if she had never been there at all.

That she would forever be waiting for Aya's return.

"I'm not used to anyone caring whether I make it back or not."

Words excruciating to hear, the tears flecked Eirinn's cheeks as she looked back to Aya. How could that possibly be Aya's reality? She had yet to figure it out. Aya was so much of everything, so smart, so funny, so impossible not to desire. How could no one else be waiting for her?

"But it's all right." Seizing her hand, Aya pulled it to her lips, pressing a warm, lingering kiss against her knuckles. And, even that enough to weaken her, Eirinn worried Aya might have too much power, that she was *too much* of everything. How was she supposed to survive her? "I have learned my lesson. I'm a hermit from now on. This is my world now. I live inside these four walls. They are my hovel and my sanctuary. I shall never be seen in public again."

If only it was that simple. Fear and dread swirling through the stairwell, Eirinn reached for Aya's shirt again, head coming to rest against one strong shoulder. Even with Aya there, safe and whole before her, nothing was resolved. The specters from her dreams had come to torment her for a reason. They weren't all just delusions.

"What?" Aya urged her head up, and it should have been comfort, the gentle touch against her chin. But it only reminded Eirinn how much she had to lose.

"The police came here," she said, watching the reality sink in on Aya's face.

"When?" Aya asked.

"This afternoon."

Which proved Aya had been right not to come back there. Not straight away. What would have happened if she had been there when the police came? Would they have found Aya hiding? In the wardrobe or under the bed? Would they have dragged her off to gaol?

Would Aya have even been willing to hide? Somehow, Eirinn doubted that. More likely, Aya would have climbed out a window and tried to escape down the side of the building, vanishing just as she had in the marketplace or falling to further pain and injury.

"How did they know to come here?" Aya wondered.

"People saw us together. I go to that market every week. They know I live in the neighborhood. It was only a matter of time before they knocked on the right door."

Nodding, Aya accepted the sense in that. The weight of their problem. Without comment, but with plenty of silent introspection. Watching her stew in her thoughts, Eirinn had never so much wanted to crawl inside someone else's mind.

"Then, I guess I'll have to go."

"What? No!"

"Eir, I can't stay here. It's too dangerous. For me, for you, and for Rand."

Fear stealing her breath, tears rising to strangle her, Eirinn clutched at Aya's clothes to hold her in place. She couldn't argue the point. Aya staying there *was* dangerous. For all of them, but especially for Rand. These men - the police and the banker - were absolutely convinced a man had to be involved in Aya's crimes. If they found Aya at the flat, Rand would be such an easy, convenient target for them. How could Eirinn let that happen? How could she put Rand at risk to keep Aya in Paris with her? Would it matter if she insisted Rand couldn't possibly have been involved, that they were always together? She was, after all, just a woman, unreliable in the eyes of the court, and, in this particular instance, actually lying.

"How long until you finish your studies?"

"What?" Eirinn husked.

206

"I'll go to... Strasbourg. I've always thought it lovely, and no one knows me there. Then, once you have your license, you can come and find me."

"No." Hearing Aya's solution, it was instinct for Eirinn to dissent, to sob and cling tighter to her. Just that morning, she had been wondering whether they could do this, if they would want to do this, build some sort of life together. It hadn't occurred to her they might not have the choice.

"Please... please, don't cry." Aya's plea would have been far more effective if tears weren't falling from her own eyes. If she didn't look so mournful, so utterly filled with regret. "It can't be that long."

Any length of time was too long, Eirinn realized in that instant. Neither of them knew what tomorrow might bring, what would happen in the next weeks or months or years. One of them might get sick or hurt. One of them might die, and, if that happened, she didn't want to be in Paris with Aya in Strasbourg. "I don't want that."

"Well, I don't *want* it," Aya said.

"No. I mean, I refuse it." Eirinn found her footing, her fortitude, and it surprised Aya. Her vehemence. Her absolute, unflinching conviction on the subject. As certain as Aya was that she would have to leave to protect them, Eirinn was equally certain that was unacceptable to her. "I am not staying here without you."

"Eir, I cannot stay here."

"Yes, I know."

Aya looked confused. Adrift. As if she was searching for a lamp in a dark room. Then, the light flicked on, casting the walls in the starkest of light. "What about your license?"

"I don't care about that."

"Yes, you do. You must. This is your dream."

Is it? Eirinn questioned herself. To stay in Paris? To get her medical license? It had been just days before. Was it still?

"Dreams change." Reaching out, she traced the contours of Aya's face, and after everything - every line followed in a textbook, every person they had helped restore to health - touching Aya felt like the most essential thing her hands had ever done.

"I'm afraid you'll come to regret this decision," Aya uttered.

"Are you planning to make me?"

"No."

"Will you?" Eirinn asked her. Aya was, after all, the one who had lived the bigger life, who had traveled the world and did things others only fantasized and wrote about. Eirinn was only in Paris because she couldn't get what she wanted in England.

"You must be madness personified if you think that's even possible," Aya said. "I always did believe in angels. I never thought I would meet one."

"I'm not an angel."

"Are you sure?"

Arms tightening around her, Eirinn sank, surrendered, into the safe circle of Aya's embrace, wondering what either of them was thinking. Were they really going to do this? There was some commitment to this moment. They could always undo it, somewhere down the road, if it proved a reckless decision based on impulse and necessity, but for now... for now they were choosing each other. Over everything else.

"You wouldn't think that if you knew how much I wanted to slap that grin off your face when you first got here."

Head tossed back, the sweet, rich sound of Aya's laughter vibrated the weak light and shadows against her throat. "I wouldn't have cared. When you run to me, I don't care if you slap me or kiss me or curse me. Just as long as you always run to me."

Winding her arms around Aya's neck, Eirinn pulled Aya's lips to hers, and she knew she always would.

Incorrigible

Chapter 27

CAROLINE

1886

The road to redemption was paved with small acts of kindness. At least, that was what Caroline kept telling herself over the next several days, because small acts were all she had the means at the moment to do.

She couldn't buy Lei and her new friends gifts or take them out for fancy tea dates. She couldn't even invite them over for tea in her own home. But she could take a load of books off their hands and carry them through the halls or jump to clean a spill they had made at the table.

"We forgive you, Kid," Francie felt the need to state plainly one night - more of a bark really - when Caroline rushed to retrieve the tumbler she inadvertently flung from her hand while emphasizing a point in her story. "You like us. We like you. We've kissed and made up. Stop acting like you work for us. It's gettin' weird."

"Sorry." Caroline rose from the puddle of whiskey and small pebbles of broken glass that had chipped off the tumbler's edge with flushed cheeks and renewed embarrassment.

"I mean, you can finish gettin' that one for me."

"Do not, Caroline." Stella pointed a firm finger to hold her in place. "Clean up your own mess, you drunken louse."

"Ah. You drink the stuff too, you bloomin' hypocrite."

"Yeah. But I don't drink myself stupid. Admittedly, I have a considerably longer way to go."

"What'd you say?" Francie teetered as she stood.

"Nothin'," Stella said.

"I got it. I got it." Francie forgot all about the insult as she waved Caroline out of her way.

"Watch the glass." But, still, Caroline stayed close, worried Francie would topple herself right into the fire when she bent to retrieve her mess.

Otherwise, that was the end of it. Caroline's friends forgave her for putting unkind names to them, if they had ever held it against her at all, and things went back to the way they were before their unfortunate encounter in the map room.

"Caroline. Could I have a word?"

Except for her standing with Dr. Todson. In Caroline's own estimation, that was. Aya had said she needn't do anything to make the matter right, and, by all outward appearances, that was true. Dr. Todson's behavior toward her hadn't changed in the least. She was just as munificent. Just as warm and as gracious. But penance wasn't for the wronged, it was for the wronger, and for days Caroline dwelled upon it, what small act she might do that would put her square with Dr. Todson when Dr. Todson owned everything she saw and could touch. One couldn't pick flowers from another woman's garden and present them to her as offering, could she?

"Yes, of course."

Before Caroline could come up with the answer to that, Dr. Todson came to her. It was just after dinner, at the time Dr. Todson usually made her rounds to say goodnight before retiring up the stairs. Sometimes with Aya. Sometimes on her own. To bathe or to read from the stack of books next to her bed. That was how Caroline always envisioned her, tucked in, readers perched at the end of her nose, book open in her lap.

Following Dr. Todson across the grand hall, Caroline glanced back, relieved to find Lei had lingered inside the door. To say she was nervous about talking to Dr. Todson was a felony understatement, but she did feel less so with Lei in the room.

"How are you?" First question Dr. Todson asked her, it was so simple, so genuine in its concern, Caroline nearly burst into tears right then. She just wanted to do her penance, to be allowed to atone for what she had done. Why was everyone being so preemptively kind?

"I'm fine," she uttered.

"Are you?"

Have you taken any more laudanum, Caroline? Are you a chaotic mess again? Should we be tying you up and talking you down?

Hearing the words not spoken, Caroline dropped her gaze to the floor, noticing a small, black scuff on the toe of Dr. Todson's otherwise pristine cream-colored lace-up boot, and felt the extraordinary urge to fall to her knees and spit-shine it back to perfection. "Yes. I'm doing much better. Thank you."

"Good," Dr. Todson murmured, her tone so gentle it was almost punishment in itself. "I've received a telegram... from Thomas."

Declaration enough to snap her head up, Caroline instantly lost focus. Solidity. Back and shoulders dissolving, her head felt as if it bobbled on her neck.

"It arrived this morning. Mr. Poke collected it on his trip into town." *A telegram? From Thomas? Why? Why now?*

"Are you all right?" Dr. Todson's voice sounded muted. Standing immediately before Caroline, she blurred. Lost her shape. Along with the outlines in the paisley wallpaper behind her. If Caroline put her hand out, she was certain it would go right through both. "Caroline?"

"Mm," Caroline shortly hummed, all she could manage for several baffled seconds as she endeavored to compile her fragmented thoughts. "What did it say?"

"He's coming for a visit," Dr. Todson said, and Caroline either nodded or bobbled in response. What else would the telegram be? Unless something (else) tragic had happened, why would Thomas even write if not to, in some way, interfere? He certainly didn't miss her.

"Did he say why?"

"To see to your condition and the state of your mind. That was what he said," Dr. Todson softly stated. Without conviction. And, absently, Caroline felt the warm, wet lines that streaked her face, the rise of a sensation inside pulling every rib and muscle taut in her back and chest, clamping around her windpipe.

Yet, somehow, she wasn't quite there to feel it at all.

"Caroline." Dr. Todson's hands came to her arms, sturdy, if imaginary, and, salt on her lips, Caroline recognized the choking sensation she felt as fear. Was Thomas coming to retrieve her? To take her back? As quickly as her life changed, would it change again? Would she soon be back in the house in South Kensington? *Her house.* In a life she hardly lived? *Her life.*

Remember how you wanted that, Caroline? her own mind mocked. *Not even weeks ago? You wanted your world back. What little there was of it. Congratulations, you're a prophet.*

"Let's just take it one step at a time, all right?" Dr. Todson tried to hearten her, to give her strength, and, on top of everything, it was just too much. The proverbial last straw. Playing the role of the camel's back, Caroline broke, guilt rising up in heaving gasps she couldn't swallow back down.

"I'm sorry. About everything. About what I said to you."

"I know." Dr. Todson's hand moved from where it grasped her arm to touch her cheek, and Caroline wept harder. "It will be all right. It will." Dr. Todson hugged her then, but that only started the tears anew and it was minutes before Caroline could get herself even somewhat under control. "Are you going to be all right?"

Caroline was going to be scared. Until Thomas came, she was going to be worried and restless and crawl inside her skin. She already felt her nerves beginning to vibrate, recognizing the threat.

"Yes." Remembering Lei waiting inside the door, she glanced back, watching Lei come to slightly more attention, seeing the concern on her face, and knew, at least, she didn't have to be alone.

"Are you sure?"

"Yes." It gave Caroline some strength. Though, her knees still wobbled and she felt decidedly faint. "I'll be all right."

"All right. Well, if you need me, you know where I'll be." Dr. Todson glanced to Lei too, waiting for her to make it across the room to them before she let Caroline go. "Try to get some sleep, all right?"

"I will," Caroline promised.

"Goodnight."

"Goodnight," Lei said, and Dr. Todson left them, carried across the hall on a series of steady, muted thuds. "What happened?"

Without pause, Caroline burrowed into Lei, feeling Lei's arms close instantly around her. And, while it couldn't stop what was coming, couldn't make it any less fearful or worrisome, it did make it infinitely easier to bear.

Chapter 28

EIRINN

1872

Eirinn had never been nervous to come home. She had never had cause to be. She still didn't, she knew - well, part of her knew - as she let herself through the front door, reaching back to encourage Aya inside when Aya seemed reluctant to follow.

"Eir!" Happening through the front hall, Bally threw the objects she carried into a juggle as she saw them, fumbling for a moment before dropping everything onto the bench of the hall tree to rush Eirinn's way. "Why didn't you tell us you were coming home?" she asked as she gathered Eirinn into an almost ferocious embrace. "My goodness. We don't have a thing ready for you. I don't even know what we have in the kitchen."

"It was a spur of the moment decision. We would have practically been here by the time a telegram made it to you."

Not entirely true. After they fled Paris, they spent several nights on the coast of Calais before boarding the ferry on to Dover. Eirinn had more than enough time to send word of their impending arrival, had she so chosen, but she didn't want to give anyone in London too much time to deliberate, to wonder why she was coming home, or to formulate too many questions.

Are we going to pretend to be friends? Aya had asked one morning as they linger in bed, staring out the window that overlooked the sea. *Just a couple of gals being pals? It's all right with me, as long as you also say I have sleeping fits and can't sleep alone.*

No. I would never ask you to do that. Eirinn wouldn't. She would never ask Aya to live a lie for her, or even a diluted version of the truth. But it wasn't just Aya she was thinking of when she made her declaration. She didn't want to live under such an onus herself. If she couldn't tell her parents about Aya, who could she tell?

"Well, at any rate, I'm certainly glad to see you, Dear. Hello." Bally glanced to Aya in the foyer.

"Hello," Aya said in return, and, though she could scarcely conceive of it, if Eirinn were to put an emotion to the soft utterance, she would say Aya almost sounded nervous.

"Bally, this is Aya. Aya, this is Mrs. Ballentine, Rand's mother."

"Ah, yes. I can certainly see the resemblance." In an instant, Aya's natural charm found its way. "It's nice to meet you, Mrs. Ballentine."

"Oh. Call me Bally, Dear." Bally clasped Aya's hand between her own, which was as good as an endorsement, even as she glanced past her toward the door. "Rand's not with you?"

"He went around back. I think he meant to surprise you," Eirinn said.

If she had one regret in any of this, it was that - cutting short Rand's time in Paris. She had told him he could stay, that she would sort it with her parents and Bally. Rand could find work in Paris. He could keep the flat. He had worked so hard over the past few years, he had the means to start a fresh life wherever he wanted.

I'll just get into trouble on my own, he uttered when Eirinn mentioned it. *I should probably get to packing.*

Eirinn didn't know if Rand actually believed that, if he was scared, or if he just preferred to be where he had family around him, but she still felt the brush of guilt, knowing he wasn't done with Paris when they left it.

"Well, I'll just go and let him," Bally said. "Your mama is upstairs in her bed."

"Is she all right?" Eirinn instantly worried.

"Not feeling very well today, I'm afraid. But she's been resting for hours. I'm certain she's doing much better by now. If you'll excuse me." With one last squeeze to her arm, Bally gathered the items she'd dropped on the hall tree and went off in search of her son, and Eirinn turned to Aya, watching her dark eyes move about the foyer, the heavy inhalation that expanded her chest, the uneasy exhalation that pushed it past her lips.

At least she was breathing.

"Are you all right?"

"Me?" Aya broke out her million-pound grin. "Of course. Never better."

Anyone else might have believed her. Just days ago, Eirinn might have believed Aya, she sold the lie so well.

"We're going to be fine." Reaching out, she brushed a wayward hair off of Aya's cheek, hoping she conveyed exactly what she meant. *They* would be fine. Whatever happened, the commitment she had made to Aya in the stairwell in Paris was just that - a commitment. It could not be torn asunder by legal statutes, fire-and-brimstone, or disapproving parents. And if her parents disapproved, well... Eirinn weakened a little at the unlikely but still possible possibility, then they wouldn't be who she thought them to be anyway.

"Eir."

Eirinn would have waited another minute, or several, given Aya more time to adjust to the situation, if it wasn't for her name softly called from the top of the stairs. Turning around, she saw Mama standing on the landing, dressed in her usual day dress and smiling down at them.

"Mama." Her own nerves pulsing, she smiled back, moving around the curved banister and up the stairs as Mama padded softly down them.

"What are you doing here?" Mama asked her, pleased, but surprised.

"It's a bit of a long story," Eirinn answered as she met her somewhere in the middle, and Mama hugged her one-armed, other hand clinging to the railing to make sure they didn't both go toppling down the stairs. "How are you feeling?"

"Oh, I'm fine, Sweetheart. I'm fine." Pulling away from her, a trace of delight, almost amazement, lit Mama's face. "My. Paris must have agreed with you. You look positively radiant." Then, as if putting the two things together, she glanced over the railing to Aya. "Hello."

"Hello." Aya practically gulped in return.

"Mama, this is Aya, my..." She had every intention of easing into it. Not outright lying, but downplaying, temporarily, her relationship with Aya. Just until she had the chance to sit down with her parents and talk to them first. But watching Aya stand there, proud, confident, but clearly anxious, in her home, her parents' home, the home she grew up in, walking its halls, dreaming of a future that seemed and felt impossible, she couldn't. She couldn't obscure what Aya truly meant to her. What Aya was to her. Not even temporarily. Not even until her mother was no longer standing on stairs. "My love."

Flash of surprise flaring Aya's features, it melted into a hesitant smile as Aya held her gaze, and Eirinn knew she could face anything. Endure anything. She could even look back to her own mother, who was staring at her with a sort of dazed comprehension, as if her mind understood the words just fine, but the rest of her would take a moment to catch up.

"Well..." Lifting a hand to Eirinn's shoulder, Mama gave it a light squeeze as she moved her out of the way, and Eirinn gripped tightly to the railing to keep from losing her footing as she whirled to watch her descend the stairs.

"Aya." Mama walked right up to her, looking Aya up and down with absolutely no discretion at all. "It seems you and I have A LOT of catching up to do. Let's get some tea, shall we?" Arm thread through Aya's, she turned to guide her from the foyer. "You can come too, if you'd like," she called on their way out, and, not sure until then whether or not she was invited, Eirinn tripped her way back down the stairs to follow.

Chapter 29

CAROLINE

1886

Hands trembling, Caroline brushed the skirt of her mended dress, gaze moving over the smooth plait of her hair and the rest of herself in the mirror. Outwardly, she looked the same, same clothes, same face, as when she came. All except her eyes. They were brighter, more aware, and saw both the good and bad in her reflection.

Her body was thicker here, in Surrey, skin less sallow, a combination of fresh air and less frequent bouts with pain. But when had she gotten all of those lines that were etched into her face?

She was old, Caroline accepted with a sigh. Much too old to be scared of her own husband.

"Are you ready?" Dr. Todson was waiting in the hall when she stepped outside her door, and, though she wasn't, wasn't sure she would ever be, Caroline made the effort to pretend. "Rand's already gotten Thomas settled in the reception room. They're just waiting for you. I'll be in the library when you're finished."

"All right." Caroline nodded, grateful for Dr. Todson's presence there. She had told Dr. Todson she didn't need her, that she would be just fine on her own - she was certain Dr. Todson had more important things she could be doing - but it was a lie, Dr. Todson knew it was a lie, and Caroline might have been grateful for Dr. Todson's ability to see right through her most of all.

"It will be all right."

Lei had offered to be there with her too. To stand by Caroline's side and hold her hand. She had even offered to walk her down the stairs, to wait in the parlor or a reading room on the first floor instead of going back down to the workshop. But Caroline didn't think she could endure that. Lei. She had no idea what Thomas was coming to the house to say, but it felt prudent to remain as dispassionate as possible. As stoic. Until she couldn't anymore. Lei would be highly deleterious to that end.

"Don't worry, Caroline."

Even Dr. Todson was challenging her efforts at stoicism, prodding her desire to run and hide or to fall into her arms and weep. So, with one last curt nod, Caroline turned and moved for the stairs, hoping, at some point, her resentment would take tighter hold and help to ease the dread.

"Caroline. There you are," Rand said at her entrance, standing to welcome her into the reception room. The room in which she last saw Thomas. The room where she went bestial on him and clawed at his face.

But Thomas looked the same too. Marks healed, he wore the same suit he was wearing the day he dropped her off, and it was impossible for Caroline not to entertain the notion she had imagined everything. That she hadn't spent weeks, but mere minutes, in this house. That it had all been some feverish hallucination. It would almost make more sense.

"Caroline." It was only Thomas's shock that assured her time had, in fact, gone by. Only she who was obviously, markedly different.

"Hello, Thomas," she said.

"You look... very well."

"Isn't that why you brought me here? To get well?"

Flummoxed, Thomas nodded. What else was he to do? It wasn't what he expected, for her to look better - healthier - than she had when she came to this house, but he could hardly say it wasn't what he expected. He couldn't say he was looking forward to her coming out in a dirty frock with stringy hair and ashen skin. Bruises, perhaps. Rips to her clothing and terror in her eyes.

"I'll be right outside." Rand, in his false role as doctor, looked very much like he would like to give Caroline a hug, or her hand a fortifying squeeze, as he left her alone with her husband, pulling the door closed behind him, and Caroline sat in one of the armchairs like a civilized person as Thomas looked her over repeatedly. Searching for signs of what exactly? she wondered.

"How's Oliver?" Him so distracted, it would be up to her, apparently, to commence the conversation.

"Fine," Thomas vaguely answered as he at last found his way to a chair.

"Is he?" Caroline pressed.

"Yes, he's fine."

"He'd better be." There, in his presence, Thomas so full of shock and confusion, Caroline discovered she wasn't that scared of him after all. She was more annoyed, really, by his face. The familiar blandness of it. The lack of visible scarring. Thomas wanted her out of his way, and she was out of his way. The least he could do her was the courtesy of leaving her alone. "Why are you here?"

"Well, I see they haven't corrected your brashness any." Beyond his shock, Thomas fell into familiarity too. "But even still, you'll be happy to know I've come to bring you home."

Panic gripping her, instant and icy cold, Caroline fought not to shudder. To tremble. To react too much at all. But react she did. On the inside. Heart quivering, lungs constricting, she struggled to draw even half a breath.

"That's quite the change of heart." Tucking her hands beneath the edges of her skirt, she pressed her nails into her palms to redirect the torment and managed to sound almost casual.

"It was never my intention to lock you away permanently, Caroline. I just wanted you to get the help you so desperately need. I think we understand each other better now." Thomas stood. Reaching into his inside jacket pocket, he unfolded several pages, producing them to Caroline with a pen. "I need you to sign this."

I've come to bring you home? More like, *I've come to extort you.* It took Caroline no more than two lines of the document to huff a laugh, not even in disbelief, expecting nothing more or less of him.

"You want me to sign the house over to you."

"I think it best the only real property we own be under the control of someone in his right mind, don't you?" Thomas asked, and the fuse caught, Caroline's anger sparking instantly to life.

So, that was what this was about. Money. Always money with him. She had almost convinced herself it was the other thing this time, the thing he might know she knew and could one day blurt out in polite company. No one would believe her, of course, not crazy Caroline Ajax - *Oh, her poor, handsome, long-suffering husband* - but she might sow just enough doubt in their minds to turn their knee-jerk sympathy for Thomas into knee-jerk mistrust.

"Why? What does it matter? I'm in here. I can't do anything with the house."

"That's the point, Caroline. In here, you can't, but out there you can. Do you want to come home or not?" Growing quickly frustrated, Thomas paced the floor. As he always did when they fought. Or, rather, when he took issue with something she did. Caroline cared so little about their arguments, she rarely had a word to say back. Most of the time, she just wished for him to stop talking.

"Has my father stopped my allowance?"

"No."

"So, you should be sorted financially. Why do you need the house?"

From his resounding huff and the way he raised his hand to scrub at the stubble on his chin, it was clear Thomas hadn't thought this far ahead. Hadn't expected any pushback from her. Her freedom on the line, he thought Caroline would sign any paper he put in front of her. Immediately. Gratefully. And it might have worked, were she in Hell.

"What have you done, Thomas?

Gambled with the wrong men and lost. That was the nature of it. That was always the nature of Thomas's poor decision-making. Money. Money, money, money. Greed was his deadly vice. No legitimate lender willing to give a man with a terrible track record who was dependent on his wife's marital portion a loan, he turned to illegitimate sources, men who would front him the quid at steep interest rates with his life as collateral.

This wasn't the first time Thomas had backed himself into a dingy back alley since they'd been married, and, in the past, Caroline always felt obliged to help him. He had never been an ideal husband, or a halfway decent one for that matter, but there was no denying he had become a worse man the longer they stayed married. Caroline always felt some guilt over the fact, some responsibility for Thomas's dwindling judgment. She had *been made to* feel guilty and responsible for the choices Thomas made. As he was forced to put up with her defects, she was forced to put up with his.

But she had always wondered what would happen if she didn't help Thomas, if she didn't go begging her father for money on Thomas's behalf, and let those thug lenders come and take their due instead. If Thomas was in trouble - and it was quite apparent he was - with no other means to repay them, she supposed she was going to find out.

"If you need money, just ask my father for a loan. That's what I always did."

Tick in his jaw growing more pronounced, Thomas glanced away, and Caroline was surprised by the satisfaction she felt as the realization struck her.

"You did. He said 'no' to you. Huh. I guess he doesn't trust you. Gee, I wonder why."

"If your family had just been honest with me from the start -"

"About what?" Caroline asked him.

"You know what."

Yes, indeed. Caroline did know. "Me, you mean? I was a twenty-four-year-old heiress with no other interested suitors. How much more obvious could we have been?"

"No one mentioned you were perpetually ill and probably barren."

"Would it have mattered if they did? I would have looked just as appealing to you with the giant pound symbol next to my name."

Thomas swooping on her like a bird of prey, Caroline recoiled as he grabbed the arms of her chair. For an instant, she *was* scared of him. Again. As scared as she would have been back in London. Knowing what he had done, what he had the inhumanity to do, she had good reason to fear him, and she might have seen her life flash before her like the scenes on a zoetrope. In some small way, she still did. She saw Sarah. Oliver. Lei.

Then, she remembered where she was, and when she remembered where she was, she remembered the house and everyone in it was on her side. Rand was just outside the door. Dr. Todson waited for her in the library. Lei was downstairs in her workshop. This wasn't the world Thomas came from. There was no neutrality or blind eyes for him here. They might act the part when necessary, but, one scream, and Caroline was certain Rand would come bursting through that door with a veritable army at his disposal.

Even Aya would fight for her before she would let Thomas hurt her, Caroline felt without doubt, and it gave her power, realizing even her worst enemy at Dr. Todson's would be more willing to stand up for her than her best friends back in London.

It also didn't hurt that, up close, she could see Thomas did carry some scars from their last encounter, small white indentations where her claws had left marks in his cheeks. Holding the deed between them, she waited for him to take it back. "Would you prefer I tear it up?" she asked when he didn't, and, fury warping his face, Thomas ripped the deed out of her hand and took a step away, sweat pouring from his hairline as if they had been in a physical altercation.

"Don't make me do something I don't want to have to do."

"Like what? Poison me with arsenic?"

Like a mouse caught in a sudden sweep of light, Thomas froze, contemplating what to do next. Before a slow, heinous smile came to his lips. "You're mad, Caroline. You don't even know what you're saying anymore." Slipping the deed back into his pocket, he passed his hands over his hair, smoothing it neatly back into place. "Maybe you're too comfortable here. Maybe if you are someplace less... accommodating... you'll have a change of heart."

So much for strength. So much for power. Threat sinking in, Caroline's entire body went liquid until she was certain she was going to cascade right off the chair and onto the floor. Because he could do it. Just as he put her in there, Thomas could take her out. Whenever he wanted. At his whim. And put her wherever he wanted her next.

"I've sent Oliver to Eton." Not content with the threat alone, he lobbed one last cruelty her way. "Where he should have been all along."

"He isn't ready." Caroline felt the tears that blurred her vision drip onto her cheeks.

"He'll survive." Thomas went out the door, and *What was that?*, Caroline thought. Another threat? An admission?

"Mr. Ajax." She heard Rand stop Thomas in the hall. "Is everything all right? Would you like some tea, and we can have a follow-up conversation?"

"No tea," Thomas grunted in return. "It's supposed to rain. I want to get back on the road. But I'm not going far. I'm getting a room in the area. Letherhead, most likely. I'll be looking for a new place to move Caroline."

"A new place? Sir, I don't understand. I assure you, your wife is getting the finest possible care here."

"I want her closer to London."

Bedlam. Thomas wanted her in Bedlam. Or somewhere like it. He wanted her tortured in a socially and morally acceptable way until she did as he asked. And he had all the authority he needed to do it because a younger, stupider Caroline once said "I do" to some semblance of a normal life.

"Are you sure you don't have a moment we could talk?"

"No. I told you I want to get on the road."

The conversation moving away from her, down the hall and toward the front door, Caroline sunk in on herself. Into the chair. Through it. She was almost on the floor when Rand came back to the room.

"Caroline? Are you all right?"

In that moment, Caroline didn't have the thoughts she would have expected to have. To run. To escape before Thomas could come back. Or she did, but they were weak and fleeting. Ideas for later contemplation. Faced with her imminent expulsion, only one thing proved immediate, one need absolutely essential.

"Caroline!"

Ignoring Rand's call, she rushed from the reception room and down the ground floor hall, pulling open the door to the basement and stumbling blindly down the stairs.

"Caroline! You know you shouldn't come in here without..." Lei started to scold as she burst through the workshop door. Before she saw Caroline's face. And recalled where Caroline had been. And her bigger worry superseded her immediate one. "Are you all right?"

No, Caroline was not all right. And she may not be tomorrow. Or the day after that. But today... today, she was still there, and Lei was there, and she watched Lei's expression warp from worry to surprise as she marched straight up to her, hands sliding onto the sides of her neck, and pulled Lei's lips to her own.

At first brush, all sorrow evaporated - all fear, all worry - the longing and awe that seized her mind, her body, leaving no space for anything else.

"Caroline." Lei pushed her softly away, but the gentle pant of Lei's breath against her lips was like a church bell tolling its invitation.

"I want you." Lei's eyes went slightly wide, showing like the heavens, dark and filled with divine secrets. And Caroline felt beyond affection. Beyond lust, or even need. She felt ravenous, a desperate, gnawing hunger unlike anything she had felt before. Unlike anything she knew she could feel. "Can we go upstairs?"

Lei's eyes going even wider, trails of stardust weaved out to wrap around Caroline, holding her together when she could so easily fall apart. "Yes, we can do that," she said.

Chapter 30

EIRINN

1872

Mama and Aya got on well. It wasn't all that much of a surprise. They had many interests in common. Art. Music. The offspring of the Todson bloodline.

Until she was sitting with the two of them at dinner, Eirinn had no idea how much it would mean to her, whether her parents took to Aya, but there was something undeniably comforting about watching the two women she loved most in the world relate with such natural ease.

"Sorry. There was a bit of a carriage mishap." It was only slightly past seven-thirty when Papa made it to the house, but, so hungry from the day's journey where the food was unappetizing and the pickings slim, Eirinn and Aya had already started in on Bally's famous cawl cennin, Eirinn's favorite comfort soup from her childhood, before he came into the dining room. "The brougham lost a..."

Spotting Eirinn sitting in her usual place at the table, absolutely not where he expected her to be, Papa's face broke into a near ecstatic grin. "What are you doing home?" He rushed to embrace her, and Eirinn stood to be embraced. "Did you know she was coming?"

"No. It was very much a surprise for us all," Mama told him.

"A good surprise. It's so good to see you, Sweetheart."

"You too, Papa," Eirinn said, and he hugged her again, just seeming to notice Aya where she waited beside her.

"Hello. I'm Simon Todson."

"Aya Kobzari."

"It's nice to meet you, Miss Kobzari. Are you a fellow student?"

"No, Papa. Aya is my -"

"Companion," Mama cut her off. "But we can talk more about that in a minute. Let's go into the kitchen and get you a bowl of soup." Rising from the table, Mama smiled at Eirinn and Aya as she took hold of Papa's arm, practically dragging him from the room, and all the good feelings Eirinn had been basking in since they arrived at the house, from Mama's immediate grace to Bally's cawl cennin, turned cold in an instant.

It wasn't like Mama. To put words into her mouth. Or to stop them from coming out of it. To lead Papa off to talk on their own. When she did, it was almost always because Eirinn had asked for something that required some discussion. Now, Eirinn didn't know what they could possibly discuss. She had asked for something, she supposed, in a roundabout way, but Aya was already there, and she wasn't going anywhere. Not without Eirinn.

Then, perhaps that *was* the discussion, Eirinn glanced to Aya, trying not to look too concerned. Too unsure. But she was unsure. Beyond unsure. The thoughts being exchanged on the other side of the door were a source of rapidly creeping anxiety. They crawled up her legs and stole her strength.

What are they saying? It occurred to her she didn't have to just stand there in clueless worry, and she went to the kitchen door, pushing just enough that she could hear through the infinitesimal crack without the door looking open from the other side. She had lived in this house long enough, and had always been curious enough, that she knew just how far she could push without being caught.

"...hired a companion?" Papa's voice the first thing she heard, Eirinn settled soundlessly against the doorframe. "I thought she was insistent she didn't need a lady's companion in Paris."

"Does Aya look like a lady's companion to you?" Mama asked him.

"Well... no," Papa acknowledged. "But leave it to Eir to find someone outside the registry, right? Someone as rare and unorthodox as she is."

"I'm glad you feel that way," Mama said, and Eirinn waited for it. "Because Aya is not an employee, Simon. She's Eir's companion."

Seconds ticked by in the quiet London night.

"Her partner."

More seconds.

"Her lover."

Silence. Stretching. Long and deep. So deep Eirinn could hear the scrape of the ladle against the bottom of the soup pot, even as her mind went charging off in a riotous clamor. What would she do if Papa said the wrong thing? Where would they go if he said Aya couldn't stay there? Or, worse, if he said something that made Eirinn not want to stay?

Maybe she should just go back to the table.

"Eir is in a relationship? With a woman?"

"She is in love with a woman," Mama said, and the words took even Eirinn by surprise. Because she hadn't told Mama that. She hadn't even told Aya that. It was implied, more than implied she supposed, in the fact she had abandoned Paris, her studies, every plan and known desire she had ever had to abscond back to England with her, but no one had said the words. Not until now.

Suddenly warm, Eirinn looked to the table, breath seized by Aya's ambiguous gaze, before her own gaze was drawn to the soft rhythm of Aya's thumb where it ticked against the wood.

"What is she thinking? Have you asked her?"

It was dichotomous, the words she heard and what she felt as she looked at Aya - one so full of doubt, the other so assured - and, for a second, she lost all strength, gripping the doorframe as she faded against it.

"No, of course I haven't," Mama said.

"Were you waiting for me to do it?"

"No." Mama's voice turned hard. Frigid. "You will do no such thing."

"Corinne, I know we have been lenient with her, but we cannot just allow her to -"

"Allow her?" Edge to Mama's voice sharpening, it paused Papa for a moment.

"You know what I mean," he said at last. "You must know what will happen if people find out."

"They'll have words to say, I imagine."

"They'll have more than words. Cor, this is dangerous. Has she even considered the -?"

"She's happy, Simon," Mama stated softly, so softly Eirinn almost didn't hear, and it quieted Papa again, quashed whatever argument he was about to make. For several long seconds, nothing but the slight chill breezed through the crack in the kitchen door. "She was practically glowing when she arrived here. You should have seen her."

"I do see her," Papa returned, and, swallowing, it occurred to Eirinn it *was* that obvious she was in love with Aya, at least to both of her parents, as Mama spoke again.

"Eir's entire life has been one long struggle up a hill people have repeatedly tried to push her back down. Somehow, she has always remained optimistic. She has always remained kind and caring and loving. But when have you ever seen her without a cloud of melancholy hanging over her? That's gone now. And if you will sit with her for five minutes with an open mind, you will see that."

"I'm glad that she's happy. I also want her to be safe."

"I believe she can be both," Mama declared, and Eirinn felt some strength return. Breathed back into her on the power of her mother's unwavering conviction. "Sy, we have brought up a smart, gentle, capable woman. She knows who she is. She knows what and who she wants. And

228

she knows all too well what cruelties this world can bring. She just doesn't let that stop her. You have always told her she can be whatever she wants to be. You've proven it a hundred times. Was it not true?"

"Yes, of course, it was true."

"Good," Mama said, and there was another stretch of silence in which Eirinn could picture Mama standing with her shoulders back, head slightly tilted, letting her words sink in. "Now, I'm going back out there. Make your peace with this now or make your excuses and go upstairs. We are having a lovely dinner, and I don't want it spoiled. You have been a nearly perfect husband and father. Don't let us down now."

Sound of her footsteps moving across the kitchen, Eirinn knew Mama was coming, but she didn't rush back to the table or even slink slowly away. Taking a step back, she simply waited for the door to open, and Mama paused as she came through it, taking in Eirinn's proximity and realizing what just happened. Not at all surprised to find her listening in, she slid a reassuring arm around Eirinn's waist and escorted her back to the table.

"Is everything all right?" Aya cast worried eyes toward the kitchen.

"It will be," Mama assured Aya as she sat down in her chair, and, back in her own seat, Eirinn reached for Aya's hand, squeezing it where it fidgeted against the table, thumb moving gently against Aya's skin.

"So, what did I miss?" Less than a minute later, Papa appeared, taking the seat next to Mama instead of his usual chair at the table's head, so they would be in a better arrangement for conversation.

"Aya was just telling us about the time she spent in India," Mama told him.

"India, really? Did you see the Taj Mahal?" Papa asked.

"Yes, I did," Aya said.

"And the food! My God, the food! The curries and the samosas. Fried dough filled with potatoes, if that is not the perfect food, I don't know what is. Except for maybe olliebollen." Pausing, he winked to Eirinn, and Eirinn felt the weight of uncertainty lift off her shoulders. "I'm sorry. You were talking about India. But before you get back to that, where are you from, Aya?"

Soft smile coming to her face, Mama glanced to Eirinn across the table as she reached across the space between them to rub Papa's back.

Dinner running longer than usual, with conversation occupying so much of it, Mama kept Aya in the dining room even after the meal was finished, serving her a hot toddy and telling her about her favorite works recently acquired for the museum. No doubt Mama enjoyed Aya's company and would talk her ear off about art given the slightest opportunity, Eirinn also knew it was a diversion, a chance for her to talk to Papa alone, while assuring her Aya was in gentle hands.

"Hey, Papa."

Night growing thicker inside the walls of the house, Eirinn knew just where she would find him. And Papa was there in the study waiting to be found, glass of brandy in hand before Mama had the chance to join him for her nightly tea. Of course, Papa could just be getting an early start on her. He might well help himself to two glasses tonight.

"Hey, Eir."

It occurred to Eirinn it wasn't the worst idea, and pressing the door mostly shut, she ventured to the table where the liquor bottles lined up in a row, bypassing lesser spirits to fill her snifter with the rarest cognac and turned to find Papa watching her with a trace of intrigue. And of amusement. Though, he said nothing as Eirinn came closer, sitting down in the chair where Mama usually took her tea, across from him and closest to the fire.

"How are things at the museum?" Eirinn asked.

"Good. Very good. We have a new exhibit opening next week. A retrospective of the early members of the Society of Female Artists."

"Yes. I remember Mama telling me in her last letter. I'm excited to see it."

"I take it that means you won't be returning to Paris to finish your degree."

"No." Eirinn took a substantial sip, reveling in the burn and hoping it kicked in with some alacrity. She knew she owed her parents sufficient explanation for that. They were, after all, providing the majority of the means. She could afford to pay for her own schooling, having saved most of her earnings from the clinic, but Mama and Papa insisted her education was their responsibility. As such, they had provided the flat in Paris and paid for her tuition. Now, they were financing an empty room and a lost spot in a university program they had every reason to believe she would finish. "Not right now. Certain matters arose. I can pay you back."

"Certain matters?" Papa echoed, ignoring the rest.

"Mm hm." *Aya.* They both knew Eirinn meant Aya. She was, after all, currently sitting in their dining room, charming Mama to the fullest extent of her capabilities if Mama's occasional laugh that punctuated the otherwise quiet ambiance of the house was any indication.

It was only the rest Eirinn had cause to explain. Falling in love didn't necessarily preclude her from finishing her degree. Yet, here she was, back home, with a romantic partner and no medical license of which to speak.

"I heard you with Mama at dinner tonight."

As unsurprised as Mama had been when she caught Eirinn doing it, Papa was equally unfazed, scarcely registering her admission at all. "I'm just worried."

"I know." It wasn't as if Eirinn didn't know she had given her parents good reason to worry, or that she hadn't expected them to. She was expecting worse, to be honest. Had prepared herself for every possible eventuality, from having to justify her own feelings to being estranged.

She knew her parents' belief system - thought she knew it - their capacity for compassion. For understanding. The museum wouldn't be doing nearly so well if Papa and Mama couldn't get on, to some degree, with the misfits and outcasts of society. In their own ways, Papa and Mama were outcasts themselves.

"But you don't have to worry, Papa. Not about that. I've always known what other people might do to me for choosing to follow my heart. I've gotten quite good at dodging their arrows."

Sucking in a breath, Papa held it a moment, as if afraid of letting it go, and even in the weak glow of the hearth light, Eirinn could see the tears that filled his eyes as he did. "I never wanted you to have to do that."

"Well, I think the only way to avoid it is to do what everyone else tells you to do."

"And I suppose that was too much to ask."

"I am my parents' daughter."

"Yes, you are." Small laugh breaking past his lips, Papa sniffed and flicked a tear from his cheek with his thumb. "You absolutely are. To an extraordinary degree."

As he took a shaky drink from his snifter, Eirinn matched it with one of her own. And, for the next several minutes, they sat like that, drinking their liquor in silence, each lost to their individual reflections.

Watching the flames move down a thinly curved wood fiber in the fireplace, turning it ever so slowly into ash, Eirinn wondered if she really needed to tell Papa anything else. He was already worried. She had already given him good cause to be. Was there anything to be gained by being completely honest? *Yes*, she accepted in the very next instant. *Almost always.*

"There is one more thing."

It must have been the way she said it, her diminishing volume, the tension that plucked her vocal cords, because Papa looked instantly more concerned.

"All right."

"There's a reason we came back now, that I left Paris without my degree."

"I assumed," Papa said.

"We had to leave."

"Why?"

"Because..." Now that she'd started, Eirinn knew she had to finish, but she wasn't sure how she was supposed to get the words out. Throat thickening around the burn left behind by the cognac, it felt as if she was pushing the first syllable through a mound of silt, each letter coming a little slower and more crooked than the one before. "Because... the police... were looking... for Aya."

Papa's gaze instantly darkened, grew steely and penetrating where it focused upon her. Setting his glass down on the table next to him, he slid forward in his chair, rigidity in his form making him look like a department store mannequin.

"Why?" he asked again.

"She hurt some people," Eirinn barely whispered, rushing quickly on before Papa could take the statement and make what he would of it. "People who hurt other people."

"What do you mean, she *hurt* people?" Papa demanded.

"I mean, she hurt people." Eirinn really hoped that would be enough. She really didn't think she should, or could, tell Papa about Aya's satchel full of tricks or how she had shown up stabbed and bleeding at her door.

"How did she know they had hurt other people?"

"Because she studied them. Their lives. Their pasts. She is quite adept at reading others."

Staring at her for a moment as if she had gone half-mad, or he had, as if nothing she was saying made an ounce of sense, Papa at last turned back into a functioning human, sliding back in his chair, and where moments before he looked as stiff as a dummy, he now looked abnormally floppy, like someone put a hex on his bones and left him spineless in the chair.

"Did she get paid for this... ... ... endeavor?"

"No. Not exactly," Eirinn hedged, and Papa raised an eyebrow. But he didn't ask. He didn't have to. He was a smart man, and had once been a member of the street class himself. He knew all the possible means of getting compensated for one's work.

"Is she violent?"

"No!" Eirinn was adamant. Then, realized how ludicrous she must sound. She had literally just told Papa Aya *was* violent, that she had hurt people. But as a general statement, it was impossible to brush her with such a broad-sweeping stroke. And that wasn't what Papa was asking her anyway. "Not toward me. Not ever. Aya would never hurt me. I know she wouldn't."

She wasn't sure if Papa believed that, but he did take her word on the matter, trusting Eirinn knew the woman who slept in her bed better than he did.

"Then, is there something else you're worried about?"

"No. Not really," Eirinn said. Though there was some lingering cause for concern, it was minimal. Aya had been in England before, but not for very long, and she was certain no one would recognize her there.

"Then, why are you telling me this?" Papa asked.

Wondering that herself over the past few turns in conversation, as she watched Papa's opinion of Aya warp and falter before her very eyes, Eirinn huffed a small breath realizing why it mattered to her. For Papa to know everything. To tell him the truth.

"Because I don't want to keep secrets from you. I've never had to before, and I don't want to start now."

Her voice catching, in an instant, Papa softened. Grasped how much Eirinn needed him to understand. This wasn't just a normal conversation they were having. It was a delayed conversation. Most people did this with their parents when they were sixteen, seventeen years old. At seventeen, all Eirinn had cared about was becoming a doctor. Now, she was a twenty-nine-year-old woman, but inside, at the moment, she was a teenage girl desperate for her parents' approval.

"Is Aya planning to continue this... enterprise?"

Endeavor. Enterprise. Looking for words that weren't "vigilantism," Papa was apparently trapped in the "en" section of the dictionary.

"No. Even before the police came, she was finished."

"Because of you?"

"I don't know." Eirinn had never asked Aya that. It was clear when Aya appeared at the flat in Paris she was tired of the life she had been living. Tired of the running and the anger. Tired of trying to punish men who scarcely had the capacity to feel shame or regret. But Eirinn couldn't say she wasn't the final piece of the puzzle. Aya had been for her. Why wouldn't she be the same? "Maybe."

"Did you tell your mother this?"

"No. I know her worry is different."

"Good," Papa said, clearly one trouble off his mind. "So, if Aya is no longer going to..." Waving a hand in the air, he searched for a moment, but, apparently out of "en" words, he gave up on a descriptor entirely. "What exactly is she planning to do here?"

So, Papa wanted to know about Aya's prospects. Small grin curving her lips, Eirinn assumed that was a good sign.

"I don't know. She'll find something. She's really quite brilliant."

"Oh, I have no doubt. She was pleasant enough to talk to, and I can't imagine you settling for anything less."

Pleasant to talk to. Another flattering assessment. And one Papa didn't make about a lot of people.

"Does that mean you like her?" Eirinn asked. A heavily loaded question, she fully realized. She had just told Papa the absolute worst thing about Aya, a thing that would give any father doubts and make him send a suitor packing for the hills.

"Yes, I do." Papa sighed, almost against his own better judgment. "But it doesn't matter what I think. All that matters is that you like her."

"I love her," Eirinn declared. Simply. Explicitly. So, there would be no question. First time she had said the words aloud, they felt right. Inevitable almost. As if from the moment Aya showed up at her door she was destined to say them. "I feel... I feel as if I knew her in another life."

Her words sinking in, slowly, but profoundly, Papa smiled.

233

Chapter 31

CAROLINE

1886

She kept forgetting to breathe.

It wasn't a thing one should have to remind herself, Caroline thought, but, body so overwhelmed, it was instinct to hold her breath, to channel her resources to those places that felt the most. To find herself gasping for air and clinging tightly to Lei, hoping she wouldn't black out.

Naked, though she had never been naked with anyone before in her life, save her lady's maid when she was much younger and even then with some discomfort, she suffered the silk of Lei's skin against her own like an invasion, the press of Lei's thigh a constant throbbing onslaught between her legs.

And then there were Lei's hands. And Lei's lips. Long fingers stroking inside her. Soft licks against her collarbone that turned into possessive suckles at her nipple, and she was glad she had let Lei ease her out of her clothes - all of them - self-conscious as she felt in her own skin, because Lei seemed to want her that way, completely exposed but for the sheet that kept the heat locked between them and the rest of the world away.

"Are you all right?"

She had lost count of the number of times Lei asked her that, whispered the words against her lips, checked in on her condition though she was pressed intimately against her and could clearly see.

Yes, I'm fine turned into *Oh God, yes* to *Please, just don't ever stop touching me.* Or so arced the trajectory of Caroline's thoughts. She was certain they came out in a series of senseless moans and babbles as the euphoria racked her body, carrying her out of the room for a moment and depositing her back into it with scarcely a change. Because, when she came back down, she was still pressed skin-to-skin with Lei and that was a rapture all on its own.

Are you all right?

After, Caroline could feel the warm comfort of Lei's arm against her back as she listened to the cadence of Lei's heartbeat beneath her ear, its gently slowing rhythm, and expected the panic to set back in. To feel increasingly frantic in her own mind. To hear the minutes tick away like some giant pendulum inside her head.

Beyond the sheet and the walls, the threat was still there. Not even a threat, a veritable inevitability. Thomas had flat-out said he was taking her out of Dr. Todson's and putting her someplace else. Someplace worse. *Bedlam.* The notion went through her mind again, sending enough of a shiver through her that Lei hooked the quilt with her foot and dragged it up over them.

So, why wasn't she frenzied? Why wasn't she crying and hysterical? Screaming and throwing things at the walls? Running to find Dr. Todson and asking her to spirit her away into the night? Asking Lei to?

That was one means of escape. She could just disappear.

She ran away, Caroline could hear Rand saying to Thomas in a most baffled way. *We don't know how she got over the wall or past the guards.*

Thomas wouldn't trust it, of course, Rand's word on the matter. Her marital portion on the line - both the house and the cash allowance - he would insist on searching the grounds. Bringing in extra men. Hunting dogs even, perhaps.

But Caroline would only have to stay gone long enough for him to be satisfied she had truly vanished. Go just far enough away that the dogs couldn't follow her scent. Just beyond a river or a wide stream.

Then, she could come back. If they would have her back. Would they? Without the payment for her keep? After she brought such scrutiny upon their house?

Did she want to bring such scrutiny upon Dr. Todson's? If dogs and men came sniffing about the grounds, there were so many things they could find.

No, she couldn't do that to them. Not after all they had done for her. She couldn't run off and leave them to kick dust over her footprints. And it wouldn't matter if she did. Nothing would change. Not in any real, fundamental way. She would still be in the same predicament she was in right now. At the will of Thomas, waiting for him to return, to find her, to drown what life she had left beneath the sludge he piled atop her.

If she wanted to be rid of Thomas, truly, permanently rid of him, there was only one possible way. One legal way, at least. Caroline credited Lei's arms with giving her the idea. Lying there, with Lei, all she wanted was to make it all stop. To take Thomas out of the equation. He had power over her by the sheer fact that he was her husband. If he wasn't, she could go anywhere, do anything. She could walk right out the door of this house or walk right back in it, and Thomas would have no say over any of it or cause to come looking for her.

Idea hatching, sudden and feral, before Caroline could tame it a knock came at the door startling her out of her half-conscious contemplation.

"It's all right." Lei pressed a kiss to her shoulder as she slid out from under her, and, eyes fluttering in response, Caroline swore the entirety of the world was different than she had ever known it to be. Warmer. Less hollow. How had she been led to believe it was so very empty?

"Eir." Lei raised her voice just enough to let Caroline know who was standing in the hall as she opened the door in her wrapper.

"Lei, I'm sorry to bother you," Dr. Todson said. "But have you seen Caroline? Rand thought she went down to your workshop, but she wasn't there. We've been looking everywhere, and we haven't been able -"

"I'm here." Hearing the concern in Dr. Todson's voice, edging quite close to panic, Caroline couldn't let her go on worrying about her when she was right there, and, glancing her way to make sure it was all right, Lei stepped aside to let Dr. Todson into the room.

"Oh." Sweeping through the door in a rush, Dr. Todson came to an abrupt, abnormally graceless halt when she saw Caroline sitting in Lei's bed. "There you are. Are you all right?"

"Yes. I'm feeling much better now. Thank you."

"Good. Good." Still trying to get a handle on her obvious surprise, it took Dr. Todson a second longer to remember what else she had to say. It was clear when she did, a dark shadow passing across her face that forewarned her coming words just a little too late. "Rand said Thomas wants to take you out of here."

Lei looking sharply to her, Caroline felt instantly guilty.

"Yes. That was what he said."

It wasn't how she wanted Lei to find out. So abruptly. At this particular moment in time. Watching Lei's face go through a range of emotions, it occurred to Caroline she probably should have told her before, given her the chance to make a truly informed decision. But Lei didn't look angry, or regretful, when her expression finally settled. She only looked troubled, anxious tears coming to her eyes that accelerated Caroline's heartbeat and made her even more convinced of what she needed to do.

"Is that what you want?" Dr. Todson gently asked, and Caroline's composure fluttered - solid state giving way to the rapid beat of wings.

"No, not at all." Feeling suddenly more exposed, she checked that the quilt fully covered her where she clutched it against her chest.

"What do you want us to do?"

Question so simple, it still brought a small gasp to Caroline's throat. Tears to her eyes. She knew. Had known. Leaned on the certainty both in the reception room with Thomas, and, again, as she lay in bed with Lei. They would help her, Dr. Todson, Lei, Rand, and the others. When she became so certain she could rely on them, she couldn't exactly pinpoint, but she was certain of it. Soothed by it. And it humbled her. Permeated her. Put new twists on the thoughts flowing through her mind and directed them together, so the multiple tributaries coalesced into a single pulsating entity like a bubble of blood that formed atop a wound.

"I have an idea."

Caroline knew what she needed to do, had already made her peace with it.

"Good. What is it?"

She would give Thomas what he wanted to get what she wanted. He tried to bribe her, and it gave her the means of bribing him. Thomas would get something, but so would she. When all was said and done, she would be free of him, no longer having to worry about what he might do to her next.

Two minutes before, she had been fine with that, the tit for tat. She had accepted it as the only possible solution. Now, with Dr. Todson standing there asking what they could do, it occurred to her there might be a way to undo what she had to do. To give *and* to take. There might be a way to get what she wanted *and* make Thomas suffer for his sins.

He so deserved to suffer.

"I want to rob my husband. Can you help me?" She looked to Dr. Todson, and Dr. Todson's eyes went wide.

"You want us to help you rob Thomas?"

"If it's not too much trouble," Caroline said, and Dr. Todson blinked. Lei blinked.

"Um..." Dr. Todson uttered, but seemed to get stuck there, leaving the note hanging for several passing seconds as she stared at Caroline. "Let me talk to Aya." She moved toward the door with a somewhat aimless step, stopping again as she reached it. "Are you sure you're all right?"

"I am," Caroline promised.

"All right. Let's talk again after tea."

"Yes, of course."

Dr. Todson went out, leaving Lei standing, stunned and alone, just inside the door.

When she glanced to Caroline in the bed, Caroline pulled back the quilt to coax her back, and Lei came, sitting down to face her in her wrapper, stunned expression still on her face.

"Are you all right?' Caroline finally got her own chance to ask, but Lei didn't answer her right away. For some time, she just sat there, unmoving, hand unconsciously clutching the top of her wrapper, eyes focusing somewhere beyond Caroline's head.

"I'm confused," she admitted when she did speak. "Thomas said he was taking you away from here?"

"Yes," Caroline answered.

"You're not leaving with him, are you?" Lei looked panicked, seeming to realize if Caroline left the house with Thomas she would end up no place good.

"No," Caroline said as she reached for her hand. "I won't have to. I have a plan."

"To rob him?"

"That's part of it." Small smile flickering to her face, Caroline fell into a moment's contemplation. Daydream. Robbing her own house. Thomas ruined. It was a revenge fantasy, plain and simple. But how satisfying it would be if it actually worked.

"You know you don't have to prove anything to them, right?" The gentle question drew her back. "They'll still help you."

"I'm not trying to prove anything," Caroline said. Though, she could understand how Lei might have gotten the impression. Her next words coming to mind automatically, as they had hundreds of times before, she weighed them for only a second, determining them safe with Lei, but still nervous as they passed her lips. "He killed my sister."

"What?"

"Thomas killed Sarah," Caroline declared, out loud for the very first time, tears rising to garble her voice though she'd had a year to get used to the fact. "And Nathaniel. He picked Oliver up from their house that night. He did it somehow, I know he did."

When Lei just stared at her, Caroline could hardly blame her for looking so... put out. So... flummoxed. By any account, it was a wild accusation, a dangerous accusation, even if it was true.

"Did you tell anyone?"

"No. Of course not. As soon as I pointed a finger at Thomas, he would have pointed it back at me. Who do you think they would have believed?"

Lei didn't have to think. At least, she didn't have to think too long or too hard. A man's word and two signatures, that was all it took to devalue a woman's mind. Her competence. To label her insane and put her into an institution. A woman couldn't even speak to her own mental state. How could she possibly perceive anything outside of it?

"Your nephew..." Lei instantly thought to worry.

"He's at Eton." Caroline realized she could actually take some comfort in the fact. Oliver wasn't ready. He was too raw, too needy, to be thrown into a world with other boys who had no understanding of what he had been through. But it was better than him being in London. With Thomas. Thomas's fury. Thomas's desperation.

"So..." It took Lei several minutes to speak again, and, in that time, Caroline grew more and more enraged. At Thomas. At the police for their

238

terrible bungling of Sarah's and Nathaniel's deaths. At a world that would rather believe a kind, decent woman killed the man she truly loved and herself than that they were more likely murdered by a calculating man. "If Thomas hadn't come here... if he didn't threaten to take you away today... would this be happening right now?"

Change in subject jarring, Caroline felt the vitriol ooze back out of her as the disquiet in Lei's question took hold. She didn't want to say it.

"No," she admitted. With an appropriate amount of shame. "Not unless you had kissed me first."

Nodding, Lei looked to the far wall, seeming to expect the answer, and Caroline couldn't let her so easily slip way. Sliding her hand up Lei's arm, she gently pressed with her fingers until Lei finally looked back to her.

"I'm not brave." It was pathetic, unattractive, Caroline knew, but it was true. "Sarah used to always say she admired my strength, my daring. I don't know why, because I have never been strong. I have only ever been impetuous. All my life... my adult life," she corrected with a sigh as she realized she hadn't always been this way. "I tried to be as quiet and as invisible as possible. The only reason I ever appeared as anything more was because I would get so overwhelmed with the saying nothing, the doing nothing, that eventually I would erupt. I have never once acted on my own behalf. I have only ever reacted."

"So, Thomas came here and you reacted by coming to me?"

"Yes," Caroline confessed. But it was a sad testament to the truth. Because she wanted this with Lei, had wanted it, and it spoke volumes as to who she was, and who she wasn't, that she was too afraid to ask for it until it was almost too late.

But not anymore. Not ever again.

Sliding closer to Lei, she pressed her lips to the delicate rise of Lei's throat, the sweet scent of Lei's soap mingling with the salt in her sweat as Lei moaned softly above her, and felt desire reverberate through her again, a real revelation given that Lei had left nothing to be desired, sating her fully and completely mere minutes before. Or so Caroline thought.

So, this was what it was to truly crave someone. Utterly wanton. Shamelessly gluttonous.

"But I'm not reacting now," she whispered into Lei's ear, letting the quilt fall from her chest as she reached for the tie on Lei's wrapper, so desperate to get Lei back out of her clothes, she pulled the wrong strand first and nearly bound her up in them instead.

"Here. Let me." Lei's hands came to help, pulling the tie free with practiced ease, and Caroline was beyond grateful as the wrapper slipped from Lei's shoulders and fell to the floor.

Chapter 32

DR. EIRINN TODSON

1886

Eirinn moved through the house in a flurry of astonishment, not sure which hastened her feet more, her giddiness or her apprehension. It wasn't often she was surprised by someone. In her line of work, she had seen people behave in all manner of ways and had more insight into that behavior than most. But this time she was. In a multitude of facets. Some pleasant. Some more ominous. Either way, they all led to Aya, and she found her where she had the sudden epiphany to look, in the barn where they kept the horse-drawn carts and self-powered vehicles, nothing but hair and arm where she crouched behind the front wheel of her steambike.

"What did you say to her?"

"What?!" Fully materializing, Aya looked positively spooked by the question. "I only said I could *conceive* of being a queen's mistress, but only if I wasn't already madly in love with and committed to you."

Crossing her arms, Eirinn heaved a heavy sigh, expecting no more serious a response out of Aya. Nor the shot of jealousy that went straight through her. Still. After fourteen years. "You'd better be joking."

"I am." Aya grinned. "Who?"

"Caroline."

"Ah. Take it you found her." Dropping the spanner she held onto the potato sack next to her feet, Aya ambled around the bike's front, new tire light Lei had finished for her the day before half-attached and dangling precipitously by its wires. "Stella came in saying she'd gone missing. Told me to keep an eye on things here, as if Caroline might make off with a vehicle all on her lonesome." Smile turning to a smirk, Aya thought it a joke, the idea that Caroline might abscond, that she might steal a steambike and slip and slide her way haphazardly out of town, but, given Caroline's other recent changes of behavior, it was probably considerably more likely than she knew. "Anyway, there have been so many things," Aya said. "If you could tell me why I'm in trouble, it would help to narrow things down."

"She wants to rob her husband," Eirinn returned, and Aya barked laughter, jolly bold grin coming to her face that threatened to completely overwhelm it.

"Is that right? Good for her."

"You think this is funny?"

"No. Absolutely not. I was laughing in horror."

"She wants us to help her do it." Fingers clutching at her bicep, Eirinn's voice lost strength, volume, and Aya sobered somewhat, hint of regret coming to her face as she glanced to her hands in the light of the open barn door, taking out the rag that hung from her pocket to wipe dirt from her fingers as she drifted Eirinn's way.

"She said that?"

"Asked."

It was a cardinal rule. One of the very few they had. Keep the two things separate. That was how they made sure everyone stayed safe. Stealing from moralistically-challenged men was dangerous as a rule, but they could keep that danger as far from the women in the house as possible. As distinct. As distant. If they robbed Caroline's husband, it would bring the two into direct collision. Who knew who might get hurt by the impact?

"And since you gave her the idea you get to be the one to explain to her why we can't."

"Wait. When did we establish that I gave her the idea?"

Tilting her head, Eirinn waited. Curious. Was Aya really going to try to wriggle out of her part in all of this?

"Do you think I don't know about your spirit away with Caroline in the middle of the night?" she asked, and Aya feigned surprise, confusion. For a split second. Abandoning the act when she realized the facts were not in her favor.

"Johnny, that traitor. I gave him an entire pint of brandy. Jerez, even!"

"Yes, yes. You're the fun one with the high-quality bribes, but I see that he actually gets paid. He knows who butters the bread in this house."

"Brigit, I would say, half the time. The other half, the women do it themselves." Aya flashed a cheeky grin, and Eirinn smiled. She couldn't help but smile. Even as she softened. Weakened.

"You know we can't." It pained her to say it. She had no cause for the guilt, there was good reason for keeping their worlds as far apart as possible, but the first time Caroline had asked them for anything, any help at all, and there was nothing they could do for her.

"I'll tell her." Aya's hands came to her arms. But she too was troubled, dissatisfied by the outcome. It manifested in a near soundless sigh, in the way she stared off toward the barn wall.

"What? What is it?" Eirinn asked her.

"Did Caroline say *why* she wants to rob her husband?" Aya returned.

"No. Not specifically. But I think we both agree she has good reason."

Accepting the point with a nod, Aya's expression didn't falter. Just as contemplative as the moment before, soft wispy lines appeared at the corners of her eyes as her gaze further narrowed. Jaw clenching and unclenching as the thoughts and words sharpened between her teeth. "When I took Caroline into London..."

Eirinn jolted with surprise, her own mouth falling slightly agape. She knew Aya had taken Caroline gallivanting outside the estate grounds. She had no idea they had made it quite so far.

"I showed her General Joffreys stocking another slave ship."

"Ugh, that repugnant brute."

"I wanted to imprint upon her just the sort of people we steal from. Show her just how terrible were their crimes. How much they truly deserved it."

Explanation straightforward, it was far from simple, and Eirinn heard every nuance. "All right."

"And now Caroline wants to rob her husband. Aren't you at least curious as to why that is?"

Goddammit. Eirinn really didn't need Aya to try to convince her, because she didn't need all that much convincing. From the moment Caroline had asked, she had been wondering *why*, what exactly Thomas had said or done during their meeting to prompt such an extreme response.

"You know we can't." But it wasn't smart. And it wasn't safe. "We have a lot of other people to think about."

"I know. I'll tell her." Aya didn't argue again. Which left Eirinn in the awkward position of arguing only with herself. Why did Caroline want to rob her husband? It wasn't as if the question was unimportant. What had Thomas done, aside from the obvious, that Caroline felt deserved such severe retribution she would actually ask for their help?

"Then again..." she heard herself saying, and could almost hear the smirk Aya tried to withhold. "I suppose we should at least hear her out."

Aya's arms slipped fully around her, and she sagged into them, knowing Aya would support whatever decision she made. Would do whatever she asked her to do. That certainty, combined with the press of Aya's body against her own and the pleasant thoughts still occupying her mind, produced a sense of urgency, an urgency that only grew with each soft caress of Aya's hand against her back.

"Don't you want to know where I found Caroline?"

"I'm going to assume from the fact you're asking me that I do."

"In Lei's room." Eirinn's fingers walked slowly up Aya's arm. "In Lei's bed."

"Hmm," Aya hummed as if it was an interesting fact she had just gleaned from an article she was reading. "Were they wearing any clothes?"

"No."

Watching Aya nod, processing the information, Eirinn saw the same set of emotions cross her face that she herself had felt. Minor shock, though not true shock - the attraction between Lei and Caroline had been quite palpable, both visible and otherwise perceptible, like the buzz off a wire at a telegraph office - followed by an amused sort of delight. Chased, a moment later, by a slightly more lascivious delight as her thoughts took a decidedly carnal turn.

"Well, I can't say that does nothing for me," she said.

"We have to make this quick. I have less than an hour before I need to start tea."

Wicked smile coming to her face, Aya licked her lips like a puma on the prowl, and Eirinn felt the perilous potential of tripping over her own feet as she stumbled them backward to slide the barn door closed.

Chapter 33

CAROLINE

1886

She had asked for something preposterous - though, not nearly as preposterous as it would have been anyplace else - and now she had to explain herself.

It was much like the first day after Aya arrived at the house, Dr. Todson and Aya sitting across from her, Dr. Todson gently worried, Aya more blandly curious, while, next to her, Lei sat, like a buttress, providing support without saying or doing anything. Only they were in the map room instead of the dining room, and Caroline knew everyone differently now. Better. As more complete people. Dr. Todson. Aya. Lei...

Blushing softly, she smiled just thinking about how things with Lei had progressed, realizing she should probably get started before her thoughts could roam too far from her intended purpose.

"Thomas wants the house." It seemed the most logical place to begin, given it was the basis for her entire idea. "He came here with the deed and tried to get me to sign it over to him in exchange for taking me back to London."

"Ah. An offer you couldn't refuse," Aya quipped.

"I want to give it to him in exchange for a divorce."

"Do you think he'll agree to that?" Dr. Todson asked.

"I don't think he has any choice. He needs the money."

That was Thomas's great blunder, his fatal error, the leverage he had given Caroline quite by accident. He was desperate. That much was clear. Did she think Thomas would grant her a divorce under any other circumstances? No. She was almost certain he would not. She was much too lucrative for him. Still. In spite of his complaints. She might not have proven the fortune he expected her to be, but she was still worth a great deal more than he was.

"Then..." Caroline forced herself to go on, knowing if she didn't she would lose her nerve, talk herself back out of it before she could talk them into it. "Once he has it, I want to take it back."

"Your house?" Aya asked.

"Yes."

"Lei, Physics. Go." Aya made a careless motion Caroline's way.

"Not the *actual* house." Caroline shot her an irritated glare. "Thomas needs ownership of the house so he can use it to secure a loan. He's in a bind. He's done this before, made deals with the wrong sorts of men he's had to beg money to pay off. It always happens the same. He secures the money before he contacts them, and then it takes a few days for him to arrange payment. He won't do it any other way. These are not the type of men you tell you have their money unless you actually have it in hand."

"Mafioso?" Lei asked.

"Or other goons or crooks," Caroline returned. "When he wasn't playing at society husband, Thomas made acquaintance with all sorts of disreputable characters. He would take money from the devil Himself if He offered it."

"Did that ever put you into danger?" Dr. Todson asked, and it struck Caroline with a sort of soft awareness. That, even in this, Dr. Todson was the same, worried first for her. *She isn't like us,* Aya's words echoed through her mind again.

"No. Just disgrace. I always asked my father for the money to pay Thomas's debts, and he always gave it to me. I suppose he truly did love me... in his way."

Just not enough. Not enough for him to flout the rules of society and treat her and Sarah as equals, regardless of their abilities to bear male heirs. Not enough to protect her from the likes of Thomas, because it was easier to be rid of her than have to deal with her himself.

"So, if you sign the deed over to Thomas, once he takes out the loan...?"

"The gold will be in the house for at least a night," Caroline told Aya.

"It sounds as if you've thought this through."

"I have," Caroline said. Over and over, every second Lei wasn't actively engaging her senses.

She would sign the house over to Thomas only *after* she saw proof of his divorce petition. Only *after* that petition was entered into the courts. Then, once Thomas had possession, he would go straight to the bank with the deed and take out gold - gangs rarely worked in bank notes -

that he would take home to put into his safe. Caroline didn't know the safe code, nor have access to its key, but she trusted, for Lei and Aya, that wouldn't prove much of a problem.

"Why?" Dr. Todson suddenly asked her - or it felt sudden - and Caroline was thrown off guard.

"Why have I thought it through?"

"Why do you want to rob your husband?"

Because he deserves to suffer. The words bubbled up like water in a volatile geyser. But did they sound hysterical? Vengeful? Reactionary? What was it they wanted to hear?

"It's my house. It's the only thing my parents gave me without condition. The only thing in the world that belongs to me outright."

"And that's not fair," Dr. Todson said. "It's not right, and it's certainly not just, Thomas living in your house while you're in here. It also isn't enough."

With four words, Caroline's heart dropped. Emptied. Unreasonably, perhaps. She had asked for something preposterous. She knew it was preposterous when she asked for it. Yet, still it stung, Dr. Todson's rejection. More than she thought it would. Why did she think they would jump at the chance to help her with this?

"All of the women here have stories, Caroline." Caroline wasn't sure why Aya was suddenly the one doing the talking, but she was, taking Dr. Todson's hand as she did. "Not exactly like yours, but if we went after every bad actor the residents here have had to endure, it's all we would do. And the chance that we might make a mistake, that we might lead the wrong person back here, it's simply too great a risk. Do you understand?"

"Yes." Caroline didn't. She was hurt. She was embarrassed now for even asking it. Of course, all the women in the house had their own stories, pasts with people who had hurt or betrayed them. Why did she think hers any different?

"Tell them, Caroline."

Lei's voice soft, insistent, beside her, Caroline lost her train of thought, her poise, disbelieving as she looked Lei's way. What she had told Lei, she had told her in confidence, and she was certain Lei had to know that.

"Tell them." Lei prodded her anyway. "Tell them what you told me. You know you can trust them."

Hand on her arm, Lei gave it a small squeeze, and Caroline realized two things simultaneously. One, that Lei was only trying to help her, and, two, that she hadn't really said anything. Lei didn't announce her secret thoughts to the entire room, only that Caroline had them. And Caroline looked across the table, trying to decide if she really wanted to share them with Dr. Todson and Aya, to say the one thing out loud that might make her sound legitimately mad.

"Would you prefer I leave?" Aya asked, and Caroline sent her another peeved glare. But, as always of late, it only made her feel better, calmer, Aya's insistence on being so consistently aggravating. A new familiarity that brought a bizarre sense of comfort.

Besides, what was the worst they could do? Put her in an institution? Caroline almost laughed.

"Thom..." But her humor dried up quickly, along with all the moisture on her tongue, as she tried to get the words out. Saying them to Lei in her bedroom felt different, like whispers in a confessional, entirely separate from the real world. Here, they felt alive - official - unable to be safely tucked away once they had been said. So scared were they to come out, they practically unraveled themselves letter by letter before they made it to Caroline's lips. "Thom... Thomas... Thomas killed my sister." She expelled them all in one quick breath, and, for a moment, there was nothing.

Nothing but silence. Stunned or skeptical, Caroline couldn't tell. She was too scared to look up and see.

"Did he tell you that?" Dr. Todson asked.

"No." Lei's hand moved to her leg, and Caroline reached for it, clung to it, feeling grounded back to the earth as Lei squeezed her fingers. "He didn't have to. I just..." Lifting her eyes, she met Dr. Todson's gaze and lost her voice. Her thought. It was eerie the way Dr. Todson stared at her. Into her. Reflective almost. As if she looked at Caroline but saw mostly herself. "I just know."

"How do you know?"

Well, now they were getting into the meat of it, weren't they? More gristly and tougher than Dr. Todson probably knew. Because it wasn't some clue left behind or slip of the tongue that told the truth about Thomas. It was years of living with him, of finding out who he was and who he could be. It was being proven right, at every turn, that his cruelty could always get crueler, that there were fewer and fewer lines he wouldn't cross.

"Thomas married me for my money." Did she really want to tell them this? With Aya there to prod at it, and Lei there to hear it at all? "That's probably no surprise. I married him because he was my only real prospect. Also probably not that much of a surprise." Pausing, she gave Aya a chance. Surely, Aya had to have some zinger up her sleeve or perched at the back of her throat.

But Aya said nothing.

"The moment I proved incapable of conceiving a child, my value diminished. I was the oldest. Had I given birth to a son, we would have inherited almost everything. We would have gotten the second estate, my marital allowance would have gone up. When I didn't, we got what we got. Thomas thought he was going to end up with half a fortune. I think he still thinks he deserves it for putting up with me."

Caroline stated it plainly. Unemotionally. She had very little emotion, she realized, when it came to the facts of her own life. Thomas didn't care for her, but she didn't care for him either. He wanted money. She wanted to get on with her life in the expected fashion. Her parents were going to marry her off to a suitor at some point, if not by force, by persuasion and innuendo. Better a common fortune seeker than some sixty-year-old widower. At least, that was what she thought at the time.

"Could I speak with Caroline alone for a moment, please?" Dr. Todson softly asked, and panic bubbled up in Caroline.

No, I don't think that will be necessary, she wanted to say, shout, plead. But, watching Lei and Aya rise, she kept her mouth firmly shut, regretting opening it in the first place, nerves on edge as Dr. Todson rose from her chair to move around the table, taking the seat next to her as Lei and Aya left them alone and the door to the map room creaked shut.

"I know Thomas's visit had to have upset you," Dr. Todson began simply enough. "The fact that he killed your sister, I can imagine how much you must hate him."

"I do." Caroline felt no need to lie. She did hate Thomas. She had hated him for a very long time. Maybe always. Though, at the moment, she was mostly distracted by Dr. Todson saying "fact" instead of "if." Could it be Dr. Todson believed her?

"That is why I worry you might be making a rash decision. That you don't recognize all of the dangers involved, or you don't care."

"I do. I do care! I care about this house and the women in it."

Dr. Todson's eyes falling closed for a moment, they reopened on a soft sigh, and Caroline realized, whatever the question, she had answered it wrong.

"I'm not talking about this house or the other women, Caroline. I have no doubt about your ability to care for others. I worry that you don't always consider yourself. It's the way you put things, you see. I know you think you are speaking from a place of what you believe Thomas to be thinking. Your parents. Society. But it is still *you* who says it.

"Your value did not diminish when you failed to have a child."

I know that, Caroline wanted to say, argue, deny forthright that she had ever actually felt that way about herself. But, the truth was, for many years she had felt it. Believed it. Unequivocally. Until she came to Dr. Todson's, she thought and believed a lot of things with painful certainty that were now riddled with questions.

"I worry you aren't entirely aware of who you are. Of what you feel. Of your worth. That your mind can be -"

"I know." Caroline realized she could spare Dr. Todson some effort. Aid her in her diagnosis, if that was what she was doing.

"Know what exactly?" Dr. Todson cautiously asked, and Caroline took a breath, largely ineffective and almost impossible to expel.

"I know that I am not... well." Tears springing to her eyes, she tried to blink them away, but it was a difficult thing to confess. To admit to. That Thomas was somewhat right about her. That her parents were somewhat right. Looking to the stacked books on the shelves across the room, she watched their titles blur into illegibility, grateful now that Dr. Todson was no longer in her direct line of sight. "I am not crazy."

248

"No," Dr. Todson said, and it was exactly why Caroline could admit it. In her old world, had she told anyone this, they would have treated her like even more of a leper than they already did, because sick meant dangerous. Here, sick just meant sick. It didn't define who she was, in the same way Dr. Todson's sex didn't determine her career prospects or Johnny and the other men's desires didn't reduce them to dandies or perverts.

"I'm not... dangerous... or cruel." The sentences formed like multiple tongues in her mouth, all trying to stop one another from talking. "But I do know I am not like everyone else. Or I have come to understand the fact over the years. I know I have thoughts not everyone has. That they get away from me. I am prone to bouts of despair, and when I get them, they possess me. I feel utterly hopeless, and I often..." So often, it had been nearly a nightly prayer for most of her adult life. "I often want to die. I have fits of temper. I am angry all the time. And I have been so, so lonely in my life."

Tears dripping down her face and off her chin, Caroline pulled out her handkerchief, holding it to her nose and recalling every truth she just said - every moment of detachment, of desperation, of looking forward into death, certain there was no other way her life would ever change.

"I need help." The broken appeal surprised them both, Dr. Todson more so than Caroline, who at least had the forewarning of thinking it first. But Dr. Todson only nodded in response. "But none of that is why I want to get my house back from Thomas. Thomas killed my sister and Nathaniel. He doesn't deserve to be rewarded for that."

Caroline also worried what Thomas might do next. With Sarah and Nathaniel out of the way, her out of the way, her parents were old and would be gone soon enough, but Oliver... she had no faith Thomas wouldn't destroy anyone standing between him and the riches he felt so entitled to have.

"But I understand why it's too dangerous for you. For everyone here. If I give Thomas the house, he will give me a divorce. He will no longer be a threat to me or anyone I love, and that will be enough. If..." Realizing there was one more thing she needed, one thing that would make all the difference in how content she was with this not-entirely-satisfactory outcome, Caroline looked to Dr. Todson again. "If I can stay here."

"Of course, Caroline," Dr. Todson said. "You can stay here as long as you like."

And, sobbing her relief, Caroline discovered it really did make all the difference.

Chapter 34

DR. EIRINN TODSON

1886

Snow spread across the landscape, the sprawling two-story house with its towering portico sitting in a world by itself outside of town. Not too far outside it. In the distance, the outline of village houses and the tower of a castle blended with the background, little more than scratches of brush against paper. Intentionally non-provoking.

Aside from the red sleigh and dark horse just off-center, deep spots of color amidst an otherwise muted world, there was nothing particularly striking about the painting, nothing to dominate the eye or command the attention. That was why Mama loved it as she did, because it existed in the world without fuss, as only something simplistic can. Existing for the sake of existing. Pleasant to look at. Peaceful. Painless. Serene.

Except when it wasn't.

Some nights, like tonight, when Eirinn looked at the painting, now hung with care on the landing of her own library, she didn't see what her mother saw. She didn't see the rise of smoke from the house's chimneys or the gentle sunset on the western horizon. She saw brutality and tragedy, blood, and some of the worst memories that lived inside her head.

"I have something for you." It was a night in late June many years ago, the house in London warm, but not nearly warm enough to thaw Eirinn, despite the fire lit and crackling in the hearth nearby, when Aya came into the dining room to find her.

Sitting at the table's head, in Papa's chair, or what had been his chair until that very morning, Eirinn was vaguely aware she was tired, vaguely aware she had been sitting for some time - since afternoon? evening? - vaguely aware of Aya saying she was going out some hours before.

In the time since, Bally and Rand had been on her like flies. One minute, Eirinn would think she had finally swatted them away for good, and, in the next, they would swarm - a hand on her back or her shoulder. *Can I get you some tea or something to eat, Love? You wanna go for a walk, Eir? Get out of the house for a while?*

Even now, in the dead of night, Rand slept in the parlor just beyond the dining room door, both determined and instructed by his mother not to leave Eirinn alone, but unable to continue holding waking vigil when he'd had a long, trying month himself.

"What is it?" Eirinn asked Aya where she stood in the firelight, looking mostly like herself, but tired too. Sad. Haunted.

"You'll have to get up to see," Aya said, and Eirinn knew it was a trick, a ploy to make her move when she wanted to just sit there and feel nothing. To listen to the fragmented echoes of conversation, of laughter, from just a month before.

But it was Aya, and that alone was convincing, even before Aya reached out and took her hands to pull her to her feet.

"Talking to your mother?"

So engrossed in the memory, Eirinn didn't hear Aya as she came into the library and startled slightly at the sound of her voice.

"Sorry."

Glancing back, she watched Aya approach, swagger subdued, but still present - Aya could never quite tamp it entirely- and felt the pain of the past recede. Memories the same and just as clear as in the moment before, they simply never tortured her the same in Aya's presence.

"I was thinking about the night you brought me this painting," Eirinn said as she turned back to the wall.

"I thought you might be." Aya stepped up behind her, arms slipping around her waist, and, slackening into her embrace, Eirinn let Aya hold her up.

"I wish she could have seen it."

"So your parents would know the woman you swore was no longer a thief was still very much of the persuasion when the mood so struck?"

Considering the question, what her parents might have said, the looks they would have worn when Aya showed up with the painting in their home, Eirinn exhaled a wistful smile.

Here you go, she could imagine Aya announcing. *This is the proper one, isn't it? That Louis Arnold is a right git. He doesn't even have decent security for his revenge art.*

Not for the first time, Eirinn wondered if she should have asked Aya to steal the painting for Mama. Before.

"She would have loved it," she said. "Papa would have too. He would have said something fatherly and disapproving, but secretly he would have been grateful to you for doing something he must have thought about doing a hundred times himself."

Eirinn could only speculate as to what her parents' reactions would have been, because, by then, Mama was dead. Papa was dead. Both killed by the same man, as far as she was concerned.

The month before, there had been a rally in Hyde Park, informal, just a meeting of the interested almost, and they had gone, Mama, Bally, Aya, and Eirinn. It wasn't large. Dozens of women, not hundreds. But the ones who were there were enthusiastic. Confident. And utterly determined.

"I don't expect to see it in my lifetime," Eirinn recalled Bally saying that day. "But I do hope you'll see it in yours."

Votes for women!

Suffrage, that was the matter on the agenda.

"Suffrage to end women's suffering!" one woman called for in her speech. Just one memorable snippet from the many speeches by women that day. Those from all walks of life. Women running for office. Industrialists' wives. Schoolteachers.

And now the Great Gennie Zee!

The performer on the bill was unusual, to say the least, a shining star in London's growing club and burlesque scene. Along with having a lovely singing voice, she played more than two dozen instruments, many brought from other cultures the people of London had never seen before. During one particularly showstopping bit, she tinkered on multiple instruments at the same time, a one-woman band of stand-up bass, harmonica, kick drum, piano, and tambourine.

Even the musician's husband spoke.

"Men, if your wives want to work, I say let them work. If they want to vote, I say let them vote. Look at my life. My wife and I travel all across Europe. She does the work, and all I have to do is book gigs and sip whisky in the back of clubs. Let her be your meal ticket, I say."

That brought some laughter, perhaps even a man or two to the cause for all the wrong reasons. No one could have imagined then how honest the performer's husband was being, or that one day, once her star had faded, then her mind, riddled from overwork and the drugs she took for years to stay awake tirelessly performing, that same man would drop his wife into Bedlam.

Gennie Zee. Gennie. A playful turn on the musician's real name - Imogen.

252

That afternoon, though, music was on the air in Hyde Park. Hope. And, as always when one group radiates too much hope, it attracted the hostility of another.

Around them, they could hear the cries of men. Angry shouts. Insults. Mocking laughter. Background noise, somewhat expected, and easy to ignore. It was certainly nothing Eirinn, and she was certain most of the women around her, hadn't heard before.

Then, one man threw a stone.

Which inspired another.

And another.

Until the women at the rally found themselves running through a hailstorm on a beautiful, sunny summer day.

With Aya to guide them, Eirinn, Mama and Bally cleared the danger more quickly than they would have without her and were several blocks removed from the violence when they at last came to a stop, giving Bally's heart and knees a chance to rest.

"You're bleeding," Aya suddenly declared, and Mama reached to her head, finding the blood that matted her hair.

"I'm all right," Mama assured Eirinn when Eirinn rushed to her side, but so much blood, it was hard to believe.

"She's fine," Dr. Fillmore, Mama's regular physician, confirmed the diagnosis a few hours later back at the house. "Just in pain. One of her bad headaches. With her history and the hit she took, it's not all that surprising. Rest is the best thing for her now. And, perhaps, you will stay away from those rallies from now on."

"Perhaps, you might blame the man who threw the stone instead of a woman practicing her right to stand in a public park," Aya said from where she stood just inside the bedroom door, and Dr. Fillmore flapped his lips, visibly offended.

"I was only trying to help."

"Who exactly?" Aya asked.

"Dr. Fillmore, let me walk you out." Papa took Dr. Fillmore's arm, leading him past Aya into the hall before a brawl could break out in his bedroom, and a smile came to Mama's face, slow and somewhat loopy through her pain and medication.

"You, I like." She pointed a flimsy finger Aya's way, and Aya smiled in return.

"I'm going to go see if Rand needs any help with dinner." Glancing to Eirinn to make sure she would be all right, she went out the door too, and, left alone with Mama in her bedroom, Eirinn turned to inspect Dr. Fillmore's work.

"How are you feeling?"

It wasn't nearly as bad as it first appeared, the cut on Mama's head, surprisingly small when the blood was rinsed from her graying blonde hair. Just a tiny patch shaved and three narrow stitches, barely a hint that anything had happened at all. It was only the blood, the sheer amount of it, that had been so troubling. So convincing. She should have recognized it as a sign, Eirinn would think later. There was no physically possible way such a small wound could produce so much, which made her wonder if the blood she had seen flow from Mama's head on the street had really been there at all. Or if it had been a harbinger, a vision, an instinctive forewarning of what was happening within.

"Tired," Mama answered.

"Would you prefer I go and let you rest?"

"No." Reaching for her arm, Mama encouraged her to stay. When the ashes finally settled, Eirinn would recall that too, just how tightly Mama held to her. "Your company is the best medicine."

"All right," Eirinn said, glancing to the actual medicines lined up on the bedside table, amazed that even those weren't strong enough for the pain still patent in Mama's eyes. She knew when Mama got these headaches, nothing could truly quash them until they had run their course. Not unless Mama wanted to be drugged into complete oblivion. It had always felt a great failure on her part that she had yet to discover something in all of her studies that could render Mama both conscious and pain-free.

"Do you want me to read to you?" Eirinn asked when she spotted the book almost buried behind the bottles and vials. "Or something quieter maybe?"

"Your voice has never hurt me. Yes, read, please. That sounds lovely. I don't have much left. We can probably even finish it tonight, if you don't mind reading the end."

"Well, if it's any good, I suppose I can go back and see how it starts at some point." Eirinn took the book from the bedside table and turned to the marked page. "'Chapter 41. After that interview with Lady Clevedon in the library Richard Redmayne went in search of Sir Francis, but did not succeed in discovering him among the crowd...'"

"Everything all right in here?" Some minutes later, Papa came back to the room, waiting in the doorway for a pause in Eirinn's reading.

"Yes. Eir's just been reading the last of my book to me. Would you like to join us?"

"No." Papa shook his head. "I have some figures I should work out before dinner. I trust you'll be well tended. I'll see you both in a while."

With that, he left the room, and Mama stared after him, heavy sigh inflating her chest and exhaling shakily across her lips.

"He's angry."

"Well, I think he has every reason to -"

"At me."

"What? Why?" Eirinn fell into confusion, disbelief, as Mama's eyes turned her way, tender and slightly wistful.

"He does share some views with Dr. Fillmore."

"What? No." It sounded like an absolutely horrendous accusation. Especially coming from Mama's lips. "Papa would never say -"

254

"No, he would never say it," Mama agreed. "He's a good man. He believes in the cause, he does. He just doesn't understand why it has to be us. He has done everything he can to make our world feel different, to make us feel as if we are equal. So, why us? Why must we put ourselves in harm's way if harm has to come to someone?

"He doesn't understand a woman's heart. The way love makes us brave. Only those of us who have been loved as we deserve to be loved have the strength to fight for those who haven't. That's why it has to be us."

It was a beautiful sentiment, Eirinn remembered thinking at the time. Almost a promise asked of her and made. She had no idea how it would sharpen by the next morning, when she awakened to Papa's screams, when Mama wouldn't wake up - a ruptured aneurysm, nothing that could have been done - and then again, not even a month later, when Papa followed her into the grave.

Eirinn had always wondered how long her parents could live without each other. Twenty-nine days turned out to be the answer. Grieving each one of them, that was how many days it took for Papa's heart to succumb, for him to drift off to sleep one night and not wake up too.

"We said no more chances." It was that night, the one immediately following Papa's death, that Aya led Eirinn into the study, and there it sat, *Government House In Winter With Sleigh* - her mother's beloved painting - stolen from the depths of Louis Arnold's house.

"Just one more." Aya softly kissed the back of her neck, and the tears started to flow, streaming down Eirinn's face for the first time since she had found Papa, cold and lifeless, in his bed that morning. "I am so sorry, Eir."

Aya battering down her defenses cleared the way for other emotions too. Darker, more malignant emotions. Staring at the soft, snowy landscape, Eirinn saw it like a battlefield - awash with blood - both her parents' and the blood she longed to spill from the man who killed them, the man who threw a stone with zero regard for the suffering on the other end.

"It isn't enough."

"What isn't?" Aya asked her.

"Being a doctor," it occurred to Eirinn then. Because no doctor could have fixed this. Once ruptured, no doctor could stop the aneurysm from bleeding slowly into Mama's brain. A doctor certainly couldn't stop Papa from dying of his heartache. It was a terrible realization, that everything she had worked so hard for was useless in the face of one man's resentment, one man's brutal action. And, turning to Aya, Eirinn felt resentful herself, equally capable of such brutality. As if she could tear the man in two with her bare hands out of pure hatred alone.

"I am so tired of cleaning up other people's messes." For the first time, she felt like she truly understood Aya, how she could do the things she had done. How her anger had grown, not against, but around others, like a shield or a castle wall. She could never do everything, she couldn't change the nature of the world or stop terrible men from doing terrible things, but if she could slow them down by degree, save one or two people from suffering as she had suffered, it would all be worth it. "I want to do what you did."

"No, you don't. You couldn't do what I did. And I would never let you."

It was true. Every part. Eirinn couldn't do what Aya had done, and she didn't really want to. She just wanted more. More than the aftermath. Her entire life she had been clinging to a pan on the scales of justice by her fingertips, a lot further to fall than the men around her. She needed more weight, a way to really grab hold and give those scales a proper bloody yank.

"Still... there has to be a way," she whispered. Contemplated. As much as she could contemplate. Awake so long, and grief so raw, she felt as if she was talking in circles, making no sense at all. "To stop some bad things before they happen, doesn't there? Can we do that?"

It sounded silly. Naïve. It had to. Especially to Aya. But Aya wasn't laughing. Gazing thoughtfully at her instead, Aya's hands moved from her waist to her cheeks, thumbs sliding through the tears that flowed down them.

"Yeah, Darlin'," she murmured. "We can do that."

Fourteen years later, and here they were, standing in the product of their combined talents. They could never do everything, they couldn't change the nature of the world or stop terrible men from doing terrible things, but they could slow them down by degree, spread their ill-gotten fortunes to worthy causes, save one or two people from suffering the way that they had suffered, pull more firmly on the scales.

And in doing such fulfilling work, Eirinn lost all sight of vengeance. Most of the time.

"In some ways, she reminds me so much of Mama."

"I know." Aya pressed a small kiss to her neck just as she had back then, and, sighing deeper into her, Eirinn tried to imagine where Caroline would be right now if Thomas hadn't decided to rid himself of her and brought her there. Knowing he killed her sister, but she had no means of recourse, the idea that Caroline might have lived out her days with her sister's murderer was almost too much to stomach.

"Mama was braver. But love makes you brave."

"So, what you're saying is... if anyone is to blame for this new, spirited Caroline, it's Lei."

Small laugh relaxing her shoulders, Eirinn turned in Aya's embrace, taking in the smirk Aya wore before looking softly past her. To the books and frescoes of the library. To their home. Their life. Their purpose. "We cannot risk this place. It keeps so many people safe."

"Agreed. But?" Aya said.

"But I also want to see Thomas Ajax burn."

"I take it that means you believe her."

"Caroline has nothing to gain by telling us Thomas killed her sister," Eirinn declared. "She has nothing to gain by even thinking it. It can only cause her pain with no viable resolution. Even if a single person outside this house believed her, she already said she has no proof. And, even if she had proof, she can't testify against her husband."

Eirinn could only imagine the thoughts that must have been going through Caroline's mind over the past year. The fear. The fury.

"There was no way of knowing who killed my parents, but if I knew without a doubt..." Shaky breath heaving through her, she met Aya's gaze, and Aya nodded, already knowing. Already in agreement. Perhaps in agreement since the moment Caroline made her confession in the map room.

"We have to help her," Aya said.

"We have to help her," Eirinn echoed.

"We'll be careful," Aya promised her, and Eirinn was glad to hear her say it. Firmly. Out loud. Because they were going to have to be.

Chapter 35

CAROLINE

1886

This was not how she expected to return to her house in London. Under the cover of night. Cloaked from head to toe in black. Trousers again, no less. If her mother saw her, she would have three glorious episodes and swoon fantastically.

But even Dr. Todson wore trousers. It was a most unusual sight, the woman of such pomp and color dressed so inconspicuously that she blended with the shadows of the four-person steam coach in which they rode.

Caroline could make out Dr. Todson sitting next to Aya in the front seat only by the outlines of their shoulders and slips of their faces that looked otherworldly in the lights shining weakly off the coach's hood and in from streetlights they passed. While, in the back, she could tell Lei was still next to her by the feel of her alone.

"We're robbing your husband," Aya had announced unceremoniously when she came into the workshop the morning after Caroline made her plea in the map room.

"What?" was all Caroline could think to say in return.

"Just what I said. We're robbing your husband. First things first, when Thomas comes back here today, get him to agree to that divorce petition. I assume he'll want to move things along if he needs the money as much as you think he does."

"And if he doesn't agree?" Caroline asked.

That was the question that had been tormenting her all night and through the early hours of the morning. She had hinged everything on the certainty Thomas would capitulate to her demands because he had no other choice. But what if he didn't? If he had any other ideas at all, he might very well be taking her out of there today. No time left to flee or reevaluate. This could be a bad idea for that very reason. Maybe they shouldn't count on Thomas doing anything sensible. Maybe she should have already run.

"Then, I suppose I'll have to kill him."

"What?" Caroline's jaw dropped.

"Let's hope it doesn't come to that." Aya didn't quite answer her, or say whether or not she was joking.

Thankfully, no one had to find out whether she was telling the truth or not when Thomas returned to the house later that day. No formal announcement. No warning. Just a message sent up from the gate by Minotaur Ben using Lei's internal telegraph system.

"I will sign the deed for the house over to you," Caroline told him when they met again in the reception room.

"So, you've come to your senses." Thomas victoriously smirked.

"But I won't sign it today. I want a divorce."

To say that he was shocked paid little service to Thomas's expression. He was confounded by the announcement. Ill-prepared. And momentarily crippled by the counteroffer as he tried to figure out how to respond to it.

Then, immediately bored with Caroline's presumed antics.

"And how exactly are we to divorce. What will you tell the court? That I beat you? You expect me to admit to something I haven't done that will tarnish my good name?"

His good name. Really? Caroline could have laughed a hole through the wall.

"No. I may have to prove other forms of harm to my person, Thomas, but you need only prove harm to your pride. That is why you will petition for divorce and say that I was an adulterer."

"And how exactly will I prove that in court?"

"I'll admit to it," Caroline said, and Thomas looked flummoxed again, left blinking into space, as he tried to puzzle out the turn in conversation.

"You would admit to adultery just to get a divorce from me?"

I would give my right arm and left thigh just to get a divorce from you, Caroline kept to herself. She would let some mad scientist cut both clean off, reattach her leg knee to hip, and limp aslant the rest of the days of her life. Not her right thigh, though, with its crooked scar and recent memories. She liked that one quite a lot now.

"Who's to say, Thomas?" Thoughts of Lei's fingers tracing the pink and white skin where the light ray had done its damage, Caroline smiled sublimely. "It might even be true."

Like he had been whipped in the face with a horsetail, Thomas looked then, taken by surprise in the most comical of ways. And it was stupidly satisfying. For a brief moment. Before his suspicion set in, narrowing his gaze and darkening his brow.

"Something isn't right." Caroline tried to hold steady in her chair, urge to fidget quashed only by her certainty she couldn't. "What are you getting out of this?"

"Freedom from you." She couldn't hold back. What more did Thomas think she could possibly need from him? Surely, he recognized he was the biggest source of her continuing misery.

It might well be why Thomas would refuse. Just out of spite. Instruction barker and door slammer that he was. Who would he be without someone to despise as he despised her? Someone to blame for his own profound shortcomings?

"Are you going to pretend you haven't thought about it?" Caroline wheedled him. "What it would be like to be free of me? Your invalid, sideshow act wife? Now, I'm offering you your freedom and my house. You could even remarry if you want."

Watching Thomas's eyes spark, she knew that had to tempt him. She hoped he was thinking of Mary, ten years younger with all the makings of the perfect housewife back in London.

"Just start the petition," she said when the temptation alone didn't quite push Thomas to agree. It was that phrase - *just start* - that did it. Dr. Todson herself had told Caroline to use it, based on her knowledge of human nature and Caroline's description of just what sort of person Thomas was.

"So, if I petition for divorce..." Thomas returned almost at once. "You will sign the deed? We don't have to wait for the court to approve?"

"No, of course not. That would take weeks." Caroline knew what he was thinking. That he would have an interval. Forty to sixty days for the court to investigate their case. Forty to sixty days for him to renege, to withdraw his petition, to take possession of the house, pay off his debts, and still retain her as his wife in case he needed future leverage.

"All right." It was only that window which made Thomas agree. Only the chance to betray her again.

He never would have accepted an equal exchange, it occurred to Caroline then, a true quid pro quo without any hidden "quos." He was going to try to work this situation to his ultimate advantage, as was she, and there was nothing left but the question of who would come out victorious in the end.

Coach creeping now, slowed to a crawl on the granite setts that paved the London city streets, it barely made a sound, and Caroline suspected the sound she did hear, the soft crunch of debris beneath the dressed wheels, didn't drift far, dying out on sharp gusts of wind before it made it to the nearby houses.

It was an impressive feat. More than impressive. Even horses at their slowest walk made enough noise to draw some attention.

Did you make this? Caroline had asked Lei when Lei revealed the coach to her in the barn where it was kept with other finished and in-progress vehicles, including a steam coach twice the size of the one in which they currently rode, several other steambikes, much like Aya's but different from it too, built as they were from the spare parts of old, dead machines, and Lei's attempt at a single-person flying device that looked like it was half kite and half airship.

Modified, Lei answered her. *It's a standard coach. But it goes faster now. And slower. I also encased the tires in leather to reduce the noise and make for a less bumpy ride.*

As for the "less bumpy" part, Caroline could only assume the bumps had been worse before, because moving at top speed, even faster than Aya's steambike, along the dusty country roads of Surrey, the bumps were certainly appreciable, sending them into a soft soar for a fraction of a second each time they hit one, before bringing them back to the earth with a noticeable shudder.

Caroline did agree the coach made no noise once they got to London and slowed, moving from south of the river through Chelsea and South Kensington at a torturous, anxiety-inducing pace, not nearly enough fog for cover on the inconveniently clear and balmy night, though its sulfurous odor still hung in the air.

"All right."

Pace so slow and smell so disorienting, Caroline didn't realize they had arrived outside her... the... Thomas's house until they rolled to a stop and Aya engaged the lever for the brake with a series of small clicks. The six-foot stone walls and creeping trees that lined either side of the alleyway looked utterly unfamiliar. Not that Caroline *should* recognize them. She didn't do a lot of approaching of her old home through its back gate. In fact, she had left the house so infrequently in an unaltered state, she would be surprised if she could recognize its front without the house number to guide her.

"Everyone ready?" Aya asked, and Caroline's burgeoning nerves burst into temperamental bloom. Looking toward the stone wall, the trees reaching out and over it, she could see the outline of the terraced house through their branches, rising with the houses on either side like a dam against the purple night.

Draw us your house, Aya had said to her days before, handing Caroline pencil and paper as they met in the map room. *Outside. Inside. Each floor's layout.*

So, rudimentarily, Caroline did.

Was this what her drawing had looked like? Did she get each floor right, or did she leave something out? Something important? Would they all get caught because she had somehow neglected a room or misremembered the placement of a door?

"Hey, Water," Aya called to her, and, oddly enough, that was perfectly easy to remember. To respond to something that wasn't her own name. Perhaps, because Aya had been calling her that, and nothing but that, all week. "You all right? Do you want us to go in without you?"

"I'm going in," Caroline firmly declared, and Aya made a small gesture of surrender.

"All right. Let's go then. Time's a tickin'." She climbed out of the coach, checking with Caroline and Lei to make sure they had everything they needed and that their wraps were secure around their faces - everything covered but the narrows of their eyes - before they pressed the doors closed with soft thuds.

"If you see anyone that isn't us, just go." Aya leaned on the open window frame as Dr. Todson slid into the driver's seat, ready to command the steam pump and steering column should they need commanding. "Up one block. We'll circle counterclockwise, you circle clockwise."

"I know. Just be careful," Dr. Todson said.

"We will. I promise."

Through the open window, Aya pressed a kiss to Dr. Todson's lips, and Caroline watched them, remarkably soothed by their natural expression of affection. She didn't know what would happen once they were inside the back wall or back door, but she did trust that Aya would move Heaven and Hell to reunite with Dr. Todson.

With Eirinn.

Eir.

Air. An alias... of sorts. Though, not much of one in Dr. Todson's case. Spoken aloud, it was still just her nickname, used every day by the women in the house, but with the rest of their aliases it should blend.

"Air. Earth. Water. Fire," Aya dubbed them that first day in the map room, gesturing with an open hand toward Dr. Todson, Lei, Caroline, and then herself.

There wasn't even any indication at that point a plan might be needed. Thomas had left Dr. Todson's, thank God, without Caroline, headed back to London to file a divorce petition as far as they all knew, but no one could say what would happen when he returned. Given time to think, he might just turn the carriage back around, reappear with renewed vigor to whisk Caroline away, to take her home, to find other forms of persuasion that required no compromise on his part.

"Better to plan for nothing than not to have a plan," Aya said, and it surprised Caroline, to be quite honest. In the time she had known her, in the hours they had spent together, Aya didn't exactly comport herself as the conscientious type. "When Thomas does come back with that deed for you to sign, we'll have bloody little time."

Caroline took that to mean Aya had every confidence Thomas *would* come back with the deed, that he would use it to secure the gold from the bank to pay off his lenders, that everything would go quite as expected, and they would actually have something to steal.

The four of them. Just the four.

"It's safer for the other women in the house if they know as little about this as possible," Dr. Todson explained, but, still, it made no sense. In fact, in Caroline's own deductions, it seemed the unwisest possible decision.

"Should you really be going?" she asked Dr. Todson.

"Worried I'll slow you down?" Dr. Todson teased, but Caroline wasn't joking. Not even remotely.

"What happens to the house, to the women, if you don't make it back here?"

"The house will go on."

How? Caroline instantly wondered. *If its very heart has been ripped from its chest?*

"She might not have the degree, but Blanca could easily obtain one. She has the mind for it. She can see to the women, and Rand will take care of the day to day matters. The house is bigger than us. It will survive. Everyone will be all right."

"But who will see to Blanca?" It might have been unfair, reminding Dr. Todson how Blanca relied on her too. How she took appointments with her, twice a week every week. Confided in her. Needed her there.

"They will see to each other," Dr. Todson said, convinced, it seemed, of her own proclamation, but worry still prevalent in her eyes as she took a deep breath and released it on a sigh. "But let's just be smart, and make sure we all get to come back home."

Yes. Exactly. Caroline sighed too. This was Dr. Todson's home. Aya's home. Lei's. It could be her home now. Her life. And what a strange and beautiful life it would be. She had scarcely been born into it, and even she worried about losing it.

"I don't understand."

"Well, if something unexpected happens and Aya has to disappear for a time, I'm going with her, so it only makes sense for me to come with you, even if I am completely useless as a thief."

"No, I mean..." Caroline lost her words, nerve wavering too as Dr. Todson looked her way. "I don't understand why you would do this for me. Why you would expose yourself, the house. You already said it was too risky."

"It is risky. It's very risky," Dr. Todson confirmed.

"So, should we even be doing it? Shouldn't we just wait and see what Thomas does, and then... I don't know."

For a moment, Dr. Todson just sat, gaze drifting off, thoughts seeming to pile in on themselves, before she looked back to Caroline. "Do you remember me telling you about my mother's headaches?" she said, and that was how Caroline learned about Dr. Todson's parents, about the man who threw a stone, and how they were alike in that way, having both lost some of their most important people to violent acts of men determined to have their own way.

"But I didn't have to live with my parents' killer," Dr. Todson concluded, and it racked Caroline down to her ankles. Blew a chill into her bones she couldn't shake.

She had had the thought many times herself, in a much more self-flagellating way. What sort of person could just continue to live alongside Thomas, in the same house, in the very next room, without *doing* something? How could she just go along as if nothing heinous had taken place when she knew with everything in her what Thomas had done? What was *wrong* with her?

"Plus, you and I both know Thomas is never going to keep his word. As long as you are married to him, you have no power." Dr. Todson captured her gaze, and Caroline wasn't sure if she was speaking in generalized terms or was inside her head again. "We have to do something to try to force his hand."

"But..." Caroline's breath seized, heart clenching and aching, then beat with powerful thumps of comprehension. So, Dr. Todson thought as she did, that Thomas would get the deed, get his money, and still come for her.

Could they even stop him? Really? What means did they have? They could take the gold, but then what? Thomas would just be in even more debt, be even more desperate, and she would still be his wife. God, he would probably sell her outright if he thought he could get away with it.

"Everything's going to be all right, Caroline." Pulled from her thoughts by Dr. Todson's hand on hers, Caroline tried to focus. "Trust us."

"I do. It's just..." It all seemed so unpredictable. How were they to make any assumptions at all? As smart as they were, Dr. Todson, Lei, and, yes, Caroline was forced to acknowledge, even Aya, none of them could predict the future. They couldn't know what Thomas would do once the gold went missing. He might well suspect Caroline first. He had already made it clear he was suspicious of her motives.

"Stop overthinking it." Dr. Todson turned off the tap in her head, at least for the moment. "That is all I am asking you to do. Let us do the worrying for a while."

Why? Why would you do the worrying for me?

"Good surprises, Caroline." Dr. Todson gave her hand a small squeeze. "Just keep expecting good surprises."

Good surprises. Caroline was trying, but it was hard to imagine what good might come from being a trespasser in her own home.

264

Was such a thing even possible? Could one trespass in a house that may no longer bear her name, but was still her legal residence? If her husband lived there, so did Caroline. So, did it matter if they cut the bar on the back gate or Lei picked the lock of the back door? She did so, after all, with Caroline's express consent. What laws had they really broken? So far.

This way. Leading the way through the ground floor with Lei and Aya, past the food stores and kitchen, through the dining room and into the entrance hall, Caroline felt like a ghost, a phantasm, a thing that once belonged, but now walked the house like a memory. Or had she always been a memory here? Had she ever really lived inside this house's walls? She was certainly alive there now, ghostly though she may feel, unless Ghost Caroline also had a pounding heart and breaths that sounded far too loud inside her head.

Stay to the right, Caroline motioned to Lei and Aya at the foot of the first set of stairs, favoring the wall herself as she put one boot on the bottom step.

When she laid out the diagram of the house, she couldn't recall every creak and groan of the stairs, which ones were the worst offenders, but walking up them she remembered instinctively, pointing out each as they climbed. There were some benefits to her headaches, it seemed. In her effort to avoid it, she knew every spot in the house that made any noise, and they drifted upward as silent as a breeze, though her growing anxiety made each step just a little bit heavier than the last.

Maybe she *should* have let Lei and Aya come in alone. They probably weren't nervous at all.

"Where does everyone sleep?" Aya had asked her in the map room, Caroline's drawing of the house laid out before them as they waited for Lei and Dr. Todson to arrive.

"The staff quarters are on the top floor."

"How many live-in?"

"All of them. Four. Winnie, Jane, Ivor, and Floyd. Also, Thomas's cousin, Mary. She sleeps on the floor below in a guestroom. Here. Just above Thomas's room. Though she may be sleeping with him by now, if he's had any luck at all."

Statement giving her pause, Aya restarted with a small snort, making both notations on the drawing. In her own special characters, or at least no sort of shorthand or symbolism Caroline had ever seen before. Caroline suspected anyone who got their hands on the map would be hard-pressed to decipher it as anything more than a crude drawing of a common terraced London home.

"So, this is Thomas's bedroom here?" Aya pointed to the front chamber, the largest and most prominent on the second floor.

"Yes. My room." Caroline pointed to the smaller chamber with no street frontage adjacent.

"And this third one at the end of the hall?"

Memory of casual teas and soft late-night knocks coating her throat, Caroline thickly swallowed. "My nephew, Oliver, was sleeping in there. But he's away at school now."

"Good." Aya marked the room as empty, and Caroline supposed for their immediate purposes it was. "Where will the gold be?"

"The main safe is in the first-floor study." Caroline pointed to the spot on the map, and Aya marked it with what appeared to be a crude chicken. "But Thomas has a second safe... in his bedroom."

Hand hovering atop the drawing, Aya went instantly still, before turning in what seemed an abnormally slow and deliberate movement to look at Caroline. Incredulous, as if she thought this was something Caroline might have mentioned before. At the very start, for example, before they launched into the planning of what was clearly an imbecile's undertaking.

"No chance the gold will be in that study safe, is there?"

"I doubt it very much."

Near growl escaping her throat, Aya turned back to the drawing.

"Well, wouldn't want it to be too easy," she said as she marked the spot, and Caroline wanted to offer her a way out. *Maybe this isn't such a good idea, then?* she could say, and Aya could reconsider. Change her mind. Bow out. Though, she doubted Aya would. Every out she had offered them thus far had been unceremoniously rejected. They might have declined to rob her old house when it was first suggested, but, once agreed, they were clearly determined to see the matter through.

"Thomas's sleeping habits?" Even now, Aya went on as if Caroline hadn't just announced their target was dead in the center of enemy territory.

"He's a very heavy sleeper, so that's the good news."

"Optimist, are you, Water? Eir been rubbing off on you?"

Smiling a little, Caroline certainly hoped so. There were far worse temperaments she could catch.

"Thomas drinks at least a half a bottle of liquor every night before bed," she said. "And it has its desired effect for the first few hours."

"Early to bed, is he?"

"Late. Always. After midnight at least. Usually one or two o'clock. Sometimes later, if he's been out. I always heard him come to his room."

"Clip-clopper, is he? Guess that means we'll know in advance if he's still awake."

"Most likely," Caroline said. But she could make no promises. She had never been able to determine whether Thomas's late-night banging about was drunken carelessness or done with intention. Either way, being woken by a fright from her sleep all but guaranteed Caroline would have a headache come morning.

"How are the walls and the floors?"

"How do you mean?"

266

"Solid? Will they hear us two stories up if we have to, for instance, subdue Thomas?" Aya asked her, and the question blanched Caroline. Then, utterly enthused her. Visions of holding a pillow over Thomas's face as Aya hog-tied him in bed filling her mind, it took her several extra seconds to think the matter through.

"No. They won't hear us. When we first moved into the house, we had to install a bell in my room. I woke up ill with some frequency, and Winnie never would have heard me calling for her."

"And this Mary on the third floor? Will she hear the sounds just below her?"

"It depends. When someone's in the rooms above, you can hear their footsteps, but they're muted, easy to ignore, so I doubt small sounds will wake her. A scream or a slam, though, she is likely to hear."

"No slamming doors. Gag Thomas." Aya pretended to notate, and it brought another fleeting grin to Caroline's lips. Followed by a vague sigh of acceptance. She hated to succumb, but she was starting to understand why people liked Aya.

"Are there any weapons in the house?"

"Yes."

"In Thomas's bedroom?"

"Yes." It was exactly the sort of question that made Caroline want to change her mind, to refuse to cooperate further. But she felt as if they had reached a point of no return. Maybe from the moment she opened her mouth. Whatever she did now, she had set something in motion that was going to happen with or without her, and everyone would be safer if she told them everything she could. "A revolver."

"And does he keep that revolver loaded?"

Not usually. Caroline didn't think. But what was usual anymore? Money owed. Lenders ruthless. No one to go begging Daddy for money on his behalf. "I imagine right now he is."

"Right," Aya said, because it only made good sense. "Well, let's all try not to get shot then."

Try not to get *shot.* Bully advice at any time. But this time, they had guns too. Of a sort.

At the top of the second floor stairs, where the main bedrooms waited, including Thomas's with its safe and revolver and dominant size and position, Caroline squeezed Lei's light blaster tighter against her to keep it from swinging into anything as she gripped the banister with her other hand, finding it practically slick in its spotlessness.

Everything in the rooms and foyers they had passed through a little brighter, a little shinier than when she left, even in darkness, it seemed Thomas was having his way at last, keeping a tighter, cleanier household in her absence. Caroline could only imagine the number of hours it took each day to keep the dust permanently in the air from settling on anything. What a thankless, wasteful task, she thought as she shook her head, glancing from the ajar door of Oliver's vacant bedroom to the closed door of her own former room. Newly dark glean making it sink deeper into the wall, it looked even more like a cell now than an actual cell.

Caroline! the aggressive tap at her shoulder seemed to impart, and Caroline barely stifled a jump as she glanced back.

Yes, that's the one, she indicated with a silent nod when Aya tilted her head toward Thomas's bedroom door, and Aya went immediately past her, moving them forward toward the room and the bottom of the next staircase, which lay just diagonal each other on the wide landing.

Watching her slink ahead, Caroline waited for Aya to find something - a creak in a floorboard, a loose post in the banister she forgot to warn her was there - but she should have known better. Aya moved as quietly as a cat, testing the floor with the tips of her toes as if they were whiskers, expending none of her lives on such a simple task.

When she reached the corner of the banister, where it curved and started upward toward the third floor, she stopped, waving Caroline and Lei past her, nearer to the door of Thomas's bedroom, and, for a moment, they all stood in silence.

It *was* silent. *Not even a mouse stirring*, as the beloved poem said.

Just what Aya was hoping to hear, nothing, she gave them the signal - *In quick. Out quick. Quiet as can be.* - and rotated to the stairs to keep watch. And Caroline and Lei had nothing left to do but tiptoe up to Thomas's bedroom door.

"Something I can do for you, Water?"

"Bloody hell," Caroline swore beneath her breath, and swore her latest talent was getting caught traipsing about when she thought she was being entirely undetectable. It did not bode well for her taking part in her first burglary in just a few hours' time. Perhaps, Lei was right. Perhaps, she was more of a liability than an asset. Of course, Lei hadn't put it into such harsh terms. "Sorry. I don't mean to bother you."

"You're not." Aya looked back from where she knelt in the grass next to the small pond, only the lights from the house to illuminate her or light the way through the gardens. Along with the candle she had just lit and set out, on a floating holder, into the water. It was at that moment Caroline realized she might be invading on something private and tried to leave without interrupting. Unsuccessfully, as tended to be her recent way.

"What are you doing?" She took a few steps closer as, waving out the matchstick, Aya stood, face illuminated for a moment in the sporadic yellow flame before it snuffed out.

"Offering to the gods," Aya said, and Caroline didn't know why it struck her so unexpected, but it did. Aya simply didn't seem the type to lean on gods, she supposed. As she hadn't seemed the conscientious type just a few days before.

More and more, Caroline was beginning to realize she had no idea what type of person Aya was.

"Seems an appropriate time to make one." Glancing to the neat spread of votives and matchsticks laid out on a swath of fabric next to the pond's edge, she remembered the mandala that had hung from the bedframe in Dr. Todson and Aya's room, looking out of place next to Dr. Todson's books of science, but, perhaps, just where it was meant to be. "Which gods?"

"Does it matter? It's all the same, isn't it?"

"Yes, I suppose it is." Caroline could practically hear the collective gasp of everyone she had ever known back in London. Their whispers - *On her way to Hell now for sure, that one* - as if any of them had done anything remotely deserving of Heaven themselves.

"I, um..." She had just followed Aya out into the deepening night when she saw her step outside after dinner, wanting to talk to her for a reason she couldn't entirely explain. To make some sort of peace with Aya, perhaps. To make her amends everywhere they needed making. "I just wanted to thank you. For everything."

"Don't thank me for everything until everything works," Aya firmly declared, almost as if she thought Caroline was putting a hex over the entire mission.

"For taking my side earlier then," Caroline quickly amended. If there was some sort of thieves' superstition, she certainly didn't want to step all over it.

"Why wouldn't I?" Aya asked, and Caroline shrugged, thinking the answer fairly obvious.

There had been some disagreement earlier that day - well, for the past several days really - as to whether Caroline should go into her former home.

Lei was of the firm mind 'No.' *Aya and I will be faster*, she said.

And take on all of the risk, Caroline argued in return.

Maybe it does bear some logic to have the person most familiar with the house with us. It could make things go considerably more smoothly, Aya had settled the debate earlier that night.

"You know, I don't always side against you just to side against you, Water. I usually genuinely disagree." Aya's smirk scarcely shown in the meager light of the house.

"Still, you could just as easily have agreed with Lei because she's your friend."

"Are you saying you and I aren't friends?"

"Are we?" Caroline reasonably asked. "I barely know you."

That was considerably more her fault than Aya's, she knew, but it was still a fair thing to say. Over the weeks she had been there, Caroline had gotten to know almost everyone in the house, at least to a point beyond mere acquaintanceship. Now, she was about to commit a serious crime with a woman whose surname she hadn't even learned.

"What do you want to know?" Aya asked her.

"I don't know." Given free rein, it was instinct to backtrack, to be slightly embarrassed by her own overt nosiness. But Caroline did know. Had literally just had the thought. "What's your last name?"

"Bit boring." Aya was duly unimpressed. "But Todson, for all intents and purposes. It's been many years since I've used anything else. But as for my family name, my mother's name, which I'm assuming is what you're asking, it's Kobzari."

Mother's name. Which meant Aya hadn't taken on the name of her father. There had to be some story to that, but a more complex one than she had likely earned, Caroline pressed on more generally.

"Where were you born?"

"Ireland."

Ireland? Squinching her eyes, Caroline didn't mean to cast doubt, at least not so obvious of doubt, onto Aya's account of her own life - wasn't this the very reason she was here? to build trust between them? - but nothing Aya said agreed. Two things she had learned about Aya, just two, and already they didn't go together.

"Kobzari doesn't sound very Irish to me. You don't look Irish either."

"Noticed that, did you?" Aya smirked, not teasing her on purpose, Caroline didn't think, but still enjoying making her turn in circles. "My mother was Romani."

Ah. Now they were getting somewhere that made plausible sense. "And your father?"

"A flaming redhead with more pride than sense. Or so I was told. I have no memory of him."

Caroline couldn't tell whether Aya was sad or not about that fact. She stated it rather indifferently. Still, she broached her next question with an abundance of caution just in case.

"How did that happen? Your Romani mother and Irish father?"

"My mother's tribe migrated to Ireland to take work on the farms. My mother got friendly with the son of a local farmer. I was the result of those very friendly relations."

"Oh." Caroline warmly flushed. Would she ever get used to such candor?

"Born with the blight of '44."

"Oh." Mood instantly changing, something like phantom hunger clutched at Caroline's stomach, despite the fact they had finished eating mere moments before.

The blight. The potato blight. The Irish Famine. Famine. Just the word was uncomfortable to think. To have no access to the most essential thing that separates life from death, for everyone, equally, it had to be the most agonizing state to endure.

She tried not to imagine it. Aya. Without food. Or with the meager scraps of it. Trying to maintain her vigor, her brashness, her irritating cheekiness. It would be impossible. No one could be strong on the verge of starvation.

270

Of course, Aya wouldn't have been as she was now. She would have been just a girl, not even a girl, a baby - an infant - so small she would have absolutely no chance of fending for herself under such bleak conditions.

"Hey... Water." Suddenly concerned, Aya took a step her way, and Caroline glanced up, seeing her through blurry eyes. "Don't worry. I wasn't there."

The breath burst from Caroline in instant relief.

"It was clear from the start how things were going. To my mother, at least," Aya said. "She was pregnant again with my sister, and her tribe was leaving the island for the continent. Nomadic by nature, it was easy for her to follow them. But my father, he was tied to the land."

"He wouldn't leave?" Words lining up one at a time, it took Caroline a moment to put them into order. "Even for you?"

"My mother didn't give him the chance. She knew he wouldn't, or wholly believed it, and she was afraid he would make claim to his children if she told him she was going. So, she didn't. She just left, took a ship across the sea. She trusted her instincts, and her instincts proved right."

"Wow," Caroline breathed, mesmerized almost by Aya's story. It sounded like a legend, a pregnant woman smuggling her young daughter, soon to be two daughters, away to their safety. She could practically see it unfold like a cartoon illustration inside her head. No wonder Aya was so bold, so uncommonly fearless. She had daring rooted in her very veins. Still, it couldn't have been easy for her. "Was it hard?" Caroline asked. Haltingly. Not sure Aya would like being asked. "Being Romani in Europe?"

"It's always hard," Aya said, "being something people view with suspicion, but don't understand. We weren't welcome in European society because we were Roma. We weren't welcome in our tribe because we weren't. Then, my mother died. Scarlet fever. And my sister married back into another Romani tribe. For numerous reasons, that didn't appeal to me. We said we would always be family, but we really did live in two separate worlds, and I felt like I didn't belong to either of them. I felt like I didn't belong anywhere until I stumbled into Eir's life. And it truly was a stumble. It turned out what I thought was my lowest moment was the best thing that could have ever happened to me."

Sorrow gripping her throughout the entirety of Aya's admission, slithering up and around her like a snake in the night, Caroline felt unclutched by its end. Rewarded. And strangely harmonious. The longer Aya talked, the harder it became to deny just how much they had in common.

"I think I know that feeling," she whispered, and Aya smiled. Genuinely. Kindred thread spinning its way through the space between them.

"I think you do too," she said.

One hand on the brass handle, other pressing lightly against the wood to keep the door from making the horrible popping sound all the doors in the house made when they opened, the thought came raging back, the same one she had suffered in the reception room when Thomas came with the deed - that the world around her was bogus. Had been the whole time. One misstep, and she would fall through the wall into her old bed, gripped by a headache and laudanum and the realization that the last few weeks had been nothing but a conjuring of her ailing mind.

For an instant, it tottered Caroline into a state of unmoving panic, of blackened vision and pounding ears. Until Lei's hand came to her back, real and warm upon her, reminding her she needed to move - actually move - quickly and quietly, in and out as unobtrusively as possible, and she went through the door of Thomas's bedroom.

Inside, the light from the moon and gas lamps lit on nearby houses shined through the spotless windows, illuminating their way. Caroline could see the outline of the room's main furnishings. The wardrobes. The chest of drawers. The reading chair. The small writing desk. The bed where Thomas lay, dormant in his sleepshirt, face turned toward the weak light, mouth agape and light snore covering the creaks and rustles of their entrance.

I could kill him, the thought went through her mind. She could. Thomas was sound asleep and a sound sleeper. She could look for his revolver - it had to be right there, in his bedside drawer - end him with his own gun and a single bullet. That would be one sure way of bringing everything to an immediate, definitive end.

It would also be much too loud. Would draw far too much attention. Would put Lei and Aya and Dr. Todson in danger.

Did she have the strength to kill him with her bare hands instead? To strangle Thomas to death before he could make a single sound? She did have the advantage of surprise. Was killing him the only way to ensure he could never do any more harm? Could she do it in front of Lei? The actual Lei who was really, truly there with her?

Squeeze to her arm, Caroline realized she had ceased to move again, had gotten lost inside the dangerous corridors of her mind.

The safe. They were there for the safe. And what was inside it. Starting course once more, she led Lei to the wardrobe which held it, jaw clenching as she realized Thomas had moved the heavy reading chair so it impeded the right-side door. The door would still open, somewhat, enough even for Lei to slip inside and coax the lock of the safe free, but there was no way the safe door could swing wide enough to retrieve the gold once it was unlocked.

They were going to have to move the chair, Caroline accepted with a grimace, wishing she felt a whole lot stronger as she tipped her head to let Lei know. And, nodding, Lei slid her fingers along the underside of one tufted arm, realizing it wasn't going to be a particularly easy chair to move, before reaching into her pocket to pull out a small penknife and cutting two slits into the upholstery.

272

The rips to the fabric no more than whispers in the night, they sounded agonizingly loud in the dead space, and Caroline glanced to Thomas to make sure he was still asleep as Lei tested the slits she had made. Satisfied, her gaze flicked up to Caroline, slightly obscured behind long, black lashes, and Caroline felt the sudden, inopportune press of desire.

Maybe it was having Thomas right there for direct comparison, or the moonlight that shone in Lei's dark eyes, or the clandestineness of it all. But she knew she couldn't let herself get distracted by that either, not even as Lei came around to cut the same slits on her side of the chair, and she could smell Lei, and feel her, and wanted nothing more than to bury her face beneath the scarf that concealed Lei's face and hair and take a deep, lingering inhalation.

Stay focused, Lei seemed to say as she took Caroline's hand, pressing her fingers into one of the slits she had cut in the fabric, and Caroline felt its purpose - the frame of the arm, solid wood to get her hands on instead of the squishy, slippery velvet of the chair's upholstery. Easing her free hand into the remaining slit as Lei returned to the other side, they lifted the chair less awkwardly than expected, but still with some effort. It was only in the release that they fumbled, Lei misjudging the distance to the floor and putting her side down with a resounding thud against the hardwood.

Eyes flashing again to Thomas, Caroline watched him throw a leg out from beneath the quilt as he turned half-roused onto his side. But Thomas fell almost instantly back into a steady snore. Convinced he wouldn't wake, Lei pointed to the wardrobe, and Caroline nodded, eager to be done and out of the room, as Lei went to work opening the door, slowly and painstakingly, to make sure it made no sound.

It felt like a full minute before she was dropping down in front of the safe and thumbing on the wand light clipped to the front of her shirt to cast a gentle red glow against the dial.

Turning away from her, Caroline couldn't even hear Lei beside her as she watched Thomas in his bed, both hands on the light blaster in case he got a mind to move.

You killed Sarah. Her hands flexed and unflexed on the blaster's grips. *You killed Nathaniel. You made Oliver an orphan. You tried to use me. You've always tried to use me.*

Before her thoughts could converge to seize her hands, the door of the safe popped open, and Caroline glanced down at Lei in the red glow of the wand light. Shocked. And not shocked.

You know when Aya found me in London, I was already a thief, right? Lei asked her a few nights before as they lay together in bed. *I told you there was more to it.*

Yes. I'd come to the realization. Caroline rose up on one elbow to press a kiss to Lei's bare shoulder, knowing Lei had forgiven her, but still wishing she could take back everything she had said to make Lei feel as if she had to explain herself. *You did tell me you could pick a lock in school, and you broke into a vault the night we met, so, honestly, I had all the pieces. I was the one slow in putting them together.*

Watching Lei pile gold bars, layer of felt between each one to keep them from clinking together, inside two separate carpetbags unfolded from her supplies, it occurred to Caroline that knowing Lei was a thief couldn't prepare her for just how *good* Lei was at it. How seamless. How fast and how flawless. All the dexterity Aya possessed in her feet, Lei possessed in her hands. It wasn't an entirely new revelation - she had experienced the dexterity of Lei's hands intimately - but safe completely emptied in less than two minutes, it was still an impressive thing to witness.

Seconds later, Lei closed up the carpetbags and pressed the door of the safe closed, giving the dial a soft spin to secure it, and rose to hand Caroline one carpetbag before easing the door of the wardrobe shut.

Taking the bag with one hand, Caroline felt the small tug at her shoulder. *It should weigh about twenty pounds*, Lei had estimated the weight of the gold bars in total, if Thomas was able to secure as much of a loan as they thought. Hefting half that weight, Caroline wasn't sure if it was ten pounds or not, but she marveled at the fact the gold was there at all. Exactly where they expected. Exactly on the night they felt quite sure it would be.

Everything had gone perfectly to plan. Everything was quick and efficient. Thomas didn't even wake when they dropped furniture right next to him. It was absolutely the easiest thing in the world to rob her own husband - Caroline stupidly, arrogantly thought.

So, it was partly her fault, and a reckoning of the universe, when a scream came from the landing and Thomas stirred more forcefully in his bed.

Terror. It was all Caroline could feel. But not the same terror she had felt before, that everything was unreal or they were in danger themselves. Second scream piercing the darkness, only to be muffled an instant later, she felt the truest terror of all. Love. It burned raw and desperate up her throat, trying not to cry out in return.

Feet hastening to the open door, she was vaguely aware she still needed to be quiet, still needed to be sensible, but, screams possessing her ears, she didn't know if she succeeded as she reached the dim light of the landing and spotted two figures in the now open doorway of her old bedroom, the larger restraining the smaller, the smaller squirming and whimpering in fear.

"Fire! Easy!" Caroline meant to whisper, but it felt like a shout as she rushed on the lightest feet she could across the hall. "Don't hurt him!"

Small figure stilling instantly, Aya eased her grip, and Oliver blinked and trembled up at Caroline.

"Aunt Caroline?" Tears ran down his face as Caroline dropped to her knees, tugging the face wrap down around her chin so he could see for certain it was her.

"Shhhh," she said too late as Oliver fell into her arms, his own thin arms wrapping around her neck and holding on tightly, as above their heads the rapid creaks of footsteps moved across the ceiling and a thump close by had to come from Thomas's bedroom.

"Let's go!" Aya said.

"You're leaving?" Oliver choked out a sob as Caroline dragged his arms from around her neck, and Caroline didn't know what to say. What to do. He wasn't supposed to be there. Thomas had said he wasn't there!

Glancing up at Aya, she pled for guidance. For help.

"Fine." Aya knew what she was truly asking. "But we have to go! Now! Go! Go! Go!"

Back on her feet, Caroline grabbed the carpetbag in one hand and Oliver's hand in her other, dragging him after Lei toward the top of the stairs. They were all but there when Mary made it to the second-floor landing and Thomas staggered confused into his doorway.

"Light!" Aya cried out, and Caroline closed her eyes, yanking Oliver to her to shield his eyes as best she could.

In the next instant, the flash turned the insides of her eyelids pink and green, a gunshot punched her ears, and there were two screams. Mary's, Caroline assumed, and Oliver's.

"It's all right," Caroline whispered to him.

"I can't see!" Oliver sobbed back.

"I've got him." Aya came immediately around them, hunching on the stairs to pull Oliver onto her back. "Go," she said, and they all pounded down the stairs, noise the least of their concerns as Lei glanced back to make sure everyone was still coming behind her and the sound of Thomas staggering toward the stairs spurred them onward.

Reaching the top just as they reached bottom, Thomas took another blind shot. The stained glass window next to Caroline's head shattered, and Oliver screamed again.

Sweat turning cold on her skin, Caroline worried he had been hit. She wanted to tell him it was all right, that it would be all right, but she didn't know that, couldn't make such a bold promise, and she knew Thomas couldn't hear her speak.

A few seconds and one last staircase later, they reached the ground floor at an advantage, Thomas slowed by his lack of sight on the stairs, and Lei led them back the way they came, through the entrance hall and dining room toward the back of the house.

They had made it to the kitchen, nearly through to the stores and the back door, when the back stairwell door burst open and two figures came careening out of it, the taller of the two wielding a dangerous-looking ax while his shorter sidekick brandished what appeared to be a wooden sword.

Lei instantly raised her light blaster.

"No! Wait!" Caroline grabbed her arm without thinking, lucky she didn't blind them all in the process. But she knew these men, and they knew her. At least, they did as soon as she spoke and they stared harder into her only half-covered face.

"Miss Caroline?"

Oh, God. What have I done?

Recognition filled Ivor's and Floyd's faces.

Everything had been going so well. They had the gold. They had Oliver. They had gotten away unharmed and unidentified. Until now. Why didn't she just let Lei fire her light blaster? All it would have done was blind the men temporarily.

Instead, they were caught. She was seen. They were caught, and she was seen. Seen with Oliver. Seen with a weapon. Ivor and Floyd probably even knew what was in the carpetbags she and Lei carried.

Together, the men lowered their weapons and stepped aside.

"Miss Caroline." Floyd smiled at her, and Caroline reached out to squeeze his arm as the sound of Thomas's clambering chase reached the kitchen and they had no choice but to resume their mad dash for the door.

When they made it to the alley, Dr. Todson still waited with the coach, despite the disturbance and windows now lit up in nearby houses. Little surprise. The gunshots had probably woken half the street.

"Is everyone all right?"

"We're fine." Aya dropped Oliver into the rear of the coach with Caroline and Lei before climbing into the driver's seat Dr. Todson vacated for her.

Doors barely shut, they took off in a lurch, and Oliver made a small cry of surprise, no idea where he was or what was happening to him.

"It's all right." Caroline hugged him against her, worried about his thin gown and his bare feet as she rubbed his back and felt the shivers that racked his body. "Are you all right? Did you get hurt?"

"No." Oliver sniffed.

"Then, it's all right."

Was it though? Tears dripped from Caroline's own eyes.

What would happen now?

She was seen.

She had taken Oliver.

She had taken the gold.

Ivor and Floyd knew she was there.

Coach careening down the alleyway, no doubt waking everyone in the neighborhood who wasn't already awake, Caroline felt tossed about by its movement. Unmoored. Unbalanced. Unable to breathe. Until Lei slid across the seat, arms wrapping around both her and Oliver, keeping them warm and steady as the coach slowed a little at a time, puttering scarcely back to a crawl.

It felt nonsensical, slowing down when they needed to get away, tiptoeing when they really ought to run. But Aya knew what she was doing, and Caroline knew why she was doing it. Once out of immediate danger, they had to disappear again, vanish into the night, and that meant moving slow and soundless through the London streets.

"Are you all right?" Somewhere in the middle of Chelsea, Oliver's vision returned, and he nodded in response to Caroline as he blinked about the coach in confusion. In wonder. He had seen steam carriages on the streets of London before, Caroline was almost certain, but she doubted he'd ever had occasion to ride in one. Even if he had, Oliver had certainly never been in a coach like this, and they hadn't even reached top speeds on the open roads yet.

But he asked no questions.

No one asked any questions, nor said anything more, as they crept through the last streets of Central London and across the Albert Bridge.

Some distance away - from the Thames, from the factories and tenements of the South Bank - Aya brought the coach to a stop. Grass stretching beyond the soft lights, trees looming and turning to shadows outside the windows, they had to be in one of the recently developed parklands, but Caroline got little chance to take in their surroundings before Aya cut the lights and engine completely, leaving them in silence and darkness.

Deep, but not absolute.

The moonlight, even through the trees, turned everything in the car gray instead of black, so they all looked like sketched figures in a poorly-printed newspaper.

"Is everyone truly all right?" Dr. Todson could wait no longer, turning in her seat to look at them as she asked, gaze lingering on Oliver as general murmurs of assurance met her question. "What happened?"

But no one, not even Aya, answered her.

Turning like Dr. Todson instead, Aya looked back at Caroline too, at Oliver, at Caroline and Oliver, before resituating once more to stare out the front window of the coach. At some point during the drive, she had unwound her face wrap so it bunched and dropped around her shoulders, and Caroline could see the tight line of her mouth, the illustrated clench of her jaw, but she didn't know what either of those things meant.

"Should we go to the harbor?" Dr. Todson hesitantly asked, and Caroline's heart shuddered in response.

Was this their plan? If things went wrong? To get out of England? To go straight to the harbor and onto a ferry? Disappear? Leave the house and everyone in it behind? Completely upend their lives?

But, then, did Dr. Todson and Aya really have to do any of that? Did Lei?

The only people in the car Ivor and Floyd recognized were Caroline and Oliver. Aya could just as easily take *them* to the harbor, put *them* on a ferry, send a telegram to Thomas saying Caroline had escaped, absconded in the night. Whether Thomas believed that didn't matter. Caroline would be gone, so what proof would he have she hadn't?

"Aya?" It was clear Dr. Todson didn't want to press, but they were running out of time. Out of cover. After midnight when they left Surrey, it was now closer to sunrise than to the dead of night. Soon, the sun would start to trickle over the eastern horizon, bathing the world in a soft pink and orange glow. Day would come and people would come looking for the coach that had caused such a commotion in South Kensington before dawn.

Recognizing the fact, Aya powered the engine back up and put the coach into gear.

"Where are we going?" Dr. Todson asked her.

"Home," Aya said.

"Aya," Dr. Todson breathed, no way of knowing what had happened inside the house, but knowing there had been gunshots and they had to flee in a hurry and they came out with a child they didn't go in with.

"It's all right, Darlin'," Aya murmured, looking over at Dr. Todson in the reflection of the coach lights, and Caroline had to be wrong, had to be - what possible reason could she have to be happy right now? - but she swore she saw the trace of a grin on Aya's face. "Let's go home."

Chapter 36

DR. EIRINN TODSON

1886

Thomas Ajax was not a mystery. He arrived exactly as expected. Without warning. That very evening. "Trying to bark up a collie-shangle," according to Ben's illustrative description telegraphed up from the guard shack.

Even the two uniformed men of the Surrey Constabulary came as little surprise.

"Police!" Caroline exclaimed earlier that day, after they had time to rest up, not that anyone did much resting, and gathered to go over the potentialities in the upstairs study.

"I'm not saying that it will happen. I'm just saying it's possible," Aya said. "I've never seen anyone more dogged than a rich man convinced he knows something."

"He might very well know something," Caroline worried.

"Yes. He very well might," Aya conceded. But she was little concerned about it, and didn't really believe it. And it was exactly that unshakeable conviction that had soothed Eirinn as they lay in bed throughout the late morning, trying to sleep, but no chance that would happen until Thomas, and whatever Hell he decided to bring along with him, was put to bed first.

"Then, why did you even bring us back here?" Panic crackled off Caroline like grease in a frying pan.

"Don't worry, Water. You are not leaving this house today," Aya told her. "I promise you that."

"They're here." Sounds of horses and carriage disturbing the air of the foyer as they came to a stop outside, Rand glanced to Eirinn where she stood on the landing at the top of the stairs, and Eirinn nodded for him to open the door when the knock finally came.

Just the two of them waiting in the entrance hall, there was a sense of nostalgia to it, the danger - the police hadn't been to a home they lived in since they came looking for Aya at their flat in Paris - but, this time, they were far from alone. In the grand hall and parlor, the residents gathered, as they always did this time of night. In a few minutes, they should be sitting down to their dinner, not waiting for Thomas Ajax to disturb their peaceful evening, but Thomas was there, furious and demanding, so peace would just have to wait.

"Mr. Ajax," Rand greeted with a bright smile that warped into a feigned look of surprise when he saw the two constables who accompanied Thomas to their door. "Good evening. Mr. Ajax, is something wrong?"

"Yes. I need to see my wife."

"Yes, of course. Please, come in." Letting them by, Rand looked to the two constables as he closed the door behind them. "Hello. I'm Rand." He held out his hand to the first.

"Constable Farnham, Surrey Constabulary," the constable said as he took it.

"Constable Spindley," the second man introduced himself in turn.

"Where is she?" But Thomas had no time for such niceties. Glancing from doorway to doorway, the muscles in his neck stretched taut as light voices drifted from both sides of the hall.

"Who?" Rand asked.

"My wife," Thomas repeated in exasperation, and Eirinn started her slow descent down the stairs, breaths falling in time with her steps, deep and deliberate. "Caroline. Where is she?"

"Oh. I believe she is in the -"

"I want to see her. Right now." Thrusting a furious finger toward the floor, Thomas apparently thought he could make Caroline appear on command. "And I want to speak to Dr. Todson."

"Yes. Hello again, Mr. Ajax." Eirinn put on her dazzlingest smile, and Thomas's gaze jerked upward, face going muddled when he saw her.

"Who the hell are you?" he asked, and Eirinn brought herself to an abrupt, overly-dramatic halt, eyes widening in feigned befuddlement, hand rising to her chest.

"Mr. Ajax. Do you not remember me?"

"No. Should I?"

"I'm Dr. Todson."

"What?" The question fell like a boulder from Thomas's mouth.

"Sir, that's Dr. Todson." Moving nearer his back, Rand pressed flush against Thomas, words quieted into his ear. Though, not nearly quiet enough for everyone in the foyer not to hear. "You really don't remember her?"

"What? No, I don't remember her."

"Mr. Ajax, we have met twice before."

"What?!" Thomas might have said more, thrown words around in support of his denial, if it wasn't for the appearance of the others in the foyer, the residents trickling out in their dinnerwear from the grand hall and parlor, looking as soft and harmless as kittens, puzzled looks on each of their faces.

Likewise perplexed, Thomas stared back. Disconcerted. Outnumbered. Then, increasingly irritated as he turned to the only two men in the room who were not Rand. "Listen, I don't know what is going on here, but I have never met this woman before in my life. That is not Dr. Todson."

Well, that is a very bold and incorrect claim to make to two constables of the law, Eirinn lightly tisked in her head.

And it was obvious the constables had no idea what to do with it. Glancing about them - at Thomas, at Eirinn, at the women flooding the flanks of the foyer - they looked completely out of their depth. As if they had been tossed into a murky lake, poor swimmers, and had no idea which way to paddle toward shore.

"I'm sorry to have to ask it, Ma'am..." Constable Farnham was the first to spot land ahead. "But do you have any proof of your credentials?"

"Yes, of course." Under normal circumstance, Eirinn would have been miffed by such a request, knowing the constables would never ask a man for the same proof, taking him instead at his gentleman's word. But, at the moment, she was just happy to prove Thomas wrong. Officially. Irrefutably. And she did take some consolation in the fact Constable Farnham at least buffered his question with apology. "Blanca, would you mind?"

"No. Not at all, Dr. Todson."

Her title reiterated, Thomas visibly flinched. "Where is Caroline? I want to talk to my wife!"

"I'm right here," Caroline said from where she stood in a group of residents just outside the parlor door. And, squinting her way, it seemed to take Thomas a moment to recognize her between Francie and Stella.

"Where is it?" He stomped her way when he did.

Feeling the pulse of worry, Eirinn glanced to Constables Farnham and Spindley, observing how the two men stood, how they watched, hoping they were prepared to act on anyone's behalf. They didn't look particularly loyal to Thomas. They mostly looked mind-boggled, both baffled by events as they unfolded and to find themselves amongst such a lovely group of proper, well-dressed women.

"Where's what?" Caroline asked.

"You know what," Thomas said.

"No, Thomas. I have no idea what you're talking about. If I did, I wouldn't be asking you."

Flawless. She was flawless. Near unimpeachable. Whatever fears Caroline had when they first returned to the house, and as they waited around for Thomas to appear, she had apparently found a way to dispel, or at least tuck safely away, so they in no way impeded her performance of innocence.

"I know you were there," Thomas said.

"Where?"

"At our house this morning."

"What?" Now, it was Caroline's turn to look baffled. To laugh. A helpless, humorless laugh. As if she didn't know how else to respond to that. "I wasn't at your house, Thomas. I was here. Where you put me. Couldn't have left if I wanted to."

Perfect. Eirinn's eyes cut to the constables again, hoping they were paying adequate attention. It should make sense to them, what Caroline said, given they had just come through the estate's deterrents themselves. Through the guard gate and the expansive grounds. And Ben, their Titan.

Bring their attention to the security, Aya had told Caroline earlier. *But only if you can make it sound natural. It will help them realize just how ridiculous Thomas's claims are.*

But Thomas's claims aren't ridiculous.

No. And you're not crazy, Aya said. *Consider it recompense.*

"Here it is, Dr. Todson." A moment later, Blanca returned to the foyer with the framed license out of Eirinn's office.

"Thank you," Eirinn said, passing it, at once, to Constable Farnham, who mumbled a small "thanks" of his own before skimming the document's details. Slowly and painstakingly. Eyes moving over each line. Miniscule movements of his lips sounding out the longer words.

"Let me see that." Nearly a minute passing under Constable Farnham's perusal, Thomas tromped himself back across the foyer, reaching for the frame with impatient hands.

"I have quite got this part." Constable Farnham held out an arm to block Thomas and Eirinn's license out of reach with his other.

"And as for the proof that it's mine…" Eirinn said to Constable Farnham, and to Constable Farnham only. "Everyone here can attest to the fact that I am Eirinn Todson. You will also find me listed in the Medical Register. Along with my sex."

Constable Farnham's gaze flicking up, something mulled about his expression as he nodded and looked back to Eirinn's license, curious change coming to his face and a tilt to his head that soon revealed itself as recognition. "Hold on. Todson. Are you the same Dr. Todson who donated the libraries to the schools in Peaslake and Shere?"

"Yeah!" Constable Spindley gave Constable Farnham's shoulder a firm slap, as if he too had been trying to place the name. "And all the flowers at the county clinics."

"Yes, I am." Eirinn let a dash of hope trickle in. It wasn't why they did it, but, in her experience, it seldom hurt to be charitable. "But it isn't just me. It's a community project. The residents grow most of the flowers themselves."

"That's real nice," Constable Spindley said, in all earnestness, glancing around at the residents as if recognizing they too were deserving of his gratitude.

"Sorry. This is yours." Realizing he still held it, Constable Farnham handed Eirinn her license back and tried to come to official attention. To be professional. To stand firm and unaffected. But, gruff exterior crumbling all at once, his face split into a near-giddy giggle. "We had no idea you was a... I mean, I never met a lady doctor before."

"Well, we've been out here for some years. You should have stopped by."

"I sure would like to bring my daugh..."

"Hey!" Thomas shouted to regain the constables' attention. "This may be Dr. Todson. But I have never met this woman before today! If she is the doctor, I was deceived! Hoodwinked! This place is a fraud!"

"She's the doctor." Constable Spindley's face was a muss of confusion as he looked to Thomas. "We just walked by her name next to the front door. You expect us to believe you left your wife here without ever meetin' her?"

Ah. Eirinn did wish she had a good cup of tea, so she could take a hearty sip.

"This!" Thomas marched over to Rand, and Eirinn noticed Aya had made it to stand with Rand next to the front door. "THIS is the doctor I met."

"Are you a doctor too?" Constable Farnham asked Rand.

"No, Sir. Not that I'm aware of," Rand said.

"You told me you were a doctor!" Spinning on him, Thomas forced Rand to take a step back or end up chest to chest with him. But Aya took an equivalent, nearly invisible step forward. Too many unpredictable movements, and Thomas had no idea just how quickly he would end up on the floor. "You introduced yourself as Dr. Rand!"

"Is that true?" Constable Farnham asked.

"If he says so, Sir." Rand gave a helpless, pitying shrug. "That's not how I recall it."

"He's lying. Tell them!" Looking back at Caroline, Thomas tried to order. "Tell them how he introduced himself as Dr. Rand."

"I was being committed against my will, Thomas," Caroline said. "I have very little recollection of that day."

Head shaking, Thomas turned back around. Huffing. Furious. "You're lying." He stared hard at Rand.

"What possible reason would I have to lie, Sir?" Rand stared back like an innocent schoolboy who had no idea how he ended up in the headmaster's office.

"Have you ever heard this man say that he's a doctor?" Looking around for a corroborating witness, Constable Spindley landed first on Aya.

"Rand? A doctor? No." Aya snorted. Then, leaning into Constable Spindley's confidence. "He does sometimes like to call himself 'The Sheik.' But we all have our fantasies."

Seized with a snigger, Constable Spindley flushed aggressively pink, completely enraptured by Aya. Her beauty. Her unflappable charm. And Thomas fell back a step, all fury fading from his face. Then, all confusion. Until there was nothing left but horror.

"Oh my God." Gaping around, at Constable Spindley's laughing face, at Aya, at Rand, at the women all around him, he backed slowly toward the center of the room - away - as if any one of them might be catching. "You're mad. You are all mad."

But the only one who looked mad was Thomas, turning and pointing fingers as he was. Unfurling right beneath the noses of the constables. In another venue, with another audience, he might have been in a Shakespearean tragedy, waiting for the spotlight to deliver his big soliloquy.

Before he spotted Caroline again, and the rage renewed his motivation.

"It was you." Accusatory finger thrust in her face, Caroline didn't budge. "I know it was."

"I don't know what you saw, Thomas, but I can assure you it wasn't me."

"I don't understand. Why do you think Caroline was at your house last night?" Eirinn asked Thomas. To draw his attention. Worried by how close he stood to Caroline, by how frighteningly unraveled he was beginning to look.

But, of course, Thomas couldn't answer her. Couldn't admit what made him suspect Caroline in front of the constables. Couldn't confess that he had taken money from crooks he was running out of time to pay back.

"Did anyone see her there?" Aya asked Thomas next.

"I did!"

"You *saw* me?" Caroline questioned, one eyebrow raised and waiting, and Thomas hesitated. Reconsidered. Considered saying he did. Considered what would happen if he said he did and they could prove for a fact Caroline wasn't at his house.

Do you think he saw your face? Aya asked Caroline earlier.

If he did, not well enough. Caroline was convinced.

"I know it was you," Thomas changed tacks. "Because you took Oliver!"

"What?! Oliver is missing?" Seizing the lapels of Thomas's jacket, Caroline's panic was half real, built up from weeks of worrying about her nephew under her murderous husband's care. "I thought he was at Eton. You said he was at Eton! I swear to God, Thomas, if you did something to him..."

"You know I didn't because you took him last night!" Thomas shoved her hands away.

"Hold on now." Constable Farnham seemed to realize he was quickly losing control of the situation. That it was growing louder and more animated. Closer and more dangerous. "Can anyone verify this woman's whereabouts last night?"

Francie and Stella raised their hands. The women around them. Rand. Aya. Eirinn. Imogen raised both of hers, grinning with all her remaining teeth, delighted to be a part of it.

"And I assume those whereabouts were here?"

At the nods from the residents, Constable Farnham sent a sideways glance to Constable Spindley, and Eirinn felt truly sorry for the men, they looked so painfully embarrassed. If there was any part she hated, it was this. The lies they had to tell. They were the only thing that ever felt wrong. Because they swept up everyone, villain and bystander alike. There was no way to separate the two.

"Right. I think we're done here," Constable Farnham said.

"Wait! You're just going to believe them?"

"Two dozen witnesses say your wife was here."

"But they're all crazy women!"

"And a doctor. And..."

"Doctor's assistant, Sir," Rand said when Constable Farnham glanced his way.

"And the cook," Eirinn added. "The housekeeper. The guard on-duty last night who would have seen Caroline had she left."

Hand rising to his forehead, Constable Farnham might have been trying to rub the shame away, but Thomas only looked more livid, more rabid, far more the man who hobnobbed with ruffians than any society husband.

"I don't know how you did it." His breathing sounded halfway across the foyer as he turned to Caroline. "But I know you did it."

"I was here, Thomas," Caroline stated again. Coolly. Though, scarcely calm, voice and shoulders tremulous with a fury she had been suppressing for half her life. Even more so over the past year. "It must be terrible to know something, but have no proof."

No time to blink. In the next instant, Thomas reached up under the hem of his jacket. The shape of a holster was just distinguishable in the shadow of his arm.

And Eirinn smiled.

As he clutched at empty air.

Confused, Thomas patted the holster. His waistband. His pockets.

Glancing to Rand, Eirinn watched him flip back the front of his jacket, revealing the butt of Thomas's revolver tucked into his own waistband, pickpocketed, or pickholstered, Eirinn supposed, to perfection just as Aya had taught him.

"You bitch!" Thomas turned the blame on Caroline, wrapping his hands around her throat and sending her staggering backward.

At once, Eirinn ran toward them. The constables ran toward them. Aya and Rand ran toward them. But Francie and Stella were already there, thumping Thomas so firmly about his head and neck, he had no choice but to let go of Caroline and fend for his life.

"All right, Ladies. We'll take him off your hands." Constable Farnham pulled Thomas out of the fray as more and more of the residents started to join in, and Constable Spindley came to his aid, each man holding one of Thomas's arms as they dragged him away toward the door.

"No! Wait! She did it! She broke into my house! She stole my gold! It's here somewhere! Oliver is here! You have to search the house! Search the grounds!"

"We're very sorry about this, Ma'am. Doctor." Constable Spindley looked from Caroline to Eirinn and back again.

"What fault is it of yours if you've been lied to?" Eirinn asked.

"ME! I'm the one who's been lied to!" Thomas thrashed wildly about in the constables' clutches, looking for something - anything - to stop his inevitable denouement. Gaze passing over Aya, Aya raised both her hands, mimicking the grips on Lei's light blaster and winked at Thomas as she pretended to fire. "Did you see that?" Thomas grappled at Constable Farnham's arm to try to make him look. "Did you see what she just did? She was there! She's one of them! She's the one who shot me!"

"Been shot now, have you? Where's the wound?"

"No!" Running out of foyer, Thomas made a last, spirited effort to cling to the doorframe, but the constables just kept on pulling, dragging Thomas out of the house and down the stone steps to their waiting carriage.

"You all right there, Princess?" Francie asked as Rand closed the door behind them, and Eirinn looked to see Francie and Stella holding Caroline steady. "You rich girls, I swear, yer more delicate than glass. I don't know how ya walk on your own feet."

"She didn't get a lot of sleep last night," Eirinn gently defended Caroline as she moved their way.

"Ah, she knows I'm kiddin' her. I got nothin' but heart for this one." Francie prodded Caroline in the side, and Caroline produced a compulsory giggle in response.

"Are you all right?" Reaching them, Eirinn laid a hand on Caroline's forearm.

"Fine," Caroline said. But Eirinn could feel her trembling. Minutely and invisibly, but still altogether anxious.

"He's gone. Away from the house at least," Aya announced as she came their way.

"Was that really necessary?" Eirinn asked her, trying to look disapproving, but she could feel the satisfaction that colored her face. If anyone deserved a little gratuitous taunting, it was Thomas Ajax.

"It was. It really was." Aya was nothing but proud of her little gun-mimicking stunt.

"Do you think this will work?" Caroline asked them. "That Thomas won't come back here?"

"If he does, he'll be hard-pressed to find any allies," Aya said. "And he has no proof."

"But how? Ivor and Floyd…"

"Clearly like you a great deal more than they like him. Can't say that I blame them."

They're loyal to her, Aya had told Eirinn that morning. *She's been good to them. They won't tell anyone Caroline was there.*

And you're willing to stake everything on that? Eirinn asked.

I am, Aya declared.

"But still…" Caroline worried. Shook harder under Eirinn's hand.

"There is one other new factor," Eirinn said. To try to calm Caroline. To settle her mind. Or, at least, to give her something to think about other than what might go wrong next. "Thomas did just physically attack you in front of two officers of the law." It was quite by accident, and hardly an ideal happenstance, but it did provide some potentially positive utility.

"I can petition for divorce," Caroline realized.

"Yes." Eirinn nodded. "And I imagine you won't have much trouble getting it approved with two constables as your witnesses. We can also petition the magistrate first thing tomorrow. I trust he'll issue an order of protection on the word of two local lawmen."

"Thomas won't be able to come after me again?" Caroline whispered. But it sounded more like a wish, a prayer, a whimsical hope set forth on the wind than an actual inquiry.

"He would be an idiot to try."

"Which means he almost certainly will," Aya declared. "But, if he does, the guards will have every authority to stop him at the gate."

"And if he brings another gun?" Caroline quietly asked them.

So, she did know. She did know what Thomas was looking for when he went searching about himself. Whether to threaten Caroline or shoot her dead on the spot, thankfully none of them would ever have to know for sure. Eirinn did have her nauseating suspicions.

"Then, he'll regret it," Aya said. "They might not all look as intimidating as The Titan, but I assure you even the guards who appear harmless are not. You really think Johnny's super-scopic ears are all he's got going for him? That man could tackle an elephant and still show up on time for tea."

Laughing, tears streamed down Caroline's face, and she seemed to believe that. To accept it. That Johnny and Ben and the other guards would protect her as they protected all of the women who lived in the house. That she was safe there. With them.

Tentative footsteps entering the hall a moment later, they hastened into an all-out sprint, and Caroline turned in time to catch Oliver as he ran straight into her, arms winding around her waist.

"It's all right." Caroline pushed the hair from his eyes as she looked down at him.

"Is it?" Lei asked, approaching more cautiously behind Oliver.

Someone must have alerted her to the fact it was safe to come out of the basement. Rand or Blanca, most likely, using the controls on the wall to signal down to the workshop.

Had it gone the other way, had there been the need to flee or to hide, that same system would have alerted Lei to seal her workshop door and take Oliver and the gold out the back passage to Ben and Phileas's property and wait for Thomas and the police to leave. They had prepared for everything.

"What happened?" Lei asked.

"Thomas made himself look like a right ass in front of..." Aya started to answer.

But, by then, Lei was near enough for Caroline to reach, to grab by the shirtfront and pull to her. And Caroline did, seizing Lei's lips in a kiss that was as surprising as it was zealous.

It wasn't as if the residents didn't know there was something between Lei and Caroline. But Eirinn doubted Caroline was normally one for such public displays of affection. And Oliver looked gently and genuinely bewildered as he gazed up at them.

"Hells fire, Caroline! Give the girl back her tongue. How's she supposed to eat?" Stella asked.

Breaking apart on a laugh, Caroline and Lei held each other's gazes.

"It's all right. I'm not that hungry," Lei murmured.

"Same," Caroline husked.

"Well, I *am* hungry," Francie declared.

"Yes. Yes." The pronouncement shook Eirinn back to her senses. "It's time for dinner. Let's all get into the dining room."

"Come on, Oliver." Aya tugged him away from where he still clung to Caroline's waist. "You sit with me. We're going to have a merry ole chat about adults and the strange things they like to do with each other."

Caroline looked absolutely horrified that Aya might be the one to teach her nephew about the more intimate aspects of human nature. And equally grateful to Aya for taking him off of her hands.

"I'll race you," Oliver challenged Aya.

"I'll beat you," Aya returned.

And they set off, careening through the room like two bowling balls, all but toppling those unlucky enough to be in their path.

"Right, then…" Watching them vanish through the door to the grand hall, Eirinn turned back to Caroline and Lei as the flow of residents moved around them. "I guess someone should go and tend to the children. Has Aya thanked you for bringing her a new playmate yet?"

"No, not yet." Caroline laughed.

"Well, I'm certain she will. Goodnight."

"Eir?"

Caught by the arm, Eirinn was surprised anew as she glanced back to Caroline. And even more pleased. In all the weeks she had been there, it was the first time Caroline had called her by anything other than her formal title.

"Thank you," Caroline said, holding tightly to Lei. For comfort. Out of affection. But not for support. She could stand on her own.

"You're welcome," Eirinn said.

Chapter 37

CAROLINE

1886

Dear Mother and Father,

As I am sure you must have heard by now, there was a robbery at my former home in South Kensington. I say former, because, shortly prior to that, I was compelled to transfer the deed over to Thomas.

Thomas claims some gold went missing. I am in no position to attest to the truth or lies of that. However, something quite more important went missing that same night. As I do not wish to worry you unnecessarily, I am contacting you to assure you the other item is not, in fact, missing, but is safe here with me. It is quite well-suited to its new environment, and has no interest in being relocated at this time.

In other news, I have filed a petition for divorce with the court. I have every expectation it will be approved.

I am well. I hope this finds you the same.

Your Daughter,

Caroline

Our Dearest Caroline,

It is a great relief to receive a letter from you. We have thought of you unceasingly over the past weeks, and have made inquiries about our dominion in regards to your current predicament. But we were uncertain you would receive our letters, and were informed by several knowledgeable solicitors that it was very unlikely a court would overrule Thomas in his decisions about your welfare.

We feel a great deal better knowing you are well.

We were, in fact, informed of the burglary at South Kensington prior to the arrival of your letter. Our knowledge came from the London police, who showed up at our door asking of your whereabouts. We told them, as far as we knew, you were in a home for women in the Surrey countryside. We also told them we suspected Thomas of nefarious intent, and mentioned his propensity for lying. They had no further questions after that.

It might interest you to know the items from your house are not the only things that have gone missing. Your husband has been unseen for several days.

Men have been asking about him in the neighborhood (according to your most prying neighbors the Peabodys), so it is believed he may have fled the city. Possibly, England entire. It is a dangerous endeavor, making acquaintance with those whose interests are singular.

Presuming the house in South Kensington will soon be lost to the bank or burglarized by thugs seeking repayment, we would like to offer you the Willow estate. We understand it may hold bad memories for you, as it does for us all. As such, the possibility of selling the estate is also under consideration. Have you any opinion on the matter?

You are also welcome to come and live here at Oakwood with us. Once your divorce is approved, we will happily provide transport to gather you and any belongings or additional items which need relocating from Surrey.

At any rate, your marital allowance remains intact. It should prove sufficient to keep a household of your own, if none of the above options prove preferable. Please, let us know if you need more.

If you would keep us apprised of where you are and how you are getting on, we would be most grateful.

Your Loving Parents

Dear Mother and Father,

Thank you, truly, for the continuation of my marital allowance, which I suppose is now simply an allowance, for you should know my divorce petition has been approved by the court. I am now considered a feme sole in the eyes of the law.

The fact that Thomas has not been seen and was unreachable by the judge certainly had some bearing on matters. Where do you think he is? A beach somewhere, perhaps?

While I very much appreciate your offer to live at either one of the family estates, I intend to stay where I am. (It is my opinion you should sell the Willow Estate. I will never visit it again, and Oliver should not inherit the house where his parents died.)

You asked how I am getting on. I told you I was well, but the truth is I am getting on quite happily. More happily than I have ever gotten on before.

Oliver (whom I feel we can refer to safely by name now) is, likewise, incredibly happy here. Thriving, in fact. He takes lessons in French, bookbinding, psychology, gardening, and physics, just to name a few. Should he want to return and live with you, I will let you know.

I would not say no to an increase in my marital allowance, nor to the proceeds from the sale of the Willow estate. I assure you, both will be put to good use.

Good health and good fortune to you both.

Your Loving Daughter,

Caroline

Dearest Caroline,

We understand. If you have found some happiness, cling to it. We regret that you have not had your fair share.

We are pleased to hear Oliver is doing so well. We did worry a great deal after his parents died, but you provided him a sort of understanding only you could, by being exactly as you are. Ever true to your emotions. Ever genuine. We suspect he would not be doing nearly so well without your influence.

What we are trying to say is, you are a good daughter. We are sorry we have not been better parents.

Please, do visit with Oliver when you can.

Your Loving Parents

P.S. As to your former husband's whereabouts, we haven't a clue, but feel it matters little since it is only a temporary stopover on his way to Hell.

P.P.S. Your marital allowance has been increased as requested. We will forward the proceeds from the Willow estate if and when it sells.

They were, by far, the kindest words she had received from them in many, many years. Perhaps, even overly indulgent.

It seemed losing one child had made them recognize the value of their other.

The girl lay in the small reading room. On the puffed-up fainting couch. Weakly sedated.

Rooms had opened up at Dr. Todson's Home for Women, and they had a place for her now.

"Sofia?"

Bolting upright, a small mewl sounded at the back of the girl's throat. She was so young, this one. Barely sixteen. Sixteen, and already written off.

"It's all right," Caroline said as she stepped into the room. "My name is Caroline. I'm here to help you."

Of course, Sofia didn't believe her. Why would she? She had been dropped at a madhouse in the Surrey Hills. Away from her family. Her home. Her life.

"I need you to come with me."

"Where?" Sofia asked in a whimper.

"I'm taking you out of here."

"How?"

"Come with me, and I'll show you. Can you stand?"

"I don't know," Sofia said. But she could. With enough will and someone stronger to lean on.

In the beginning, Caroline hadn't understood the purpose of this ritual. Its point. Its significance. Now, she did. It was a cleansing of sorts, a fresh perspective, escape from one's preconceived notions into a strange and wonderful new reality.

Sofia was the second resident in a month to come to Dr. Todson's Home, and there were still rooms for more.

Caroline's parents had asked if she needed more money, and the answer was *Yes*. The house could always use more. The generous increase to her allowance had already funded two cottages at the edges of the estate. Still within the property walls, they were no more than sleeping quarters, but had freed four rooms in the main house already.

Francie and Stella took one cottage, getting into skirmishes nearly every night when Francie drank too much and had to be loped back through the gardens to sleep.

Caroline and Lei shared the other, with a room of his own for Oliver.

They still spent most of their time in the main house, Lei in her workshop and Oliver with his lessons. He was learning so much, and was so genuinely enthused by his uncommon education, there was even talk of opening a school not far off the grounds if the Willow estate sold and Caroline's parents were true to their words.

Francie volunteered as headmistress. *I did it for two days up north once before they runned me off,* she said. *I don't think I ever got paid for that one.*

"It's all right." Sob echoing beside her as they stood in the open door of the basement, Caroline gave Sofia's waist what she hoped was a reassuring squeeze and tried to capture her darting gaze. "I know it looks dark and frightening, but there is only different light down there."

Sniffling, Sofia said nothing, but continued to cry as Caroline led her through the doorway and onto the stairs.

"Just give me a minute." When they made it to the vault, Caroline leaned Sofia gingerly against the wall. But she was far too confident in her estimation. Turning to the switches and dials, it was clear Lei had been the one to set the pattern, and it took minutes to even begin to figure it out, which way to press them to get the door to open.

If you want to be good at this, you have to be challenged, she could hear Lei say. And Caroline was challenged. Quite cruelly. At least ten minutes on, she was still flipping and sliding levers, before the latch finally gave way and she could spin the wheel to free the light from inside.

"Sofia." Inviting her over, she offered the girl her arm, and Sofia looked stunned as she grasped it. Wordless. But, at some point, she had stopped crying.

"Do you want to know how long?" Sitting in the velvet armchair at the vault's center, Eir bit back a laugh as she asked.

"I think I'd rather not," Caroline said.

"Lei told me she was going to make it difficult for you. You should consider it a victory that you got in at all."

"And a good thing too. I would hate to be the one to asphyxiate you."

Letting go her laughter, Eir tucked the watch into the pocket of her vest before she turned her attention to Sofia. Her brown eyes focused and attentive. Her smile soft and sincere.

"Hello, Sofia," she said. "I'm Dr. Todson."

Elements of Truth

There are many minor historical truths and asides in this fictional novel, both large and small. Two of these truths are so integral to the story, they deserve further mention.

1. Elizabeth Garrett Anderson

    Elizabeth Garrett Anderson was a real person. She was the first woman to be licensed to practice medicine in Britain, a license she obtained through the Worshipful Society of Apothecaries, who, due to their charter, were obliged to accept her as she had obtained the necessary certificates through private study.

    The Worshipful Society of Apothecaries truly did amend their charter to disqualify private study for admittance immediately after, effectively making it impossible for other women to follow in Anderson's footsteps. This included Sophia Jex-Blake, who was making her own splash in the advancement of women's education in Scotland.

    With no positions available for a woman in Britain's hospitals, Elizabeth Garrett Anderson started her own practice in London before opening St. Mary's Dispensary for Women and Children at 69 Seymour Place.

    She received her medical degree from the Sorbonne in Paris in 1870 (they opened their medical school to women in 1869), making her the first woman to be licensed as a doctor in France as well. Shortly after, she was appointed to an official medical post in Britain. Another first.

    Throughout her career, Anderson continued to advance the role of women in medicine, and, in 1874, founded the London School of Medicine for Women with Sophia Jex-Blake. In 1883, Anderson became dean of the school, which was eventually absorbed into University College London.

    Personally, Anderson was active in women's suffrage, and retired to Aldeburgh, eventually leading a successful campaign to become the city's mayor. Yes, she was the first woman in Britain to hold that position too.

2. *Government House In Winter With Sleigh*

Government House In Winter With Sleigh (1855) was one of several paintings by artist C.L. Daly. For decades, the painting, along with Daly's other works, were attributed to two separate men, Charles L. Daly and John Corry Wilson Daly.

In 2014, a man visiting an arts center on Prince Edward Island, Canada, recognized the signature on the painting as that of his great-grandmother, Caroline Louisa Daly, which prompted the center curator to look into the museum's attributions.

After extensive research, curator Paige Matthie determined the gallery had no basis for their attributions (or, rather, misattributions) of C.L. Daly's paintings. If anything, the investigation proved their attributions highly unlikely. There was no indication Charles L. Daly ever visited Prince Edward Island (where the house in *Government House In Winter With Sleigh* is located) and no indication John Corry Wilson Daly painted at all.

In the end, Matthie determined Caroline Louisa Daly the most likely artist of the paintings. In 2017, the Confederation Centre of the Arts held an exhibition titled *Introducing Caroline Louisa Daly*, properly attributing Daly's works to her.

Author's Note: While the painting and its history are true, I took liberties with the size. It is watercolor on paper, and not nearly large enough to fill a landing wall.

About the Author

Riley LaShea is the author of a bunch of novels in a bunch of genres that so frequently combine into a single book, she spends a lot of time thinking, "Now, how the hell do I categorize this?"

She currently lives in Las Vegas with her wildly sarcastic, yet oddly charming spouse Shawna, but we'll see how long that lasts. The location... not the wife.

Sources

Canadian Press, The (2017, Jan 17). P.E.I. artist's work wrongly attributed to men for years. The Hamilton Spectator. Retrieved from https://www.thespec.com/entertainment/2017/01/17/p-e-i-artist-s-work-wrongly-attributed-to-men-for-years.html